FILTHY RICH

THE FIVE POINTS' MOB COLLECTION: TWO

SERENA AKEROYD

Copyright © 2020 by Serena Akeroyd

All rights reserved.

No part of this book may be reproduced in any form or by any electronic or mechanical means, including information storage and retrieval systems, without written permission from the author, except for the use of brief quotations in a book review.

❃ Created with Vellum

PLAYLIST

If you'd like to hear a curated soundtrack, with songs that are featured in the book, as well as songs that inspired it, then here's the link:

https://open.spotify.com/playlist/1lMPgtAzKxkjRQaHLxH2NF

To Snake Eyes.
Two words.
Thank. You.
Two more: much love.
Gem
<3

AUTHOR NOTE

OKAY, darlings,

Few things...

Filthy is the prequel to this book. It doesn't have to be read to enjoy Eoghan's story, but hell, if you like this, why not give it a go? ;)

Secondly, you pronounce the names like this:

EOGHAN - Owen

INESSA - Ih-nessa

AOIFE - EE-Fah

I truly hope you love this walk on the wild side with the Filthy Feckers. This might be book one, but you may be happy to know that The Five Points' Collection is actually going to encompass some of the characters in the Satan's Sinners' MC universe. ALL books will be standalones. They do not have to be read in order, but you'll have a damn good time if you do.

Much love to you all, and I hope you're staying safe and staying SANE during this madness!!

Serena

xoxo

THE CROSSOVER READING ORDER WITH THE FIVE POINTS

FILTHY
NYX
LINK
FILTHY RICH
SIN
STEEL
FILTHY DARK
CRUZ
MAVERICK
FILTHY SEX
HAWK
FILTHY HOT
STORM
THE DON (Coming Soon)
THE LADY (Coming Soon)
FILTHY SECRET (Coming Soon)

PROLOGUE
DECLAN

I THOUGHT I'd loathe her.

She was fucking Bratva, and the Russians were pigs. Violent, trigger-happy dumbasses who wouldn't know if they were swinging their dicks or someone else's.

I figured that was down to the leadership. Vasov was a prick, and his *sovietnik* and *obschak*, the money man and head of security and enforcement, weren't much better, but Inessa Vasov? The leader's daughter? A kid who'd been promised to my brother to seal ties between the Bratva and the Irish Mob?

Nothing like her father.

She was delicate and beautiful. He was a fat fucker with beady eyes. She had the grace of a ballet dancer and spoke like an American Princess Diana. He stomped around, flat-footed, and the only grace he had was what he said over dinner before we ate. His voice? Fuck me, it grated. All guttural and snappy, none of the fluidity of the Irish singsong I was used to.

I wasn't supposed to be here tonight.

Eoghan was.

This was supposed to be the first time he met his future bride, a year or so after the contracts had been signed, but I was here instead because he'd taken a job, at half price, just to get out of the country, just to avoid his future. Only there was no avoiding this future. What Da wanted, Da got, and that was what went down when you were psychotic, but also when you were the head of the Family.

Yeah, capital F.

The Irish Mob wasn't a democracy, and Aidan O'Donnelly Sr. had made his decree.

Eoghan was to marry the sixteen-year-old daughter of Antoni Vasov the second she was eighteen.

And when I said 'second,' I meant it. The poor bitch wasn't even going to get a birthday party. She was going to be getting married on her eighteenth.

Vasov was a prick.

Confirmed.

I'd watched her dance down the stairs in a dress that made her look eighteen, nothing flashy or trashy, if anything, she looked like a politician's wife, and the truth was? I knew Eoghan would get a hard-on for her.

Sure, it was creepy to say that when she wasn't eighteen, and I was no kid fucker—I'd slay any man in my crew who fucking was too. But I could see the roots of the woman in the girl, and knew she'd wreck my brother.

He was particular—so was she. Just watching her eat, especially after viewing her father's charming eating habits, was enough to see that. The precise way she snapped out her napkin, the way she handled the silverware. Then, there was how she got to her feet, like a lady. The way she moved, like a lady. I bet she'd taken ballet classes or some shit like that.

Without even moving a muscle, I knew her room would be pristine, and she'd be like living with a doll.

Eoghan thought he needed that, and while he did to a certain extent, he liked to touch more than he liked having things on pedestals.

Although, Inessa had the kind of beauty any man would worship.

And she was smart. Fuck, she was so smart that I almost envied my prick of a brother. The guy who wouldn't face facts and who had forced me to step in for him.

I'd seen her entire being drop when she'd been introduced to me and she'd realized I wasn't Eoghan. She'd hidden it well though. Again, more of that grace my brother would get a boner for. She'd been polite, kind, and well-spoken. Everything her father wasn't.

Eoghan was definitely a lucky man.

After the interminable meal was over, where we'd eaten purple fucking soup, some kind of weird pork dish, and some fucking bright red Jell-O that hadn't tasted too bad—but who the fuck served Jell-O at a meeting this important?—we retired to a drawing room.

Ma had kept Da contained for the most part, but when Vasov began grace in Russian, the Catholic in my father had bristled. It had reminded me of that scene in *The Devil's Advocate*. Where Al Pacino, as the devil, went into church and approached the holy water which fizzed and bubbled at his presence.

Yeah, that had been Da right about then.

My lips twitched at the thought.

Ma had, as usual, been as graceful as Inessa, but considering she had about five decades of dealing with Aidan Sr. under her belt, I figured that wasn't much of a feat. She'd managed to contain him, especially when Svetlana, Vasov's much younger wife, decided to ignore anything Ma had asked her about the upcoming wedding. Pretending to speak only Russian, forcing Inessa to translate, had worn on Da's nerves.

Fast.

Nothing was more dangerous than that.

With her bright blonde curls topping her head in a way that made her look like a fucking meringue, Svetlana was lucky they weren't dripping purple—Da had no issue punishing women who were disrespecting Ma, and tipping the violet borscht over his hostess' head was the least he was capable of doing.

The meal had been long, but when we retired to a drawing room that looked like something Tsar Alexander could have jacked off in, I was sad we had to continue the charade of getting along.

Robin egg blue walls, all with heavy moldings that were a bright, gaudy gold, lots of paintings of fucking dogs in old frames that screamed money, if not class, in a place like this, with furnishings that made me wonder if they'd break if we took a seat on them. And Inessa? Oddly enough, she suited the place.

She was like a crystal figurine in a crystal palace.

Untouchable.

It was weird. Unnerving. She had none of the recklessness I'd expected, nothing that told me she was actually sixteen.

I moved over from the doorway, tracking her as she took a seat beside the fireplace in a spindly chair that she fit in well. With her tailored dress in a creamy peach color that offset her beautiful hair, and made the green of her eyes pop, she was so fucking still, it creeped me out.

When I was closer, taking the stool at her side and stacking my elbows on my knees, leaning over as I did so, I stared at her shoes, knowing full well that no sixteen-year-old would pick them. They were tall with a small platform. Nude.

Fucking nude.

Who wore that shit unless you were Kate Middleton?

A couple of my crew had kids her age, and they were into neon shit and fucking Snapchat… It made me wonder what they were hiding, and if she was so quiet because her parents had told her to be, which would make sense. She couldn't be happy about the wedding, could she? No kid wanted to be forced to marry a guy she'd never met.

But when I finally shot her a look—maybe it was the light from the fire that did it—I saw something on her arm.

Something that, when she saw where I was looking, had her reaching over to cover the skin.

Bruises.

Figured.

I sighed heavily. "Oh, girl."

She swallowed. "Please, don't say anything."

What could I say? "I'm sorry."

"I shouldn't have talked back."

The wooden words had me flinching. I knew another kid who'd said that to me once upon a time... It had made me do some stuff I regretted. Had made me want to be a protector when that wasn't in my nature, and look what happened? I'd wrecked my entire fucking life.

For a second, I felt tongue-tied. Violence was a part of my life, and Inessa's too, it seemed. But we tended to shield our kids, at least the men did in front of Da. He'd kneecap them if he found out there were kids being beaten in the Family by our crew.

Once they became 'made men,' it was different, but until that point? Kids in the Five Points didn't need the authorities to protect them. Not when they had their very own boogeyman protecting their asses.

I stared down at my feet. "Not much consolation, but Eoghan's a good man. He won't treat you that way."

"He didn't come here tonight."

Yeah, I could see why that was going in the con column. I couldn't exactly blame her for feeling that way either.

I cleared my throat. "He's away on business."

Her jaw tensed, but I saw that register—knew she knew I wasn't lying—and also knew she'd more than suit my brother. She understood the score. That was rare, even with daughters in our world who were kept in cloud cuckooland by overprotective daddies sometimes.

"I thought your father was lying."

I snorted. "Da doesn't lie. He doesn't have to."

She blinked, then shot my father a look. He was nursing a shot of vodka like it was poison. Maybe to him, it was.

"Looks normal, doesn't he?" I muttered, and saw her lips twitch.

"Surprisingly, yes."

"He's not," I said dryly.

"I know. I've heard of him."

Hard not to in this area. I shrugged. "Eoghan's like him—just not in the psychotic way."

"Good to know," she murmured, her tone rueful.

"He'd never hurt you."

"Wouldn't he?" Her smile was pained. "Isn't that par for the course?"

"No. And not with Eoghan." I hunched my shoulders, feeling awkward. I really shouldn't have to be doing this—warming up my brother's bride-to-be for his sake, but fuck, Eoghan deserved a good woman, and Inessa was young enough for her Bratva roots not to have poisoned her.

A thought that was confirmed every time she looked at her father.

It was hidden well, but she loathed him. That much was clear. Even if it *wasn't* clear to Antoni.

Anyone with that level of acting skills might have appeared untrustworthy, but sue me. She gave off good vibes, and I was willing to buy into it if it was an act.

"He's not going to visit, is he?" she asked abruptly.

I blinked at her, then stared down at my shoes. "Probably not."

"For the full two years?"

"Maybe. I'll see what I can do."

She swallowed. "Please? I'd like to know the man I'm tying myself to for a lifetime."

I blew out a breath. "If it was Conor or Aidan, I'd say I could promise you and I wouldn't break that promise, but Eoghan, he's..."

"Difficult?"

Wincing, I shook my head. "Different. Not bad, not good. Just different. The war fucked him up some, but he's not bad, just likes things done a certain way, you know?"

She twisted in her seat, eying me in a way that would have put my back up if I didn't know she was my brother's. "He's particular?"

There was a zealousness to her tone that should have taken me aback, but didn't.

Inessa was shrewd.

She wanted to know her husband, not so that she'd 'know the man she was tying herself to for a lifetime,' but so that she could learn him. His faults. His flaws. His strengths. His preferences.

That she wanted out of the Bratva was clear to me, that she wanted a life that was different than the one she currently led made sense.

And because I wanted the best for my dick of a brother, I could see that and was willing to help her out.

"Very. Loves home cooking, is addicted to the Yankees, and irons his socks." Well, paid that old bat, Winnie, to iron them for him.

Her head tipped to the side. "Who's his favorite player?"

And that was the start of an odd but unusual friendship. Okay, friendship was too strong a term. We were more like acquaintances with a mutual desire for a particular end goal.

Winning Eoghan over.

Making Eoghan happy.

Even if it was against his will...

ONE

EOGHAN

TWO YEARS LATER

I HATED CHURCH.

And that wasn't something I said lightly.

I hated it with a passion, and as a Five Pointer, that sucked, because part of the position of being in our exalted brotherhood was that we attend church and confessed our sins.

Of which there were many.

On a daily basis.

Really, we should have had a hotline to the confessional with how much sin we perpetrated, but as much as my father, the head of the Five Points—the biggest Irish Mob family in the United States—donated to St. Patrick's, it wasn't enough for his entire crew to be outfitted with their own personal priests to service them.

My lips twitched at the thought, even as Father Doyle glared at me for daring to be amused within these hallowed walls.

While my father thought the sun rose and set on the old fuck, I didn't, so I glared back at him, amused even more when his cheeks blanched and he stared straight ahead.

The day my father died was the day when this old fuck was being sent to wherever they sent old priests off to.

And yeah, I saw him outliving my father, mostly because of the life Aidan O'Donnelly led.

The lives we all led.

That Da had hit the grand old age of sixty-six was pretty much a fucking miracle. I wasn't sure if I'd live that long, and maybe with a Bratva bitch as my bride, I wouldn't last the fucking week.

The enmity between the Russians and the Irish wasn't as bad as it was with the Italians—fucking hated that scum. Jesus, everyone did. They were cocksuckers who made the Albanians look trustworthy, and let's put it this way, I wouldn't trust an Albanian to look after a sandwich from Subway, never mind my territory—but the hostility between us was still bad.

Never the twain shall meet, and all that shit.

And personally, I didn't appreciate playing Romeo to a fucking Muscovite Juliet, but it wasn't like I had a choice.

Today was my wedding day.

Yeah, I was getting married, and I wasn't fucking happy about it.

It was also my bride's goddamn birthday.

Fucking eighteen.

Jesus.

I had about six hundred of New York's elite at my back, we even had the Deputy Attorney General of the state in the pews, and the hypocrisy within these walls which, ordinarily, would have amused me, instead, irritated the fuck out of me.

The place stank of shit.

I didn't give a fuck if these bastards were wearing eight hundred dollar an ounce scent, all I could smell was crap.

A lot of it.

The place was decked to the nines, both families' wealth out on display in the way it was decorated, but also, with the level of protection we had on this event—most of which I'd arranged because security was my jam. For every two guests, we had one detail covering their asses because this wedding meant something.

It was a way of formalizing ties between the Bratva and the Irish

Mob, a way of securing them too, but I knew it was also my father's way of trying to take us up to another level. The number of famous faces, of political figures in the pews, spoke clearly of both families' spheres of influence, and he wanted that—wanted his greedy mitts all over those spheres. He'd long been playing the property ladder in the city, and with our money man and close friend to the family, Finn O'Grady, working the figures, we were starting to take over shit, owning the biggest skyscrapers, holding controlling stakes of the best plots of land in space poor Manhattan.

I already knew my father was a whack job, but if I hadn't known it, this wedding proved it.

He wanted my kid in office.

Or, at least, one of his sons' kids in office.

That was the end game, and fuck, I wanted nothing to do with it and didn't have a goddamn say in it either way.

My mouth tightened as the organ started playing the *Bridal Chorus*, and the slap of my brother Declan's hand to my shoulder had me glaring at him in irritation—did the fucker think I didn't know what that meant?

We'd already dealt with Pachelbel as two kids, a boy and a girl, had traipsed down the aisle, and a herd of fucking bridesmaids had soon followed.

Even in midsummer, St. Patrick's was goddamn cold, so the *Bridal Chorus* came as a relief—my dick was about to fall off from the chill within the old stone walls.

"You look at her like that, she'll have a heart attack," Dec muttered, as he twisted around to stare at my bride.

Disinterested in the proceedings, I shrugged. "Will save me the trouble of having her as a ball and chain."

His lips twitched. "She looks hot."

"She's eighteen. I don't go in for kids."

"She's legal," Declan replied, "and, let's face it, you can't not consummate it. Da won't allow it."

"What's he going to do? Put fucking cameras in the bedroom to make sure I fuck her?"

A hissed, "Quiet!" had me glowering at Doyle.

Declan snorted. "Just bone her. She's beautiful. You should have gone to her birthday party yesterday, man. That was fucking rude. She looked banging."

My mouth tightened at the mention of the early birthday/rehearsal dinner I'd refused to attend.

Before now, I'd seen pictures of her, but every time the Bratva Pakhan, the leader of the Russian Mafia, tried to get me to meet his spawn, Inessa, I'd managed to be out of the country.

It had taken some fucking calculated risks, but I'd achieved it. Sure, there was more blood on my hands as a result, but I liked honing my skills, making sure that my abilities with a rifle were as hot shit as ever.

Plus, I had a couple of million in the bank which my father couldn't touch, and that was always a bonus.

The prick had a habit of tithing us when we displeased him.

Beneath the organ, the throbbing notes that signified a death knell for every man's freedom, under the low hum of the crowd's oohing and aahing at my child fucking bride, I heard the hushed murmur of her skirts against the floor—that was only because my senses were honed.

I also heard her father's tapping footsteps, and knew my fate was sealed.

I mean, I'd known that earlier, but still. This was it.

It was really fucking happening.

Those tapping footsteps, the shushing skirts, they signed my death certificate.

I twisted around when the scent of lilies invaded my nostrils, and though it wasn't displeasing, I hated it instantly.

Because I wasn't a schmuck, and I knew Inessa had to be as unhappy with this situation as I was, I didn't glower at her, but I kept my face expressionless as I nodded at her father and accepted her hand.

I wasn't sure how Da had managed to wear Vasov down and had gotten him into a Catholic church and out of an Orthodox chapel, but from the look on his face, he was as happy as Aidan Sr. was with the upcoming nuptials.

I knew why, of course. Women were a commodity to the Bratva. Children were property to be bought and sold, and while that was the case with the Irish Mob too, we didn't tend to pimp out our kids to the enemy.

I cut him a look, more interested in him than my bride, and when our eyes met, his flashed slightly, a flicker of something I couldn't read surging to life inside them.

Maybe he saw my lack of fear, something that probably surprised him, maybe he saw that I was so beyond over this I'd moved into a different stratosphere, whatever it was, he muttered something in Russian to Inessa, then scuttled away like the pond scum he was.

He'd fucked off to his pew where a woman I assumed was his wife—not Inessa's mother, because she was definitely too young—had taken a seat, dressed like some kind of colorblind whore in a bright green dress that was more fitting for a nightclub than a wedding. Her hat looked like she had a nest of parrots on her head, so I knew Vasov hadn't married her for her taste in clothes, but for the tits that were spilling out of the dress. Tits were thirteen a dozen in my world, especially falsies, so, disinterested once Vasov was seated, I turned to Inessa.

The first thing I looked at was her hand trapped in mine. Her fingers were slender, delicate. The skin white and soft against my callused digits. The proof of my trade was written into the rough flesh of my hands, and there'd been so much blood shed by them that it should have marred her purity in a flash. The ring my father had procured for her sat on her finger. It wasn't gaudy, which told me Ma had helped purchase it, and the clear emerald was a dark, rich green that throbbed with life.

I had to think that, with her involvement, the emerald would suit Inessa's character—Ma would know my bride more than me. She'd met the bitch, after all. That was more than I'd done. So, for whatever reason, she sported an emerald instead of a diamond, and the heavy stone suited her delicate hand.

Letting my gaze drift over her fingers to her wrist, I took note of the thin sleeve that covered her forearm, and when I saw no sliver of skin, her face held more interest to me. Only, her head was covered with a veil, a thick one. The lace so dense that it was a wonder she could see through it without tripping.

The cream color reminded me of paper that had been aged with tea, and it draped over her, covering her from head to waist, revealing only a tight bodice that was decorated with what were probably diamonds, and the flared skirt that was like fancy netting that flounced with each step. It was large, enough for the skirts to get in my way and to put a few feet of distance between us.

Her other hand was primly pressed in front of her belly where she held the offending bouquet of lilies. The sight filled me with relief, even if I knew lilies were usually funereal flowers, not wedding. That she didn't use a lily-based scent actually perked me up.

What didn't?

Why her father hadn't raised her veil.

Why her maid of honor hadn't darted forward to do the same.

I wasn't a man who appreciated weddings, but I was Catholic. Weddings, funerals, and fucking baptisms were our stock-in-trade.

I knew the score.

And I knew that, even if the Orthodox rituals were different, they weren't that different.

Even if they were, I knew my father. He'd have micromanaged the shit out of the ceremony, and he liked things done just so. He wanted the world to know the father was giving up the daughter, handing her over like a virgin sacrifice. He'd want Vasov to raise the veil, to look at Inessa, for the girl to know she was a commodity her father was willing to trade, before handing her over to the buyer.

Yeah, sick, but that was daddy dearest for you.

That was how I knew something was going on.

Something that set my nerves on edge.

I stared at her so long, I heard Dec whisper, "What's the hold up?" I could easily foresee Da cutting him looks, glaring at him and waving his hands in an effort to get him to do something, but that wasn't going to work now. Not here. Not at this moment.

Behind me, people started to murmur too, wondering why I wasn't moving. I could imagine my father's face had gone from jubilant at a successful plan coming to fruition, to infuriated as he wondered what I was waiting for.

I just knew my mother was having to calm him down, and behind me, I could feel Doyle shuffling, his cassock whispering against the altar, and the bridesmaids starting to grow uneasy as my pause went to extreme lengths.

I ignored it all, focused only on her, on the puzzle that I was about to uncover, because all my instincts were telling me something.

Something I didn't fucking like.

They were hiding her away like she was some ugly bitch, where Declan had distinctly told me she was beautiful. He wouldn't lie. Not to me. Not without knowing I'd castrate him if he lied about that.

So what the fuck were they hiding?

Whether I wanted Inessa or not, she was my property. Had been since my goddamn father had tied me into this fucking engagement.

And I knew, fucking knew what I was about to see.

So my stillness?

It was me trying to prepare myself.

Me trying to calm myself down, because if I didn't, I would slice Vasov up like a motherfucker, and I didn't care who was watching.

Deputy Attorney Generals, Lieutenant Governors, and five hundred and ninety other witnesses be damned, blood would stain the altar of St. Patrick's for an eternity if I didn't get a handle on my temper.

The bouquet trembled, and I knew I was frightening Inessa—unfortunate, but it couldn't be helped. Not now.

The sight did stir me into action a minute later, because I didn't want her fear to encompass me, didn't want her to associate me with fright. So, I reached out, noticing she flinched at the movement, and slowly began to unveil my prize.

They'd done a skilled job of it.

I'd give them that.

The makeup was pretty flawless, but my trade was blood. Broken bones. Bruises.

I knew a black eye when I saw it.

I knew a busted jaw too.

My own popped out to the side as I processed the beating she'd taken, and I stared at her wedding dress, taking in all the covering, from the wrist-length sleeves to the way that not an ounce of her chest was revealed to me.

Sure, they might have been going for the demure look, but I'd seen nuns show more skin.

My mouth tightened, and I stopped looking at her flaws, and instead, looked at her.

My bride.

She was beautiful.

Dec was right.

She was a fucking stunner.

Her face was delicate, the bones strong, but somehow fragile. Like she was a fairy. Her blonde hair was in a fancy topknot, and tiny curls bobbed around her cheeks—it was a neat updo, but the way it teased and bounced with the faintest movement reminded me of the way a woman would raise her hand to grasp a hold of her hair during a blowjob when shit got real and she got down to business.

The thought, surprisingly enough, had my dick twitching when my mind's eye switched Inessa into that role, but I pushed thoughts like that aside and focused on my future wife. Her ears sported heavy emeralds that complimented her engagement ring and her clear green eyes, and her mouth was made for sinning.

At my unveiling, the congregation hushed down, evidently

thinking the show was about to start, but when I reached for her bouquet, more whispers stirred.

She frowned at me, her brow puckering at the move, and I appreciated the push and pull as she tried to evade my grasp on the bouquet, but I ignored it. And the second our hands collided, she did too.

Her eyes transmitted her confusion, but I wasn't confused.

She was just registering the truth.

She was mine now.

Tossing the godawful lilies at the flustered maid of honor, who caught them with a gasp, I tugged her forward, being more gentle than I usually would have been, because rage was filtering through me with the purity of distilled vodka—and these fucks knew what that tasted like—and I didn't stop until we were standing opposite Doyle. I'd curved an arm around her waist, bringing her into me.

The move was not traditional, and Doyle's lips parted to scold me, but my scowl was evidently deterrent enough, because he instantly intoned, "Dearly beloved, we are gathered here today—"

As he got on with the ceremony, I tilted my head to the side. "I will make them pay for beating you."

She stiffened. "I-I...they didn't."

"Bullshit."

Another flinch.

"Don't lie to me, Inessa," I warned, and as Doyle droned on, I whispered, "They did a good job, but not good enough. You'll dance in their blood if you want."

She didn't reply, and while she was tense from the unusual hold I had her in, she relaxed somewhat at that.

If there was any consolation to marrying Bratva scum, it was that she'd been raised in the life.

She knew aggression and bloodshed were the universal language. Aoife, who was married to Finn, wasn't of the life, but she knew about the Five Points, had been raised in one of our neighborhoods, and the violence of our world still surprised her.

Not Inessa.

She was as used to it as I was, even if I doubted she'd ever gotten her hands dirty.

I twisted my fingers about said hand, surprised by the daintiness of it against mine.

My father had beaten the shit out of me just over a week ago when I'd raised hell about the upcoming wedding, but I was a man.

More than that, I was used to a beating.

Inessa?

She looked like a china doll, and while I'd never found that sexy in the past, had never found virginity or fragile women attractive, this was different.

She was mine.

I'd never put those pieces together until now.

She belonged to me.

This marriage would see to that.

She was mine to protect, mine to defend, just fucking mine.

Unlike every other aspect of my life, I wouldn't have to share her.

Not with my brothers, not with the family, not with the Five Points.

She belonged to me, and Eoghan O'Donnelly protected what belonged to him.

That was a fucking fact.

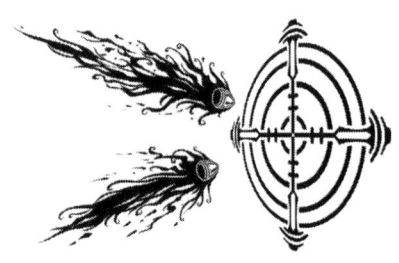

TWO
INESSA

HE KNEW.

Even as terror had filled me that he'd reject me, break off the wedding I knew he didn't want—probably even less than me, considering he'd managed to evade every single one of my father's invitations for us to meet—he'd raised my veil.

And he'd seen.

He'd seen what few men would.

He'd seen what I was supposed to hide, what fantastic makeup had tucked away, but he'd noticed. Had witnessed the truth of what had gone down a few days ago.

My heart had been beating like I'd been working out for hours on end, and by the time he'd tucked my hand into his, I wasn't sure if I was going to pass out or not. Whether it was from discomfort at his focus, fear of his rejection, or terror of being returned to my family... The latter was a fate worse than death.

I would die if I failed in this, if I shamed the family name.

So, when he tugged me toward the altar, the sweetest relief filled me, and I took a second to gape at him and take stock of the man who'd avoided me for so long. My first impression? That Eoghan was like all the O'Donnelly sons—wickedly handsome.

But the term wicked came in two definitions. Everyone in our circles knew what he, in particular, was capable of.

An expert marksman who'd been dishonorably discharged from the army, his skills were renowned—even by my father.

And Antoni Vasov didn't approve of anyone or anything.

The asshole.

But Eoghan's talents were undeniable. As a sniper, he was famous in our circles. A dubious fame, of course, but then that was the world I lived in. A shitty one.

My mouth tightened as Father Doyle—a man I'd met more times than my fiancé—began to start the service in earnest.

Undoubtedly, Aidan O'Donnelly Sr. thought he'd won some kind of boon by having the wedding ceremony in a Catholic church, and by being able to hold a traditional Catholic wedding when, really, it was a sign of my father washing his hands of me.

There'd be none of the traditions my sister would get at her wedding.

No special ceremonies like the crowns brides and grooms were given on the day, the earrings a bride received during the ceremony— Eoghan's family had given me a set that matched my ring as part of a bridal trousseau. There'd be none of the games that were played between a couple who was in love for the entertainment of their family.

This was a business transaction, and Father had made that very clear by not having a thing to do with the ceremony.

Not even to save face among our people was he willing to lower his disregard of me, and though I didn't want to be married at eighteen, I did want to be out from under his thumb.

There were only so many times an animal could be beaten before they decided to bite back, and each and every time he hit me, each and every time Svetlana slapped me and I was expected to do nothing other than take it, I was finding it harder and harder not to fight back.

Gritting my teeth was almost as painful as the bruises they inflicted upon me. Things had gotten worse recently, and it had culminated in the beating I'd 'earned' three days ago.

My entire face was numb. I was a little high on Tylenol with codeine from the pain—not just from the wounds themselves, but from the fact I'd had three makeup artists flittering around me, torturing me with beauty blenders on delicate skin.

I wasn't sure how I hadn't cried my makeup off, but it stuck. Somehow. And here I was.

Somehow.

Maybe I shivered, I didn't know, but Eoghan's hand tightened about mine, and it brought me back to the here and now.

A here and now where I was getting married.

To a man I didn't know.

To a man I didn't want to know.

To a man who had killed only God knew how many people for cold, hard cash.

I bit my lip at the thought and forced myself to think of anything other than the clusterfuck of this week, and how I'd endured my worst beating ever because I'd dared to tell my father that Eoghan was, essentially, a serial killer and that I didn't want to marry him.

Instead, I concentrated on the vows.

There was no divorce in our world.

Only death.

Either through the freedom of illness or violence.

My mother had died that way, when our house had been infiltrated by the *Famiglia*, and she'd been raped first before she'd been slaughtered like a pig.

I'd always thought that would be my fate, had always thought...

Despite myself, I turned slightly into Eoghan, curving my body toward his warmth.

He was a stranger, the aforementioned serial killer, but the people I knew had beaten me like I was a dog, so I had no place to go for safety.

And while his words weren't comforting, they sure as hell stuck with me.

"You'll dance in their blood if you want to."

My vision blurred as I contemplated that, then I thought about the fact I no longer had to answer to my father.

He wanted me to listen out for things, keep him in the loop, but I didn't want my new, relatively safe haven to be tarnished by my being a spy, so there was no way in hell I was going to do that.

And if I avoided him like the plague, there was no way he could ever expect that of me.

Well, that was naïve.

He could expect it of me, but I didn't have to give it to him.

All week, loathing for him had burned in me like a fever. It had distracted me from the upcoming marriage, and I'd focused only on getting away from him, on getting out of the house that was my prison in Brighton Beach...and after that, when I was wed, to getting away from Eoghan. To running and starting a new life for myself.

But now?

I could dance in Father's blood?

I tightened my hand around Eoghan's, turned my attention to Father Doyle, who was glowering at Eoghan over something—I didn't know what. Eoghan didn't seem the most reverent of people. Far as I could tell, he didn't give a damn for rules, which meant he either wanted this wedding—which I highly doubted—or someone had some power over him.

Having met my future father-in-law, I knew who that someone was.

I couldn't blame him.

Aidan Sr. was scary, and I said that when I was a Pakhan's daughter.

When I was the daughter of a woman who'd been slain for being married to said Pakhan...

Scary and me were friends.

But Aidan Sr.'s eyes said it all. He was insane. I wondered if his family knew it, and if they did, if they were as terrified of him as I tried not to be.

Like any predator, they distrusted fear, respected strength. The second I lowered my guard, showed Aidan Sr. I was scared, was the second he'd pounce. I just didn't know what that might entail.

Eoghan tugged on my hand once more in the silent communication I was slowly getting used to, and I realized I had to get involved in the ceremony.

I'd read up on the Catholic ritual, so I repeated the words the priest intoned, then I headed to a pew to the side of the altar where Father Doyle began a sermon about the power of marriage and how it could bring peace to a world filled with strife.

Fitting, but I highly doubted most of the congregation knew just what kind of peace it was bringing to the city.

A truce.

Between the Bratva and the Irish Mob.

Sure, they weren't the only players in the city. There were the Albanians, the Triads, and the *Famiglia*, but today's union bound the separate brotherhoods together in a way that would reap misery on the other factions.

Even though I was kept out of the business, I knew that much.

I wasn't an idiot, even if my family treated me like I was one because I had issues with the violent world I lived in.

"Who did it?"

His voice was like silk, whisper soft as it slid over me. I jolted in surprise because my focus had shifted when Doyle had started droning on—I knew my concussion wasn't helping me appear lucid—and quickly shot him a look. I just realized he hadn't let go of my hand, and his fingers tightened—not punishingly, but enough for me to feel his grasp.

"Why is it important for you to know?" I half-mouthed, not wanting to disturb the ceremony.

"It matters to me."

I knew I was his property, knew what my father had done was

essentially like giving Eoghan a backhanded slap, even if I was an unwanted bride, even if the beating was the only reason I was here today, but...

A united front, a merging of the Bratva and the Mob, would make us stronger.

Safer.

And I really didn't want to die like my mom had.

I didn't want to be raped by scum who hurt me just because they hated my husband.

I didn't want to be butchered like an animal, even though I'd had no say whatsoever, just like she hadn't, in whom she married.

Tears pricked my eyes at the thought, and I dipped my chin, whispering, "They can't touch me anymore."

He stiffened at that. "You're damn right they can't."

I froze, a little horrified at how loud his voice had been. A hush fell over the church, and Doyle stopped mid-sentence and twisted around to glare at Eoghan again—this was getting to be a theme of the day—before he flared his eyes in warning and returned to the full lecture.

Despite myself, my lips twitched, and I whispered, "Your irreverence is showing."

He snorted. "That's one word for it. Doyle can't stand that I don't give a shit about this crap."

"Why are you here then?"

"Because, like your father, mine rules with an iron fist. He might be an old bastard, but he's handy with them."

"You were beaten too?" My mouth rounded at that, and I gaped at him, unable to believe it.

Eoghan was...

He was, well, like a warrior of old.

I could see him in a kilt with a claymore on his back, could see him on horseback with armor covering him.

Sure, his features were a little baby faced, but his eyes? Those dark brown orbs held a multitude of secrets, and I got the feeling most of them were terrifying. His body was taut and trim, and the tails he wore—a long suit jacket with a 'tail' at the back—fit him to perfection. He gave off a slender appearance, I guessed, but there was something coiled about him. Like he was just preparing to spring into action.

And from his response to my very well hidden, expertly concealed bruises?

I figured that was pretty apt.

He had dark hair, so dark it was almost black, and his brows matched. They hooded gleaming eyes that, I got the feeling, saw everything and missed nothing, and his jaw was clean-shaven but, judging by the faint tan on his cheeks, he usually had a short beard.

The notion intrigued me, as did his handsomeness.

I'd known, at some point, I'd be married off to someone. Sure, I'd never thought it would be when I was eighteen, and I'd never thought I'd be married to a goddamn Irish man, but to be wed to a handsome guy who wasn't thick around the waist, smelled of potatoes that had been lost in the back of the kitchen cabinets, and drank more vodka than water?

Yeah, technically Eoghan was a dream.

A technicolor one.

"You're staring."

His lips twitched, the dusky peach flesh moving, enticing me to smile with him.

I hadn't expected any kindness from him.

If the Russians hated the Irish, that was nothing compared to what they felt for us. I'd known I was walking into enemy territory today, but, of course, life was full of surprises.

My 'home' camp had treated me worse than Eoghan who, the second he'd seen me, had stopped glowering at me, and had started glaring at the world like he was pissed at it and not me.

I couldn't even begin to describe how much of a relief that was.

Not to be in his crosshairs? Bliss!

And the truth was, if he could keep me safe?

I'd do anything, be anything he wanted. I'd even stay, I wouldn't run.

I just wanted away from my family, I just wanted a life of my own, even if it was still curtailed by being a wife to a high-ranking lieutenant in a crime family.

"You're very handsome," I whispered, my voice husky.

He arched a brow. "Thank you." His voice was toneless, but his eyes gleamed with humor.

I felt gauche, very young and stupid, until he leaned into me, pressed a kiss to my temple, and whispered, "A handsome groom for a beautiful bride. We're going to make the congregation weep."

It was my turn for my lips to twitch, and I grinned at him, liking the softer side he was showing me, and hoping and praying, even though I knew both were stupid and dangerous, that maybe we could have something together.

Maybe we could take this arrangement and make it work for us.

Even if we led shorter lives thanks to our affiliations, we still had a long time on this earth to be tied together. I didn't want to spend every day miserable, and that kiss? His tenderness? While surprising, they filled me with dreams I shouldn't have.

That I was foolish to have.

THREE
EOGHAN

DECLAN CLAPPED me on the back mere seconds after Father Doyle, the boring bastard, declared Inessa and me man and wife.

I shot him a look over my shoulder, saw he was grinning at me—seeming to be genuinely pleased on my behalf—and rather than scowl at him, I shot him a wary smile before I turned back to the aisle and Inessa, and I started down the path that ran by the pews and into the South Transept.

We had to sign the registrar next, so we followed Doyle to the side chamber where the legalities would be dealt with. When we entered the small room, it was empty, but I knew people would be filtering in shortly.

People like my father and hers.

Though I'd kept a hold on my temper throughout the ceremony—just—now that I was out of there, I felt like a pressure cooker that'd been left on the stove for too long.

I was going to burst.

And I didn't intend for Inessa to be on the receiving end of that tonight.

I knew she was a virgin, knew it like I knew my fucking name, and there was no way I was blowing off my rage on her body when she was new to this shit.

I needed a long, hard fuck, but I wasn't going to get it.

Also, I wasn't going to scare the shit out of her. She was my wife, whether she or I wanted her to be, and we were going to be stuck together for a long ass time. No way did I want her flinching every time I fucked her. Not only would that drive me insane, but it would kill my boner.

I was a dangerous man, and I knew it. I owned it. But even though she wasn't my chosen bride, I'd never hurt her.

The fucker who had, on the other hand, I didn't have any loyalties to.

"Who did it?"

She jerked in surprise at my question—like she'd thought I was going to drop it or something.

She'd been staring around the side chamber like it housed a museum-worthy exhibition.

Spoiler alert, it didn't.

There was a table, a chair, some flowers on said table, and aside from a lectern with a bible on it, that was pretty much it.

"It doesn't matter," she replied, her voice low. Husky.

It pleased me.

In fact, it did more than please me.

It was sexy as shit.

Though there was no hint of the motherland to her tone—something I was relieved about, because I hated fucking Russians and didn't need the reminder she was one whenever she opened her goddamn mouth—neither was it the high-pitched drawl I was used to from New Yorkers I had on my speed dial. Although she was from Brighton Beach, she spoke like a lady, I guessed. Nothing brash about her, from her voice to her face to her wedding dress.

Demure.

Gentle.

It made me want to break the conditioning she'd been forced to adhere to, made me want to ruffle her, and...

Well, safe to say, do things I felt sure she wouldn't be happy about.

"Was it your father? Or that slut of a wife of his?"

Her eyes flashed for a second—in anger? Then she snorted and raised a hand, clapped it to her mouth, and giggled.

Fuck.

That sound did shit to me.

Sure, it reminded me that I felt like I was robbing the goddamn cradle, even though Dec had reminded me for the twenty millionth time that she was legal, that today was her birthday, but also, I liked it.

It suited her.

I'd only just been thinking of rumpling her, and there she went and did it for me.

Her eyes sparkled as she whispered, "Svetlana *is* a slut, isn't she?"

There was braggadocio lacing each word, like she was being daring, like she had to whisper just in case someone was listening... but no one was listening.

And they wouldn't.

I'd just locked us in here.

The second part of the ceremony, the shit that made this legal, wasn't about to go down until I had answers.

I wasn't necessarily a patient man, but Inessa, by the justification that she was mine and that I had to look after her because she was my wife, deserved patience.

"Yeah, she's a slut. And those nails look like they could do damage," I rasped, leaning back against the door. I might have looked relaxed, but I wasn't—if I found a single scratch from those claws on Inessa's body later, I'd be pulling them off each goddamn finger.

As the bloodthirsty thought drifted through my mind, I crossed my feet at the ankles, and I saw her take in my posture, and recognize my game—I wasn't moving until she told me what I wanted to know.

She blinked, fluttering long lashes that weren't fake, even if the rest of her makeup was, and whispered, "I don't want to cause trouble."

In all honesty, she couldn't have picked anything worse to say.

I gritted my teeth. "I won't hurt you."

Her eyes turned sad, and she tipped her head down. "They all say that."

Rage flushed through me, and I surged onto my feet and stalked toward her, not stopping until she backed up and into the desk, and I had her pinned in place.

With a delicacy that I was only known for when it came to killing people behind a scope a thousand yards away, I reached up and held her chin in place. "I will never hurt you, and no one else ever will either."

She tugged her chin free from my two-fingered hold, and something told me that behind the war paint she had slathered on, she was blushing—not with nerves, but anger.

"Don't make promises you can't keep."

I hadn't said the word 'promise,' but the childlike request had my mouth turning down at the edges.

"My father never beats my mother," I proffered, hoping she'd find comfort in that. "And Finn, who you'll meet later—"

"I know who Finn is. I know most of your family," she commented dryly. "It's just you I don't know."

I shrugged, unapologetic. "I didn't want to get married, and I sure as fuck didn't want to get married to an eighteen-year-old."

Her eyes widened, even as she muttered, "Be grateful the age was specified. If Papa could have, he'd have married me off to you at sixteen."

My top lip curled in disgust. Disgraceful bastard.

Though she'd shrugged off my hold on her chin, she hadn't moved away, and though her skirts were between us, my body leaned into hers, her heat leaching into me and mine into hers.

Mingling.

Morphing into one unit.

"He did it, didn't he?" I repeated, just needing confirmation.

"Svetlana started it." Her words were matter-of-fact, showing me my wife was smart enough to sense that I wasn't going to back down from this. "But Papa finished it."

"Don't call him Papa in front of me. Papas," I mocked, "don't do this shit to their kids." I tipped my chin up as she had and stated, "We didn't want each other, but we'll get along well if you don't piss me off."

"And what if you piss me off?" She huffed. "Like you are now."

The spirited question surprised me and had me grinning. "Then we'll get along even better, won't we?"

She stilled at that, her eyes darting over my face as she studied my smile.

I noticed Inessa looked at my face a lot. Like she was trying to read my expression... Then, of course, I got it. Call me fucking slow, but I could sense she read a face to read the mood.

Her fucking father was going to pay.

I didn't give a shit that she'd been his longer than she'd been mine. The second that fucking contract had come to exist between our families, he should have treated her with fucking kid gloves.

She reached up, surprising me further by letting the tips of her fingers trail over my smile.

When she stopped, tilting her head to the side, I asked, "You aren't scared of me?"

The notion was unusual. Most people were scared of me outside of the family. With good reason. I was a lethal motherfucker. And I'd kill anyone who got in my way.

But this young kid wasn't.

I mean, she had been. I'd seen that back at the altar.

Especially when I'd taken a long ass time to raise her veil.

Now?

Something had changed.

Because I intended on having sex tonight, I wasn't going to complain about her defenses lowering, but I was definitely curious.

"You're not the biggest monster I've come across."

Her words floored me.

Fucking floored me.

And not because I was jealous either.

Our eyes met and held, and out of nowhere, a flame soared between us, arcing into being.

The lust came as a surprise, but the depth of it?

Annihilation.

It razed me to the ground.

Then the doorknob twisted, a knock at the door sounded, and a grumble in Russian clued me in to the fact that the families were out there.

A hearty laugh sounded next, and I knew that was my father. He'd be amused, thinking I was trying to bone my bride before I even signed my life away, but I wasn't.

I wanted answers.

The doorknob rattled again, and I ignored it, though she didn't. Inessa tensed, gulping, and that angered me even more.

So, I straightened up, pissed that the burn of heat between us had chilled, and I stalked away. Unlocking it quietly, I pulled open the door just as someone shoved it. When Vasov, her cunt of a father, almost toppled into me, I reached out to stop him and took advantage.

Within seconds, his arm was behind his back, and I jerked upward. Svetlana the Slut screamed as I dislocated her husband's shoulder.

"You'll lose your fucking hand if you touch my wife again," I growled over his screams that had guards surging forward and guns being drawn.

My eyes darted over to my father, and while I had expected some anger, I wasn't altogether surprised to see the excitement in his eyes.

He was a sick fucker too.

We both shared that trait.

He waved a hand at the guards to back off, but I saw Bratva hovering around, and knew they'd get trigger-happy if this shit wasn't handled quickly.

His words were calm, too calm, when he questioned, "Vasov, is my son's bride wearing bruises?"

The Pakhan was howling as he clutched his shoulder, telling me the pussy didn't enter the field all that much anymore.

We were all foot soldiers, even if we had gone up the ranks and were riding it out at the top. We were used to pain, used to bleeding for the cause, but Vasov had grown soft.

And while it was only physically I was talking about, I figured that softness would have infiltrated every aspect of his life too.

That was the way of it.

It was like fucking blight. Once it hit one spot of a crop, it would fell an entire field.

I wondered if the blight spread past his family, deeper than poisoning just the man, but maybe his territory too. A chink had to exist in the Bratva's armor if this was the making of the man they called Pakhan...

A flurry of Russian came from Svetlana, who darted forward to attack me. My mother, God love her, stuck out her foot so the bitch went flying.

I laughed, amused by the scene, and Da followed me. Ma shook her head, and Father Doyle, standing in the corner, sighed. "It's a sinful day to be fighting, Eoghan."

"I'll make it up to you, Father," I rumbled. "I'm sure the church needs a new stained-glass window or something."

When his eyes gleamed, I knew I had holy forgiveness for my soul, but it didn't stop me from adding to the tarnish on it by jerking Vasov's arm higher, forcing his whimpers into a whole other octave, and stating, "I mean it, bitch. You touch her again, and I will slice off your hand and throw it to my dog. You fucking understand me?"

He didn't reply, just cried out his agony. Svetlana, on the floor, called something to Inessa in Russian, and I wasn't surprised when her voice, calm as anything, intoned, "Eoghan, that's enough, don't you think?"

I twisted to look at her over my shoulder, scowling at her calmness. "He hurt you."

"And you've hurt him." Her smile was soft. "Thank you."

She meant that.

Those two words...they were genuine.

And again, that flame arced between us, and even as my dick grew hard, I released her cunt of a father to stride over to my new wife.

She knew I'd protect her now, knew I'd honor her, so there was no better time to sign her life into my keeping.

And mine into hers.

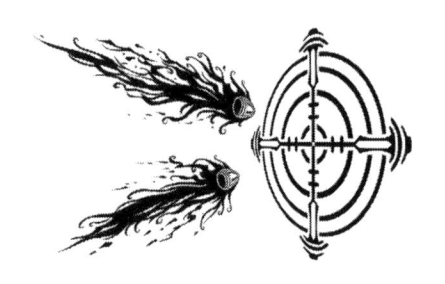

FOUR
INESSA

I'D KNOWN, because I'd listened to the organizers plan the reception, but it was non-Russian to the core.

We didn't have any of the usual traditions that were part and parcel of a celebration such as this one—there wasn't even the traditional recanting of, "*Gorko! Gorko! Gorko!*" which was the declaration after the first toast for the couple to kiss, to chase away the bitterness of the alcohol used in the toast.

The only Russian aspect of the event was that there was free flowing vodka, and that was mostly because my father's men, who were in attendance, might have started a riot if they hadn't had the free bar to soothe the very anti-Russian celebration.

Still, all told, it hadn't been a bad party, mostly because every time I'd felt the strain of my new circumstances, I'd looked over at my father, who had his arm in a sling, and who sported the face of a pissed off bear who'd been awoken from hibernation two months too early.

Straightaway, that sight cheered me up.

Eoghan mostly ignored me during the meal, which was delicious but not enough to tempt me to eat more than a few bites, and I was strangely okay with his silence. I had Declan, the best man and Eoghan's brother, to my left, and on Eoghan's right, he had my maid-of-honor, Veronika, a boring cousin who had a wicked temper when crossed.

I wasn't the only one he was ignoring, because he evaded her every attempt at conversation, and just sat there, brooding, slouched back in the seat that was like a throne as he watched over the events.

The place was done out classily, I'd give the organizers that.

The parquet floor had over eighty round tables dotted around in a formation only they knew, and each was decorated with overflowing centerpieces that consisted of the freshest of flowers with ivy trailing over the linen as they demarcated the settings between diners, almost putting people at a point on a clock face.

The head table was at the back of the room in a very fancy hotel that, I got the feeling, was a front for the Five Points—a genius, wasn't I?—and the dance floor was bordered by the tables, creating a huge semicircle. Overhead, large pieces of netting and fabric had been swathed like something from a pasha's cavern, rich silks and such draped here and there with more foliage swirling into being, heavy chandeliers dripping with crystals refracting light, and hidden inside a heavily gilded kind of box, the DJ played tunes that were alien to me at these events.

Soft notes. Jazz. Sinatra. Some classical music. None of the robust songs I was used to hearing.

A part of me wondered if I'd ever hear them again. Father had made it clear that the second I was married, I was no longer Bratva, but I was expected to feed him information out of loyalty to the brotherhood that had raised me.

So, technically, I was now Five Points. I'd be attending Catholic ceremonies and events, not Russian ones.

Would Father let me attend my sister's wedding when her time of sacrifice came?

I had to wonder, even if I knew the answer already.

"You're looking way too miserable for a girl who has a plate of chocolate in front of her."

Declan was surprisingly cheerful, and even though he kept shooting glowers at Eoghan, it seemed like usual, he'd appointed himself as the official family greeter. Like he was the one charged with smoothing things over because Eoghan couldn't be expected to do it himself. He'd been doing that for years, but it wasn't like Declan was going to be living with us. He couldn't keep doing that on his brother's behalf.

Eoghan had made it known, quite clearly, that he didn't want a wife, and yet, he'd gone to great and dangerous lengths to honor me. To show me the kind of husband he'd be.

The only thing I didn't believe?

That he wouldn't hurt me.

All men hurt women.

I knew that just as I knew I was a Bratva daughter in a Five Point family who would never truly trust me.

I was the enemy. The Trojan Horse they believed would betray them at the first chance...

An outsider, and a dangerous one at that.

Because Declan was trying, I murmured, "I don't actually like chocolate."

My wry comment had his brows lowering. "Thought all bitches liked chocolate."

Nose crinkling at his phrasing, I muttered, "Well, maybe all bitches do, but I don't."

His eyes twinkled, but what surprised me was Eoghan's chuckle. "You teach him some manners, Inessa. You'd think he was raised on a pig farm with that mouth of his."

Declan's eyes widened to such a degree he looked like he was in a cartoon. "Me?" he boomed, pointing his finger at himself. "Me? I'm the one with the mouth of a sailor?"

Eoghan grinned—I saw, because I cast him a look to see if Declan was joking or not—and stated, "Ma would be so ashamed."

Declan growled, "We all know I'm her favorite."

Eoghan laughed, and the tenor told me Declan wasn't telling the truth. "I'm the baby."

"And don't we fucking know it." The second he finished, he winced. "Sorry, Inessa."

My lips curved. "I've heard worse."

Eoghan growled, but I ignored him—he kept doing that. A part of me wondered if I'd married myself to a wolf, but that was ridiculous.

He was just a grouch.

But I could deal with grouchiness, could even deal with a man who was more likely to scowl at me than smile, just so long as he didn't hurt me.

And there were so many ways to hurt me that he probably didn't even know.

I gnawed on my bottom lip at the thought and turned to look at my new husband, who was still slouched on the throne we had at the top table like he truly was a king, and I was his queen.

But I wasn't royalty.

How could I be?

"What is it?"

His focus swerved onto me with the precision of a laser, making me gulp, even as I appreciated the way his gaze softened the second he'd traced over my expression.

I would never mistake him for a kind man, but at least he wasn't being mean to me.

"You look bored."

He blinked. "You only prevaricate about family. Have you noticed that?"

There was a lot to prevaricate about where they were concerned.

I blinked back at him. "I prefer to be honest."

He slipped forward, resting his elbow on the armrest. "Interesting, considering if there's a point in our lives where I won't trust you, it's with them and where they're concerned."

I slipped closer, not stopping until our noses were barely an inch or two away from one another. "You can decide whether or not to trust me, I can't control what you think or feel."

"Just like I can't control what you think or feel." He hummed. "Little bird, are you going to fly back to your nest with little twitters?" he mused, reaching up to cup my cheek.

The second his fingers brushed the skin there, little shivers danced down my spine.

"What kind of twitters?"

"You know what kind." He narrowed his eyes, and his hand moved to cup my throat. He didn't put any pressure on it, didn't even tighten his hold, but the weight there was...interesting.

Instead of making me feel like I was choking, and I knew what that felt like, he made me feel...

Bound.

The sensation was unusual, and I let him take the weight of my head off my neck by tipping it to the side.

I knew I'd shocked him, even if he covered his surprise with a quick flare of his eyes.

"You have to know what Father wants from this match."

"What he wants, he isn't necessarily going to get," he rasped, and his words had my brain whirling.

"Is that why you've been quiet?"

He snorted. "Plotting your family's demise? No. Even if your fucker of a father deserves it." His lips thinned. "I'm quiet because I hate crowds."

The admission surprised me. Not just because he was admitting to a weakness, but because crowds were a part of our lives. "We're raised with them."

We were. We were used to, by necessity, large, overbearing events.

In our world, we lived fast and died young.

The goal, of course, was to die young without someone else's blade in your heart.

"I still hate them," he replied with a shrug, and I appreciated the little tidbit, the insight into his mind.

"Why?"

"Want to use it against me?"

The suggestion had me laughing a little. "How can I do that? Should we go on a safari so you can be stampeded by a herd of wildebeest? Because, let's face it, this crowd is probably more dangerous than them."

"Huh?"

I figured that would stump him, so I grinned at him, and the sight had his eyes darkening from chocolate brown to almost black. My visceral response to that was unnerving, so I ducked my gaze, and muttered, "Never mind."

He surprised me by grunting. "I don't like bullshit."

My brow puckered. "Does anyone?"

"I have less patience for it than most."

I thought about that for a second. "You're a—" I cleared my throat. "The things you do, they require patience."

"And silence... I'm good with that."

He broke off the conversation by glowering at a server who tried to pour some more wine for him. I hadn't even realized someone was nearby, but he had, so I took the chance to study him. I had a lot to learn about my husband, but I was willing to.

Funny how, as I got out of the limo this morning, traipsing into a church that was bedecked with a thousand flowers and more ornamentation that didn't suit my style but declared to the world how wealthy our families were, I hadn't wanted to know him at all.

Had wanted to go out of my way to irritate the man who'd avoided me for years since the betrothal contract between us had been signed.

He could have eased me into marriage, courted me.

But he hadn't.

He'd kept it as a business deal, telling me what he thought about me without even having to look at me, without even having to whisper a painful word.

Then he'd seen my bruises, then he'd dislocated my father's arm, and I'd known my husband was no ordinary mobster.

How did that not deserve a truth? Some trust? Some gratitude?

So I blew out a breath. "He wants me to tell him things."

My voice was low enough for not even Veronika, who I could imagine was trying to eavesdrop, even if her English was shit, to hear a word.

Hell, my statement was soundless, especially over the sounds of "New York, New York" playing in the background.

"And are you going to tell him anything?"

"My loyalty comes with a price," I informed him.

"How high a price?" I saw distaste flutter into his eyes, and his mouth curved into a quick, derogatory flash that told me what he thought of that answer.

Simply, I told him, "You already paid it."

He tensed, then his gaze drifted from my eyes and over my shoulder to where our families were sitting at the tables nearest ours —his to the right of him, mine to the left of me—and when his lips curved softly, I knew he saw my father wearing a sling formed of black silk that a *boyevik* had run out to purchase for him.

"Your price is that low, little bird?" he rasped, and maybe I was crazy, but I could hear the lilt of Ireland in the words. "I did that for pleasure."

"You did that for me," I countered. I knew I was his property, but he could easily have let it slide. Hell, most men wouldn't have even noticed beneath the heavy makeup I was wearing.

But Eoghan did.

Eoghan was different.

I liked different.

I licked my lips at the thought and wasn't unaware that his gaze drifted to my mouth.

A shaky breath escaped me, and I felt the sweet surge of desire trickle through me.

I hadn't expected that.

Hadn't anticipated that I might want him.

That my body could come to crave his.

But here I was, my pussy getting slick, and all because this man had his hand about my throat and his gaze was focused on my mouth...

Would wonders never cease?

For a second, it was like time stood still. The heat from the church, before he'd dislocated my father's shoulder, seemed to appear once more, swirling about our feet like a volcano had just erupted between us.

I wasn't sure where it came from, didn't even think about questioning why the feelings were there. Though I was a virgin, I knew enough to recognize what I was experiencing. I'd touched myself, had used vibrators, so desire wasn't new to me.

What *was* new?

That the desire in me was inspired by this man.

A man who'd been like a specter in my life for so long that I'd been pretty sure some days that he didn't even exist, that it was all a joke.

But as the wedding neared, as the details were finalized, I'd come to realize that was wishful thinking.

Still, the way he made me feel, both physically and sexually, had to bode well, didn't it?

I hadn't come here today thinking my groom would turn me on. I'd half-expected to be repulsed by his dark nature, his reputation having already preceded him. I'd anticipated wanting to run away even more.

But that was the last thing on my mind.

Maybe I was the slut my father had accused me of being.

The thought nearly poured water on the flames flickering between us, but before it had a chance to outright wreck it, the music came to a gentle halt as the sound of a spoon flicking against crystal pinged around the massive space.

Evidently, it was coordinated, because the sheer mass of humanity that was in attendance didn't demur and instantly fell silent.

Obedience, ha. We were all on a leash. Even Eoghan.

His fingers squeezed my throat, letting me feel the pad of each digit, and rather than be threatened by the move, it felt good.

Oddly...right.

And yeah, I knew that was weird, but nothing about today had turned out like I'd expected. I'd thought I was leaving the house of one brute and entering the house of another, but Eoghan, though his eyes hid a multitude of sins, didn't give off the same vibe.

I only prayed my instincts on that score weren't totally wrong.

He relinquished his hold on my throat, and I felt as though all the stuffing had disappeared from my bones as I almost slouched in my seat. He smirked at the sight, a quick twist of his lips that made my heart flutter, before he reached for my hand and bridged our fingers together.

Together, like royalty, we faced the room as the speeches began.

His hold on me was firm.

Hot.

Possessive.

And oddly enough, I didn't mind.

Not one bit.

FIVE

EOGHAN

I WAS ON A PROMISE—I could feel her ease with me, knew that when I took her into the bedroom, we'd probably enjoy something I'd been dreading since I'd learned I was being forced to marry into the Bratva.

Virgins weren't my thing. 'Deflowering' them? Even less so.

But Inessa? She was like no virgin I'd ever come across. Just remembering the heat between us, the way she'd sank into my hold made my dick ache.

So as I stepped out of the elevator with my new wife's hand in mine, I immediately froze at the sight before me because that promise of a semi-decent night in the sack? Ruptured beyond belief.

Before, it had been an advantage to walk straight into the apartment that I'd been gifted by my father after a successful mission. Now?

I regretted it.

Wholeheartedly.

Inessa, at my side, tensed and pulled her hand free from mine, and I couldn't fucking blame her.

Outrage blurred into fury as I stared at the scene ahead.

"How the fuck did you get my entrance code?"

Leticia, frozen against the sofa, didn't unthaw at my growl. If anything, her eyes turned into big, round, terror-filled globes as she stared at me, quivering.

Her tits also quivered, and because she was naked, every inch of her on display, I got a very private show of everything else that quivered too.

Inessa, like the goddamn queen she was—either that, or she was some kind of fucking saint—stalked past me and headed straight down the hall. I knew she didn't have a clue where she was going, because she'd never been in the apartment before, but her intent was to escape, and I couldn't fucking blame her.

She didn't even slam the door when she went into, unluckily for her, the first room down the hall—my bedroom.

She just closed it quietly.

Quietly.

When she deserved to slap me, fuck, stab me. If anyone had disrespected me to this level, I'd probably have sliced their throat from ear to goddamn ear.

"Shut your fucking legs," I snarled at my now ex-mistress.

She didn't obey, but when I stalked toward her, she immediately snapped them closed, then finally defrosted and began to scuttle around the sofa.

"If you make me catch you, you'll regret it," I threatened, not about to take any bullshit.

I knew Leticia well enough to know that the freak got off on being chased, pinned down, and fucked—something that, sometimes, I was quite amenable to doing, but this was different.

She'd come into my home without an invitation, on my goddamn wedding day. What the actual fuck?

So no way in shit was I building up her arousal, even accidentally, when my new wife was a door away.

Leticia froze, and I saw she'd run over to her clothes which she'd left in a puddle on the floor.

The sight irritated me even more.

She knew I hated when she did that. How was I supposed to get a boner when there was mess on the fucking floor?

"How did you get in?" I snarled, my fists bunching at my sides.

"I-I saw you put it in a few times. That's how I knew the code."

While the answer made sense, while it was logical, I knew it was bullshit.

I stared at her for a second, tipped my head to the side, and demanded, "Get out, and don't come back."

Her eyes flared wide, reminding me of a deer in headlights, and she whispered, "Until you call me, baby, okay. I won't let you down again."

"No," I countered firmly. "Don't come here again. Get the fuck out and don't come back for good."

"But—"

"No fucking buts," I growled.

"What about my stuff?" she whined, making me frown at her.

"What stuff? You never brought any shit with you."

Her brow puckered. "Some make up. In the bathroom."

My mouth pursed into a tight line.

Sabotage.

That was all this could be.

Walking home to her naked, then her bringing shit with her that she stacked in my bathroom? A bathroom I had to figure Inessa was using right about now?

Someone was behind this, and while Leticia wasn't a total dumbass, she wasn't smart enough for this shit. If she was, she'd have figured that starting off married life with a mistress in my home wouldn't have been at the top of today's to do list.

"Fuck. Off," I growled, pissed beyond reason that my fucking mistress had been weaponized against me.

She was a good actress, so I wasn't surprised by the crystalline tears that began to roll down her cheeks at my anger.

Maybe a few years ago, I'd have believed that, believed her sorrow was real. But I was older, and I had Finn's Aoife in my life. Aoife was a real woman. She cried, and when she did, her face turned pink and splotchy because everything she did was genuine.

This bitch?

The exact opposite of genuine.

Shit like that hadn't mattered to me before, especially not with the women where the only things we shared were sweat and a rubber, but now? It irritated me.

In fact, it did more than that. It irritated the fuck out of me.

Finally unfolding my fists, I scrubbed a hand across my chin as she stared at me, not goddamn moving like I asked, and when I released a grunt, that had her jerking into action and scurrying away like the snake she was.

I didn't twist around to watch her go. Instead, I followed her movements in the mirror over the mantelpiece.

I never trusted the sluts I fucked, but Leticia had just lied to me.

About accessing my fucking apartment. My home.

How the hell had she done that?

Who the fuck was she working for? Not only people who'd given her the key to my place, but who'd sent her here on today of all days.

As the doors began to open, I didn't flinch, because I knew the elevator hadn't been called since Inessa and I had exited from it, but I moved to grab my weapon just in case someone was waiting in there. Crazier shit had happened, and I didn't intend on having my head blown off—not today, at any rate. The notion that Inessa was there, twenty or so feet away, potentially in danger, didn't sit well with me either, but I wasn't about to let the slut scurrying away like a frightened mouse think I was scared about showing her my back.

The elevator was empty, and she scuttled inside, flipping me a bird she didn't know I could see before the doors closed again—only then did I turn around and move.

The dashboard in the entranceway allowed me to change the code to my apartment, and I had to admit to growing lax. After Finn's home had been infiltrated a couple of years ago, Conor, our resident whiz kid with everything tech, had put all kinds of protocols in place to save our asses from ourselves.

I wasn't usually lazy, but I'd admit to not giving much of a fuck about my security in recent days.

What with leaving the country frequently to fulfill jobs, and when I was here, getting into fistfights with my father over this fucked up wedding, I hadn't really thought about changing the passcode.

Which someone had taken advantage of.

But who?

I tapped a few keys, initiating the resetting feature, and with a touch of whimsy I wasn't known for, used today's date as the code.

Once that was done, I had three options.

Figure out who the fuck had thought it was funny to send my mistress to my new home when they had to know I'd be bringing my bride back with me—half of goddamn Manhattan knew what was going down today.

Or figure out if that same person was the fucker who'd given her the code to my residence.

Or go and appease Inessa.

The fact I wanted to appease her even a little was testament to the way I'd appreciated her comportment today.

She might have been eighteen, but not only had she acted like a lady in the face of all the shit that'd gone down, I figured she deserved my respect.

I knew for a fact that any other bitch who came into her new house and saw some other cunt with her legs spread wide as she sprawled back on the sofa like she was in some kind of porn shoot wouldn't have just walked off.

They'd be nails out and claws deep in the other bitch.

I rubbed my chin again and, though she deserved an apology, decided to ruin Conor's evening first. I'd seen him eying up some

Bratva pussy and knew I needed to save him from himself—what could I say, the Bratva were fuckers, but they bred hotties.

Inessa was no different.

After I reached for my cell and connected the call, only a few seconds later, my brother ground out, "Aren't you supposed to be dick deep in your wife? Like I was trying to be in Klara?"

I rolled my eyes. "Consider it my way of giving you a pre-emptive thanks. If you fuck her, you know Da will have you by the ballocks."

"But what a way to go." He whistled, and a feminine giggle sounded in the background. Unlike Inessa's, it was contrived. Nothing like the pure, sweet sound she'd gifted me with back in the registrar's room.

The thought made me ache a little, and I wasn't a man made for aching unless it was thanks to a bullet wound to the belly or something.

Uneasily, I stared at the city ahead, seeing a side of it few ever would. This high up, the ground was a blur, and the skyline was awash with lights you only ever saw in photos. In the flesh? It was a thousand times more magnificent.

I'd been all around the world, holed up in tiny places, high up and away from the rest of humanity, but never had I seen a view that compared.

I strode over to the wall of windows to overlook the city that never slept.

This was my home in more ways than one. This city was ours. Hell's Kitchen was only our playground.

"Eoghan? The fuck? You just called and go heavy breathing on me? I have someone to do."

Anger washed through me, making me see red again. "Got back to Leticia sitting in my apartment."

The words had silence filtering down the line.

All my brothers knew how particular I was about my personal space.

I figured it was thanks to a childhood of hand-me-downs and the like—we might be rich as fuck, but Ma was a shrewd mare. No way was she going to buy the youngest of her five spawn new gear when she had plenty of old stuff sitting around.

I was used to everything being recycled, everything having belonged to another of my brothers—until this place.

It was mine.

All mine.

Everything was new, everything had my stamp on it, and even though I'd asked a decorator to help me with it, I'd micromanaged her down to the ornaments she'd put on my mantelpiece and the knobs she'd used on the kitchen cabinets.

Conor knew I wasn't going to give the code out to some slut I was banging.

Fuck, it would take me a few days to trust Inessa with the code—and she was my wife now. She was going to live here, and since I didn't want her to think she was a prisoner, I had no choice but to give it to her. But not one of my brothers knew the code, no one did except for me.

Until Leticia, and whoever had given it to her, because as much as she had a pussy that could suck cum out of a cock better than a mouth, she was no rocket scientist.

"Shit."

While there was nothing funny about this situation, my lips twitched at Conor's curse, and I heard shifting and shuffling around as he evidently started climbing out of bed.

"Yeah. Shit."

"You just couldn't figure out our system had been compromised forty minutes later, could you?" he grumbled.

I snickered. "Forty minutes, my ass."

"You questioning my staying power?" he grumbled again.

"No, I'm questioning your interest." Forty minutes? No way could Conor hold interest in some random bitch for that long.

If he knew me, I knew him.

Conor was particular.

In his own way.

And Klara, who I remembered from the bridal party, with her dark hair and long limbs, while beautiful, wasn't Conor's type. He liked big, busty broads whose tits he could dive in without coming up for air for hours.

That kind of woman would hold his attention. Not a skinny bitch like Klara.

He cursed under his breath. "I'll be on my way home, Klara." A shriek sounded down the line, and he grunted again before he muttered, "Fucker."

"That aimed at me, or at you?" I inquired, amused to hear my brother's evening nosedive like mine had.

I twisted around and stared at the room Leticia had just marred, then I pulled a face.

I was going to have to buy a new sofa, and that pissed me off because the current sofa was really fucking comfortable.

Out of respect to Inessa, I could see no other way around it, but I'd miss the bastard.

It was oversized white leather, took up three-quarters of the fucking room, and stared straight onto a TV that made cinema screens look puny.

Grumbling to myself, I stepped over a sheepskin rug, and grabbed some M&Ms from the bowl I had on the console table that backed the sofa.

"Bitch hit me with her heel," Conor groused when I heard a door slam in the background.

"You deserved it."

"And how the hell would you know that? Watching the action, were you?" he jeered.

My lips twitched as I popped another M&M into my mouth. Crunching down on it, I told him, "You might have the attention span of a gnat, but you always make it worth a bitch's while."

"It's creepy that you know that about me."

"Know creepy shit about all you fuckers. You know that."

He huffed. "Sicko."

"Yup," was my cheerful retort.

There was a reason I was my father's favorite, even if I hadn't been feeling like his goddamn favorite with the arranged marriage.

Birds of a feather...and all that.

I'd inherited most of the crap that made him a lunatic, and while I had a better handle on it, one thing I didn't have?

Ma.

Lena O'Donnelly was calm, rational, and level-headed. Everything my da wasn't. Though she had little to do with the business, outside of rallying the womenfolk together when times grew tough and all the women had to go on lockdown for their safekeeping at our compound, I had a feeling she was the reason my father was on the brink of hitting seventy.

Without her calming influence, he'd have been dead twenty years ago.

Of course, I wouldn't be married if that was the case. Aidan Jr., my eldest brother and our father's namesake, wasn't the type to force his brothers into arranged marriages, even if that was the number one way of uniting enemies.

There was a bittersweet irony to the fact that I'd be better off with Da dead...at least, by that logic.

Conor grunted, and the sound dragged me away from the darker recesses of my mind. "You have any clue who it might be?"

"The usual suspects. I'll start digging," he muttered on a sigh, and I heard the thud of his fingers on his phone screen that told me he was already working on shit.

"Do you think the whole system has been compromised?" I queried.

"I hate to say it, but yeah. Potentially. Fuck. I had so many firewalls on our security systems that I don't have a goddamn clue how they could be broken—"

"Maybe they weren't," I said softly. Conor had lost a lot of bonuses when someone had hacked our security a couple of years back. I highly doubted he was bullshitting me.

"Then how?"

I shrugged, not really knowing where I was going with this, but... "There's a camera in the elevator. Could someone have hacked that?"

I appreciated the notion even less, to be fair. I'd done a lot of shit in that elevator...including transporting dead bodies down it.

Unease slithered through my veins when Conor muttered, "It should be all tied together."

"Maybe it wasn't." I blew out a sigh. "Just figure it out, Conor. Please?"

"Why do you think she was there?"

"From the little she was wearing, she wanted to fuck."

"She was naked?" he blurted, his surprise clear.

"Yeah, legs spread wide...that's how I walked in. Inessa saw it—"

"Aw, shit. That sucks."

He wasn't joking, which surprised me. We were a close-knit family, but we were guys. If we could rub salt in the wound, we often did. Which meant my brothers were giving Inessa the benefit of the doubt. That came as a shock considering her ties, but I figured the fact I'd maimed her father today made them pity her.

Not ideal, but better than outright loathing.

From our own experiences, we knew not to always pin the sins of the father on the sons. For all the sins we'd committed, they were nothing to Aidan O'Donnell Sr.'s. That was why he was obsessed with church and confession. He figured that was the only way he and Ma would be together in the afterlife.

Crazy, yup. But I'd already called him a lunatic for a reason...

"Yeah, it does."

"I like her."

Conor's declaration had me raising a brow, especially as it had tapped into what I was already thinking. "You do?"

"I think you do too," he countered, ignoring my question. "Otherwise, you wouldn't have broken Vasov's shoulder—"

"I didn't break it. I dislocated it."

"Well, by the time Da was done with the story, you'd dislocated it, broken it, and incapacitated him for life."

Despite myself, I had to chuckle. Sure, I was still pissed at my father—last week's beating had bruised my ego—but you had to appreciate a man who'd kissed the Blarney stone without ever having set foot in Ireland.

"Well, I didn't. He'll heal. More than the fucker deserves."

"What happened?"

"He beat Inessa."

Conor whistled. "Your hotspot."

"Yeah," I rumbled. "Anyway, can I leave this in your hands?"

"Of course, *deartháir*," he said softly, evidently sensing my irritation had surged again, trying to appease me.

Not a one of us was truly Irish. Only Brennan had visited the old country, but it was in our bones. Our blood. We only used Gaelic at heightened moments, and that Conor used it then?

Told me he understood.

I bit the inside of my cheek, then muttered, "Wish me luck."

"Da isn't the only one who kissed the Blarney stone at birth." That our thoughts were attuned once more made my lips twitch. The whole birds of a feather thing usually pissed me off, but today, Conor was right on the money. "You'll talk your way out of it," he stated confidently.

I didn't reply, just mumbled, "Later," and cut the call.

Maybe he was right, but the difference was, I didn't want to talk my way out of shit.

Inessa deserved an explanation, but what could I say? She knew this world, knew how it worked...

I blew out a breath, then twisted around and decided to get this over and done with.

Tonight was going to end a lot shittier than I'd imagined. I'd had two willing women waiting on me when I came up here—Inessa had warmed up after Declan and I had encouraged a couple of glasses of wine down her throat over the course of the day. Not enough to incapacitate, but enough to relax her—and then Leticia. Now? I had zero.

"Fuck's sake," I muttered under my breath, before I inhaled and went to atone for a sin I hadn't even fucking committed.

If this was marriage, it already goddamn sucked.

SIX

INESSA

AS I STARED in the mirror, I was surprised by what I saw, even if the bruises weren't new to me.

I'd known when I walked through the door that this space was Eoghan's bedroom, and seeing all the female shit in here had twisted my guts, but I wasn't about to complain, even if the sight surprised me. I couldn't easily imagine Eoghan sharing his space with anyone—he was too self-contained—but I was too grateful for the makeup products to get snippy over it.

Over the length of the day, the makeup plastered on my face made me feel like I was slicked in oil, and the tender flesh beneath had started to throb, reminding me of the pain I was in.

So, here I stood, having used my new husband's mistress's makeup remover, in my wedding dress, bruises on full display.

I was making a statement.

I knew that.

A dangerous one.

I stood here, covered to the max—and by contrast with what I'd just seen, the max was the truth—but somehow more exposed than his mistress had been.

I wasn't surprised when he slipped into the room and into the doorway without me noticing. He had the tread of a panther—perfect for his work, I supposed. He stood there, looking pissed off and agitated, then our eyes connected in the mirror, and shock hit him first, then more rage as he broke the connection and swept his gaze over me.

Father and Svetlana had done a number on me, that was for fucking sure. I looked like I'd been tied to a garbage truck and dragged over Brighton Beach for hours on end.

When Eoghan's usually impassive features began to scrunch up, I looked away, dipped my chin, and began to clear up the cotton pads I'd used to clear off the makeup.

A part of me hadn't been sure if he was actually having sex with the woman we'd come across in his living room, and though I hadn't heard anything, I was oddly relieved to notice that he was as neatly dressed as he'd been when I'd left him behind.

I had no rights to him.

Not really.

He had all the rights in this relationship.

He could fuck whoever he wanted, could even impregnate them, and I didn't have a say in the matter.

Me?

If I so much as looked at another man, that man might end up dead for daring to 'eye fuck' a Five Points' man's bride, and me? Only Christ himself knew what punishment I'd get for my sins...perceived or otherwise.

If Eoghan was anything like my father, he punished sins that hadn't even happened. *Just in case.*

It was easier to maintain a hold on things if everyone was terrified of you, and that was how Father ran his family and his business.

I mean, I wasn't going to make a saint out of Aidan O'Donnelly Sr. I pretty much knew that was how he ran his empire too—Eoghan's beating told me that—but there was a family at the heart of everything.

I'd seen it today.

Had seen Eoghan's face when he danced with his mom, and how all his brothers had gone out of their way, when the dancing had started, to try to make me smile.

Aidan Sr. hadn't felt me up like I'd seen Father do to the new bride of Antoni, my cousin and Father's namesake, and I'd been treated with a level of cautious respect—like I was a bitch, of the canine variety, that they weren't sure would bite them or not.

Beyond that, I'd seen the brothers joking, slapping each other on the back, laughing and grinning at random stuff like people who loved each other did.

At least, that was how it worked in the movies.

And thus far, that was pretty much the only kind of functioning family I'd seen—in film.

And while we were both rooted in the upper ranks of criminal empires, which were an entirely different breed of kin, where blood and bone were sacrificed on the regular in the family's name, I could see the difference.

There was love there.

Love in the O'Donnelly's hearth.

I bit my lip, then winced when it pulled on the paper stitch I'd uncovered beneath ten tons of lipstick. There was another, more ragged one, on the bridge of my nose, and I had various little pieces of miracle 'paper' that had been used to hide a multitude of sins.

Not my own, of course.

My father's, although the split lip was a parting gift from Svetlana.

"I should have sliced his throat."

Eoghan's rasp sent shudders down my spine.

Not in a bad way, but a good one.

Yeah, odd, I knew.

But, in my own way, I was immune to violence. Hearing his statement didn't make me cower, didn't fill me with fear.

If anything, I liked it.

I responded to it.

Fucked up, but true. Because that growl? Signified safety. Protection. And I'd never had that before. Certainly not from my father. He was too high up the ladder to touch, but Eoghan could touch him. He *had* touched him, and I wasn't sure I'd ever be able to convey just how grateful I was for what he'd done for me today.

Though I had that in mind, I let my gaze drift to his once more, sending him a silent message, one I wasn't sure he'd be able to interpret.

Men always hurt women.

He wasn't mine—sure, in name he was, but we hadn't had sex. We didn't know each other. We'd barely spoken all day, and what we had discussed wasn't exactly talk of love.

Eoghan couldn't hurt me more than my father had, at least, well, he could sexually, but I didn't get that vibe from him. Still, pain...that was all men like him gave to women like me. I was telling him I knew that. Showing him what I'd gone through already, and silently asking him not to treat me the same way.

He stepped forward, still looking as neat as he had when I'd arrived at the church. In fact, it was uncanny how put together he was, especially in the face of my own appearance.

His suit wasn't even rumpled, the sleeves showing few creases. If anything, he looked so immaculate and tidy that I wondered if, halfway through the day, he'd changed suits or something. His hair was still well-coiffed, and even his chin was stubble free.

Mentally, I filtered through the day's events, trying to see if it was possible for him to have gone off and fucked someone, then changed clothes and showered—but, as far as I was aware, he hadn't. Yeah, while that sounded insane, it was possible. Antoni hadn't noticed Father eying up and fondling his new bride because he'd been fucking her maid of honor! I'd caught them at it in the bathroom.

So while it was distinctly doable, I didn't think he had. Nor had I seen any giggling women trying to make eye contact with me, rubbing my nose in the fact that my groom had just slept with them—and trust me, in our circles, that was exactly what would happen.

He came to a halt a few inches away from me, but I could feel his heat, his warmth sinking into me like I was freezing, even if I wasn't.

Then he raised his hands, let them hover over my shoulders for a second, and I watched him, watched him hesitate, before he bridged the gap.

He stared at me, and I stared at him, then his fingers traced up and down my arms. My sleeves got in the way of direct contact, but it still felt good.

"I'm sorry."

I tilted my head to the side, not willing to allow him to use the word 'sorry' as a whitewashing tool. "For what?"

His eyes narrowed, but his top lip quirked to the side. "You're not going to let me get away with shit, are you?" Before I could answer, he rumbled, "Probably for the fucking best."

I arched a brow, then winced when that did all kinds of things to the bruises and cuts on my face. He saw it. Of course. But his soothing hands didn't change in pace or strength. Not by an inch did his reaction surge through him, changing how he touched me.

His level of control surprised me, and I'd admit, it appealed to me on a base level.

I was used to hot tempers, raging moods, and backhands that were triggered by a wrong word... Eoghan wasn't like that.

My throat tightened, and I merely replied, "I can be as silent as you want."

His brow puckered at that. "I don't want a doll for a wife."

I smiled. "That's exactly what my father said you'd want in a woman."

"Yeah, well, as much as the fucker knows about us, I doubt he comprehends the kind of woman I'd like to marry, and considering I haven't married any fucking one, he knows shit." His nostrils flared. "I don't know what I want in a wife, honestly, but I can guaran-fuck-ing-tee that I don't want you to be scared to say a word.

"I already told you I won't hurt you—"

"I know. I believe you." Not physically he wouldn't.

He froze at that. "You do?"

"You don't have the temperament for it."

His eyes flared wide, and amusement filtered into those dark chocolate orbs. "Sweetheart, you haven't heard my rep."

"Of course I have. I know you're one of the best snipers in the country. I know that, if you hadn't been discharged, you'd probably still be in the army. As you said, Father knows a lot about you. And I do too."

"Learning all my weaknesses?"

"And your strengths," I answered truthfully. "I already told you he wants me to spy on you."

"And you also told me that you weren't going to say anything to him."

"I won't. I have no desire to ever see him again," I told him genuinely.

He released a sigh that made the wisps of hair around my head dance. "I can't blame you." One hand smoothed over my shoulder, and I wished I could feel him. Wished the sleeves and the bodice weren't there, getting in the way of direct contact. He moved up and traced his fingers over my throat. "There will be times we have to see him—"

"I know. I was just saying."

He dipped his chin. "I'll never leave you alone with him again."

I frowned at that. "You can't make a promise like that."

"Just watch me. I'm a stubborn man, Inessa. You think you know me, but you don't. You'll learn though. I like things done a certain way..." He hesitated, and I knew where he was coming from.

"In all things," I surmised slowly, not making it a question when I already knew the answer.

There'd been nothing about the women in his life in the files Father had me read. I'd seen nothing about his proclivities or his preferences. The files had been an attempt at making me a perfect mate for a man who could tie his organization to Father's, and I was the means and the sacrifice. I had to make sure that the 'merger' was successful.

That meant I knew more than he even imagined.

Just not that.

I cleared my throat when he nodded. "You know I'm a virgin."

"I know it."

"Whatever—" I cleared my throat again. "Kinks you have, maybe we should work up to them?"

His shoulders started shaking, and for the first time today, I saw my husband laugh.

For a second, I wasn't sure what the hell was happening. Wasn't even sure if he was having a stroke or something.

Not once had he done more than grin at me, and even that had been in unusual moments. While his other brothers had laughed and chuckled at jokes, he'd stood there, listening in, watching the crowded room like he was measuring it up for marks.

Which, at the time, had fit, considering he was in a room loaded with Russian enemies.

Still, to see him laugh now, on the topic we were discussing?

I wasn't sure whether to be offended or not.

I thought I'd been pretty tolerant tonight. Coming here to some whore with her legs open as a welcome to my new home wasn't exactly ideal!

Had I shouted at him?

Had I even bitched at him over it?

No!

"I can feel your anger," he stated softly, still chuckling, even as his eyes danced—not with amusement this time, with heat.

The sight of which made my heart stutter.

Oh, shit.

He liked that.

He liked my temper.

I swallowed, and he watched the move.

"I'm not going to fuck my wife when her face is full of bruises, her mouth is covered in dissolvable stitches, and she favors her right side—"

I winced, because I'd tried really hard to cover up that I had a bruised rib.

His eyes narrowed. "You'll come to learn that too, Inessa. I don't miss anything. Not a single fucking thing. You'd best remember that it's not wise to lie to me, as I'll never forget every word that spills from that pretty mouth."

Curious, I tilted my head to the side. "Do you have a photographic memory?"

He shrugged. "I'm eidetic, sure. But more than that, I can replay most conversations I have with people like it's a movie reel." He removed his hand from my arm, making me instantly miss it when his heat disappeared, and he tapped his temple with his forefinger. "Like I said, I forget nothing."

"That sucks."

He snorted. "Yeah, it does, but it comes in fucking handy in my line of work."

I could imagine.

Blowing out a breath, I turned around, closing the space between us even though that wasn't my intent.

Staring directly at him, not using the mirror's reflection, my belly pressing against his, I murmured, "The vows meant nothing to you today, did they?"

"I'm Catholic by force, not by choice. It means nothing to me, but I go through the motions because it's expected of me."

I pursed my lips then twisted slightly, and reached for the scissors I'd noticed standing upright in a glass on the vanity.

It was a room made for a man, lined with gleaming, marble sinks that were formed out of the stone, and brushed silver plumbing fixtures that added an elegant twist to the dark space. The vanity mirror was large, about eight feet wide, and ran from floor to ceiling with the vanity hovering in the middle like it was by magic. To the left, a showerhead was stuck in the middle of the ceiling, and to the right, there was a door which I knew led to the toilet as I'd used it earlier.

But the vanity housed several dishes and such that he used to store razors and things, so I grabbed the scissors, which I imagined he used to trim his beard—the beard he'd shaved off today, the faint tan lines on his skin told me that—and opened the blades wide. All along, he watched me. He didn't move, even though I knew he saw me grab what was, essentially, a weapon.

But there was no worry in his face, no concern. If anything, he was curious.

I raised my hand, turned my palm so it was facing him, and stated, "Your vows don't mean a thing to me. I'm not Catholic. I'm Orthodox. So I'm going to make a vow you'll understand."

His eyes narrowed. "Blood?"

I dipped my chin, and quickly sliced across my palm. Blood instantly spilled, and I let it. This dress meant nothing to me. I had enough pictures to show any little girl I might have in the future, so I allowed the drops to fall, let it stain the expensive couture gown, and whispered, "I vow that I will not betray you...so long as you don't betray me."

The addition had him blowing out a breath, but he grabbed the scissors from me and mirrored my action.

Blood spilled once more, more of it staining my dress, and he stated, "If you think I've betrayed you, before you think to break this vow, you will talk to me about it first."

It was interesting he'd sliced his palm before he'd made that statement.

"I don't want you slicing my throat because you think I've done something I haven't," he clarified. "Misunderstandings are a common occurrence."

When I nodded, he reached for my hand and plastered our palms together. Our fingers bridged, blood seeping and surging between them, staining our hands, sinking into his calluses, sliding down my clear skin.

"I vow not to betray you...if you don't betray me." He pulsed the muscles in his hand, squeezing then releasing. "Long time since I did anything like this."

"With your brothers?" I guessed.

He smiled, and I knew he was thinking back to the memory. While it was kind of a curse to remember everything, it had to be cool to never forget stuff like that.

It was human nature for the good to blur and for the bad to stick out like a sore thumb.

For myself, I wished that when I thought of my mom, I remembered all the times we baked together, the times we'd played dress up, and the times she'd tugged the blankets around me before sleep. But I didn't. My memory instantly went to the one sliver I should forget.

His jaw tensed. "The stuff in here isn't mine. She brought it over tonight."

Pain flashed through me. "Why? Did you think I wouldn't—" What could I say? He'd just vowed not to have sex with me? Maybe—

"Hush," he rumbled. "It was a setup, but we're working on figuring that out."

I hadn't expected him to apologize, so the absence of one came as no surprise. However, his reply *did* shock me. Not only because he'd explained something that was business-related, but because it made no sense.

Why would someone sabotage our wedding night?

Before I could even think about if it was the Italians or the Albanians, he ruptured my thought processes, by murmuring, "You know I'll protect you, don't you?"

Taken aback, I mumbled, "I-I guess."

"No guess about it. I don't promise to be a good husband, Inessa. I just promise that you won't hurt when I'm around."

Somehow, that meant more to me than the vow we'd just sealed together in blood, and I thought he knew that, because his eyes softened, and he murmured, "How do you feel about burning this dress?"

A grin twisted along my mouth. "Sounds like fun."

"Little arsonist," he teased with a soft laugh, chucking me under the chin like he was an uncle and I a favored niece. "Do you need help getting out of it?"

"Just the ties."

He arched a brow. "Are you okay with me doing that?"

I nodded. Because I was.

He'd said he wouldn't touch me tonight because of my injuries, but I knew he didn't expect it also because of what I'd walked into...

Eoghan, I was coming to see, in his own way, was a man of honor.

Sure, it wasn't the kind of honor that most people thought of, but in my world, any honor at all was like digging in your backyard and finding a trove of treasure and not a dead body you'd buried there six years earlier.

And while the evening had promised to go downhill from the second the elevator doors had opened, if anything, Eoghan had sowed the seeds of something he probably didn't want or need, but which I freely gave.

Trust.

It was nothing more than a fragile sapling right now, but if he tended it?

It would turn into a mighty oak, and everyone knew about those kinds of trees. They withstood even the worst of storms.

SEVEN
EOGHAN

AS I WATCHED the rerun of last night's Yankees game, I saw Inessa tapping away on her phone and tried not to look like I was doing exactly what I *was* doing—reading her messages.

Though I'd gone out of my way to avoid learning anything about her, it was in my nature to absorb information, even if I didn't want it.

The file Conor had collected on her back when the wedding had been a seed in the whack job garden that was my father's fertile mind, had been something I had managed to avoid for over three months. Then Declan, after meeting her, had started singing her praises, and I'd been left wondering what the fuck she'd done to impress my misogynistic brother.

I'd read the file, but it hadn't shown all that much. Was I supposed to get a boner over an A grade in English Literature? That her GPA was 3.9?

I mean, fuck.

She'd been a kid.

A fucking kid her father had effectively sold to us.

So, because seeing that shit had pissed me off, I'd set a couple of the crew on her, and they'd actually managed to keep track of her when she'd done any sneaking out. What they'd failed to report?

That Inessa was being beaten.

Some days, I thought I was like my father. A little fucking nutty. Some days, I thought I was still the soldier I'd been trained to be—dedicated and disciplined. Then others, I was neither, a man capable of seeing between the lines of the law and refusing to accept something just because it was an order. But I was pretty sure, amid the chaos of my character, that I wasn't a good man.

Even so, had I known she was being beaten the way she was?

I felt certain I'd have married her the second it was legal, and I'd have shoved her in another apartment for her to grow up in.

Knowing that her favorite food was some Russian shit called *pelmeni*, her best friend a kid called Lisandra who, more often than not, got Inessa into trouble, and that she'd watched *To All the Boys I Loved Before* eighty times on Netflix, hadn't prepared me for the woman who'd become my wife.

At the moment, sitting there, curled in a ball on the other end of the sofa, it was like she was there, but she wasn't. So far, she hadn't driven me insane, which came as a surprise.

I'd thought she'd grate on my nerves, but she hadn't. Didn't.

She just read. A lot. Worked out. A lot. Stared out of windows. A lot.

The sniper in me would watch her look out of her princess tower, wondering what she was thinking, even as I feared how open a target she was making herself.

Yeah. Feared. You read that right.

She was nothing to me. Not yet, at any rate. Maybe not ever. But the way she stood there? Staring out onto a world like she wasn't really a part of it? Looking into the ant-like lives of people going about their business? It got to me. And made me glad we'd invested in bulletproof windows that were military grade.

I half wondered what she was thinking about, but equally, I knew.

We hadn't left the apartment since the wedding, and she hadn't mentioned Leticia once, nor had she asked about going out—either to shop, for food or clothes, or to eat out at a restaurant. Tomorrow, Winnie, my housekeeper, would come for the first time, so we'd have fresh produce and more meals, but in that time, she hadn't even asked to Uber in something.

She was a conundrum. Someone so okay with her place in this world that she didn't expect much else, and fuck if that didn't mess with my head.

I'd never wanted to be married to someone so young because I was jaded, because I'd lived. Being with someone who hadn't? At all? What the fuck was I supposed to do with someone like that? Someone so different from me, someone with nothing to say?

"I can feel you watching me."

Her eyes were on me at this point, making me realize I was staring at her, and she was staring back, and I hadn't noticed.

Shit.

"If you want to know something, ask."

I had to admit...I liked how blunt she was. Not coarse or crass, not defiant or in your face, but she didn't bullshit, and fuck if that wasn't enjoyable. Especially when I was used to women who'd tell me I had a fifteen-inch cock if it meant I'd buy them a pretty necklace.

"Maybe I don't have anything I need to know," I countered, just to be difficult.

"Then what are you staring at?" She winced, like she realized something, then her hand went up to hover over her face. "I forget the bruises are there."

"They don't hurt?" I sat up, the leather creaking beneath my ass as I raised my legs onto the seat when I angled around. Even with my legs flat out, we were far apart, and when I gave her all my attention, she seemed to flush, and I liked that. I enjoyed making her doll-face respond and react.

Shattering her mask.

"Some."

I knew from past beatings that bruises became tender before they got better. So, her 'some' also told me she was a fucking trooper.

It was like a nest of toads had somehow managed to rear a majestic butterfly—how the fuck had she been spawned by Vasov?

I actually thought that was one of my major issues with her. I felt like she was too good to be true, and if something was too good, then it was usually a lie. I kept expecting her to trip up, and given time, maybe that would happen...but I wasn't sure. I actually found myself hoping this was the real her, because this woman? I felt like I could be with her without wanting to top myself and her at the prospect of forty fucking years together.

Yeah, no divorce in my world.

Sucked to be me, right?

"How about your nose? That had to hurt."

"I'm—"

Used to it.

Fuck. Her wariness cropped up, as did her shoulders—hunching around her ears like she was regretting speaking.

"You had surgery?"

Her eyes caught mine. "Where?"

"Don't BS me now," I chided, folding my hands over my belly. "Your face."

"I don't approve of plastic surgery," she said primly.

"No, not to get massive tits, I mean to fix what he fucked up."

Her cheeks blossomed with heat in earnest.

I'd thought as much.

"Just my nose."

"Fucker," I rumbled. "He touches you again, I'll fucking gut him."

"I wouldn't be averse to that," she replied, and her tone was so cheerful, I almost laughed.

That she defused my temper had me inwardly reeling, but instead, I muttered, "I was reading about this movie."

She blinked. "Which movie?"

"Something about a chick whose diary, I don't know, falls into someone else's hands or something? The sequel just came out on Netflix, right?"

That had her eyes widening. "You've heard about *To All the Boys I've Loved Before?*"

I clicked my fingers like I'd never heard of it before. "Yeah. That's it."

Her mouth rounded. "I wouldn't take you for a fan of—"

"I like comedies," I defended.

"You're not a comedy person," she denied, squinting at me. "You're all action. I've seen the Netflix recently watched list."

She said that like she was listing my crimes.

"Everyone likes a change."

I got the feeling she was onto me, but fuck. I could watch some sappy as shit movie for her after what she'd been through, after her fucking sucky birthday that had ended with the sight of a slut's snatch.

Christ, I really needed to think about getting her a birthday present.

Trouble was, you had to know someone to get them a gift, and I didn't know her. Sure, I knew about her. Knew shit. But that wasn't the real her.

She was more than her file.

"You'd be down with watching something like that?" she asked shyly.

And despite myself, my lips curved. "I mean, if you want to? The game's almost over anyway."

"I didn't mind," she replied. "I'm used to sports being on. Father has a screen in our private dining room, and we always had Mets games on."

My nose crinkled at the thought I shared a similarity with that cunt, though I had better taste than him—fucking Mets fan. Should have known he was dead to me from the start—then I tossed her the remote. "Find it." I cleared my throat. "Want some popcorn? I think I have some."

Her eyes flared wide. "Like, a movie night?"

Jesus. The way she responded was like she expected no kindness from me at all. Like I was offering to take her to Tiffany's and give her free rein in there.

"Yeah. Like a movie night."

She shot me a half smile. "The sequel's out now, so we could watch both."

I had to grin as I got to my feet. *Give an inch, and they take a fucking mile.* "Why not?" I said magnanimously, tossing it over my shoulder as I strolled into the kitchen.

How fucking bad could it be?

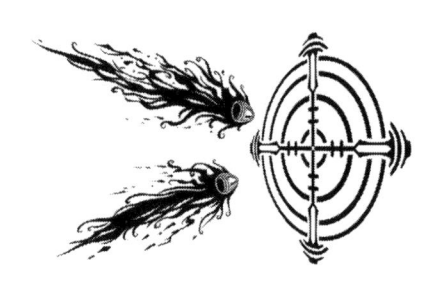

EIGHT
INESSA

THE FOLLOWING morning after our movie binge, I wandered into the kitchen and braked to a halt.

There was someone in here, and she was cooking. My nose twitched as I scented that gross smell of frying beef and onions, and my eyes widened as I took in the sight of the old woman, her hair tied into a kerchief, cheeks flushed, eyes narrowed as she squinted down at a well-worn recipe book.

I had to assume she was Eoghan's housekeeper, but damn, couldn't he have prepared me?

The older woman spotted me before I could duck out, drag Eoghan from the gym, and demand he introduce us. Her squinty look moved from the book to me, and as she raked her gaze over me, I knew, immediately, I'd been found wanting.

I stared at her.

She stared at me.

And truly?

I'd had fewer hostile looks at my wedding, surrounded by enemies, than this woman graced me with now.

Damn, I'd woken up in such a good mood too. Watching movies

with Eoghan had been a blast, and even though he'd been mind-numbingly bored through my YA flicks, he'd sat there like a trooper and hadn't even fallen asleep once.

I wasn't all about the YA, but I loved the books that were tied to the Netflix movies, so they were some of my faves, and I'd relented afterward—we'd indulged in a couple of action movies before we'd crashed around three AM.

That was why I was awake so late. Eoghan too. But it was clear the housekeeper mistook the reason for our late awakening and disapproved.

I mean, we were on our honeymoon, for God's sake. *You were supposed to have sex.* Not that we had. I was surprised we hadn't yet, but I knew that was down to my bruises still.

Shit.

I forgot about them again.

My hand clapped to my cheek, and I muttered, "Eoghan didn't do this!" That I wanted to defend him, after he'd gone so far to protect me, might have seemed weird, especially to staff who were paid to look the other way anyway, but this mattered to me.

I didn't want her thinking badly of him.

"Of course he didn't," the woman snarled, and the vitriol in her voice had me staggering back a step.

Jesus.

"My Eoghan would never do that."

My brows rose. "Are you related?"

"Known him since he was a boy. Been keeping house for him since he got out of the army." She sniffed. "He deserves better than a Bratva bitch for a bride, but that's the way the cookie crumbles." At the word 'Bratva,' she spat. Just off the counter and toward the floor, but eww.

"I beg your pardon," I whispered, unable to believe she'd not only spat but had called me a bitch without even knowing who the hell I was.

"You heard me."

I had heard her, but my ears were still ringing, and my surprise was difficult to contain.

Unsure what to do, but knowing that walking out and tattling to Eoghan might make things worse, I rearranged things mentally. I was going to make us a smoothie, but now, with a housekeeper who loathed me under my roof, I suddenly realized I couldn't trust her.

Not her food, nor the chores she undertook to make my life easier.

Would Eoghan take her side? I couldn't see that, not when he'd treated me so fairly, but also, I knew I had to expect this reaction from other people who were old-school Five Points. There was a lot of bad blood between our families, our brotherhoods, so I knew I'd face this more than I'd like.

I gnawed on my bottom lip as I moved around her, aiming for the fridge. The day before the wedding, a delivery van had arrived at my house and had taken all my belongings from my father's home to the apartment. So all my stuff was here. Everything from my personal jewelry to old schoolbooks and the protein shakes I used.

Because cooking wasn't my strength, and I knew I'd have to feed Eoghan breakfast, I'd taken to making us shakes with my products, even though I figured he'd be the kind of guy who had protein shakes with raw eggs and gross stuff in them. But with the housekeeper's food potentially containing saliva—I mean, that might be reaching, but I wasn't taking any chances for the moment—that meant I'd have to start expanding my culinary repertoire.

Wanting to groan at the thought, I grabbed the avocado, lettuce, ginger, and apple from the crisper, tucked the almond butter under my arm, along with the almond milk, and hiked it over to the side where the blender was.

The kitchen was giant, beautiful, a marvel—if you liked cooking. All marble counters, an oversized island with a stove and a sink where I usually did my prep, but I tucked myself to the side. I winced when I had to use a drawer on the island where she was working.

When she actually shoved me aside, I just stood there, my mouth working. "Excuse me?"

"I should think so," she scoffed.

And yeah, she'd totally mistaken my meaning.

My jaw tensed as I glared at her, well aware she was completely ignoring me. "Who the hell are you anyway?" I ground out.

And when she ignored me some more, I grabbed her arm and forced her to look at me. The hatred in her eyes wasn't something I was comfortable seeing, but fuck, it didn't hurt my feelings. There were many people who loathed my family. I could just chalk this bitch down as another one.

"I'm Winifred. Eoghan calls me Winnie."

I scowled at her. "Well, Winifred, you can dislike me all you want, but you need to remember—this is my kitchen now. My roof. You do not treat me with disrespect, even if you hate my guts." I wasn't about to let this old bitch walk all over me, but neither could I make her like me.

"Eoghan pays my wages."

"Yeah, he does, and if I tell him I have a problem with you, if I tell him what you just did? We both know you'll be looking for new employment."

Winifred sniffed. "He wouldn't believe you."

"He would," I told her resolutely, and something in her eyes shifted, like she knew I was telling the truth. But within a flash, her chin was up, and I knew the only thing that was going to happen here was my patience was going to be stretched thin.

I had no desire for the woman to lose her job, especially when the Bratva and Five Points had been enemies until this marriage, and I was fair by nature. So, rather than get mad, or throw my weight around, I stated, "Treat me with disrespect again, and we'll have an issue."

Though she grunted as a reply, when I reached for the knife drawer again, she didn't bump into me. She avoided me. And Christ, I considered that a win.

Even as I wondered if she'd have to be fired eventually or if I could win her over—and if I even wanted to go to that much trouble with a woman who was supposed to be my staff—I got to prepping the shake.

It was only a little thing, but I liked to give the glass to Eoghan. It made me smile, watching him sniff the drink. Not like it was poison. Like it was weird. Girly. I could just imagine him thinking that, to be honest.

He wasn't like I'd imagined, and yet, he was what Declan had promised.

Fair.

Kind.

Cold.

I kind of wanted to warm him up, even as I was grateful for his fair spirit and kind nature. Take last night...there was no way a man like him would ever, in a million years, watch my favorite movie unless he was trying to be nice. But watched it he had. Suffered through the sequel he had.

Who did that?

What kind of made man did that for a bride he didn't want?

Eoghan.

I blew out a breath as I used the back of a spoon to rub off the skin on the ginger root, then I plopped it into the mix along with a couple of heaps of my protein shake mix, which I pulsed with the chopped up apple. The soft avocado flesh and lettuce I added next, along with the nut butter.

Having fed him a tropical one, a berry one, and a green shake so far, I knew he preferred sweeter ones, which came as a surprise because he didn't seem to touch any other kind of desserts. The fridge was free of all snacks, as were the cupboards, and the only things that were in there was the stuff I'd brought with me.

Someone had unpacked the boxes.

Had it been Winnie?

The idea of her touching all my stuff, when she hated me, made me want to wash it all. Disinfect it.

Was that overkill?

I pulled a face, even as I grabbed the mason jars I served the shakes in, poured out the mix, and then, without a backward glance and leaving the dishes for Winifred to clean up when normally I'd have handled that myself, I exited the kitchen.

Eoghan was just leaving the bedroom, and he was freshly showered too. He smelled expensive. Yeah, weird. But he did. Like heat and sandalwood with a tang of musk. It got to me. His scent was powerful, and when I thought of what he smelled like in the morning? When I woke up close to him?

It was even headier.

And the heat of his body? So close to me? It was like sleeping with a furnace—in a good way. I always needed an electric blanket when it wasn't summer, but with Eoghan there to warm my feet up? Who needed to waste the electricity?

"Breakfast," I greeted him, shoving the jar in his direction.

His nose crinkled at the distinctly green color. "Not the berry one?" he complained, making me smile. I'd known that was his favorite so far.

"No berries to put in it," I informed him.

A grunt escaped him as he accepted the jar and muttered, "Thank you, Inessa."

"You're welcome, Eoghan."

He took a sip, pulled a face. "Tastes like a garden."

"It's good for you."

"So they say." He stared at me for a second, a small smile curving his lips as he reached over, running a finger over the crest of my cheek where a particularly gnarly bruise was still blossoming. That felt way too good for a little whisper of a touch. "You're looking better," he rasped, making me wonder if that touch affected him just as much as it did me.

"Few more days," I confirmed huskily, "and they'll be gone."

"A distant memory." His eyes darkened for a moment, like he was thinking of my father, then they cleared as the sound of pots clanking in the kitchen echoed into the living room. "Oh, shit. Winnie's here."

Before I had a chance to say a word, he grabbed my hand and tugged me into the kitchen.

"Winnie? I'd like you to meet Inessa."

"Why, what a pleasure it is to meet you, Inessa!"

The sweet tone stunned me, but the calculating gleam in the bitch's eyes told me that I'd lost this round. Fuck, I'd overplayed my hand.

"A pleasure, yeah," I said gruffly, even as I wanted to kick myself for being so myopic as to warn her about tattling on her to Eoghan if she treated me badly. Of course, she was going to be kind in front of him so that if I did snitch on her, Eoghan would think I was making it up.

Old bitch.

"Winnie handles everything in the apartment, Inessa. From the food to the chores, so whatever you need, just tell her, and she deals with it. If things get to be too much for you, Winnie, with the extra work, tell Inessa, and she'll see about hiring someone else." His smile was kind. "Inessa needs some berries for our morning shake—"

"Raspberries, blueberries, and strawberries." I tipped my chin up as I shot the housekeeper a false smile. "I'll make you a list."

And whatever the hell she bought, I'd wash it.

Twice.

NINE

EOGHAN

THE SUNLIGHT FILTERED through the bedroom, and while Inessa was curled up at my side like she'd been for the past six nights of our marriage, my focus wasn't on her, on the smooth skin of her shoulders and upper back that were revealed to me with her camisole. If I sat up, and peered over her, I could even see her braless tits which were smushed together now that she was lying on her side. I didn't look at the long legs which were curled up, thanks to her fetal position, and her feet, the soles of which were pressed against my calves like she was either trying to keep them warm or trying to connect with me.

She was an odd thing.

That was what I'd learned in six days of marriage.

So young in some things, so ancient in others.

The cut on my palm could have been childish. After all, blood oaths died out when you passed eleven, didn't they?

But the intention behind it? Yeah, it did more than she realized.

It also told me her capacity for pain was high. That she wasn't unaccustomed to bloodshed—either her own or someone else's. And, as a result, that violence was as much a part of her upbringing as it had been in mine.

The only trouble was, if Ma had had a girl child, that girl would have been cosseted from the womb to her coffin.

Not just by Da, but by all her brothers.

We'd have done more than spill blood to keep her safe. Didn't matter whether it was because of some little fucker in kindergarten threatening to pull her pigtails, or a husband who thought he could get handy with his fists.

Any sister of mine would have been shielded from the Devil himself.

That Inessa hadn't pissed me off.

So, the gesture, while childlike, interested me. I often found myself staring at it through the day, and when I woke up, the scabbed over wound was the first thing I looked at after I'd checked Inessa was asleep.

Her presence in my bed wasn't something I'd anticipated.

But, at the time, it had seemed natural to let her get into bed with me. After we'd stripped her out of the dress—leaving her in nothing more than a teddy that had my dick hardening, even as the bruises on her limbs had it softening faster than if she'd kneed me in the balls—and had set fire to the gown, letting it burn on the shower floor before I doused it with water to stop the alarms from blaring to life. She'd stood there, smirking at the destroyed dress which was partially in tatters, somewhat blood-soaked, and mostly burned to smithereens, and something about the moment had gotten to me.

Especially when, a few seconds later, she'd yawned.

I'd grabbed her hand, tugged her out of the bathroom and over to the side of the bed I didn't sleep on, and said, "Let's get some sleep."

She'd blinked up at me, showing her true exhaustion now that she was bare from the makeup she'd been wearing all day, and hadn't demurred. Climbing, like a good girl, into bed, and cuddling up on her side.

By the time I'd rounded the damn mattress, she was already fast asleep.

Me?

I'd been left wondering how the day had derailed so much. And six days on, I was still confused as fuck.

I had a bride who was barely legal, my bed was full when I always slept alone, I was technically on my honeymoon and I hadn't had sex once, and I'd be going back to work shortly.

The past week had been spent acclimating ourselves to one another. Almost like she was a lioness who'd been tossed into a cage with a lion, we'd been sniffing around each other, trying to work out the other's limitations and the way we rolled.

For the most part, I figured I'd done pretty goddamn well for myself.

She didn't talk all the fucking time, in fact, I often found her glued to her phone—not because she was on social media, pulling duck faces into the camera every twenty fucking minutes, nor because she was doing irritating shit for TikTok, but because she was reading.

She'd even shushed me. *Shushed me* when I interrupted her.

What the actual fuck was that about?

She wasn't scared of me at all, either because of our wedding day or because she thought I was kinder than her father—which I wasn't, but to her, I would be—and that had resonated when she'd ignored me until she'd read to the end of the chapter.

Then, and only then, had she looked up at me, and asked, "What is it? I'm in the middle of a book."

She couldn't cook for shit, and we'd started ordering in as a result, but she was very good at making cocktails—something her father had wanted her to learn. Although, they weren't froufrou cocktails, which made sense, I guess. That he'd had her mixing drinks for his colleagues made me wonder if she'd overheard anything about those business deals, and wondering if her vow of loyalty to me, promised in blood, would extend to her telling me about anything she might have heard.

I got the feeling that, if I treated her well, she'd mold herself around me, morphing into exactly what I needed, and while the idea appealed, I wasn't sure what I wanted. Or needed.

Until now, I'd wanted to be single, and there wasn't much she could do to help me on that score, was there?

I wanted sex on the regular, and not sex that a virgin would be okay with either. Her face was finally almost healed up, but I'd made a vow to myself, no bloodshed required, that until the last fucking bruise had disappeared from her pretty face, I wouldn't even kiss her.

That vow was wearing on me.

Hard.

Especially when she came to bed wearing sleep shorts and camisoles that weren't enticing at all, yet somehow were sexier for it.

This current getup was teasing my morning wood something fierce—blue and white striped shorts that reminded me of men's boxers, and a bright white cami that had a little lace at the deep V between her tits.

The notion that I wanted her to sleep in my boxers was an irritating one.

How did you ask your wife to do that?

To wear your shit?

And considering I hated sharing anything, did I even want to get into that?

Even if the prospect of seeing her in my stuff did things to my cock that a woman wearing thigh highs and leather stilettos didn't manage.

With a grunt, I rolled my head away from the sight of her and stared back up at the ceiling. Even though she didn't require much management, was neat enough to appease even me, she was still there.

Sharing my space.

Breathing the same air as me.

And it was weird.

Because I didn't mind it.

Eying the slice on my palm again, the irritating desire to slip our hands together, to unite the slits once more, flittered through me.

I wanted the scar to be a nasty one.

I wanted to see it every fucking day, wanted her to see it too, and be reminded of the weird ass night of our wedding, when two strangers had taken several steps toward knowing one another.

Wondering when I'd turned into a pansy, I rolled off the bed and slouched out into the hall.

Not for the first time, I stared at the sofa, irritated by what Inessa must think every time she sat on it, and came to a decision.

The place needed overhauling.

New bed, new sofa...in fact, I needed to make a list of every place I'd fucked someone.

At the moment, I intended to give her all my loyalty. Until that changed, I decided that this was a prudent step.

I didn't really give a shit about that whole 'happy wife, happy life' crap, but—and it was a massive but—I figured making her happy would take us down a path I actually wanted to take.

The prospect of being tied to a woman who wouldn't flinch when I returned home with a bullet wound, of bringing an enemy back without her being goggle-eyed at the sight, was infinitely appealing.

A woman who knew the score, a woman who'd been raised in the life and who got it without wanting to pass out or puke every time shit got real.

It all sounded expedient, but that was marriage, wasn't it? Supposed to be convenient when it was arranged?

Thus far, it hadn't been, not particularly, but I wasn't too put out. I especially liked how clean she was, how neat. It suited me and made me realize how good a match we could be if I was decent to her.

And I didn't mean if I beat her or not, even though I knew that was standard in the life, but if I treated her with kindness. It wasn't too hard. I wasn't a total bastard. Aoife, Finn's wife, liked me, and so did Jen, her friend. Although she checked out my ass more than I checked out hers, so that was a little different. But if I could be friendly with Aoife, I didn't see why I couldn't do that with my wife.

Rubbing my chin as I carried on with my mental note about which furniture needed replacing, I went to the gym, which was just off my office, and realized that most of the gear in there needed replacing too.

Fuck.

I had sex in a lot of places that wasn't always my mattress.

To be fair, I didn't intend for that to change, so I figured I could christen a lot of new furniture in that way...

When the matter of Inessa's hymen wasn't an issue.

Fucking virgins. I didn't get what the appeal was.

As I headed to my treadmill and began my workout, I carried on with my mental note-taking until Inessa walked in.

She was sleepy and kept stretching, and had changed out of the fuckable sleep shorts and cami into some yoga pants and a sports bra that turned her tits into perfectly round globes, that did things to me no workout gear really should, especially not when a man was running at six miles an hour.

Oranges, eat your heart out.

She ignored me, as was her way. It didn't piss me off, if anything, I appreciated it. Neither of us were morning people, but we had routines and we weren't going to get in the other's way.

Just like she had for the past six days, she went to the cross-trainer. Her phone went into the slot, her AirPods made an appearance, and she started her own training.

I knew she was listening to audiobooks, knew it because, sometimes, her cheeks would turn pink and not from exertion, and she'd laugh. Far as I knew, there weren't many songs that could inspire both reactions in someone. I mean, I could have asked, but if I asked, she'd talk, and that wasn't why we were here.

We were working out.

But, not for the first time, I found myself with questions, and I wasn't a man who liked waiting on answers.

Though I liked working out alone, hence a personal gym, she was something to look at. Better even than the news.

After forty minutes, I switched to free weights, and about twenty minutes later, she stopped her cross-training.

I knew she'd go for a shower next, and then would make breakfast—a protein shake. Though hers tasted of girly shit, she'd started making me one too, and I wasn't going to complain. Putting shit in a blender seemed to be about as much of a cooking repertoire as she possessed.

Before she could wander out, when she'd stacked her AirPods back in their case, I turned around as she did so and stated, "Tomorrow, I'll be back to work."

Her arched brow was a silent, 'So what?'

My lips curved, and I continued, "I want you to go shopping."

"For food?" She scowled. "They deliver, and what they don't, Winnie can bring here. Why do I have to go to the store?"

"If you listened... I want you to buy new furniture."

"New furniture," she repeated flatly.

"Yeah, new furniture." I cleared my throat. "A new sofa, new bed. I'll make a list of what I want."

She folded her arms across her chest, plumping up her tits and making my tongue stick to the roof of my mouth as she did so. "Why?"

Why?

"Isn't it obvious?" I retorted.

She shrugged. "Not to me. I'm not so naïve that I don't know you've fucked your way across every inch of this place. Eoghan, it's your home. Why wouldn't you have?"

"I want a fresh start," I declared, a little taken aback by her blasé attitude.

I mean, I'd just been thinking how a wife accustomed to this way of life was a boon, but still, it came as a shock.

"It's your money," she muttered, hitching her shoulder.

"Yeah, it is. So, I'll get the list, and you can do whatever you want to the place. No painting though, or refurbing. I hated having that done the first time, and most of the shit is new anyway. I only redid the place a couple of years ago."

"There's no need—"

"Inessa," I growled, the dumbbells clinking as I dropped them back on the bench. "There's every need."

She huffed, but showed no fear at my tone, and muttered, "I'm going for a shower."

Considering I'd expected more gratitude than that, I watched in amazement as she swanned off, that tight ass of hers rolling as she moved down the hall and back to what was—incredibly enough to me, at any rate—*our* room.

"That was unexpected," I mumbled to myself, shaking my head at her even as I watched every step she took until she disappeared.

The thought of her under the shower always gave me a boner, so I returned to my workout.

When my phone buzzed just before I grabbed the free weights, I peered at it, saw it was a video call from my brother, switched on the TV, and cast the call onto it.

I scowled at Aidan Jr. "What the fuck do you want?"

"Is that any way to greet your brother?"

I rolled my eyes. "I didn't think you got up before nine."

He pulled a face, and I instantly stopped giving him shit.

I knew what that meant.

On Finn and Aoife's wedding day, there'd been a drive-by shooting. Aoife and Aidan Jr. had been caught in the crossfire. Aoife had lost her spleen, and Aidan had a fucked up leg for his pains.

All these years later, he still had issues with it. And that face meant it had kept him up half the night.

I'd seen his knee a few times since the accident, and it was messed up. In fact, that was being kind.

He'd had more pins put in that bastard than a pincushion.

"How's married life treating you?"

I rolled my eyes. "You really give a fuck?"

Aidan scowled at me. "Of course I do. You're my fucking brother, aren't you?"

"Thought you'd disowned me."

He snorted. "When you were six. I took you back into the fold when you were six and a half."

Grinning at him, I shook my head a little at his bullshit. "The folks have been surprisingly quiet."

"Finn and I had to delete your number from both their phones." He grinned back at me, and even though he was in his early forties, the handsome fucker didn't look it right then. Pain had aged him, but his smile took away some of that. "They're not pleased, but they understand why we did it."

"To give us space?" I snorted. "Yeah. I'm surprised it worked."

"Ma tried to strong-arm Aoife, but other than that, they've behaved. I think Da wants it to work."

"What makes you say that?" The idea had me frowning at him.

"You know what he's like." Aidan shrugged before he rocked back in the seat I knew was his office chair, thanks to the view at his back of a shiny skyscraper I recognized. He wasn't at home, but in the office complex which was a front—a means of making our business a little more legitimate.

And I said a 'little more,' because we were bent as fuck.

"No, I don't."

"If anyone knows Da, it's you. You're too similar for either of your own good. It makes you his favorite, but also, it means he gets you more than any of us ever did." Aidan pulled a face. "He wanted you wed a lot sooner than this, Eoghan, you have to know that."

I narrowed my eyes at him. "What's he been saying?"

"Nothing, but I know him. God help me."

"God help us both." I picked up my weights again and started my training.

"Fuck, I miss squats," Aidan rasped.

"You looking at my ass?" I joked, but only to lighten shit. Aidan had found it hard working out ever since Finn's wedding day massacre, and I knew the only place he found any peace was either on the back of a horse or in the pool. It was why Da had built him a house close to the family property—he had an Olympic-sized pool now, but even that didn't help him with his pain management.

It went without being said that we knew he had issues with drugs. So far, he was controlling it, but the second it went either way, we all knew Da would be in his face. I wasn't looking forward to that day. Aidan had it miserable enough with the pain he was in on a constant basis. Cold turkey too?

That was going to suck, and even if I gave him shit, I loved him and didn't want him to suffer.

More than he already was, at any rate.

"It's a fine ass," he promptly replied. "But that one over there is nicer."

I peered over my shoulder and saw Inessa walking down the hall to the kitchen.

I scowled back at Aidan, who grinned at me. "Declan was right. You are possessive of her." He rubbed his hands together. "That's a good sign."

"Are you all playing fucking matchmaker or something? Far as I know, I'm already hitched to the—" I broke off at the word 'bitch.' Inessa was many things, but that wasn't one of them.

Aidan's eyes flared wide. "Holy fuck, you can't call her a bitch. This is deeper than I thought."

"Don't read too much into shit. I've only known her six days!"

My feathers were definitely ruffled, and I dropped the free weights on the padded mat I was standing on, ignoring the heavy clanking, and grabbed my towel and a water bottle from the fridge that was tucked into the recessed cabinets beneath the TV.

"You just call to piss me off?"

"No, to see the state of play." Aidan's expression turned serious.

"You could have known her longer. It's your fault you only met on your wedding day."

"What did I have in common with a goddamn teenager?"

"Nothing, but you'd know her better than you do now."

"I know enough. She's quiet, reads a shit ton, can't cook for crap, is neater than me, and doesn't talk too much."

"The perfect wife," Aidan teased, and I laughed at that because his eyes were twinkling and it was good to see.

They were often clouded with either pain or drugs, and the sight did my heart good.

I took a deep sip of water first, then rubbed my face with the towel. "I like her," I told him. "She doesn't irritate me, and that's a major step forward."

"You going to try to make a go of things?"

"What are we? Women? Since when do we talk about relationships?"

"Since my baby brother got fucking married! That's when."

I shrugged. "Not by my choice."

"Doesn't matter. She's yours now. Da said that would change things, and he was right."

"What else has the old bastard been saying?"

Aidan laughed at my growl, but his lips stopped twitching when he said, "Da implied that you needed to settle down."

"You don't say," I groused, and I waggled my hand at him. I didn't particularly like the sight of the titanium wedding ring on my finger, but I wore it because all married men in the family did.

The whole Catholic thing was a fucking joke sometimes.

It didn't stop men with said rings from boning anything in a skirt that wasn't their wife...

Hypocrisy. That was why I hated the church. Our lives were one big round of it, and it stank like shit, and I was way too clean to appreciate that.

"He said the only thing that has kept him on the straight and narrow is Ma—"

Before he could carry on, I hooted out a laugh. "You mean to tell me he thinks the life he's led is straight and narrow?"

Aidan's grin was sheepish. "Apparently. Can you imagine what he would have been like without Ma?"

"Fuck knows."

"Well, he seems to think you're on that path. So, by that logic, when you're sixty-six, you'll be even worse than Da."

"If any of us live that long."

"Don't be maudlin."

I shrugged. "Not being maudlin. None of us lead good lives, do we? It's not like we're spared violence on the regular."

"We're New Yorkers. There's violence everywhere," was his retort, which made no sense to me, because he was the one with the worst injury in the family.

Hell, Aoife was on daily doses of antibiotics thanks to that drive-by shooting that had almost claimed Aidan's leg, so with both of them as living proof that violence was part of our world? Yeah, I thought I had the right to be maudlin, especially when agony lined his face every fucking day.

We weren't just close because we shared blood, but because we'd made the choice to be... I sometimes wondered if he remembered that when he lost the fight with another pill.

Clearing my throat at the thought, I grumbled, "Did you call just so I could cheer you up?"

His grin reappeared. "Yeah. If that was right, then it didn't work."

I snorted. "I live to entertain."

"Well, right now, your idea of entertaining isn't working either. What the hell have you been doing with her? Conor says you haven't left the apartment once all week."

I rolled my eyes. "That fucker is a pervert."

"No, he's been trying to find a trace of the hackers who bypassed his firewall." Then he smirked. "But he's a pervert too."

"We've been acclimating to one another," was all I could think to say in answer to his earlier question.

I'd had no real desire to go out, to leave the apartment, not when...

Fuck.

I hooked the towel around my neck, strode over to grab the remote, and turned it down so she wouldn't be able to hear our conversation.

"Vasov beat her up badly."

"I know, that's why you dislocated his shoulder."

I shook my head. "He deserved worse."

Aidan whistled. "You were concerned someone would think you'd beaten her?"

"Maybe." I shrugged. "She could have covered it up like she did at the wedding, but—"

"That would hurt like a motherfucker."

"Exactly. And for what? To grab a coffee out in a cafe?" I shrugged once more. "Just didn't seem worth it."

Aidan sighed and, shaking his head, muttered, "How is it the brother with the biggest kills has the biggest heart?"

"Fuck that, it has nothing to do with heart."

My sneer had his smirk making a reappearance. "If you say so. I'll give Ma and Da an update. Should keep them off your backs for, oh, say...an hour or two."

"I'll expect a call in the morning, shall I?"

"Conference, probably. Ma won't be happy learning shit second-hand from Da."

I rolled my eyes. "Great."

"They care, Eoghan," he said softly, but his tone was insistent enough to have me scowling at him.

"I know they do, but they forced this shit on me. If they expect me to be happy about it, then they can fuck off."

He snickered. "Please, God, let me be there if you tell Da that."

I flipped him the bird, because we both knew how well that would go down. With that done, I tugged at the towel around my neck and muttered, "Everything's still arranged for Boston, right?"

Aidan hummed. "Yup. I'm surprised you're getting involved in that, to be honest. Thought it would be too small fry for you."

"On a regular day, it would be. But after I've been cooped up on my honeymoon? We could both do with a break from each other." That was definitely stretching the truth, but I wasn't about to admit to the reality of living with Inessa—she was no trouble. No bother. If anything, she was a nice view when I got bored doing what I was doing. Still, that didn't mean we wouldn't do well with some space and time apart.

"Does she know you're going away for a few days?"

The question had me sighing. "That means I should tell her."

His laugh said it all. "Use your fucking brain. Of course you should."

"I doubt she'd want to know."

"When you didn't come home, she would. Don't forget, she might think you're dead."

"Now who's being maudlin?"

"Thought that was the translation for realistic in your dictionary." He shrugged a shoulder. "Either way, tell her or don't, but it would be kinder to keep her in the loop."

I heaved a sigh. "Okay."

Aidan pursed his lips. "You really like her?" His surprise was clear.

"Yeah. She's decent." I tipped my chin up, not willing to discuss her further when I knew he'd be relaying it all to Ma. Maybe another time, when our parents weren't so up in my business, I'd share. I was secretive about most things. It was in my nature. But I was usually open with my brothers.

The past few years, I'd locked myself in a little. After the marriage had been arranged, I'd admit to going on more jobs, and that put me in my head more than was wise. Only my brothers could pull me out of the headspace a kill put me in, but it wasn't like they could pull their magic if I was, A, avoiding them, and B, in another country with another target in place.

"Here when you need me, bro."

Aware that he knew where my thoughts had gone, I cast him a sheepish look. "Thanks, Aid."

"Don't have to thank me. I'll see you on Sunday, yeah? Missed you at the table this week."

"Was weird not going," I admitted. Unless we were out of the country, we had to attend Sunday Roast at the folks' place.

"Surprised they let you get away with it."

"Ma wasn't happy, Da understood. Especially when I showed him a picture. He's not happy with Vasov." I bared my teeth. "Neither am I."

Aidan whistled between his teeth. "There'll be kickback from that episode at the wedding."

I shrugged. "He can suck my dick... Wait. No, he can't. He shouldn't have fucking touched her."

"There was a reason he did," Aidan pointed out.

"Doesn't take much to figure out why, genius. Still, he shouldn't have touched her. I'm not exactly a catch, and I don't blame her for wanting to pull out—"

"That wasn't the only reason why he beat me."

My eyes flared wide in surprise, and Aidan jerked too, telling me he hadn't seen Inessa appear in the doorway.

That she was as sneaky as me didn't bode well for keeping her out of my business. And, not for the first time, I wondered what she'd heard when sneaking around her old man's place, and whether or not she'd be down with sharing it with me.

"Why did he beat you, Inessa?" Aidan's voice was soft. I cast him a quick look, and saw he was taking in her face. She was beautiful, scrubbed free from makeup the way she was, but when I looked at her, critically, I knew the bruises were still heavy enough for him to get a glimpse as to how she'd been last week.

What had been black and purple was now a discomforting shade of green and yellow.

All week, she'd been sporting her bruises, and whenever I looked at her, I wanted to kill her father, then I wanted to kiss her, then I wondered why the fuck I wanted to kiss her when she looked like she did.

It was a confusing mess, and I didn't deal with that kind of shit easily.

I got boners for sexy women who didn't mind bending over where I wanted and taking it however I wanted to give it to them.

I didn't get hard-ons for angel-faced domestic violence victims.

I had my kinks, but that wasn't one of them.

Her chin tipped up, defiance made her eyes spark. "I told him it was wicked of him to expect me to marry a serial killer. But he started it. He gave Svetlana one of my mother's rings. I was supposed to inherit it when I got married. I asked for it, she slapped me." She touched her lip, telling me the 'slap' had been a damn sight more forceful than she was making out. "Father broke us apart, asked what was happening. I told him, even though I knew what would happen."

I frowned. "How did you know what his reaction would be?"

"After Mother died, we were never to mention her."

"Why?"

Inessa tilted her head to the side. "Do you really not know?"

"Know what?"

Her brows rose in surprise. "How she died?"

I shrugged. "No. I only knew that Svetlana wasn't your mother because she's too young."

"She's about six years older than me," Inessa confirmed, pressing her side to the door where she leaned against the jamb, neither in the gym nor out of it.

I wondered if she wanted to flee, if she regretted starting this conversation, but she stated calmly, "Some of Father's enemies infiltrated the compound where we live. Mother died as a result."

The pain that flashed over her face... I knew we were getting the cleaned up version.

Not that murder could ever really be clean.

I didn't necessarily appreciate her thinking I was a serial killer —but I definitely had blood on my hands. There was no denying that.

"You saw?" I hazarded a guess.

"I saw the aftermath. I got to the safe room in time, she didn't." Her nostrils flared. "When Father wouldn't make Svetlana return the ring to me, I told him he was to blame for Mother's death." She jerked her chin up, obstinacy flashing through her. "He went mad. That was when I told him I wasn't going to marry you, when I spat in his face..." She smiled. "Seeing him worried for a second was almost worth the beating."

I could feel Aidan's surprise, even though he was a few blocks away.

For myself, I wasn't too shocked. Inessa had a strange moral code, and I'd seen that only in our first day together.

I could easily imagine her standing up to Vasov, spitting in his face after he'd beaten her badly, then taking another beating because it was worth it.

The very idea of it both made me want to choke Vasov and pin her to the wall.

That kind of fire in a woman wasn't something I saw often. Women were soft things to be protected and sheltered, until they were married at least. That was when the gloves came off. They were screwed until they were pregnant, then they popped out as many kids as their husband decided he could support, and they were left to raise said brats while the man went off and fucked whoever he wanted as was his God-given right.

Inessa hadn't been cosseted or protected, and that I wanted to make up for that was strange. To me, at least. My feelings were in no way paternal for her, but fuck, she had me twisted up inside. And not in a good way.

I frowned at her, then turned to Aidan. "Don't tell the folks."

"They'll want to know," he said gently.

"Inessa will tell them herself when they ask." And ask they

would. Next Sunday probably. "Won't you?" I queried, without looking back at her.

"With ease," she agreed formally.

The confirmation had me staring daggers at my brother in warning, then, when he shrugged, I muttered, "See you tomorrow at the airport."

He hesitated for a second, then replied, "Will do." That hesitation had me wondering what he was covering up, but before I could ask, he cut the call, but his interested gaze was on Inessa all the while, and I couldn't blame him.

She'd revealed a lot about herself with a very small amount of words.

Maybe I should have anticipated that. Or maybe Inessa was not the kind of woman you could anticipate. Period.

When I turned back to face her, I cocked a brow and asked, "Aren't you going to ask about the airport?"

She shrugged. "I'm not going—you wouldn't have ordered me to go shopping if I was. I assume it's business."

My frown darkened. "Don't you want to know where I'm going?"

Aidan said she'd be worried.

Why wasn't she worried?

Inessa frowned back at me. "If you want to tell me, I'll want to know. Anyway, breakfast is ready."

"I'll shower—"

She cleared her throat. "No. This is warm. It'll get cold if you shower."

"You cooked?" My brows rose.

"It looked easy on the recipe."

Fuck, I was way too like my old man.

The idea of her cooking for me did shit to my insides.

"What is it?"

"Just eggs." She cleared her throat again—her nerves clear. "Come on. I don't want them to get cold."

Inessa twisted around before I could say another word, and I followed her, watching her leave before I stalked after her at a slower pace.

She was a looker, going or coming. From the front, she had the best tits, and her face was heaven sent. From the back, that ass and her long, strong legs... It was going to be fun to bend her over my desk and fuck that bubble butt.

I gritted my teeth as my dick hardened, and even as I wondered when I'd turned into a fucking saint, I saw her bend over the second I got into the kitchen and pull out something from the oven.

The scent of cheese and eggs was a good combination, as was the bacon that tinged the air, but nothing beat the sight of her leaning over that way.

She wore sports shorts this time. The kind women wore to go jogging in, a little loose around the thigh, tight around the ass. The move pulled the fabric taut, shaping her butt to perfection, and creating a perfect seam down the crack of her ass and to her pussy.

Instantly, I regretted waiting to fuck her because, by now, she'd have been broken in.

The sight of her bent over like that made me want to fuck her so hard that, for a second, I couldn't see straight.

It was insane, but I felt like some kind of animal who couldn't control his urges. Who scented a bitch in heat, and who thought only with his instincts.

But I wasn't an animal.

Sure, people, Inessa included, might think I was a beast because of what I did for a living, and with no guilt either, but I wasn't.

Snipers were, by necessity, cold and calm. Logical. We studied a situation that was hundreds or thousand of yards away, taking into account things like wind speeds to assess the variables of a kill shot taking formation. We could control our breathing, our fucking heart rate, all to make that perfect hit.

We were not beasts, we didn't fall to our baser instincts.

Yet here I was, doing nothing but that.

My mouth tightened as I let my fingers contract into fists once more. She wiggled her butt a little as she scooted back from the stove, and when she stood up, there was such glee on her face, that fuck, I wanted her even more.

She was proud of what she'd made. And considering I'd seen her earlier attempt at bacon and eggs, I could well understand as the scent in the kitchen was damn good.

But her triumph?

Her happiness?

Got to me like a hammer to the head.

Then she looked at me, and her smile died.

She blinked, the dish hovered in her hands, and she almost dropped it before she broke our gaze and placed it on the counter.

For a second, the only sound in the kitchen was the fan in the oven whirring as it cooled down. I felt frozen, as frozen as she was, then she raised her head, let our eyes connect once more, and she raised her chin.

I knew what that meant.

Game on.

And I was more than amped for the challenge.

That single gesture had my limbs stirring into action, and I surged forward, not stopping until we were inches apart.

She pressed her hands to my pecs, to hold me back or to touch me, I wasn't sure, but when she licked her lips, I had no choice but to lower my head.

I'd tasted her once—at our wedding.

Since then, the sight of the bandage on her lip had sunken any desire I had for her into the depths of the Hudson. I had no urge to cause her pain, even from a kiss, not when I knew sex might be uncomfortable for her at first.

But now, the little stitch she'd been sporting had disappeared. Lips healed fast, still, I reached up and cupped her chin, using my thumb to swipe across the luscious morsel.

"How's it feel?"

Her eyes grew round. "Fine."

"No soreness?"

She shook her head.

"Good," I ground out, my voice like gravel as I pressed our lips together for the first time.

So, remember that shit I'd said about hating virgins?

She hadn't been kissed either.

She didn't know what the fuck she was doing, and God help me, I fucking loved it.

She followed every move I made like she was learning the choreography of a ballet, gently mimicking each move until my own skills were thrown back at me to the point where I wasn't sure if I was the good kisser or if she was.

The way she responded, the way she followed my every move fucked with my head in the best possible way, and I could feel my already throbbing dick start to pound out a message. Every part of me wanted in her, but if she was this uninitiated, I knew I had to go slow, and my body was not okay with that.

I reached up, cupped both cheeks in my hands, and opened my mouth, prompting her to do the same. I thrust my tongue deeper into hers, nipping her lips, claiming what belonged to me and me alone.

And that right there blew my fucking mind.

Mine.

No other fucker had touched her, tasted her, kissed her, screwed her.

Every inch of her belonged to me.

I never had to share her, hadn't shared her with anyone.

Every inch of her was innocent, mine to corrupt.

Mine to teach.

If brains could orgasm, then I'd just come.

She didn't even have to do anything for me to feel that way, so this responsiveness made me feel like I was fifteen again and my dick could get hard no matter my location—be it at the gym or at the strip joint Da had taken us to, individually, when he decided it was time for our 'coming of age' celebration.

I pulled back, my breath rasping from my lips and, pushing my forehead into hers, I was satisfied that she was just as dazed, just as flustered. She didn't open her eyes, just panted against me, her lips parted, her breath brushing my chin.

She'd moved closer, her body shoved tightly against mine now, and the feel of those gorgeous tits pushed against my torso made me want to fuck them.

In fact...

That might be a solution.

I took a second to tamp down my urges, to rein in my control. Then, I ground out, "You know I want more than a kiss. Are you ready for what I want from you?"

That had her eyes flaring wide open, but deep inside those green orbs, I saw a need just as fierce as mine.

"I-I don't know what to do."

"Follow my lead," I prompted. "Nothing more, nothing less."

Her bottom lip quivered. "Okay."

"You're sure," I asked once more, wanting to be certain.

If she was a regular bride and I a regular groom, I wouldn't have asked her so many times if she was okay with this. She'd told me, quite clearly, with her body that she wanted me. But Inessa had had no say in her groom, her wedding, or her honeymoon. She'd been beaten to within an inch of her life, to the extent I was pretty sure she'd had a fucking concussion and that was why she'd been quiet most of our wedding day—not from nerves like I'd first thought, or discomfort, or unhappiness. But because she was concussed.

There were times when I wouldn't ask her in the future, when I would listen to the clear signals her body was sending me, but this time?

It was important.

This time set the scene for the rest of our lives, and for a passion this hot? No way in shit was I going to fuck things up.

"I-I'm certain."

My only consolation here was that she was used to pain, so I was hoping taking her virginity wouldn't be too uncomfortable for her. It boggled my mind how squeamish I was about that part.

Blood, flesh, and bone—both were aspects of my daily life.

But the thought of hurting her in that way fucked with my head.

She frowned, reached up, and her small hand cupped the back of my neck. "What is it?"

My instinct was to stay quiet, but when I didn't reply, I saw hurt filter through her expression. "I'm concerned about your first time," I rasped.

She licked her lips. "Don't be." Then she stood on tiptoe and licked mine. "I'm not."

Blood rushed to my head, and I swept her against me at her words. Hauling her up high, I pivoted so I could press her to the counter.

When her butt hit the marble top, she squealed, and I knew that was because it was cold.

I shoved shit aside that she'd been using to cook with, and ignored the fact that her ass was also coated with flour and what looked like sugar crystals.

My focus was on the honey between her thighs.

I pushed back, saw her there, arms and legs all over the place, zero grace, zero seduction, and it worked on me better than a lap dance.

She looked vulnerable and nervous when, seconds ago, the way she'd tasted me had been pure confidence.

I wanted that back, and I was going to show her how.

I grabbed the hem of her shorts, and she lifted her hips to help me lower them to her knees.

Seeing that she wasn't wearing any panties fucked me up even more as I saw her parted pussy lips topped with a landing strip of hair.

I reached down, rubbed my thumb over her snatch, that tiny line of hair, and rumbled, "Who did this for you?"

She swallowed, her focus on my hand, and whispered, "Someone at a salon."

"I'll do this for you from now on."

Inessa laughed, and her eyes sparkled when she looked at me.

Then, when she realized I wasn't joking, her mouth rounded into a perfect O that made my dick weep pre-cum.

"You're not serious?" she questioned.

"I'm deadly serious. No one sees this pussy but me."

Her mouth worked again. "That's not practical."

I blinked. "Why isn't it?"

"If I get pregnant, someone will have to see it then."

Despite myself, despite the ache in my body for her, I had to laugh. "I'll rethink the situation if I have to."

My thumb swiped down her parted folds, and she released a whimper that hit me in ways I knew she wouldn't understand. Her head flopped back, and I flicked her clit with the edge of my thumb, watching her body as she responded to my touch.

"Have you touched your clit before, Inessa?" I growled. I guessed she had, and I wasn't happy about it, but it was leading to the bigger question.

She shivered, either at my touch or the query, and muttered, "Of course. I have needs too, you know?" That her snark came with another shudder had my lips quirking, and when she glowered at me, managing to force her head upright to do so, I smirked at her.

"Did someone else touch you?"

She blinked, unease slipping into her, making her tense. "No."

I narrowed my eyes at that. "Are you lying to me?" Even as rage filtered through me at the notion of someone having touched her, she gulped.

"I-I used to—"

At her pause, I slipped a finger into her pussy, then arced it up and raked down her front wall, which had her eyes flaring wide. "Used to what?"

She took a deep breath. "There was a guard I liked." Her mouth trembled, and her eyes turned dazed. "It was stupid."

"What was?" That I managed to control the level of anger bubbling away inside me was a miracle. "What was, Inessa?" I commanded, wanting her to get used to this.

Wanting her to learn that I'd use pleasure as a weapon to get what I wanted.

"It's embarrassing," she moaned, and her elbows came out from under her as she flopped on her back. Her legs reared up, cupping my shoulders.

"You can tell me anything," I soothed, knowing that, with time, she'd tell me everything I wanted with little to no issue. Including information she'd gleaned about her father's operation.

Her hand moved to cover her face. "I used to—" She sucked in a breath when I slipped another finger inside her. "Oh God, I can't think when you do that!" she cried hoarsely, her legs tightening around me.

"Think, Inessa," I crooned. "What did you do?"

"H-He used to sit at a desk just off my father's office." A moan escaped her as I began to rub her clit with my free hand. "I'd go in there, and I'd—well, I'd hitch myself onto the desk."

I frowned.

What the hell was she talking about?

"Why did you do that?"

"If I put pressure on my clit, it feels good."

Understanding washed through me. "You humped the desk in front of him?"

Despite myself, despite the fact I was annoyed, I was also amused at the thought.

"Y-Yes."

"Did he touch you?"

"No. Never. But I did it a few times," she whispered, her shame clear. "The last time, he almost did, but my father nearly caught us. I knew he'd hurt him, so I never did it again."

That had probably saved his life from me.

"Did you come?"

"N-No. I don't know why I did it," she muttered. "It felt good but—"

She was a tease. An exhibitionist.

And she had needs.

Needs I was about to fulfill.

"Of course it felt good," I whispered, dropping over her. "But this will feel even better," I vowed, promising myself that I'd erase the memory of this guard from her mind.

She moaned as I fluttered my tongue along her clit, then as I flickered the tip back and forth, she cried out, "Oh God!" and began rocking from side to side, twisting almost under my hold as I forced her toward an orgasm.

Finger fucking her at the same time, I moved fast, overwhelmed her senses, and forced that orgasm out of her, wringing her dry within a minute.

When she screamed, the sound washed over me.

Fuck, I loved it when women screamed, and that my woman did that?

There was no better way to put a smile on my goddamn face.

Her hand moved down, shoving me harder against her, and I let her, let her ride my face, let her fly into her urges, and I gave her what she needed to fly freer.

Only when she came down did her hand move, and she let me pull back. My mouth was wet, my chin coated with her juices. I could fuck her now, fuck her without pain, but instead, I let my fingers carry on thrusting into her, scissoring her as I moved.

"What was the guard's name?"

She blinked, then slurred out, "Why?"

"I want to know."

My inexorable answer had her tensing. "You'll hurt him."

I rubbed the sensitive fore-wall of her pussy, making her cry out. "I won't."

"Liar," she rasped.

"No. I promise, I won't."

That had her turning still. "You promise?"

I knew how she felt about promises, and I had no issue with giving this one.

"I do."

She licked her lips. "Maxim."

I stored that away, another vow surging in my head to make her forget that fucker's name, and asked, "Do you still have a crush on him?"

"No." Though the answer came fast enough for it to be a lie, I actually believed her.

"Why not?"

She huffed. "Do you have to ask me this stuff while your hand is inside me?"

My lips twitched. "I want to know."

"Sometimes it isn't good to get what you ask for. Not every time."

"You'll learn to demand what you want," I rasped, the idea turning me on.

I wanted her fucking starving for me. I wanted her on me more than white on rice.

The idea of her ravenous, constantly cock hungry for me was a tantalizing fantasy I needed to live out.

Her eyes widened at my words, and she whispered, "I've been taught the opposite."

"Then you're going to unlearn it." I thrust into her cunt once more. "Now, tell me what I want to know."

"I saw him fucking one of the whores my father brought in for his men's use."

Disgust filtered through me. "You saw that?"

She shrugged. "His office is in our home. There's a wing for his soldiers."

I hadn't known that.

Everyone thought the Bratva worked out of a compound they owned in Brighton Beach, not at their Pakhan's home.

Something else to file away.

"What was he doing? What made him disgust you?" I moved my hand away at that question and pressed a single kiss just below the end of her Brazilian, where her sex split into two lips.

The move had her eyes softening, her lips parting, then, she whispered, "He fucked her ass."

There was more to it than that.

"And?"

She turned her face to the side. "He didn't use lube. There was blood."

"He raped her anally," I said flatly.

"Y-Yes. I guess so."

"No guess about it. Whores can be raped too."

"Not in my father's world," she whispered, and it didn't take a genius to know that she'd turned her face away to hide her shame at what was condoned among her people.

"Well, in the Five Points' world, which is now yours, that's what it was. Rape." I reached down and rubbed her rosette which was slick from her juices. "You know I'm going to fuck you here at some point."

I'd expected her to tense up, but she didn't. She surprised me, again, by pouting. "What if I don't want you to?"

"What if I make it good for you?"

That had her squinting at me. "I'll let you..."

"If?" I heard that 'if' without her even having to say it, and because I was feeling generous, since my ears were still ringing from her screams, I was willing to allow her to negotiate.

"If you'll—"

"If I'll, what?" She was young, inexperienced, and naturally embarrassed, but I was looking forward to the day when she'd just say what she wanted.

Still, I could be patient.

For the moment.

Until now, she'd been quite vocal in her own way. It was to be expected that she was less forthcoming sexually. That would come with time.

"W-Will you...can we do this outside?"

Whatever I'd expected her to say, I hadn't expected that.

Still, my cock throbbed harder at the prospect.

"If you want that, of course," I rumbled.

She swallowed, her gaze flickering from mine. "A-And you with a suit on and me with no clothes on?"

Stunned wasn't the word at her stuttered fantasy.

I wasn't about to complain, still, I reached up, cupped her throat, and forced her to look at me.

"I thought you'd be nervous talking about those things with me." Hell, about being naked. It was quite clear to me that she was demure where most women weren't. Used to hiding herself away because of her father's position and her betrothal to me.

"I-I am, but for two years, I've had nothing to do but think. And watch porn." She clenched her eyes shut. "I've watched so much porn, you wouldn't believe it. No one would go near me, no one would touch me, no one would kiss me when the betrothal agreement was in place. I-I needed that."

It fit that, from her past, she'd consider sex as intimacy, and that kind of intimacy as affection, and it actually made me glad that she'd been off limits, because she could have fucked her way through her senior year and never have found what she was looking for, would only have been a willing hole for a bunch of prick jocks.

So, I got it. I did. I wasn't mad. I was, if anything, a little sad for her.

It made me want more for her, even if I wasn't sure I could give her what she needed.

Physically, sure, but she wanted more than that. I could see it. She was crying out for care and love, affection. I could give her the latter, could even give her the first, but love?

I doubted it.

I was a soldier, a sniper—she'd said it herself—a serial killer. Did we even have the capacity for love?

That all whispered through my mind as I stared at her, then, unsure of what else to say, I focused on something else. "No more porn. Not without me."

And her smirk reappeared, her shyness and timidity disappearing, and she retorted, "Who's going to stop me?"

TEN

INESSA

HIS EYES FLASHED AT THAT, and I saw amusement warring with irritation.

He was possessive.

I'd felt that from the start. He was also finicky, particular, and downright difficult when it came to certain things.

The towels were folded just so and weren't piled, but were rolled and stored standing upright in baskets in the bathroom.

All his clothes were ironed—even his frickin' boxers and socks.

And everything had a stillness about it—sure, most inanimate objects did unless they were in *Beauty and the Beast*—but this entire place was like a museum. Like, if I hadn't come in, nothing would ever move. Not the blanket he had draped over the large sofa, which I was hesitant to touch considering what I'd found on it that first day, *skank*, or the remote controls which were always in the same place, even when he switched on the TV.

It was like he was a ghost within these walls, and it was really difficult trying to fit in.

I was neat by nature, but I spent a lot of time at home by force—I wasn't used to my own living space being so still. So solemn.

But it was the first week of my marriage, so I wasn't about to rock the boat too much and, even if I wasn't happy about having to go furniture shopping in the morning, I was looking forward to replacing the things I didn't like, hopefully making it more comfortable and slut-germ-free in the process.

Still, I liked his possessiveness, and call me nuts, but I was going to use it to my own gain.

Father had been a good man until Mama had died. Some women were strong enough to hold men as powerful as my father and Eoghan in the clasp of their hands—not in a bad way, just in a show of strength. Some women could harness that violence, could disseminate it, remind the crime lord they were a man, and make them as happy as they could be.

After she'd died? Things had changed for the worse, and ever since, with things deteriorating when he'd married that slut Svetlana, I'd realized just how large an effect my mother had on my father. The right woman made a shit load of a difference, and the wrong one? Tipped the scales and shoved an already dangerous man into another territory.

Knowing what I did, it made me want that for Eoghan, because I wanted to be happy. I didn't want to be tucked away inside all the time, I didn't want to be a broodmare or a trophy wife. I didn't want to be brought out for fancy parties, then sheltered away at home to rot.

If I made him happy, if I gave him what he wanted, all while entertaining him, he'd let me become a part of his life.

And while adultery was common in our world, I really didn't want that either, even if that would be almost impossible to achieve.

I didn't want to wonder who he was fucking, I didn't want to worry if he was using a condom or if he was getting some slut pregnant with a child who might resent the legitimate kids we had—and that wasn't as ludicrous as it sounded. Crazy shit happened all the time in our world, and when you thought about the money that was floating around, it made sense.

I didn't love Eoghan. I didn't know him. But that didn't mean I couldn't work toward attaining something that would make us both happy, and that would, given time, make us like one another.

Love wasn't something I was aiming for. Maybe, in my heart, I cried out for it, but hearts had no place in business deals. If I'd learned anything from my father, it was that, and it was time I put that into practice.

At my challenge, just like I'd known he would, Eoghan fell for it.

Of course, I hadn't anticipated his response.

I hadn't expected any of this, truth be told. I hadn't thought he'd eat me out on the kitchen counter, nor had I imagined he'd manage to wheedle that embarrassing shit with Maxim out of me. Then, when I'd told him my biggest fantasy? I had to admit, it was only because I was orgasm drunk.

What I'd achieved with my hand and what he'd done with his mouth?

Sweet fuck.

It was like nothing I could have imagined.

My hand gave me as much pleasure as a really good scratch when you had an irritating mosquito bite.

His mouth? I felt like my entire being was going to implode.

When you were shoved headfirst into that, into feeling something like that, there was no way you were going to come out unscathed.

Even now, as he began to trace his fingers around my clit once more, making me grit my teeth as the sensitive nub flared to life with a whimper because it was still tender, he chivvied, "You can watch it if I'm there."

"Porn is private," I retorted. "I might like something you don't."

His lips curved, and a wicked light appeared in his eyes. "I'll willingly reenact anything I see you watch."

The notion excited me more than I could stand, and he saw it.

Damn his hide.

I pursed my lips like I was contemplating that, and muttered, "Okay."

"So gracious," he replied, and then he dipped his chin and kissed me.

He tasted like me. Soap from the shower I'd just had, salty juices that I knew came from my pussy. I'd tasted it once or twice, knew it was inoffensive, but on his lips, it tasted different.

It tasted sexy.

A shaky breath escaped me as I surged upward, unable to stop myself from slipping my hands through his hair and holding him to me.

Eoghan, as a man, was beautiful. As my husband, he was still a stranger. But what he did to my body? What he'd made me feel this week? Safe? Protected? Somehow, all of that morphed into a need so powerful, because I knew that he'd make me feel good.

My friend, Lisandra, had lost her cherry to Myles Harrison in our class, and she'd been sore for a week afterward—plus he'd told half the locker room, and she'd been humiliated.

Eoghan wasn't a little boy.

He knew what to do with his body, knew what to do with mine, and I was a willing student because I was so beyond ready for sex that I knew if he didn't put his dick inside me soon, I was going to go crazy.

He chuckled at my kiss, at first, then, when he seemed to sense how hungry I was, he stopped laughing. His tongue thrust into my mouth, flicking against mine, making everything inside me wonder what it would be like for something else to be doing that.

I shuddered, clasped my legs around his waist, and seconds later, he was hauling me up and into the air.

I didn't care that the frittata I'd made was going to be cold, nor did I give a shit about the cooling breakfast muffins. My brain was on orgasms, on sex, and on Eoghan.

In that order.

He smelled like sweat and man, and that was kind of heavenly. Especially when he returned to the bed where the nest of covers I'd made before I'd left the room scented of us too.

He placed me on top of it and gradually pulled back. I only let him go because he still wore shorts, and I wanted him naked.

I'd seen flashes of him without clothes on this week, when he was in the bathroom before he got into bed, and he had a towel around his waist—through the sliver between the door and the jamb, I'd seen him put on boxers.

His body was a machine. I'd never seen as many muscles in someone's arms and back. His entire form was strong though. Delicious with it. And I looked forward to tracing my tongue over each muscle.

I guessed I should be nervous, but I wasn't. My hormones, the fact that Eoghan was hot as hell, and that I didn't have a say in who would be the one to take my virginity meant all this was expedient.

Yeah, romantic, but I was so far past that, it was unreal. Romance had no place in my world, and that I hadn't been married off to a sixty-year-old with a bigger beer belly than a pregnant woman meant I was about as hot for Eoghan as he was for me—virginity or not.

When he stood in front of me and shucked out of his shorts, I bit my lip at the sight of him. His cock was thick, long, and hard. Very hard. In fact, it stood up in a way that had to be uncomfortable.

"It'll fit."

I rolled my eyes. "I'm not scared of it."

He grabbed it, jacked off, then questioned, "Why are you staring at it then?"

"Because it's the only dick I've seen before?" I snorted, then leaned up on my elbow. "Plus, it looks painful."

"It can be." He leaned over, grabbed my other hand, and dragged my fist over his, showing me how to grip him, hold him.

I liked that he didn't make me feel like an idiot for not knowing any of this. He made it...natural.

And then I thought about that, and whispers of truths began to make sense.

Eoghan was particular in all things. Why wouldn't he be in this?

Maybe, whether I was a virgin or not, he'd show me how he liked it, finding no shame in commanding his pleasure.

I wouldn't put it past him.

And, despite myself, it made me determined to bring him to his knees. To learn every fucking thing about him, every ounce of whatever gave him pleasure and dole it out to him.

To make him mine long before I became his.

Only in that path was there safety.

Only down that road was my future secured, and I refused to live a life that mimicked my childhood.

"It's throbbing," I mused.

"In time to my heart." His hips thrust forward when I squeezed harder, and his head tipped back slightly. "Fuck."

His voice was thick—pleasingly so. The sound actually made my pussy clench.

He was so controlled in most things that the desire to break that hit me.

Don't walk before you can run, Inessa, I told myself, even as I knew I was adding that to my to-do list.

Curious, I dipped my head forward to taste the bead of pre-cum that appeared, but the second I did that, his hand was in my hair and he jerked me back.

"You taste me when I'm clean," he growled with fire in his eyes, making me jolt. Especially when my roots protested the abrupt move.

A gasp escaped me when he didn't stop until my head was all the way back, and he demanded, "Understood?"

Maybe I should have been scared, but I wasn't.

An urge hit me, an urge I knew would make any shrink squirm in their seats, but I rolled with it. Rolled with what I needed.

If this was a lesson, then Eoghan could be my teacher, and he could make this okay.

I reached for his other hand, raised it to my throat, and encouraged him to hold me there.

His eyes flickered for a second, his glance going to the sight of his fingers around my neck, then he rasped, "I won't hurt you."

"I know."

I did. That was why I trusted him with this. Trusted him to break memories that were forged deep in my psyche.

The sting of my roots, the faint pressure around my throat, it felt...good.

Right.

I blew out a shaky breath, letting him take the weight of my head, feeling somehow so vulnerable at that moment, when I'd been riding a high.

It really did feel good though.

Felt like...

Christ.

Like I was bridging a gap between us.

Making him see me. Inessa. His wife. His woman. Not just a hole, not just a pussy. His.

His nostrils flared like our thoughts were on the same track, and then he slowly climbed onto the bed, his knees making the mattress bounce slightly as he rolled me back and leaned over me.

One of his knees moved then as his elbow took some weight, and he slid my legs apart, making a place for himself between my thighs.

His dick instantly pushed itself against my pussy. The thick heat resting against tender flesh.

"Are you on the pill?"

The question had me blinking at him. "Shot."

He nodded. "Neither of us is ready for a family."

I liked how he didn't make that a question. I was too young, even though I knew it was pretty standard in my world to get pregnant quickly. I liked that he wasn't going to force a child on me, and it had been a calculated risk telling him about the shot, which I'd gotten by sneaking to the doctor on a lie. I'd have earned myself a worse beating if my father had learned of it.

He rolled his hips, letting his cock surge against me, rubbing my clit with every move. He carried on, not stopping until I was rocking my hips, seeking more. His mouth caught mine, his lips tasting mine, then he let go of my hair, and I knew to prepare for it.

His hand went to his dick, and suddenly, his thickness was there.

I swallowed, forced myself to relax, and bit my lip as he began to push inside me.

It hurt. But it wasn't terrible. I'd endured worse.

A shaky breath escaped me, one that mingled with his as he carried on kissing me as he pushed all the way in.

When he was there, fully, I didn't stop to think, I just reached down, grabbed his butt, and dug my nails in, urging him on.

He bit my bottom lip as he muttered, "No. Give it a second."

"Need more," I grumbled. Him just hovering there, filling me, made me even more aware of how overfull I was.

He seemed to get it, the smart man that he was, so he pulled out.

Slowly.

I shivered, whimpered.

He pushed back in.

Slowly.

I moaned, shuddered.

My nails dug deeper into his ass, pressing him for more, needing more, not even knowing what I desired, then he began to move.

Harder.

Faster.

Not too hard.

Not too fast.

Just right.

Just what I needed.

A shocked breath escaped me, a sharp gasp that had my head rocking from side to side, pulling at his hold on me as I tried to absorb the sheer welter of feeling he was making me experience.

A sob escaped me as he did this thing with his hips, burrowing down somehow so his pelvis ground into me, and like that, sparks began to burn behind my eyes.

The feeling was insane, so much more than when he'd gone down on me.

My mouth opened, and I stared blindly above as the sensation he forced on me pushed me from overwrought to insensate.

And then, his tongue slipped into my mouth, and his fingers tightened on my throat, and sensation returned in an explosion that had me screaming with the ecstasy filtering through my body like it was a drug I could get addicted to.

Like *he* was a drug I could get addicted to.

If that was the case, I knew I'd need to make him a junkie too. Even as my brain flooded with dopamine, I knew that this had to be mutual.

If I was ensnared, he had to be as well.

So, I thrust my tongue against his, tightened my pussy around his cock to the point of pain, because my body was still sparking from my orgasm, and I didn't stop, rubbing myself against him, urging him on until he came.

His orgasm was silent.

So quiet, I wasn't even sure he'd come, then I realized how still he was, and when he sagged on top of me, I'd admit to being a little freaked out by how contained his release was when mine was so violent.

Pushing that thought aside, I curled my legs about his hips, wanting him close, but not wanting to crowd him with octopus arms.

When he fell asleep on me, his heavy weight wasn't displeasing. If anything, it was a comfort.

So I nuzzled my face into him, appreciating the scent of us more than I'd expected, and decided to sleep too.

With him inside me.

And for some weird reason, it felt good.

ELEVEN
EOGHAN

I DIDN'T BELIEVE in fate, because to me, a man made his own destiny.

That being said, everything about this situation was starting to feel off to me.

Everything about her felt like it fit with me. She gelled. And while some of it could be contrived, I didn't think she could maintain a twenty-four seven façade to make me think she was perfect for me.

She was smart enough, granted, but I'd seen too many sides to her in the past six days. Moments of vulnerability, joy, surprise, and need.

I also got a read on her that she wanted this to work. I had a feeling, sex wise, she'd do whatever I wanted to tie me to her, and because her pussy was like crack, I'd let her carry on believing that.

And yeah, I considered myself a fortunate man because Inessa showed all the signs of having an incredible sex drive, so letting her burn off her hormones on me was no punishment.

She'd woken me up yesterday with her fingers around my dick, and the second I'd become aware, she'd moved on top of me.

She was the aggressor, but I knew I should have left her alone. I wasn't lying about her cunt being like crack.

One taste would never be enough.

I tugged at my bottom lip as I thought about her as she'd been earlier this morning. She'd been naked, her body splayed on the sheets, exhaustion riding her after another round of sex as I left the bedroom and made my way into the gym.

She didn't wake up like she'd taken to doing, and when I'd showered in the guest room after quietly grabbing some things from my closet, she still had shown no signs of life.

I'd admit to feeling smug as I left her a note on the hall console. One that detailed the code to the elevator—a code I warned her against sharing with anyone—a number she had to call when she wanted to go out, her guard's name, a guy called Limerick, and listed the pin code to her new card as well as the furniture I wanted her to change while I was gone.

My trip should only take five days, and there was a lot of shopping to be done in that time—but I made it clear I wanted it done before my return.

I hoped to fuck that I wasn't about to come home to an apartment that was styled for a teenager with bean bags or some shit, but it was an extension of trust.

One I hoped she passed.

Conor broke into my thoughts by slipping a file across the table.

I jerked to life at the sight of it, frowned, and said, "Already read it."

"I know."

I blinked at him. "Why are you here anyway?"

Usually, Aidan came with me on these things if I needed help.

Conor shrugged. "Da's orders."

I rolled my eyes. "Because you'll be a lot of use when it comes down to it."

He flipped me the bird as he sank back into the comfortable bucket seat.

The private jet was a luxury, one that made it very easy to fulfill my missions.

You'd be surprised how many opportunities there were for a sniper, and the jet enabled me to fly across the world, earning a mint, even as we infiltrated organizations around the globe.

Sure, my identity was a secret, but that I worked for the Five Points wasn't.

Everyone knew about the Whistler.

I hated the fucking moniker, but it had stuck when some kid had told the police the only thing he'd heard before one of my victims fell was the whistle of my bullet.

I called bullshit on that, but who was I to complain? Pathetic nickname or not, it gave me a rep that was very lucrative.

Da had probably funded half the plane's price tag with the commission fee he made by connecting me with clients.

Conor's dark hair rustled against his shoulders as he pushed his head back into the cushion when we hit some turbulence—the fucker hated flying. The caramel leather augmented how pale he was, and I had to snort.

"Are you being punished? Is that why you're here and not Aidan?"

He grunted.

And I laughed.

Again.

I guessed it fit. Aidan had hesitated yesterday on our call when I told him I'd see him today. Figured this would be why.

"For the code situation?" I asked.

"What do you think?"

Da didn't often punish Conor. If he did, it was by cutting his bonuses. Conor liked money, loved spending it, and had a thing about hoarding it. Hitting him in the wallet was a surefire way to get him to behave.

Deciding not to be a prick, I muttered, "Da's out of order."

Conor pulled a face. "I fucked up. Twice now, someone has gained access to one of our homes."

"Coding isn't something that stays still," I reasoned. "I mean, it takes constant monitoring, and you can't do it all."

"No, I can't, but I let us down, so I get it. I'm just lucky you didn't get hurt." Conor's mouth twisted. "That prospect is worse than Da making me fly or him cutting my wage for a while. I can deal with all that—going to your funeral isn't something I can handle."

I wanted to joke, but where this was concerned, we didn't.

We were Irish. Used to emotions.

So I just said, "It didn't happen."

"And it won't." He scrubbed a hand over his face. "I had firewalls up so high that not even the Russians should have been able to get into it."

"Teenagers can break into the NSA database, Conor—it happens. Da's too old school to realize that."

"Doesn't matter. Not where our safety is concerned." He frowned down at the table. "It's making me wonder if I'm good enough."

Because Conor was all about tech, I scoffed at that. "What about all the times you keep us safe, *dearthair*? Does this take away from that?"

"Yeah, it does. You could have been killed. For whatever reason, they, whoever the fuck they are, wanted to mess with your bride's head. As it stands, well, that didn't happen, but it could have messed with things."

I thought about that for a second, then thought about how right that was. "Conor, do you think it's a woman behind this?"

"A woman? What makes you say that?"

"I mean, it doesn't help us narrow things down really, but let's face it, another woman would think to hurt Inessa like that. A man wouldn't. A man, in our world, knows that Inessa wouldn't be hurt. She's been raised in the life. She knows the score.

"A woman outside of the life wouldn't know that." Then I told him what Leticia had said. "She'd brought make up and shit with her, cleanser. Like she was there for a stay or something. It was in my bathroom."

His eyes flared wide. "Fuck."

"Yeah. Fuck." He knew how particular I was.

If I told him Inessa was sleeping with me and sharing my bathroom, he'd probably shit a brick.

I scraped my chin, scratching at my cheek from where the stubble was starting to itch as my beard grew back in, before I mused, "It doesn't narrow things down, like I said, but it makes it seem less organized. Less from one of the Families."

"The *Famiglia* wouldn't use someone who wasn't on their payroll."

"Who the fuck knows who's on the payroll? They're not like us. They have markers everywhere. Maybe that's what this is. Someone they've called out a marker on."

"I'll need to look into a way of figuring out who would be able to compromise my code, then use that to filter back to the *Famiglia* and any ties there might be to them."

"Is that doable?"

Conor shrugged. "It'll be hard, but I know that code was strong, Eoghan." His earnestness reminded me of when we were kids, and Da had whooped one of our asses and we'd defended ourselves to each other for back up. "There was no way even an excellent coder should have broken it."

"Well, a marker out on them would probably make them work harder to excel even more. You know their markers are bound in blood."

Conor's gaze turned distant, and I knew he was thinking about just who could do it. Who could have broken his code.

I left him to it, left him to figure it out, because he needed to. Fast.

I didn't blame him, not like Da evidently did, but Conor needed to get a handle on this situation quickly before one of us really did get hurt because of it.

So, letting him focus, and even though I knew the file front to back, I pulled it toward me and started reading through it.

It was an easy hit.

Some fucker had just been released from prison. He'd murdered a few women, tortured them, and yet was being released, thanks to a DNA lab tech who'd fucked with some of the evidence. In the end, it meant there'd been a mix up, where he'd been identified as a dead prisoner when he was very much alive.

With one of the two surviving victims dead by her own hand, and the other having run off to fuck knew where, Josiah Landers was about to pay his debt to society by becoming a corpse.

And I was more than okay with being his executioner.

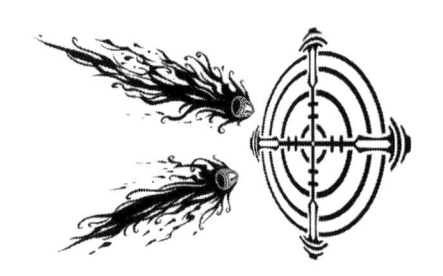

TWELVE
INESSA

"HE JUST LET you have the card, and that's it?"

My friend's surprise matched my own.

I showed her the list I'd snapped on my phone, and her brows lifted at the sight of all the things I had to buy... Essentially, an entire living room and bedroom suite.

"Yeah, I know, right? And he wants them by Friday." I shook my head. "I'm not sure if he thinks I'm a miracle worker or—"

"Maybe he thinks you'll drop his name?" Lisandra whispered. "I mean, everyone knows the O'Donnellys. People will probably jump into a breakdance if you ask them to."

Because the idea amused me, and I could tell she wanted to test it out, I snorted. "You sound jealous."

"Why wouldn't I? You're one of them now," she joked, elbowing me in the side as we wandered into a furniture store that, truth be told, I'd bought most of my bedroom furniture from when I'd been given the choice as a birthday present when I was sixteen. Of course, that had been to soften the news of the fact I was engaged...

That was probably the last time Father had tried to soften anything.

I'd grown up fast that day. My age in no way reflected how ancient I felt sometimes.

I'd seen more in my time than some eighty-year-olds did, and I was glad there were people who were spared the shit I had in my memory banks.

For a moment, I envied Lisandra, then I stopped it because she had her own woes, and at the moment, we weren't deep in misery, eating our weight in Halo Top, we were shopping—her favorite pastime. Me? I wasn't that big of a fan, but I liked doing it with her. It was the only time I felt normal.

Levigne's had a lot of ethnic articles in their stock, more of a beach vibe than the city slicker stuff Eoghan had. But he shouldn't have sent me shopping for him if he didn't want my taste to reign supreme in our home, right?

Somehow, that thought had me freezing in place, long enough for Lisandra to step forward, then to look back at me when I didn't move.

"What's wrong?" Her brow furrowed like she thought there was something wrong with me.

"I just thought… I have a home now. Like, my own place."

Her lips twitched. "You need to invite me over. I need to see it."

I shrugged. "I wish I could."

She curved her arm around my shoulder. "I know, I know. You're Vasov's daughter." She mock-shuddered. "Now you're Eoghan O'Donnelly's wife. I'm surprised you're still speaking to me."

I knew she was hurting about not being invited to the wedding, but none of my few friends had been there.

It hadn't been a wedding of love, but of arrangement, and though I hadn't been able to explain that to Lisandra, it didn't take a fucking genius to figure out that an eighteen-year-old and a thirty-year-old only got married to tie two dynasties together.

And while the dynasties were illegal, the fronts weren't.

The Vasovs were renowned industrialists. We had dozens of steel factories along the East Coast.

The O'Donnellys were property magnates.

Ha. All of it was funded on blood money. Nothing was legal or above board, and while some New Yorkers might surmise that, no one outright said it.

"Let me get to know him before I shove you in his face."

Lisandra pouted. "You make it sound like I'm a bad influence."

I grinned at her, even as I shook my head. She was a walking Barbie with curly blonde hair that bounced with each step, an ass tighter than a Georgia peach, and a waist that made me envy how tiny she was. Her face was delicate, her features elfin, and she had every boy at school panting after her. Until Myles had come along and ruined shit for her, which meant she was anti-men at the moment.

I loved her because she wasn't tainted by my world, but she was definitely not a good influence.

Every time I'd been slapped around this year by my father had been because of her—a party she insisted I come to, a double date she insisted I go on with her which, of course, had been before the Myles incident.

Still, it was worth it.

I wasn't about to let her go to parties or dates without me as a wing woman, not that I could do that anymore.

I wasn't free—I hadn't been single for two years, but I could get away with some stuff because Eoghan hadn't given a shit about me or what I did with my time. He'd made that quite clear over the two years of our engagement. Most of the dates I'd gone on had resulted in a slap or two, but nothing too bad. I was actually concerned about her when she went to college, because fuck, she was dangerous when she was drunk, and she was used to my being sober and DD as well as her lifesaver.

I'd saved her from being date raped twice this year, and the thought of her being hurt terrified me. She had an addictive nature, and I knew she wasn't going to do well without me. It wasn't like I could do anything other than worry, either, so I was definitely holding onto the time we had left together before she went to college like it was precious.

As I stared around the furniture shop, peevishness to redesign the entire apartment in stuff I knew he'd hate hit me. Girly, frilly, froufrou shit. But even as I wanted to make him pay for the two lost years where we could at least have become friends, where I wouldn't have to start married life having just turned into an adult and with a stranger at my side and in my bed, and for the fact that I couldn't have a normal life and go off to college with my bestie, I knew it would backfire on me.

So, I blew out a breath, and muttered, "We'd best get going."

"Money to burn, baby, my favorite kind of day."

I grinned at her, loving that she was more enthusiastic about this than I was.

It felt weird, redecorating Eoghan's apartment without any input from him. It made me feel like I was nothing more than a decorator, which I guessed wasn't his intention. He just hadn't made it feel like this was for my benefit, like it was about me making the apartment my home.

A little pissed at my inability to figure out why this redecorating business irritated me more than it pleased me, especially after my welcome 'home' after the wedding day from hell, I shoved it aside. I wasn't one for dwelling, but I'd been in a mood ever since I'd woken up to an empty apartment.

Tangled in the sheets, my body sore and well used after a busy night, I'd felt like a slut. A cheap whore he'd discarded after a one-night stand.

Just the thought had me biting my lip, even as I grabbed Lisandra's hand and tugged her into the store.

Of course, my mood wasn't improved when the assistant looked at me like I was a child, her eyes roving up and down me as she calculated how much my outfit cost—and I knew. It cost forty dollars, because I wasn't dressed to impress today, neither was Lisandra.

I could almost feel her dismiss me.

Thank God for my bud, though.

She sniffed and demanded, "Can I speak to the manager, please?"

The assistant, dressed from head to toe in white, with wide-flaring tailored pants and a slim-fitting camisole that showed everything while somehow looking business-casual, frowned. "May I help you?"

"Yeah, by getting me the manager. I don't like how you're looking at us—"

I snorted at Lisandra's complaint, amused by her outburst, then, by chance, I saw one of the assistants I'd worked with two years ago.

His eyes lit up at the sight of me, and I gave him a small wave. He was only a few years older than me and was the store owner's son. I'd had a little crush on him at the time, back before crushes had become verboten—well, not for me. For them. Eoghan wouldn't have done anything, but Father would have castrated him if he so much as went near me.

"Inessa?" he called out, like he was confused.

To be honest, I was surprised he remembered my name. "Yeah, hey, Jack." Okay, so I remembered his too. How lame was I?

The assistant frowned at me, then at Jack. "Is everything okay, Mr. Levigne?"

"Yes, of course. Inessa is..." His words waned. "I think I just saw you in the society pages, right? You're married to Eoghan O'Donnelly now?"

I could sense his disappointment, even as I saw the assistant eying me up even worse than she had before.

Lisandra sniffed. "Suck on that, bitch."

Barely refraining from laughing, I told Jack, "Yes, and I'm looking to redecorate our place. Can you help me?"

"Of course—"

"No, Mr. Levigne, let me—"

"No," I snapped, glaring at her. "Jack, I'd like *you* to help me."

He eyed the assistant who was trying not to glower at me, then shrugged as he led me back toward his office where we were seated by a desk.

The store was set up as a show room. Different pieces for different rooms tucked into a tiny space. They had catalogues, though, from different designers that came from all over the world, and some of my favorites were based in India.

When Lisandra and I had taken a seat, I smiled at him when he asked, "Would you like a coffee?"

"Please."

After he'd asked Lisandra, he told the assistant, who brought us our cups a few moments later.

When she'd disappeared, I informed him, "She's bad for business."

He tensed, evidently surprised by my remark. "Huh?"

"Don't play dumb, Jack," I said dryly. "You had to know how she was looking at us."

"We've had no complaints before," he countered stiffly.

"Well, you're getting one now," Lisandra inserted with a growl. "Two, in fact. That woman is a class A bitch. You're lucky Inessa saw you, because she'd have been striding out that door two seconds later if she hadn't." Under her breath, she muttered, "I'd have made her."

I knew Jack didn't like that we were complaining, but the woman had judged us on our appearances and had found us wanting. I actually knew how Vivian had felt when she'd walked down Rodeo Drive and the shop assistants had refused to help her in *Pretty Woman*.

Being found wanting was something I already felt most days without her needing to add to the shit on my shoulders.

Just knowing that Eoghan O'Donnelly's name was enough to make her judge me even more put me on edge.

I should be going to college, heading off to live in a dorm, enjoying frat parties with Lisandra, and raving the night away.

Instead, I was married to a property magnate who, in truth, was a serial killer for cash.

It was enough to break a woman out in hives.

I took a sip of my coffee, letting Lisandra bitch. I figured she had a crush on Jack, which, despite her anti-man phase, fit. He was her type, so I let her work her shit, flirt a little, then he started to look flustered because, even during the aforementioned anti-man phase, she was a lot to handle. I decided to save him by saying, "Jack? Can I look at the Haneli catalogue, please?"

He blinked, shuffled through the catalogues he had in a drawer in his desk, and passed it over to me.

When his attention switched back to Lisandra, I figured he was into her so, with a smirk, I left them to it as I perused the articles from a designer I'd already purchased several pieces from.

They were expensive, but, considering Eoghan lived at the top of a high rise in Manhattan, I figured he could afford for me to splurge.

As I eyed the long, super wide sofa that was pretty much a bed for the living room, which came with these neat, Indian-style carvings on the armrests, I'd never really know what prompted me to look up.

But when I did, peering through the open door, I saw him, and my heart sank.

A part of me knew Eoghan couldn't keep his promise, but the only way he could stop my father from getting to me was if he was dead.

My mouth flattened when I saw him standing in the store, staring at me like I was the enemy and not his daughter—which, in a way, I figured I was now. Technically, at least.

He wore an expensive suit with that black silk scarf that told me Eoghan's damage to his shoulder had been extensive because, in my world, we didn't wear shit like slings or casts for long. At least, we didn't go out with them on. Flaunting a weakness was asking for trouble.

Of course, things changed when a daughter with a recalcitrant husband left the house for the first time in a week…

I vowed, then and there, to dump my phone.

He obviously had a trace on me, and I wanted to slap myself silly for not figuring that out sooner. I also cursed my idiocy in ignoring Eoghan's demand that I contact a guard to chauffeur me around.

I'd seen his keys that hung by a console table beside the elevator, and that Aston Martin had Lisandra's and my names all over it.

The need for speed and a bit of freedom to spread my wings was going to cause me a world of hurt. I could just feel it.

His eyes narrowed on me the longer I stared at him without getting to my feet, and while a part of me feared the aftermath that was coming to embrace me, I wasn't scared.

This was too common an occurrence to be scared.

Mostly, I was mad at myself for being in this situation.

Eoghan's stupid promises had made me lose track of what our reality was.

I couldn't believe that in a week, he'd undone years' worth of training, which told me something—I wanted to believe in him. Wanted to think he could do the impossible.

And that was dangerous.

Hope was dangerous.

Deadly, even.

I knew Father could drag me out of here, could shove me in his car and take me back to the house, but would he?

He didn't give a shit about the employees in the store, nor did he care about things like security.

He could take me, and his goons, who'd be hovering outside, would be there to threaten anyone who tried to call the cops.

Assessing the situation and coming up with only one solution, I got to my feet, placed the catalogue on the desk, then stated, "I'll just be a minute."

Lisandra frowned at me, not because I'd interrupted her flirtathon, but because she was curious why I was leaving.

Maybe something was etched into my expression, because she twisted around, saw my dad, and shot me a look.

"Everything okay?"

My smile was tight. "Never better."

Her concern was clear, but she nodded, and I felt her gaze on me as I trudged out of the office and past the snooty assistant.

The second I approached my father, he grabbed my arm. I didn't wince, even though it hurt. I locked my pain behind a mask, refusing to let him beat me in that way.

I wasn't like Camille or Victoria, I didn't cower or whimper in the face of his fury.

Tipping my chin up when he jerked me over to the side of the warehouse that was farthest from the assistant, I almost breathed a sigh of relief when he didn't drag me outside.

That he didn't told me he was frightened of Eoghan, and more relief filtered through me at the realization.

God, I was so glad Eoghan was a serial killer. Okay, sniper. Same difference.

I mean, I knew I shouldn't be happy that my husband had killed a lot of people, but fuck. What a lifesaver.

Irony—well aware.

"What did you say to him?"

I didn't bother backtalking, didn't bother giving him the deadeye. If anything, I kept my face blank and stated, "He saw the bruises."

"You lie," he growled out, his face turning purple like he'd been squeezed. He used to be a handsome man, and I knew most of his kids had his looks, me included, but I looked more like Mama with my coloring and shape. My sisters were all curves, me? I was a little like a ruler with butt. My tits were small but round, and I could rock the shit out of a bra, nothing more, nothing less.

Still, I looked like Mama, and I knew he almost held that against me.

I got it.

He'd loved her.

Adored her even.

And he'd gotten her killed.

He'd been the reaper of his own misery, and to a man like my father, guilt did not sit well on his shoulders.

He was losing his hair, and it was thinning at the sides too, his face held lines from stress but not laughter, and at the moment, on the brink of apoplexy, he looked like a massive beet in a black suit.

"Not impossible," I countered calmly. "He saw the bruises."

"I paid to make sure he didn't."

"Well, he did." I almost snapped those words at him, but managed to pull it off at the last moment. "I said nothing. I had no time to say anything."

His eyes widened at the thought, then they were back to squinting at me. "In the church, with the register—"

"He saw the bruises," I repeated. "You touched his property."

That had a hiss escaping him, and even as outrage flushed through him, I saw the calculation in his eyes.

He knew Eoghan was right.

I had been his property.

The second Father had signed me away two years before my damn wedding day, I'd become Eoghan's. Father had to protect my chastity, had to keep me locked away, because if any taint fell on me, that would fall on him.

And Eoghan would be well within his rights to rain hell on my father's shoulders.

"You shouldn't have angered me," Father snapped, out of the blue.

Angered him?

He wasn't the only one outraged now. "You promised Mama's ring to me!"

"I gave it to Svetlana," he countered dismissively. "Eoghan can afford to buy you a thousand rings. Let him—"

"That was Mama's! *She*," I spat, "has no right to wear something that belonged to my mama!" I pushed into him, the fragile connection to my beloved mother, to a Papa who had been kind and gentle, making me forget for a second that this father was not those things, and his hand snapped out.

Like always, it went to my throat.

He pinned me to the wall, hard enough for me to know I'd bruise, and he squeezed.

It was hard, God, so hard not to claw at his wrists, to scrabble at his fingers, but I didn't.

Wouldn't.

Couldn't.

Instead, I stared at him as he snarled, "Your mother's jewelry is mine to give to whom I wish. Do we understand each other?"

Oh, I understood all right.

I understood that, by hook or by fucking crook, I'd be stealing it back from him. I knew he kept it in his safe in his home office, and I didn't give a shit if it meant I had to lie my way back onto the compound to get it.

I'd fucking take the pieces she loved, and I'd wear them in goddamn public. Shoving my theft in his face.

Maybe he saw my mutiny, I'd never know, but his fingers tightened to the point where narrow tunnels appeared in my eyes.

My lungs' craving for oxygen reached a fever pitch, but I refused to struggle.

I wouldn't give him the satisfaction.

Instead, I glared my loathing of him until his eyes flashed like the monster he was.

It was then when I realized there were two types of monsters in the world.

Eoghan was one variety.

My father another.

And while I had eighteen years with this bastard, I'd have a lifetime with Eoghan, and I was suddenly very grateful for the fact that I had to get married so young.

Eighteen was the opposite of ideal, but I didn't care.

It got me away from this evil bastard.

My defiance had his fingers pinching into my throat with a force that made me feel like he could tear through the skin, then someone called out, "Pakhan."

I wasn't sure whether it was a warning or to prompt my father about an upcoming appointment, but he backed off.

For those intense moments, our gazes had been locked on one another, nothing else intruding. Nothing in the world getting in the way.

But the second he heard his title, he twisted around, and I saw it was Maxim.

My old crush.

Great.

Two old crushes under the same roof while my parent was trying to kill me...

Not exactly ideal, was it?

He stared at Father, not looking at me, and I knew there was no reason for him to call out, none other than to save my father from choking me to death in a furniture store just off the East Side.

Without another glance at me, Father snarled, "Cover that up, and if you let him see, next time, no one will be around to save you when I punish you."

He stalked off, and I slumped into the wall as I tried to get air into my lungs.

Father veered off in a different direction to the lane in which Maxim was standing, so when I shot him a look, our gazes connected.

His was concerned, but I tipped my chin up, silently telling him I was okay.

He frowned, glanced at Father, then flared his fingers in a small wave before he shuffled off, striding after his boss and leaving me the hell alone.

Only when they'd left did I truly sag into the wall and let myself collapse to the floor.

For a second, I breathed a little too hard, a little too long. It was like over breathing. Trying to make up for the air I'd lost, trying to suck down what had been denied to me.

I wasn't surprised when Lisandra found me a few minutes later, and her arm came around me even as she crouched down at my side.

"I hate him," she whispered, pressing her cheek against mine.

"Me too," I rasped, and I winced at the sound of my voice.

I sounded...choked.

How fitting.

She tensed, then muttered, "We should kill him."

Her words had me smiling, even as I reached up and touched my throat. "How bad?"

Her bottom lip was sucked between her teeth. "Bad. Like really pink and white, kinda. Splotchy." She removed the scarf she'd been wearing like a jaunty handkerchief around her neck, and carefully rearranged it around mine to hide the marks.

It wasn't the first time she'd had to watch my father punish me, nor was it the first time she'd helped me cover up in the aftermath.

She didn't understand why I didn't go to the cops, didn't understand why I let him do it, but the Bratva Pakhan did what he wanted, authorities be damned.

And I figured that was in my eyes, that she picked up on that, even though she didn't really know who my dad was, because she came from a world where criminals didn't go to the best schools and rub shoulders with kids like her.

She just thought I was the same.

Elite.

Rich.

I wasn't.

I just played at being like her.

But even though she wasn't aware of all the details, she knew enough not to get involved. I'd warned her that he'd make it harder on me, and that I'd have to lie to her when it happened if I thought she was a threat to the status quo. And that was something she'd taken seriously.

"Are you going to tell Eoghan?"

The question surprised me. "Why do you ask?"

"Because" —she winced— "you can see his fingers. There's no way that's not going to stick around for a few days."

Despite my earlier resolution not to hope, I decided that was my best option.

To hope that Eoghan came back from wherever the hell he was just in time to see my bruises.

Because although I couldn't do anything, though I couldn't nor wouldn't go to the cops, my husband was a man few would defy.

He'd warned my father.

He'd dislocated his fucking shoulder, and that hadn't been enough to teach him a lesson.

And call me bloodthirsty, but I couldn't wait to learn what Eoghan's second lesson would be...

I said none of that. Instead, I murmured, "I won't tell him, but if he sees me when he gets back, then I'm okay with that."

Lisandra frowned. "Why won't you tell him?"

Because phones had ears...

I cleared my throat. "Don't worry about it. I need a coffee. A big one. Not that stupid espresso we just had. And then I need to get a new phone."

She scowled, taken aback by the direction of my thoughts. "We only just got new phones."

Yeah, and Father had put a tracker on me.

"I want the new rose gold version."

Like a little magpie, interest flickered in her eyes at the prospect of something shiny.

Amused, I muttered, "Come on. I saw enough to know what I wanted from the catalogue."

She blinked. "You did?"

"Yeah, you were too busy flirting up a storm—"

"He gave me his number." She grinned at me. "We're going on a date this Friday."

I laughed. "I thought you were off men."

She sniffed. "I'm off boys. Jack isn't. He's a man."

He was cute, I had to give her that, but a man? No. He wasn't. I knew what a man looked like, what one felt like, and I knew Jack and Eoghan were like two different species.

The thought made me feel weird.

I'd already compared Eoghan to my father, and Father had been found wanting. In this instance, Jack was found wanting too, even though, just ten days ago, I'd have preferred to be with Jack. Someone simple and bland and easy.

Nothing about Eoghan was easy.

But that didn't stop me from sending up a silent prayer for him to come home.

ASAP.

THIRTEEN

EOGHAN

I WAS SUPPOSED to be gone for five days.

Three days, and it chafed.

Why?

I couldn't say.

Okay.

Lies.

I knew why.

She didn't answer any of my fucking messages. Not a single goddamn one, so when I was supposed to be trailing Josiah Landers to make sure that his habits hadn't fucking changed, instead, I was checking my phone like a pussy.

I knew she was on that goddamn thing all the time. Her books were on it, so were her audiobooks.

So...

Why. The. Fuck. Didn't. She. Text. Me. Back?

The kill shot was anticlimactic, because I was too fucking pissed off at my goddamn wife who couldn't answer a text and who was ignoring my calls.

What was the point in having a wife if she didn't message back?

If there was anyone who should reply, it was her.

It wasn't like I'd left things in a bad way.

Three orgasms?

For a virgin?

Fucking hell, she'd won the sex lotto!

So her gripe with me was not only unfair, it was an irritating glimpse into married life that I wasn't appreciating.

I was supposed to kill Landers on the fifth day of my job. Instead, I did it on the third. When the bullet tore his brain apart, I was already cleaning up my gear, breaking the rifle into several parts, and fitting it into the cello case that I used to transport my gear around while Conor took a picture of the corpse on the ground for us to send to the client.

An hour later, when I received the payment from a guy who only went by the name Martinez, and whom I'd known back when he'd ran Los Lobos, a once pennyante gang that he'd transformed into an army, I was already on the Dassault Falcon, winging my way back to the city.

Conor bitched and griped at me for pushing the schedule forward, but I didn't care.

I wanted to know what the fuck was going on.

It was, therefore, not a cheerful Eoghan who walked through the elevator doors into his apartment four hours later.

If anything, it was a man who was not happy about being led around by his cock by his eighteen-year-old wife after only eleven days of marriage.

The new furniture surprised me.

Enough that I jerked back at the sight of it.

It wasn't to my taste.

That was my initial impression.

There were none of the clean lines I appreciated, none of the hard angles and smart leathers I preferred.

But...it was comfortable.

It was also clear she'd only received the delivery of furniture this morning or the day before.

The sofa was still at an odd angle, which made me wonder why the delivery drivers hadn't arranged it for her before they left. The sofa was massive, which was a plus, it was also a dark beige with flecks, which I didn't like, not when the fabric was linen. Even someone like me spilled shit from time to time. But I could see why she liked it.

The mink back wall, the dark mauve side walls, all complimented the cream/beige linen, and the teak wood armrests offset it perfectly. A leather cube armchair had been replaced with a winged back armchair that matched the sofa's carvings, but was in a mink a shade darker than the walls.

The TV was still suspended, but beneath it was a new console, and it was that shabby chic shit that I didn't necessarily appreciate, but it gave the area a more comfortable feel.

I'd had no carpet on the ground, just a small sheepskin rug, but that was all different now. There was a large, dark brown one underfoot, and it spanned over half the room with a swirling pattern that reminded me of leopard print without the delineated circles.

There were several free standing lamps that were dotted here and there, some roughhewn, upstanding logs that she had lamps on too, and behind the sofa, another console table, this one metallic, yellow gold to the point of being brassy, with a glass top and a large bowl of purple flowers that floated on water.

All in all, it wasn't me, and I wouldn't have said it was her, but it didn't have another woman's pussy juices on the gear, and I didn't hate it—so it was a win.

I wondered if she'd bought the sofa with the notion of having sex on it, because it screamed bed to me. I could even, God help me, imagine her curled up on one side and me on the other as we watched another movie or something.

The very idea had me pulling a face, which made me realize she was here.

Watching me.

"You don't like it."

The flat statement had me cutting her a look. I didn't appreciate that I hadn't known she'd approached—still, she could be quiet when she wanted. I'd learned that the other day during my video call with Aidan.

But any annoyance I'd felt at her not answering the phone surged into outright fury the second I clapped eyes on her.

I almost understood what that phrase 'a sight for sore eyes' meant.

She wore short shorts in black denim that offset the pale cream of her skin, and an oversized sweater that mocked the revealing nature of the shorts. It was big and baggy, shapeless, cashmere and expensive... It was also loose around the neck, somehow framing the marks I hadn't put there.

I knew my strength.

While she'd encouraged me to put my hand to her throat, I hadn't touched her with such ferocity.

Which meant someone else had.

My nostrils flared at the sight of her. My dick went to full mast, even as my primitive response to her being injured put my mind and body at war.

"Who?"

Her mouth pursed. "You know who."

That Vasov had made me break my promise to her not only outraged me, but it prompted immediate action.

"I'm going to assume that when the family was invited to meet with you, they were never taken to the true address?" I queried carefully, even as I fought the desire to go over to her, to kiss those marks, to soothe the pain she must have felt during their creation.

"You would be right," she replied.

"Where does he live?"

She didn't hesitate and gave me the address. Something settled inside me when I knew she'd been expecting this.

She'd been waiting for me to return.

To make Vasov suffer for his crime.

"I'll make him pay," I vowed, my tone cold, but my eyes heated as I burned her with a look filled with a promise for redemption.

Her smile was small, soft, but I liked the look of it on her. "I knew you would."

The beast that had been stirred at the sight of her throat relaxed at her words. Knowing she was aware I would avenge her injury calmed me enough to ask, without a hint of anger, "Your phone?"

She bit her lip. "I don't have your number, and when I realized Father could follow me, I smashed it."

"He put a trace on you?"

She nodded. "Yeah. He was in the first store we went to." Inessa cleared her throat, and it was almost cute how she moved her toe inwards and buckled her knee as she looked down at the ground. "I can take the stuff back if you don't like it."

"It looks comfortable."

That was all I could say.

It didn't offend me.

Which was probably more of a compliment than anything else.

She stared up at me at that, then a chuckle escaped her. "It is. I also bent over backwards to get this stuff here in time."

What she meant was it had cost me a fortune to get the items here, but I wasn't about to complain.

"I appreciate the effort you spent bent over—next time, I'd like to be in the vicinity when that happens."

Heat shimmered in her eyes, and it washed over her cheeks too. Watching her come into herself, blossoming into a sexual creature, actually made me happy.

Especially when I was the only one who would ever get to see her like this.

I didn't let her blush surge too high before I muttered, "Tell me your new number."

She blinked, recited it.

"Did you cancel the old contract?"

That had her tipping her head to the side. "Not yet."

"Don't."

"Why not?"

"Do you have the old phone?"

"Yes. It's in the kitchen. Smashed up, doesn't have much functionality, or I'd have grabbed your number from it and sent you a message, but it turns on and off."

"Good. Keep it charged and turned on. Let him think you're here most of the time."

She rolled her eyes. "I *am* here most of the time."

"Apparently not." A thought occurred to me. "I didn't hear about this from Limerick."

When she averted her gaze from mine, I knew what had happened, goddamnit, and I spat, "You're not to leave the house without him again, do you hear me? Christ, Inessa. Do you think I give a shit if you go shopping all day or if you spend half your afternoon with friends? I set him on you for your protection. Which you evidently need."

For a second, she looked mutinous, like she wanted to argue, but how could she? I was right. And she wore the marks to prove it.

"I just wanted to do something normal with my friend," she whispered, her defiance shriveling into dust. "That's all."

I softened at her words, because nothing about her life was normal right now. Hell, it never would be either. Still, she had to know that she couldn't just leave the house without someone on her.

It had been beyond stupid, more reckless than anything else.

"What if it had been one of the *Famiglia*?"

She closed her eyes and turned her head away from me. "I get the picture. You don't have to ram it home."

"Apparently I do." I wanted to stride over there, but shaking some sense into her wasn't going to make shit better. "I'm going to deal with your father."

When I turned around, she whispered, "Can I watch?"

Despite myself, my lips twitched in amusement. "You're not ready to see what I'm about to do to him, Inessa. You may think you are, but you're not."

I pushed the button, grabbed some keys from their place above a console table, and walked into the elevator the second the doors whirred open. When I turned around, her gaze was fastened on me, and even though she still sported the blush of arousal, and the frown of irritation, the flash of hero worship in her eyes couldn't be feigned.

The only trouble was, I was no hero.

The doors closed, and the desire to punch something overwhelmed me. Those fucking bruises...

Were they a taunt?

A message?

Or was the prick so stupid that he thought I wouldn't find out about them?

Whatever the reason behind them, he'd pay.

He'd pay with blood.

Even as I felt torn up inside, I stared impassively at my reflection in the doors before I was let out into the garage.

Heading over to an Aston Martin that Da had bought me for my birthday two years ago, I slipped behind the wheel and thought about my next move, but whichever way I planned it, it would be considered an act of war.

Vasov had only wanted to save face at the wedding, but if I did what the bastard deserved, it would be a declaration.

And while I was okay with that, my family might not be.

Still, I wasn't going to change my path, but I could alter it.

Slightly.

Rubbing my chin, I reached for my cell and got Declan on the line.

"'Sup."

I rolled my eyes. "Since when were you down in the hood?"

A laugh rattled out. "You'd be amazed what you pick up when you hang around with the youth of today—oh, wait, you'd know that."

"Just know I'm flipping you the bird right now."

"I'll bet. I can feel it all the way over here."

My lips twitched, even though I was still irritated as fuck. "You know what Eagle Eyes is packing right now?"

"The MSG90."

I crinkled my nose in distaste. "Do we have one in storage?"

"Why?"

"I want to pull a hit and make it look like Eagle Eyes did it," I replied patiently, using the dumbass name the only other sniper worth his shit went by. Where the fuck people came up with this crap was beyond me.

Declan wasn't slow, but his tone was musing as he asked, "Vasov?"

"Yeah. He hurt Inessa again."

"Fuck's sake. Why? When?"

"She went out without her guard. I need you to arrange something—maybe get the apartment beneath us? So the guard is always on hand?"

"I can do that. Especially if you go ahead with this. You sure it's wise to take him out?"

"Oh, I'm not taking him out. I'm sending him a warning he can't ignore."

Silence hummed down the line. "But you still want it to look like the Italians did it—"

"Yeah. War's been brewing among us for a while. If this is the trigger, then they look like the aggressors."

Everyone knew Eagle Eyes had ties to the Italians. People said he worked on a marker the *Famiglia* held over him, but I'd long since stopped believing that.

Maybe it had started that way, but our business was lucrative.

"We should talk to Aidan at least."

"He'd sanction it. He already saw the state of her the other day. If he saw her neck, he'd want to ram Vasov's balls through his throat."

"That bad?" Declan grunted. "Fuck, Eoghan. I don't know. This is a decision with repercussions."

"Yeah, but the war won't be between us, will it? It's the Italians and Russians that'll be at war."

"Bullshit. You want the Bratva to think that, but you'll rub this shit in Vasov's face. I know you—you forget that."

I pursed my lips, appreciating that he did, in truth, know me well.

"Vasov will be glad to have a scapegoat."

Dec clicked his tongue, but he didn't try to dissuade me. "Come to the compound. I'll hook you up with the gun."

"Thanks, bro."

We both knew I could have gone alone, but my presence at the warehouse that housed our armory would raise questions without Declan or Brennan there too.

That wasn't my side of the business.

An hour later, I was heading away from the compound where our shipments of weapons were stored, and onto the address Inessa had given me.

I wasn't sure what I was walking into, and Declan had offered to come with, but he knew I worked best alone, and there was little threat to me when I slipped into the shadows.

The only danger I was truly in was boredom when I had finished my setup, waiting for the perfect hit.

When I approached the streets near the compound where the Russians hid in plain sight, I found a neighborhood of red-brick McMansions that were along an avenue that led to the ocean.

The street behind had a few high rises, wide rather than super tall, and when I drove by the end of the road where Inessa had lived, I let my gaze scan the periphery without slowing down that much.

While the street was much like the other I'd passed, instead of low fences, or even none in some cases, there were brick walls. High ones that separated the houses from the street, revealing roofs and the upper parts of the building, nothing more. At least, not from the road.

Inessa hadn't said there were several houses on the compound, but it was myopic of me to think theirs would be like ours.

I took the long way back just in case their guards would recognize my very memorable car, and looped two streets behind where the high rises were and selected one that, experience told me, would be a good place to use as my base.

Having never appreciated Brighton Beach, I didn't anticipate enjoying the next few hours as I grabbed my cello case, this time with a different gun in it, and hauled it over to the building's gate.

Buzzing a random button, I waited for someone to answer. When no one did, I repeated it a few times until someone responded, "What?"

"Here for emergency plumbing," I stated, my tone pure Staten Island.

"I didn't call anyone."

"Not you. Apartment below. Not answering the buzzer."

A huff sounded, but the gate clicked, and I pushed in. I pressed the same apartment buzzer and they, very kindly, let me in too.

The building wasn't poor, but neither was it affluent, even though I knew they'd have a small sliver of an ocean view.

The hallway was bare and basic, lined with posters advertising babysitting and dog walking services. There was no graffiti, which I took as a good sign.

If we'd secured the Russian compound, this building would be on our radar, and we'd own the top floors.

One of the reasons why we controlled the real estate around us was to ensure that snipers wouldn't be able to get to my da while he was eating his eggs for breakfast.

Everything in the vicinity was low lying, and his fences were higher than Rikers'.

In case I was wrong and the Russians held the top floor, I made my way to the sixth floor, which was halfway up.

The elevator spat me out into a corridor lined with a puke green carpet, and it opened into the middle, so there were ten doors to my left and ten to my right.

I went right first, which was actually further away from the Russian compound.

Stepping down to the end, I noticed the last one had flowers and shit outside the door, so that was out, the next had a kind of shoe cleaner shaped like a hedgehog, and the third had scratch marks on the bottom of the doorjamb, which meant a dog lived in there.

Skipping the fourth because of the dog in the third, I knocked on the fifth door and came up with a bullseye.

No answer.

Taking a chance and settling my case against the wall, I pulled out my kit and worked on opening the door. Fifty seconds later, inside the apartment, I smiled to myself.

It was barren.

Whistling happily at the sight, and knowing I had time to plan because it was vacant, I set up my rifle.

It didn't have the gloss or glamor of mine, but it was decent kit. I eyed the scope, adjusted it, set it up as well as I could for a tool I didn't like, and then peered out of the window, seeing the Russian compound which was nearer to the ocean. I also saw that oceanside, there were lower walls.

Dumbfucks.

Didn't they realize people had boats?

You couldn't be in our line of work and appreciate a view—not when people would exploit the view to get to you.

Picking up my rifle, I eyed the houses once more, then turned back to the apartment.

The kitchen and living room were one open space, but the kitchen window was wide enough to encompass the U-shape of the counters, meaning I could set up on there with the window open and have a higher hunting ground.

It'd be uncomfortable, but I'd been in worse spots.

Arranging myself took another ten minutes, but when I was content, I peered through the scope once more, and waited.

That was all I could do for the moment.

Wait.

And watch.

Monitor what was, essentially, my family.

Hours passed.

The light blurred, fading out as night swirled in. Streetlamps turned on, creating a glow that made my eyes ache. I acclimated, waited some more, and then a car appeared at the top of the road.

A Bentley.

No, it couldn't be this easy, could it?

My mouth curved into a smile when the car pulled up outside the gate. The guard stopped to speak with the driver before opening the aperture. As the vehicle rolled inside the drive, for a moment, I was blind—the Bentley was hidden. Then it pulled out and stopped before a house with a portico and large columns that told me Vasov had a taste for the classics. As the car came to a final halt, the driver climbed out first, opened the door to the passenger's side, and there he was.

My father-in-law.

For a second, my heart pounded so hard that blood rushed in my head, but ruthlessly, I held my breath. Accustomed to the whirl of the adrenaline rush and the need for calm, I focused, then tapped the trigger before slowly squeezing once I'd aimed.

Seconds later, Vasov started to crumple on the steps that led to his house.

Before he could fall over fully, I let another shot rip three seconds after the first.

As guards poured out, panic hitting the Bratva base at the sight of their downed leader, I leaped down off the counter, quickly disassembled the rifle, stored it away, and made my way out of the apartment and toward the exit.

I hurried because the guards would be making sweeps for the

sniper behind the attack, and made it into my car with a few minutes to spare, pulling off onto the parkway when men began running around the corner of the street, guns raised like they didn't give a fuck if people called the cops.

With a smirk, I switched on my playlist and blasted Alkaline Trio out of the speakers as I opened the windows and sped home with one thought on my mind—just let Vasov hurt Inessa again when he didn't have knees to stand on.

FOURTEEN
INESSA

I GOT the call before Eoghan arrived home.

Even though I'd been expecting it, I hadn't expected what Victoria was telling me.

"Papa was knee-capped!" she was shrieking, half deafening me, even as I wanted to laugh.

Trust Eoghan to do something weird.

I didn't know him well enough to consider this standard practice, but what I did know about him was that he didn't think inside the box.

"Is he okay?" I asked flatly, as I stirred the sauce in the pan, grateful I'd gone to the effort of watching another recipe video on Facebook and had decided to make it just in case Eoghan came back home early from his trip of vengeance.

After all, I'd already pissed him off by not taking a guard with me when I went shopping with Lisandra—stupid, too stupid to live, I feared—and then by not answering his calls or messages when he'd tried to get in touch, which I had to assume was the case or he wouldn't have asked about my cell.

Food was the least I could do.

But now that I knew the details of what he'd done for me, I figured some limp red sauce wasn't the way to go about showing my gratitude.

As I stirred the concoction in the pot, eying it dubiously, I inquired, "Are you okay in the house?"

"Of course." She tutted. "That isn't the point. You don't sound cut up about it, Inessa!"

Her chiding tone had me grimacing. "If you'd seen what he'd done to my throat, Victoria, you'd know why I wasn't all that sympathetic. If Maxim hadn't called out his name, distracted him—"

"Why do you have to taunt him?" she whined. "I don't understand you."

"And I don't understand you," I snarled back. "For God's sake, we're not dogs to be whipped. Hell, I wouldn't do what he does to us to a dog!"

"Just do as he asks."

"Obeying him isn't something I have to do anymore," I muttered.

"You're still his daughter," Victoria reprimanded sharply.

"If I never have to see him again, it's too soon."

"You have to visit him in the hospital! He's been knee-capped, Inessa."

"That you even know what that means at your age tells me how shitty a father he is. He choked me for the last time—"

The beeping of the elevator made itself known, and I muttered, "He sold me into marriage, well, he can't blame me for making the best of what he gave me. My love to you, Victoria, and if you contact Camille—"

"She's on her way."

"She is?" I arched a brow, thought about that for a second, then added, "Give her my home number?"

"What's wrong with your cell? I tried your number—"

"He was tracing me, Victoria, that's how he knew how to follow me."

She snorted. "You're naïve if you didn't foresee that."

I shook my head. "This conversation is fucked up because it sounds like you're condoning every wrong move our father has made."

"I'm not. A lot of it, Papa does for our protection."

At her defense, I grunted under my breath. "You can choose to think the sun rises and sets on him, but I don't. I love you. Take care. I have to go."

I didn't wait for her to reply, instead, I almost slid out of the kitchen on my sock-clad feet and moved into the living room.

It was almost a similar stance to earlier when he'd returned. He stood there, staring at the living room like he'd been plopped onto Mars without even being anally probed first, and I watched him—the socks and a super shiny floor were my secret weapons.

I was actually super proud of myself and what I'd achieved in his absence. Lisandra and I had managed to work the furniture out of Jack by getting him to take the goods off another person's order. I'd facilitated things with a nice little bribe, and Lisandra, by the look of Jack's face, had helped things along by what appeared to be her giving him a blow job but what had probably been a kiss.

She claimed her tongue was magic, and I almost wished I was gay so I knew what she did. I figured I needed magic on a man like Eoghan, who stared at the world as though he was seeing it through a filter.

What that filter actually filtered, I didn't know.

Bullshit?

Maybe.

Emotions?

Could be.

But I knew he had feelings. I'd seen the love on his face when he spoke to his brother the other day. I knew he cared for his parents fiercely—because a man like Eoghan didn't allow himself to be beaten by his father unless there was love between them.

And yeah, I knew that was a weird kind of logic, but in our world, we were violent.

Eoghan had just knee-capped the goddamn Pakhan of the largest Bratva brotherhood in the Northeast! He wasn't scared...so why would he be afraid of doling out the beating back on his dad?

So, no. I knew he felt stuff, and I just had to figure out how to make him feel something for me that wasn't related to my being his property.

The only way I could think to do that was with sex, but also, I couldn't be too easy. He was used to easy sex. Sex, violence, and blood were as commonplace in my world as carrots and onions were in the world of someone normal.

As he looked at the furniture, stared at the new living room I'd turned from a showroom into a home, I eyed it from his perspective, but I was pleased with it. There was comfort in the oversized soft furnishings, everything was warm and made to want to snuggle up in. I figured I'd be the one spending more time here than him, so I'd gone for comfort.

Every gilded cage needed cushions.

"Thank you."

My words were husky, but they were all I could think to say, all I knew to utter in the face of what he'd done for me.

The statement had him jolting, then narrowing his eyes at me. "How do you do that?"

I grinned, lifted my foot, and showed him my socks. "Ever seen *Risky Business?*"

He snorted, but his face softened, going from harsh to, well, less harsh to be honest. "I have, but I'm surprised you know what it is."

My nose crinkled. "I like old movies."

"*Risky Business* is five years older than me," he said dryly.

A sigh escaped me. "Oops."

"Yeah. Oops." His lips twitched, but he waved a hand at the room. "It's growing on me."

Like mold.

Great.

I eyed him a tad warily. Father would do this. He'd say he liked something, would reel you in, then he'd slap you...

But Eoghan wasn't like that.

I had to have faith.

Ugh, wasn't that just another word for hope?

"It is?"

"It is." His nod was decisive. "It's not to my taste, but it's welcoming."

"I'm glad you think so." I cleared my throat. "I mean, I'm very happy that you like my taste, but, you know, my father? Did you—"

"You should know not to ask me about business," he chided.

I rolled my eyes. "My sister just called. She's frantic."

He shrugged. "I don't know what you're talking about."

My brow puckered. "I know it was you. Any other sniper would have brained him, never mind gone for his knees."

Like he was tired of the conversation, a conversation I hadn't anticipated because I'd thought he'd crow, he strode forward and brushed past me.

He headed into the bedroom and froze at the sight of the bed which was, I'd admit, majestic.

This place had had an overhaul too, and now it looked fit for a Maharajah.

The headboard was one and a half the size of the queen-sized bed. It was filigreed and covered in knots and detailed work that formed tigers and roses and all kinds of beautiful carvings. It was whitewashed too, and the covers were resplendent and thick with lush cyan velvet undertones that offset the gold and rich chocolate brown rug that went underfoot. There weren't a lot of cushions because, even though they looked fancy, I wasn't the kind of person who could be bothered with taking them off every night and putting them on again in the morning, but the duvet and comforter were in jewel tones that caught the eye.

I'd changed the curtains too. The simple drapes that had shielded blinds were now a rich purple. Nightstands made out of driftwood with large, moon-shaped globes for lamps stood at the side of the bed, and at the foot, there was an old-fashioned steamer trunk that I'd had overnighted on eBay.

When he froze, I wasn't sure if he liked it. Then, he seemed to shake it off and traipse into the shower.

Before he'd left, we'd had sex.

But if I'd anticipated any intimacy to grow from that, it couldn't when he was in another city.

So, if I'd known him well, I'd have followed him into the bathroom, but I didn't. I hovered, awkwardly taking a seat on the steamer trunk, before huffing and returning to the kitchen.

The sauce was still simmering, and it actually looked nice. I just wasn't convinced about the anchovies in there as a base which was, apparently, the traditional way, but I'd never tasted any fishy ragu before.

Another huff, and I boiled the water, then set some pasta to cooking.

By the time it was al dente and not mushy—I was pretty proud of that feat—Eoghan was strolling into the kitchen looking far too scrumptious for my own good.

Jesus.

He wore boxer briefs.

That was it.

Boxer briefs.

Dear Lord.

Every single muscle was on display, from his eight pack to his faintly hairy calves. I mean, they weren't like a werewolf hairy, but just faintly prickled with it. He didn't have a hairy back like Father, which I was so beyond grateful for, too, when he twisted around slightly to grab the towel around his neck and dry off his still wet face before looping it over his head once more.

"What are you doing?"

I scowled at him. "Thought you were smart."

His lips twitched. "I also thought you couldn't cook."

"I can learn, can't I?"

"It smells like fish and ragu."

I rolled my eyes. "I followed the recipe."

"I really need to introduce you to Aoife."

"Finn's wife?"

He nodded. "She has her own bakery and is a really good cook. She can teach you."

I stabbed the wooden spoon I'd used to stir the ragu in the air at him. "You haven't tasted this yet. It might be good."

"Might being the operative word. Anyway, Winnie can cook for us. She should have left things in the fridge…"

She had.

Winnie was still treating me like I was scum, and I guessed, to her, I was.

Maybe she wouldn't spit in Eoghan's food, but I wasn't taking any chances.

Apparently, Eoghan was better at reading my emotions more than I thought, because, soft enough to tell me he'd read between the lines, he murmured, "Ah. I'll talk to her."

There wasn't much aggression in his voice, which told me he'd be kind but firm, so I jerked a shoulder. "I get it. I'm the enemy still. I have to prove myself."

"You won't do that until you have a child," he replied flatly. "And I don't want one. Not yet anyway. Maybe not for years."

My brows rose. "Really?"

"You're still, I'm very much aware, part child yourself." His mouth tightened. "Ma had issues from having kids so young. I won't put you through that."

Whatever I'd expected him to say, it wasn't that, and call me crazy, Jesus, call me insane, but that made my heart flop around in my chest.

In a day, the guy had flown home, took out my father's kneecaps to make him pay for putting his hands on me, protecting me from the monster in my life like no one else could, and then he went and said that?

I was a broodmare.

That was my job in life. My role.

And yet, here he was, treating me like a woman. *Like a person.* Not just a walking womb.

Fuck.

Maybe someone else wouldn't get it, but I couldn't stop the tears from prickling my eyes. It was stupid. So stupid.

So fucking stupid.

But a quivery breath escaped me as I stared down at the ragu, which was a big, fat blur.

I knew he hadn't seen my reaction, because he'd headed into the fridge like he hadn't just rocked my goddamn world, then muttered, "What's your sister's number?"

"Why?" I asked after I'd swiped my hand over my face. Tears were still thick in my throat as I tried to formulate an expression that was close to normal. Turning to look at him, I found one way to switch gears...

His butt.

Yum.

"Because I want to know when he's awake." He peered at me over his shoulder, and evidently caught me staring at his ass in those obscenely tight boxer briefs, because he smirked at me.

"Why?"

"You ask a lot of questions, don't you?"

"Probably why he punished me more than my other sisters."

He tipped his head to the side at that. "Other sisters? How many do you have? I thought you only had one."

"Father wished he had other kids. Preferably a son," I muttered.

"Why? Not the son part. That's standard. What happened to your sister?"

"She rebelled," I told him simply. "She's six years older than me.

But the last I heard, she lives with an MC as some kind of..." My brow puckered, distaste filling me at what I knew of the life.

"Clubwhore?"

That he surmised as much from my expression didn't altogether surprise me. Men of his stature had access to such women, but it pissed me off that my sister was a whore.

"Yeah."

"Which MC?"

I scowled at him. "Why do you want to know?"

He finally retreated from the fridge, pressed into the wall at its side after he found a glass, and did the unthinkable—drank from the glass.

Not a bottle.

He even put the toilet seat down.

I wasn't sure if I *had* married an alien. Far as I knew, men weren't good at that stuff.

"Sinners or something. I don't know. We don't talk that much."

"Why not?"

"She knows I'm mad at her."

"Why?"

"Now who's asking so many questions?"

"I'm curious. Aren't I allowed to learn about my new wife and her family?"

I rolled my eyes. "Are you interested?"

"Of course. I want to know everything about you."

That had me rearing back. "Huh?"

"What?" he countered.

"You didn't want to know about me before."

At my remark, he shrugged. "You weren't interesting before."

"Now I am?" I sputtered, standing there in socks, shorts, and a sweater, with more bruises than a heavyweight wrestler from the neck up.

I felt anything but interesting.

I felt like a disaster.

"Yes." He blinked. "Why wouldn't you be?"

"Because we had sex?"

He snorted. "I've had a lot of sex."

That stung. I mean, I knew that already, but I didn't need him to tell me that.

Because he'd hurt me, wounding me with his laissez-faire response, I bit off, "And how would you feel if I said that to you?"

His expression darkened. "I'd want to kill whoever touched you."

"Well, I don't have that option. I have you and a butcher's knife close at hand." I bared my teeth at him. "I dealt with the slut on the first day because I'm not an idiot. Your wunderdick hasn't made me stupid. I know how this works. Don't shove my face in it, and I won't have to shove this knife down your throat."

His brows lifted at that. "Such violence."

But he didn't move away.

Didn't, by an inch, show that he was discomforted.

If anything, he looked amused. I sniffed at him and turned away, but as my gaze drifted down his body, I happened to notice he had a boner, which made me whip my head around swiftly.

His soft laugh and his arousal confused me. To be honest, what I'd threatened him with confused me.

I knew my place. I did. I was okay with it. But I wasn't okay with him bringing it up.

I wasn't violent by nature, but something about the way he'd dismissed what we'd done…it hurt. Especially after the way he'd just considered my feelings like I existed and wasn't just a walking babymaker.

When he moved behind me, his heat hit me like a furnace. I tensed up, and his hand came to my waist, the other to my arm. "I'm sorry. I didn't think."

"No. You didn't," I said woodenly. "Verbal disrespect is an abuse in and of itself. I won't treat you so poorly, so you shouldn't treat me that way."

He was quiet for a second, and I didn't shrug him off or move away from him, but I carried on stirring my sauce like if I peered into it, it'd act like a crystal ball.

Shit, I had more of chance of seeing into my future if I looked into fishy ragu than the crystal!

"You're right."

"It happens from time to time," I muttered. "Neither of us wanted this, Eoghan, and I know that, for you, it's a—" God, what was I? "I mean, maybe you're ashamed of me. Not just because of my ties, but my age, but I won't do anything to shame you. I've been raised to do the opposite."

"I never thought you'd shame me," he countered gruffly. "But in all honesty, I've shamed myself. I never meant to hurt you by saying that. I didn't think and, I mean this, Inessa, I won't say anything like that again."

"Thank you," I whispered. "When my father was doing what...he did," I mumbled hesitantly, "I was thinking how unlike him you were, and how, though I didn't want this marriage, I was so glad because I knew you'd keep me safe."

"You thought that when he was doing that to you?" he rumbled with disbelief.

"Yeah, I did, because I knew you'd make him pay." My grin was wasted on the ragu. "And you did. Whether you admit to it or not, I know it was you, and I'm beyond grateful. If the fucker can't stand, he can't strangle me again."

"You know it'll cause issues—"

"War. I know. It might even..." I blew out a breath. "He has to get back to work soon after, or he'll lose everything."

"We can bring your sister under our roof if he falls."

"Thank you," I whispered, finally twisting my head over my shoulder to look at him. "I appreciate that."

He shrugged. "She's family now, isn't she?"

My lips twitched. "She is."

A sigh escaped him as he let his gaze scan my face. "What am I going to do with you, Inessa? You don't fit into the niche I want to put you in."

I shrugged. "You think you fit in mine? Maybe instead of trying to push square pegs into round holes, we shouldn't take each other at face value."

"Friends first?"

"Friends." I licked my lips. "But with benefits?"

His snort had me grinning at him. "I'm down for that."

"Good," I retorted. "I'm still sore, but maybe tomorrow?"

His hand dropped to my hip, which he squeezed. "I haven't slept in seventy-two hours, Inessa. Don't worry, the only thing I want to do in that pit you made for us is sleep."

"You don't like it?" I asked with a wince.

"I do. I especially like how big it is. You worked a miracle on this place. I appreciate it. Really. I do. And I'm glad you made it to your taste because there's no way I can ever really apologize for what you saw that first night, but I can try to make it up to you."

"J-Just make sure it doesn't happen again. This apartment might be just a roof to relax under, a place for you to sleep, but this is my gilded cage, Eoghan," I told him softly. "I know that, and I'm not bitching—"

"I understand." His hands squeezed me again. "This is your place."

"No, it's ours. If you'll let it be," I muttered, unsure why I was even clarifying that.

The prospect of him having a second home, one with a mistress in it, filled me with pain.

I knew Svetlana had been Father's whore before she'd, somehow, managed to get him to put a ring on her finger.

That Eoghan probably—

The pain in my stomach flared out of nowhere. Eoghan wasn't mine. He never would be.

But me?

I was all his.

He'd become my world, and when we had children, they'd be my everything. The small sphere of my future depressed me, but I knew I had to make the best of it, or what was the point?

I might as well just slit my wrists and try to escape like Cammie had. Of course, she'd failed, but my attempt wouldn't be a cry for help.

It would be the desperate need to escape a life that was more like death row without an end date in sight.

FIFTEEN
EOGHAN

SHE'D BEEN quiet ever since the night I returned home with her father's blood on my hands, and truthfully, I didn't like it.

She was pretty mouthy, something I was surprised hadn't been leached out of her, but even though her focus had been on her books and audiobooks again, it was different.

I thought our conversation in the kitchen, followed by the beyond bizarre ragu we'd shared, and our tumbling into sleep together in a bed that was fit for a king, had changed things.

Well, it had, but not for the better.

Which surprised me.

I thought we'd cleared the air, and yet, she seemed sad. I knew it wasn't about her father either.

It was about something we'd discussed.

Even as I was pulling into the ward in which Vasov was being kept, and I saw the guards lining the walls, I pondered what had gone wrong.

We were going to my family's later on today, and I'd have liked for her to have been her relatively chirpy self.

Instead, she was downcast at my side, her shoulders hunched as we walked toward her father's room.

The sight of her had the guards relaxing somewhat, but they still moved their hands to their weapons—smart boys, with a killer walking toward them.

"Inessa?"

Her name being called out pissed me off, as did the subsequent conversation in Russian that excluded me.

She didn't really look at the guard, but he was young, not ugly, and from the blush on her cheeks, it didn't take much to surmise he was Maxim.

"Inessa wants to see her father," I stated, speaking over them, not willing to bullshit around too much.

No one was late for Ma's Sunday Roast. Not unless it was on pain of death.

And, I had to admit, I was curious what the little gift boxes that were sitting in the trunk contained.

Though I'd asked her what the gifts for my parents were, she'd just smiled at me and said it was a surprise.

Which probably meant it was something weird that I didn't need to know about.

I was kind of praying for vodka. That was fitting, right?

Maxim's eyes narrowed at my statement, but Inessa merely twitched her shoulders, said something else, and Maxim opened the door, letting us inside.

Vasov was hooked up to machines, lines coming out of him from every orifice, but as the door opened, his eyes flared wide.

I understood.

If I was in the hospital, the only way I'd ever truly be able to sleep was if they drugged the shit out of me. We were in constant danger, and being here was a vulnerability that no one needed.

Aidan had gone through this nightmare after he'd been shot, but he had more allies than enemies, unlike Vasov, who ruled through fear.

Da was a bastard, but he was a kind one. If a husband died, leaving a wife penniless, that woman would never have to worry about bills, either until she died or remarried. He was charitable and generous with his bonuses come Christmas, and while he was a psychotic piece of shit with a knife, you were only on the receiving end of that if you betrayed him. Otherwise, you were rewarded for your loyalty.

Ruling solely through fear worked, but it meant you could never expose any weakness.

Hence Vasov's current predicament.

He couldn't afford to languish in here for weeks on end. He had to get fit, recuperate, and little things like physical therapy would need to be done behind closed doors and over an extended period of time. I didn't doubt he was paying for knee replacements, but again, time was of the essence.

With the biggest barracuda down, it was only a matter of time before smaller ones came to nip at him in his weakened state.

I had no pity in my gaze when I glanced at him, and Inessa didn't seem to be that sad either as she cast him a single look before whispering, "Cammie!"

So, this was the sister who had fled home, turned into a club-whore for, ironically enough, the MC with ties to us, and who was, technically, a Bratva princess just like Inessa.

I would have probably been married to her if Camille hadn't been such a letdown for her father, and while the other sister was beautiful, she didn't have that special something that Inessa possessed. She was more my age though, and that was the only thing I wished was different.

The eleven-year age gap wasn't terrible, neither was it ideal. Especially when she was as young as she was, and deep inside, I was old. So fucking old.

The two sisters hugged, even though it seemed awkward, and Victoria, the youngest, hurled herself into Inessa's arms the second that awkward embrace was over. She was only thirteen or so, but they all had a maturity about them that was undeniable.

I recognized it.

It was the same with young boys in our world. At nine, or thereabouts, it was like the curtains were ripped from our windows to reveal the real world.

It sucked.

And in all honesty, I hoped for better for my sons if I ever had any, but it was a fact of life.

When Victoria had squeezed Inessa hard enough to make her grimace, both sisters glared at me, then their father.

"I think I'd like to speak to your father alone," I rumbled.

Victoria stiffened at that. "What right do you—"

"Don't argue, Vicky," Inessa chided, tapping her nose. "Do as Eoghan says."

"He's not my husband," she muttered rebelliously, making my lips twitch.

"Nor is he mine," Cammie rasped, eying me warily.

"Regardless of those sorry truths, I'm Inessa's, and I'm here to speak with your father."

"The nurses don't want him upset."

"Leave us," Vasov rumbled, and there was exhaustion lacing each word as he sucked in a deep, pain-filled breath.

Considering I knew the pain Aidan was in, and that I'd been with him along every step of his recovery, the irony was I knew what Vasov had ahead of him.

I didn't envy him.

Aidan had it bad enough with a fractured patella... I'd purposely shattered Vasov's.

Nor did I feel guilty about it.

The sisters traipsed out, but as Inessa went to join them, I grabbed her hand and tugged her to my side.

I wasn't sure why when this was men's business, and her curious gaze definitely questioned my judgment, but I ignored her, and instead, focused on her father.

"Vasov," I greeted, rather unnecessarily.

"O'Donnelly."

Inessa's hand tightened on mine, and I sensed her confusion, as well as her concern.

But I felt neither.

She needed to be here for this.

She needed to see her father downed.

The monster, as she'd called him the other night, put to bed.

Forever.

"They say Eagle Eyes was behind your hit."

"That's the chatter," Vasov muttered.

"Wonder why he went for your knees and not a kill shot."

Inessa tensed at that.

"My lucky day," Vasov growled, anger filling his eyes at my insolence.

I reached down and placed my hands on the metal rail at the foot of the bed.

The position placed my fingers very close to his feet.

I saw him take note of that, saw him eye me, then Inessa, and he began to scowl.

"Where is my welcome?"

His command had her questioning, "Where's Svetlana?"

"At the compound, I think."

Inessa hummed under her breath. "Sounds about right."

Though Vasov groused with annoyance, I stated, "You put your hands on my wife, Antoni."

His eyes flared wide, but though anger filled him, and he glared at Inessa for a second, he didn't for long.

I reached for his foot and pulled.

Not even that hard, but enough for his entire body to strain, for his face to turn white, and for his eyes to bulge. Everything about him tensed and pulled taut as he fought the instinctive scream that tried to fall from his lips.

A scream he couldn't afford to release with the guards outside.

When he was merely panting through his pain, I smiled at him genially. "Now, I warned you in the church. 'You do not touch her again.' Those were the words I used, I think, Inessa?"

"Yes, Eoghan. You warned him."

"But he didn't heed my threat, did he?"

"No," she replied unnecessarily. "He didn't."

I sensed her satisfaction, even as she'd recoiled at her father's evident agony at my simple torture.

"I wonder if he's learned his lesson now?"

Vasov's eyes were back to bulging. "You did this?"

"Yes, and I gave you a nice little scapegoat—Eagle Eyes—to put the war where it needs to be.

"I'm not your enemy, Vasov, and no one in the fucking world would blame me for doing what I did when you mistreated my property that way." I felt Inessa tense, but I ignored it. I no longer thought of her that way, two weeks of marriage making me dispel the notion and see her as an entity and not an object as she'd been up until my wedding day. Still, Vasov would understand my meaning only if I termed it that way.

"I barely touched her—"

"You touched her period. She's mine to touch," I snarled, my temper snapping off its leash at his paltry excuse. "You don't lay a fucking finger on her, or I'll consider this my barely touching you, and the next time, I'll blow your fucking head off. Do you understand me?"

He gulped, then glared at Inessa, but my hand snapped out to reach for his other foot, and he cried, "I understand! I won't touch her."

"Good. You won't even fucking look at her with malice. You will leave her alone. You will not expect her to spy on us, because if you think we're that fucking stupid, you're mistaken." I bent down, leaning my elbows on the rail once more as I declared, "You can blame me, and you can start a war with your new allies, or we can fight the scourge in our city. A family who everyone hates. Or, by blaming me, you can make the men under you wonder exactly what you did to your daughter that had me punishing you in such a fashion."

His nostrils flared at that. "You fucker."

I smiled. "I know." I stood, reached for Inessa's hand, and as I squeezed it, said, "Say goodbye to your father, Inessa."

Her voice was blank, free of emotion, and I had to admit, I gave her credit for that. "Goodbye, Father."

She turned away before I could say another word and, smiling at Vasov who was glaring at me with all the loathing in his blackened soul, we retreated from the ward.

Camille had her arms folded, her gaze on her feet. She was too thin and looked like she was cut up about something—her hands clasped her elbows like she was comforting herself, and her shoulders were faintly hunched. I recognized the sight of someone in pain, even if it was emotional and not physical. Considering her father's skills at parenting, I had to assume it wasn't his being shot that put her in a depressed frame of mind. Victoria was bristling at her side, bouncing on her toes like she wanted to smack something.

I knew how the Russians treated their womenfolk—like dolls. The girl needed martial arts or something to help her control her temper. I recognized it because I'd been that way. One big bundle of energy, and I'd had anger issues until Da had shown me how to beat the shit out of a punching bag.

Still, that wasn't my place, so I nodded my chin at the *boyeviks* guarding the private ward, wondering what position Maxim held because he seemed to be above them but was still given only guard duty at the hospital, as Inessa hugged her sister farewell.

"You have my house phone?" she was saying to Camille, who cut me a look before nodding. "Don't be a stranger."

"I won't be."

That seemed to surprise Inessa, because she frowned. "You're not going back?"

"I have things to tie up, but no."

"Why not?"

"Does it matter?" Victoria snapped. "She's coming home!"

"You won't like Svetlana—"

Inessa's predication had Camille's mouth twisting. "I've dealt with worse sluts than her."

Inessa tensed, but Victoria evidently didn't get the double meaning, because her gaze swung between her sisters like she was at the U.S. Open Finals.

Sensing an argument brewing, I called out, "Inessa?"

She twisted back to give me her attention, then nodded when I merely cast her an expressionless look.

"We have to get going."

She stiffened a little more, then blew out a breath and muttered to her sisters, "We'll speak soon." A quick hug for each of them was the only other farewell she granted them before she was huddling at my side, having rushed over to stand next to me.

I didn't let her waver—I grabbed her hand and slipped our fingers together, tangling them in a way that reminded me of our legs this morning in bed.

Married life hadn't started out the way I'd anticipated, but it was definitely interesting. I couldn't call it anything else.

As we strolled down the corridor, I felt the guards' eyes on my back, and though I itched like I was in the sight of someone's crosshairs, I highly doubted a gunfight was about to go down in the hospital. Not with the all-out preparations Lukov and Abramovicz, Vasov's right and left hand men, were currently engaged in for the upcoming war that was about to hit the streets.

As we retreated to the car—my Aston Martin again, because driving it the other day had put a smile on my face—and with a beautiful woman at my side, an enemy tucked away in a hospital bed, and the threat neutralized, what better day to blast some tunes as I drove her to my parents' compound?

She was quiet on the ride through the city, and I didn't necessarily blame her. Coming to terms with a punishment was always different than the desire for vengeance, but I knew she hadn't liked my words, and more than that, was mad at her sister.

"Did you look into Camille's past?" she asked softly when we came to a halt at some traffic lights on the West Side. It was quite good timing, considering the last song died off, so I leaned over and turned down the stereo.

"Of course." The morning after she'd told me about her, I'd contacted Conor about the missing sister. Turned out, Vasov had done a killer job of hiding her fucking existence, but my bro had found her.

She nodded. "What did my file say about me?"

"That you had a best friend with a habit of getting you into trouble."

Her nose crinkled. "That's it?"

"That's all you did, wasn't it?" I questioned curiously.

"Yeah, but...it's all blamed on Lisandra?"

"She was behind most scenarios—at least, as far as I recall."

"You know I went shopping with her the other day, don't you?"

"I surmised you'd shop with her."

"And you weren't thinking of, I don't know, stopping our friendship?"

I snorted. "Why would I?"

"If she's a bad influence?"

Shaking my head, I muttered, "No influence out there worse than that prick in the hospital bed."

Of course, it helped that I knew her friend was going to be attending NC State...a few thousand miles distance would help—

Help, what?

My thoughts ground to a halt.

Break the friendship?

I didn't particularly want that. If anything, I wanted Lisandra to be far away so Inessa didn't have anything to be jealous of.

I was well aware she was missing out on many things, and I didn't need it rammed home with her friend inviting her to parties she couldn't attend.

I wasn't going to keep her locked up at the apartment—which she didn't seem to realize, what with all her references to gilded cages— but I did need to assure myself of her safety, especially with the upcoming war. So, I changed the subject back to her sister.

"Camille, yes, I did check in on her. She's been living on the compound of a nearby MC."

"As their resident slut?"

I shrugged. "To each their own."

She huffed. "Yeah. She looked real happy back there, didn't she? All skin and bone. Cammie used to be so curvy... I wonder if she's sick."

"I don't think so. She looked unhappy, and I don't think it had anything to do with your dad being in a hospital bed."

"No. She only came back for Vicky. If Father and I have a testy relationship, that's nothing to him and Cammie."

"Why?"

"He tried to arrange her marriage to Abramovicz."

My mouth dropped open. "He's nearly seventy!"

"I guess life in an MC was preferable to that."

"And she'd have been safer in a nest of vipers," I mused.

"I guess so."

"You think she'll stay?"

"Not long. She won't like Svetlana." Her mouth tightened. "I don't much either. Fucking bitch."

"I'll get your mother's jewels back... You don't have to worry on that score." I made the promise easily, knowing that was a point of contention for my wife and her stepmother. It had been enough of a catalyst for a fight before our wedding, after all.

Her eyes flared wide. "You'd do that for me?"

Svetlana the Slut, who had money-grabbing whore written all over her, didn't deserve shit, never mind something that mattered to Inessa.

"Oh, Eoghan," she whispered when I just shrugged, maneuvering us upstate where the folks had moved a year ago after a security scare at their old property.

Unease settled inside me at her gratitude. This relationship with Inessa was unlike any other I'd had with a woman. I didn't even have female friends outside of Aoife, and Finn kept close tabs on her interactions with the family—mostly because of Da, I knew that.

With my father like a lightning bolt that could surge out of nowhere, it was safe to say that no one outside of the family knew how to handle him.

Unless you'd lived with him for years on end, no one was prepared for the deep pit he could sink into.

A shrink might say he was bipolar, maybe even manic, but whatever he was, he'd never take pills for it, and the house would exist under a storm cloud for up to a week at a time before he came out of it, turning back into the relatively cheerful man he was around Ma.

One of my biggest fears was that I would be like him. Everyone said how similar we were, and even though my wife was still, relatively speaking, a stranger, I didn't want that for any woman. Stranger or not.

Da had never hit Ma during those blackouts of his, but I'd seen her crying in the kitchen. Whether that was in concern for him or for something he'd said, I'd never asked.

Maybe I should have, maybe, with fears of my turning into him, I should have delved deeper, but all I could do was make sure I kept myself in check.

It was why, the other night, I'd been so pissed at myself for hurting Inessa's feelings.

Accidentally wounding her with words was a slippery slope that I didn't want to fall down.

A soft hand appeared on my lap. "Eoghan?"

I blinked, surprised at her touch, but even more surprised by how deep down the rabbit hole my mind had taken me. "Yeah?"

"Thank you."

Her whispered gratitude made my chest feel weird. Like it was too full.

She was...for want of a better word, sweet.

I didn't tell her that. I doubted any woman wanted to be told they were sweet. It was like the personality equivalent of cute, and even I knew most women thought being cute was a crime. They wanted to be sexy, to vamp it up. But I didn't think it was a crime.

If Inessa had been brazen, it'd have been a surefire way to piss me off and to lock her out.

As it was, she kept doing shit that made it easy to accept her presence in my life.

This whole trying to cook stuff was charming, especially as she always got one aspect wrong, and she'd look up at me with those fucking eyes of hers, all round and wide, hope filling them as she tried to please me, then when I barely refrained from gagging—and I had a cast iron stomach thanks to all the MREs I'd eaten in my time—that need to please would disappear and she'd scowl at me, biting into the dish, then, more often than not, spitting it out.

I knew she was trying to soften me up, but her nature came out, revealing her true self, and it often amused me.

The other night she'd gagged, too, when she'd tried the ragu. Apparently, she'd put a whole can of anchovies into the mix, which made it taste like some ungodly concoction I wouldn't wish on Vasov —wait, maybe I would.

Then there were the cinnamon rolls she'd drowned in vanilla extract, and they'd made the apartment smell like the Pillsbury Dough boy had let off a wet one in the apartment. They'd tasted quite good, actually, but they'd been sloppy as hell. More raw dough than cinnamon roll.

Then there was the Jell-O she could never get to set.

I wasn't sure how she did it, but do it she did.

And it always amused the fuck out of me, even if I never let her know it.

"You're welcome," I rumbled after an awkward silence had filled the space between us.

"You're not used to people thanking you, are you?"

I pursed my lips. "We take in our world. You know that."

"Oh, I know that," she said bitterly, turning her face to the side.

I hadn't meant to upset her, so to smooth over things, I told her, "I think you'll like Aoife. Everyone always likes her."

"Why?"

"Because she's..." I cleared my throat. "Sweet."

My prediction was correct.

I'd heard a little jealousy in her voice, but at dropping that one word, she smiled. "Oh."

Since when was it a fucking crime to be sweet?

Rolling my eyes as I drove off the freeway, I muttered, "The rest of the family are just overgrown boys who bicker too much."

"I can't imagine you bickering."

My hands tightened around the steering wheel. "Actually, I used to be the joker."

I didn't have to turn my head to know that her jaw had dropped. "You?"

"Yeah." I shuffled in my seat. "I know, I'm different now."

"Why?"

"Too many jobs. It taints you."

A hushed breath escaped her. "Your soul?"

I shrugged. "Maybe. But don't forget, I'm not Catholic."

"I thought we'd have to go to church this morning."

"We will next week, then we'll come to the folks' afterward."

"Why didn't we today?"

"Because of your father."

"Do they know you did that?"

"You ask a lot of questions."

"We've been through that already. You know I do."

I rolled my eyes once more. "Declan knows. And I didn't do anything."

She snorted. "Yeah, plead the fifth after that conversation with Father, why don't you?"

My lips twitched. "Wives can always testify against their husbands."

She scowled at me. "Is that a joke?"

"Apparently a bad one."

"Are you sure you were the joker?"

"What can I say? I'm out of practice."

At my shrug, she huffed. "Why would I want you to go anywhere?"

"Freedom is sweet, and you've never had any." I cut her a look, saw she was staring straight at me, and her head was tipped to the side like she was considering me and what I was saying.

"Some people," she eventually remarked, "will never be free. When you're in the life, you're always in it. There's no running away, there's no avoiding the taint." She shrugged. "I knew that. It's why I never fought the wedding."

"Because of your sister?"

"Yeah. She whored herself out for safety, what's the difference between—"

"Don't you dare compare me to a clubhouse of dirty bikers."

A laugh escaped her, and this time, the smile that blossomed almost had me crashing the fucking car. "I did at first, then I got a sight of your ass in boxer briefs and I was a convert."

I rolled my eyes for the third time in this conversation. "My butt is a lifesaver."

"Well, I wouldn't go that far, but it's sure pretty." She wolf whistled, then giggled when I glowered at her. "Anyway, before I knew you, maybe I got it. Maybe I understood, but I also knew that chasing freedom is only going to get me one place."

I frowned. "Where?

"Nowhere. We have to make the best of things, and I'd like to think we're doing that. Getting to know each other, you know?"

I dipped my chin. "Are you sure you're not trying to poison me?"

"Well, I'd be doing a damn good job of it if I was, wouldn't I?" she muttered, utterly disgruntled now. "I follow the recipes exactly."

My lips twitched. "Remind me to speak to Winnie in the morning, would you?"

She shifted in her seat. "You don't have to do that."

"Yes, I do. I'm not having her make you feel uncomfortable in your own damn home. She'll change her tune—"

"She'll spit in our food is what she'll do."

"I have cameras in the kitchen. You can watch the footage—"

"You have cameras in there?" she squeaked.

"I have them everywhere." I cut her a look. "Why? You had to know that."

Her cheeks were bright red, and what I'd mistaken for embarrassment, I swiftly realized was the opposite.

My tongue felt thick in my mouth as I rasped out, "You want to watch us in the kitchen, don't you?"

She swallowed, and her pupils were like pinpricks. "I'm weird, aren't I?"

Weird?

More like perfect.

We'd be late to dinner, and that came with a wooden spoon to the back of the head, but fuck.

It was worth it.

I spun us down a side alley about ten minutes away from my family home, and as I tucked us into the street, at the road I knew was a dead end, she stared at me.

"What are we doing?"

Her whisper inflamed me. "I think you know." After pushing my seat back, I reached for her seatbelt, unbuckled it, then grabbed her waist and hauled her over to me so she was sitting sideways on my lap. She settled there like she was made for me, and fuck, if it wasn't starting to feel that way.

Her kinks and mine?

Were one and the same.

I shuddered as she cupped my face and initiated the kiss between us. It was long yet fast, hungry and frantic. Her body writhed against mine as need she wasn't accustomed to yet flushed through her. She reached for one of my hands, hauled it to her breast, and squeezed.

"Make this feeling go away, Eoghan," she pleaded breathlessly, her agitation clear.

I made no promises on that score, because I wasn't always going to give into her desires, but instead, I dove for gold straight between her thighs.

She wore a skirt, and like a good little girl, she parted her thighs for me, letting me plunder the treasure between them.

A groan escaped her the second I rubbed over her panties, which I shoved immediately to the side. My fingers touched slick flesh, and she wasn't the only one moaning.

My cock pounded behind my fly, and even as I wondered what the fuck was happening to me, how I was parked in a dark alley, treating my wife like some kind of two-bit whore, I thrust a finger inside her slickness.

She clung to me like silk, and the notion that, once again, I was the only one to taste that cunt, to touch it, to fuck it, to hear these moans, to own them and her, made me feel like I could explode.

I wanted nothing more than to drag her outside, bend her over the fender, and to fuck her over it.

The fantasy blurred my reason, and only knowing it was bright out, that it was relatively busy, and that the street I'd parked off of held a lot of foot traffic, stopped me, because Inessa?

She was loud.

She screamed.

A lot.

Her moans would be overheard, and no one, no fucking one, was allowed to see her pleasure except for me. It was mine. I owned it.

I finger fucked her, jamming the heel of my hand against her clit, providing friction which instantly set her off. She grew wetter still as her spine arched. Her head fell back, and I latched onto her throat.

It was stupid, reckless.

But I didn't give a fuck.

I bit down, sucking on her throat like I was eighteen again and wanted my girlfriend to bear my mark. I knew my brothers would give me shit about it, I knew they'd know what it meant.

I was a possessive motherfucker.

And I'd just claimed her as mine in front of them.

But I didn't have it in me to give a shit about the upcoming teasing, about the knowing looks I was going to receive. I didn't give a shit that Da would tell me that I should have trusted him all along to pick the right woman for me.

I didn't give a shit.

I just wanted her.

I needed her.

Spearing another finger inside her had her flinching as sensitive tissues reacted to the invasion. She pressed her head back to the driver's window, and I damned the wheel for getting in the way, because if I could, I'd have—fuck!

Why didn't I drive my Hummer upstate like I usually did?

There was enough room in there to have her for my starter, entree, and fucking dessert.

My other hand clamped around her waist to the point where I had to hold back, because I knew I'd mar her delicate skin, so I put it to work, I shoved at her top, a prim little blouse that really shouldn't have fucked with my head the way it did.

I'd never been one to get off on plaid skirts and shit like that. Teacher/student kinks had never been my thing, but seeing Inessa wander out of the closet this morning looking like a Catholic schoolgirl who was in serious need of punishment had hit my cock in so many ways that I'd almost had to sit down at the sight of her.

I'd been fighting the urge to get her to suck my cock all day, but I didn't want that now.

I wanted this cunt covering my cock, not her mouth.

When she was juddering in my arms with sensation as I fucked her with my fingers, harder, faster, I pulled out, loving the noise that came with it.

Fuck, so wet.

She curved into me, pushing her face into my throat as I grabbed her panties and dragged them down her legs. The console and the stick shift got in the way, but I was patient, I had to be.

I didn't want to scare her.

She wasn't ready for me full throttle. Not yet.

Fuck, maybe never.

The thought had everything inside me whining, because I wanted nothing more than to lose myself in her but...that was for whores.

Whores didn't use mouths that eventually kissed your babies on the head before bedtime.

They weren't the ones who sat at your side in church or ate with your family.

Everything inside me went to war, and I froze, my hands on her ankle, as I thought about whether I should fuck her in the car. Whether I—

"Eoghan," she whispered, and that soft tone of voice got to me in ways I'd never be able to describe.

"What?" I said gruffly.

"I-I—" She gulped, her forehead pushing harder into my throat. Then her body rippled, and she writhed against me once more. Her hunger was a tangible thing, and the scent of her in the small cab fucked with my senses until I felt like a fucking dog with a bitch in heat.

The comparison offended every single one of my sensibilities, but fuck, that was how I felt.

Her pheromones, or whatever the fuck they were, got to me like heroin. Liquid heroin shot straight into my fucking eyeball.

A growl escaped me as I demanded, "What?"

"I-I'm empty." Her hips rocked, her butt digging into my lap, brushing my cock with her weight. It protested the move because it was already caged up when it wanted out, and her words?

Had every bit of my fucking soul coming to life.

I wasn't the most talkative of men, and in the bedroom, less so. I took what a woman offered me with her body. Reading the language she spoke with her moans and sighs, her writhing and wriggling.

But with Inessa? I wanted more.

I needed to...

"You want me to fill you up?" I rumbled, and her sharp sigh told me she needed to hear that from me.

She was a kinky little thing for one so innocent, and that made me wonder if she could be both my whore and my wife.

If there even was such a thing.

My heartbeat slalomed as she whimpered, "Please. I need you. I need your dick."

"Why?" I rasped, smoothing my hand over her soft legs, trailing my fingertips over the inside of her thighs. They instantly spread wider, like she was encouraging me to go higher, but I kept the touch light.

Taunting.

"Tell me why, Inessa."

"You fill me full," was her thick response. She grabbed my hand, dragged it higher.

"This little cunt wants my cock, huh? Wants to be stuffed?" I played with the slit that was weeping for me.

"Y-Yes," she moaned.

And I couldn't stop myself. Couldn't, even if, later on, I'd kick myself for being a fool.

"You might not like what you're asking for," I warned.

Her eyes had been closed until that point, but at my words, they flared open and she stared straight at me. "I want everything you have to give."

My nostrils flared, and though foreign needs suffocated me, I grabbed her waist, spun her around, and demanded, "Straddle me."

She did as bid, and the sight of her slick cunt, dripping...

Any other woman, I'd have cared about my pants and upholstery.

Inessa? I wanted to be covered in her cum. I wanted it on my face, on my hands, around me, soaking me through.

She went to open my fly, but I growled. "Put your hands behind your back and don't move them."

She obeyed. Instantly. I heard her grip the wheel, in fact, and I reached for the blouse, tugging the buttons open with a care I wasn't feeling, but I didn't want to disrespect her to the point where my family knew what we'd been doing. A blouse she couldn't fasten was a giveaway.

My hands were shaking as I unfastened them, but revealing the lacy bralette was more than worth the wait.

I dug deep, propping her tits on the shelf of fabric as I reached down, freed my dick, and licked around her areolae, nibbling the tip with my teeth.

With my dick out, I grabbed her hips, shuffled her where I needed her, then, grabbing my cock once more, I pushed it against her tight hole.

Fuck, she was wet and small, and I gritted my teeth as I rocked my head back against the headrest. The move put our eyes in perfect alignment as she sank down onto my dick, taking every inch of me.

The sharp cry that escaped her set my nerves alight, and I grabbed her hips once more and urged her into riding me.

She was awkward at first, and I understood that, and for some fucking reason, those swaying movements got to me more than a practiced slut would.

Every time she moved off me, I gritted my teeth hard, and when she accepted all of me, I wanted to fucking explode.

Because I was close, ridiculously, shamefully close, I rubbed her clit. I'd normally have driven us both a little crazier, but there was no way I could handle feeling more out of control than I did right now.

She stunned me by grabbing my hand, raising it to her mouth, then biting down on my palm—right where I'd sliced it during our vow. The tiny pain didn't register, but what did? Her claiming. Fuck.

Like that was all she'd needed, she exploded around me while every other part of her froze into a stillness so powerful, it dragged the cum straight out of me.

With a heavy groan, I exploded into her, but unlike her stillness, I burst into action. I drew her against me, shoved my face in her tits, and forced her to move to prolong the glorious feelings she'd dragged out of me.

Only when I'd come down from that insane high did I sag, and she slumped against me.

I knew, at that moment, I'd never been closer to someone than I was with her.

To the world, she was my possession, but the sense of belonging I felt was different than ownership at that moment.

I didn't understand it, couldn't explain it, but I figured some things didn't need to be reasoned or defined.

They just were.

She was addictive, and she'd just reeled me in.

Hook.

Line.

And sinker.

SIXTEEN
INESSA

I FELT CERTAIN THEY KNEW, even though they couldn't. They couldn't know, could they?

I mean, it wasn't possible.

Sure, my cheeks were pink, but they just looked like I'd put a little too much powder on, and while I felt sure I stank of sex, it wasn't like they were sending me knowing looks.

If anything, they were focused on my throat, which made me nervous, because I thought they were looking for the bruises my father had given me.

Only when I excused myself to the bathroom did I realize why.

As I stood there, in my new family's restroom, I had two predicaments.

A hickey was the first. A big one. It was splotchy too, and there was no amount of foundation or concealer that was going to hide it. Plus, they'd already seen it, so what was the point?

I cursed myself for not checking in the mirror before I climbed out of the car, but to be honest, I'd been so out of it that I hadn't even realized we'd arrived at the house.

Eoghan had...

Fuck, was this what sex was like? Was it always this way?

His fingers had been between my legs even as he'd driven us here, and his cum, as it left my body, he'd rubbed it into me, swirling it about my clit, sending sparks of pleasure and pain through me.

I'd been ready to fuck sooner than was physically possible, but he'd tapped my pussy with slick fingers and said, "Until later. Don't wash this off. I want to be inside you all afternoon."

The thought was beyond intense, but I actually needed to pee, so wasn't sure how I was supposed to keep 'him' inside me while I really needed the bathroom too.

It was impossible, right?

Went against the laws of gravity?

But it made me hot, and I was tempted not to pee to keep him inside—hence the second predicament.

To pee or not to pee, that was the question.

He'd raised his dirty fingers to his lips and had sucked them clean, all while I watched, and somehow, that was the hottest thing of all.

I got the feeling that if we'd been home, he'd have eaten me out, which should have been gross, but wasn't.

Nothing we did was.

And that was how he made me feel.

Like all the filthy things I wanted weren't filthy. They were normal.

I'd always gotten turned on at strange stuff. Getting off in front of Maxim was sexier to me than him actually touching me.

The thought of sex outside, with the guy fully dressed and me totally naked, hot as fuck.

But those strange triggers weren't weird to Eoghan.

If anything, he made them acceptable. He accepted me.

And he didn't make me feel dirty for it. He embraced those peculiarities, and took them into both of us, creating that explosive heat we'd both felt back in the car.

I'd never look at that Aston Martin the same way again, and there was no way Lisandra was ever getting in it either.

I just knew she'd figure out I'd done the 'deed' in there, and she'd drag the details out of me. Except I wasn't willing to share.

I was finding, quite surprisingly, that I was as possessive of him as he was of me.

Only, with him, he had no worries on that score. I knew not to be so stupid. He, on the other hand, had no limitations on his behavior, and if that didn't gut me, I wasn't sure what would.

As I stared at the mirror, looked into deep green eyes that were dazed from the morning I'd had, I whispered, "You're a fool, Inessa."

I was.

Because I was falling for him.

Falling, like someone with Stockholm syndrome, for the man who held my reins.

Who promised to retrieve my mother's jewelry from my slutty stepmom, who threatened my father and who had grievously hurt him as a punishment for hurting me. The man who, even though I didn't mean to destroy good food, patiently tried everything I made, even if it was vile. He didn't even bitch at me or call me names. Just sighed when it was gross and pulled out some of the frozen meals Winnie the Witch had stored in the freezer for him.

There was the way, at night, we started at opposite sides of the bed, yet somehow, by morning, I was always in the middle, and my feet were on his calves, and though I knew he liked his space, he didn't jerk away when he woke up in the morning like I'd scalded him.

No, he reached over, rubbed his hand down my side, tangled his fingers in my hair, and leaned down for a kiss before tugging me into the gym with him after we'd changed—in front of each other.

No him going into the bathroom anymore. Nor me either.

In three days, everything had changed. Sex hadn't brought intimacy. My dad almost strangling me to death had. Him knee-capping my father had. And him hurting me, reminding me that he'd fucked a battalion of whores in his time and that sex meant nothing, had somehow unlocked a door that had led to this morning.

That had led to this cocktail of feelings that were threatening to overtake me.

To consume me.

A tap sounded at the door, making me jump.

"Inessa?"

Aoife.

She was, like Eoghan had said, sweet. Her eyes were kind too, and when she smiled at me, it was without artifice. It was genuine, even though I was Bratva and she had to hate me like the whole family had to.

But thus far, they hadn't shown signs of loathing me, if anything, they'd just stared at my throat and the hickey Eoghan had placed there.

"Yeah?" I replied huskily, reaching up and touching the love bite he'd given me.

"Are you okay? You've been in there a while?"

I'd never understood the logic behind that. People spent a while in the bathroom. Wasn't it rude to ask if you were, essentially, taking a crap?

Because the idea that they might think I was having a dump creeped me out, I pulled the door open, looked at her, then stated, "I have a hickey."

Her lips twitched, and her gaze dropped to the offending mark. "You do. And it's very big."

I blew out a breath that had the few strands of loose hair around my face floating upward. I had it in a neat chignon, but it had looked too formal, so I'd released a few strands, but now I wondered if I should use my hair to try and cover up the hickey.

"There's no point," she murmured softly, seeming to sense what I was thinking. "They all know, and they've all jibed Eoghan over it."

"Jibed? What do you mean?"

"Teased him." She shrugged. "They're like little boys when

they're all together. Eoghan, by the sounds of it, doesn't mark his women."

Well, that was a dubious honor.

Apparently, my expression said it all, because she snorted out a laugh. "You'll get used to them. They mean no harm."

My brow puckered. "I don't understand their dynamic."

"No, I can see you don't." She tilted her head to the side. "Is it so different for you and your sisters?"

I shrugged. "We were close, but my eldest sister ran off when I was fourteen, and Vicky is almost that age now, but she's a brat. We're not close anymore."

"You probably will be when you're all older. But these boys grew up together. They're all very tight, and they help each other out. It's a different world than the one you were raised in."

I knew that without her telling me.

Her lips curved at my eye roll. "You figured that out on your own, huh?"

"Yeah, I did."

"Don't get me wrong, Aidan Sr.'s certifiable," she said cheerfully, "but we're a family. Not a brotherhood. There's a difference."

"How would you know?"

"Finn tells me things he probably shouldn't," she said wryly. "Not business, just..." She shrugged. "Interactions."

"His read on a situation?"

"Yeah."

My nose crinkled. "So, Eoghan doesn't suck on his whores' throats like a vampire. I guess I'm unique."

"You're his wife. He's bound to treat you differently."

The soft words had me closing my eyes, because I wanted that. I just wanted to be enough.

It was a ridiculous question, rude and insufferable, and she was kind and didn't deserve me to ask her things that weren't polite, but I couldn't stop myself. "Does Finn have a mistress?"

I half expected a slap, or for her to stalk off back to the dining room table. "No. He doesn't," she answered on a chuckle.

"How do you know?"

"I don't. I mean, he does things with his days that don't involve me, and I own a bakery... We're both busy people, and we have a baby together. But I know he doesn't."

"How?"

"Because what we have together is unique. Like Paul Newman said, 'Why go out for a burger, when you've got steak at home.'" She grinned. "To Finn, I'm prime beef." At my shocked laugh, her grin widened before, abruptly, it softened, and she reached over and patted my arm. "Finn and I didn't have the best of starts."

"You didn't?" Though I'd initiated the conversation, I couldn't believe we were discussing this just off the bathroom, but hell, it seemed fitting. This entire visit wasn't going to plan.

"No. He blackmailed me into sleeping with him."

My eyes rounded. "Finn blackmailed you? I mean, Aoife, you're beautiful, but Finn is..."

She grinned. "I know. He makes Chris Hemsworth look ugly, am I right?"

Her smug tone had me snorting. "Eoghan is just as hot."

"I know. The O'Donnellys are a bunch of hotties. We're lucky ladies."

Something about that statement seemed off to me, but I didn't get why, and her laughter had me focusing on what we were talking about, not just her remark.

"Anyway, he did, and look at us now. There's no reason you can't be Eoghan's prime beef too."

"The way to tie a man to you, girls, is to make him so drunk on you that he can't see anyone else."

I flinched at the sound of my mother-in-law's voice.

Oh fuck, could this get any worse?

I felt a little like a rabbit in the headlights when I turned to her, saw her amused expression, and then just wanted to sink into the ground.

"There's a reason I kept Aidan Sr. tied to me for over forty years. They get offers all the time, but they don't have to take them, do they?"

"No," I said slowly, my gaze on my shoes.

"Eoghan's a loyal boy," she continued, ignoring my shy response. "If you want more of him, just be loyal back. It's not that complicated." She hummed under her breath, and I got the feeling she and Aoife were having a silent conversation. "Anyway, child, if you still need the bathroom, go, because I want to open your gifts."

I bit my lip, nodded, and muttered, "I didn't actually go."

"No, and I'm glad to see you didn't try to hide that hickey, by the way. There's no point," she told me wryly. "Trust me. I've had decades to try, and it never works. We'll be just off the hall down there when you've finished." She surged forward, surprising me when her fingers came to cup my cheek. "Mostly gone now," she murmured, and I knew she was talking about my bruises. "I'll make sure Aidan doesn't mention them, but just so you know, my boy will never lay a hand on you."

"I-I know he won't," I whispered.

"Good." She beamed at me. "Of course, if he ever did, I'd chop off the hand that hit you." Lena winked at me, like that was supposed to reassure me, and frickin' weirdo that I was, it actually did.

Even as I knew Eoghan would never, ever, in a million years hurt me like that.

I sank back into the bathroom, Aoife's rueful smile the last thing I saw before I used the facilities.

Unlike my old home, this place wasn't gaudy. The family's wealth was clear, but not like it was in my father's mansion.

There, everything was marble and touched with an edge of gilt.

Here?

It was a home.

The hall, when I'd finished in the restroom, was lined with photos and paintings of the family. I'd never seen so many family photos in one place. There wasn't an ounce of wall left. It was kind of chaotic, but I liked it. I also liked seeing Eoghan growing from a serious young boy into a cocky teenager. Something changed when he was around sixteen or so, the cockiness grew, as did the smirks and the grins in the various shots I looked at, then, he had a buzzcut and I figured he had just enlisted.

Some somberness appeared, but his grin outshone it.

I could see, from those pics, why he'd been considered the joker of the family.

Had the prospect of being forced into marriage changed him so much?

Then, I realized how stupid that thought process was. How sexist.

Why shouldn't he hate being trapped? Why shouldn't he loathe it more than me? He was older, he'd had freedom, he'd had the taste and the bug had bitten him—to have that taken away? To have to marry someone he didn't know? Have his choices ripped from him?

We were both in this together.

It was probably the first time I genuinely felt that.

We'd been shoved into a marriage thanks to our families, and we had to sink or swim as a unit.

As I stared at what was evidently a Christmas celebration, one pre-Aoife—I figured, as she wasn't there, neither was Lena, which told me she'd been the one behind the camera—I looked at the family and was surprised to see Finn was there.

Evidently, he'd been taken into the fold, but he was O'Grady, not O'Donnelly. Yet, in that picture, with seven matching smiles staring back at me, a weird thought crossed my mind.

That smile was Aidan Sr.'s.

A little taken aback, and concerned, especially since Lena had just said she basically kept Aidan Sr.'s cock on a leash, I gnawed on my lip until I had no choice to stop staring and trundled down the hall to the living room.

Did Eoghan know? Was it an open secret among the brothers?

I knew better than to stick my nose in it, but still, it fascinated me. Truly fascinated me.

And I had no idea why, other than the fact that in my world, bastards didn't eat at the table with the legitimate children. They were out in the cold forever. Not always a bad thing, considering the fathers the Bratva reared.

When I made it into the living room, I saw the TV was on, blaring a football game—the Patriots vs. the Giants—and that two brothers I hadn't seen that much of, Conor and Brennan, were arguing over stats with Finn who, by the sounds of it, was actually a Pats fan.

What the fuck?

Surprised by his lack of loyalty, I nevertheless smirked at their arguing—it was a pleasure to see they could do that without actually being violent.

Heaven.

The TV took up one wall. It was massive. Bigger than the monstrosity in our living room. It was faced by a leather sectional that took up three-quarters of the room, and I knew then and there that this room was for Sundays. I couldn't imagine Aidan Sr. and Lena sitting in here on the regular, it was too big. Too uncomfortably over-sized. But for seven men, and now three women and a baby? It was just right. If the other brothers got married, it would still be large enough to fit everyone, and I had a feeling that was why the sofa was so big.

In front of it, there was a coffee table the width of a frickin' dining room table, but it was low to the ground and made out of stone. On it were the two boxes I'd brought with me.

They were wrapped by the lady in the Louis Vuitton store, because she could do a better job than me, and I bit my lip, knowing how the gift was going to go down, but still needing to do it.

A quick glance around the room showed me the back wall, opposite the TV, was just as loaded with pictures as the hall, but other than that, it was a room made for the sofa and a TV, where a baby swing stood empty in front of it.

A family room in the true meaning of the word.

While my sisters and I relaxed when we were among ourselves, that never happened with Father's presence nearby.

Yet here, Aidan Sr. was scowling at Aidan Jr. over something, while Finn was trying to explain the rules of the game to Aoife who looked both bored and amused at the same time. Lena was under Eoghan's arm, her shoulder clasped in his embrace, even as Eoghan intercepted an argument between the Aidans.

When Lena saw me, she smiled and patted the seat at her side.

I bit my lip, hating that I felt like an interloper—which, rightfully, I was—but still appreciating that they weren't going out of their way to make me feel like Bratva scum.

I mean, I felt that way because Aoife was right.

This was a family.

The Five Points was forged upon the familial links between father and sons, and between brothers.

My world?

Ties were forged in hatred and fear and spilled blood.

There was no love, only control and power.

Here? While I didn't doubt things could get nasty, because Eoghan had just blown off my father's kneecaps, it had a different undertone.

It felt wholesome.

And I knew any number of federal agencies, be it the FBI, the DEA, or the ATF would probably laugh their asses off at that statement, but it was true nonetheless.

When I perched on the edge of the sofa, I reached for the first box which was papered in pink.

Hesitantly, and with a soft smile, I murmured, "For you, Lena."

Her eyes twinkled. "You didn't have to, dear."

"I-I know you don't like my roots, but it's tradition." My smile faltered as she tipped her head to the side when she tore open the box and stared at the soft pink, open back loafers. "When we enter someone's home, we always take our shoes off—and houseguests are offered a set of guest slippers, or if they're frequent guests, they keep their own at the home in question."

Her hand slipped into mine. "Thank you."

I wasn't sure if she got the inference. "It's my way of saying you're welcome—"

"I understood, dear." A kind of fierceness appeared in her eyes. "Truly, thank you."

Eoghan snorted. "That's why you wanted their shoe sizes?"

Lena grinned. "I did wonder at that."

Aidan Sr. pinned me in a stare. "I get a pair too, then, hmm?"

"Of course." Nervously, I reached for the box and handed it to him.

Unlike Lena's, which were pink and dotted with the trademark Louis Vuitton square medallions, Aidan's were flat slippers, black leather, with the monogram on the front.

His eyes twinkled. "I've never worn slippers in my life, Inessa, but for you, I will."

Heat bloomed in my cheeks. "Thank you."

"No, thank you." He passed them back to me. "So, these are for you to take home with you, aren't they?"

I nodded. "They'll always be there for when you visit."

Agitated, I shot Eoghan a look, hoping he approved of the gift.

Maybe it wasn't flowers or chocolates, but it was my heritage. It was how we worked, and even though I wasn't particularly proud of my ties to the Bratva, I was Russian before I was Bratva, and there was no evading that.

I almost thought I'd see scorn in his eyes, but instead, I saw a heat that wasn't banked.

It seemed to pierce me like his dick had pierced me earlier, and this time, my cheeks weren't the only parts of me that were flushing with heat.

Lena broke into the moment by tucking the slippers back into the box and saying, "For you, Inessa. I'll be sure to visit soon." She hummed. "Maybe tomorrow. Eoghan says you're having a problem with Winifred. I'll have a word. Woman to woman. It'll go down better."

"Oh! That isn't necessary—"

But she didn't let me finish the statement. "It's very necessary. You're Five Points now, not Bratva. It's time Winnie remembered who her betters are."

While the steel in her voice shouldn't have come as a surprise, not when I knew who she was married to, it still did.

Aidan Sr. cackled. "I may have to join this visit. I always did like watching you put people in their place, Lena."

"Winnie's not that bad," I argued, concerned if Aidan Sr. was getting involved. "She's just—"

"Just nothing. The ring on that finger of yours changes everything, girl," Aidan boomed, loud enough to make me jump and for the baby in Aoife's arms, Jacob, to burst into tears, which had Finn glowering at him.

While the situation was beyond unorthodox, I had to laugh.

Especially when, upon rethinking things, I reckoned it entered the territory of batshit crazy. But they'd welcomed me, more than I could have imagined, and while I was still nervous, still uncomfortable with the hickey, and very aware of the fact I wasn't wearing panties and my pussy was coated in Eoghan's cum, I actually managed to settle in until Lena declared that it was time for dinner.

And the craziest thing of all?

I enjoyed it. All of it. I was grateful to be included in the family get-together, and I was even more grateful to think that, every Sunday, I'd be welcomed here again and again.

Because I was family now too.

And I'd never been so happy not to be a Vasov anymore.

SEVENTEEN
EOGHAN

THE MEAL, surprisingly, had been quite amusing, and Inessa appeared to have enjoyed herself.

Da had been on his best behavior, well, relatively speaking. For him, he'd been good as gold. A few times, he and Aidan had knocked heads, and I knew why too.

Da was getting frustrated with him.

We all knew what was going down with Aidan, but it wouldn't mean shit until he accepted what was happening too.

That was Addiction 101, right?

Until addicts admitted they had a problem, there was no doing shit for them. Even if it hurt not to get involved—and Da? He didn't do well with delicate situations. Whatever anyone could say about the man, he loved his kids with a ferocity that few could ever understand.

For all he was a psychotic nutcase, this was the other side of that coin. A psychotic love.

Trouble was, it wasn't like Aidan was a regular junkie. We all knew to avoid drugs. That had been rammed into us by Da—I could still remember the drug den he'd taken me to when I was a teenager.

I'd far preferred the fucking strip joint. Watching women sell themselves, offering me, a kid, BJs for cash? Yeah, it had stained my fucking eyes. Drugs? Fool's game.

Still, Aidan wasn't like that kind of junkie. He was in physical pain, and a man like my bro? A strong fucker who'd been raised with violence and knew what it was to piss blood several times a month because of a beating? Our tolerances were whacked.

Even now, a half hour after the meal was over and we were sitting outside on the patio, stacked around a patio table, bottles of beer in front of us as we shot the shit, his agony was clear.

He also looked wrung out. His eyes bloodshot, his face drawn and weary.

He wasn't sleeping. That much was also obvious.

But even as I kept an eye on him, I focused on what Conor was saying. "Doesn't seem like she has any affiliations."

Aidan dug his fingers into his eyes. "So, what was the whole thing for? Shits and giggles?"

Conor shrugged. "No way of knowing her motivation, but I'm relieved she's not tied to law enforcement. I thought we were fucked for a while there."

"Thanks for sharing that with me," I grumbled wryly, keying into the fact he was discussing the hacker who'd sneaked her way into the camera system on my elevator.

Conor grimaced. "We all know we have a tendency of storing stuff at your place."

"Corpses. Not stuff."

"You're the only one who doesn't get freaked out by it."

My lips turned down at the sides. "While we're on the subject. No more storing bodies at my place. Inessa is as understanding as any woman could be, but I draw the line at that. Anyway, Conor has the walk-in fridge—"

"Are we seriously arguing about this now?" Brennan groused, taking a deep pull of his beer.

Of all the brothers, he was the quietest, but like they always said, you had to watch out for the quiet ones.

My lips twisted at the thought of the things my bro got down to in his spare time, shit he didn't know I was aware of. But I had stuff on all my brothers. Not for blackmail purposes, well, not the devious kind. More of the leverage variety. Yeah, I knew that was splitting hairs, but you never knew when you might need a bit of push.

Ten years ago, for example, Aidan had somehow managed to get his hands on Yankees' tickets for their winning World Series game in '09.

I might have used some of my hoard on him—like how I'd seen him kissing Larry Duke when he was seventeen.

Aidan was as straight as they came, but in a Catholic household? Experimentation wasn't exactly permitted.

Fuck, I thought Da would prefer for Aidan to have his brain spliced than for him to be gay.

Looking back, I actually felt bad for pulling that card on him. While I'd been made, I'd still been a fucking teenager and hadn't really thought most things through. I'd just wanted those fucking tickets more than I wanted Janet O'Leary to suck my dick—which was saying something.

Still, I figured I should probably apologize for that.

When Aidan wasn't strung out on opiates, of course.

I eyed him once more, measured his exhaustion, and shook my head at the sight of him. "You figure out how she contacted my mistress?" I queried, glancing around the yard and making sure everything was copacetic.

I actually preferred this garden to the old house. It was smaller, but Ma had taken control of it. The herb garden took up eighty percent of it, with the pool and its terrace taking up the rest. Even now, as we sat here, we were amid plants I recognized as lavender and basil.

The walls were high, the perimeter solid because I'd helped plan the security for this place, and there wasn't a tall building in sight, meaning Da could swing his dick anywhere he wanted, and no one would have a target on it.

As Inessa would phrase it, it was a 'pretty prison,' but my folks seemed to like it.

Conor sighed. "That was easy. Especially for someone like Lodestar." He sounded like he was trying to be patient, which meant none of us were really listening to him—that was true.

Stuffed full of roast beef and gravy, I wasn't even sure why we were talking work. Except for the fact shit was serious right now, and this was a safe place. It got swept every day for bugs, and this place made the Pentagon look low on security.

"She did it?"

"Yeah. Hacked her phone."

"Just neutralize the threat," Brennan suggested with a waft of his bottle.

"She's not that easy to get to." His brow puckered, and he began to rip at the sticker on his dewy beer bottle. "She's good. Damn good. But as far as I can tell, she's just making mischief."

"Why would she do that?"

Conor snorted at Brennan's question. "Why wouldn't she? Hackers and hacker collectives pull all kinds of stunts. It's their idea of fun."

"They need to get laid," was my elder brother's retort.

My lips twitched. "They sound like they need to learn how to bone if that's their idea of a good time."

"When did you lose your virginity?" Declan joked, nudging Conor in the side.

He flipped Dec the bird, and growled, "This isn't about me."

"Probably still a virgin," Brennan muttered, making us all snicker.

Conor glowered at him. "Whatever—as far as I can tell, and there's no way of knowing unless I force her out into the open, she's no threat. I've dealt with Leticia but she claimed it was all a misunderstanding. Was zero help with Lodestar."

Knowing what 'dealt with' meant, I pondered that, pondered how she'd been bought off by the hacker. "She has footage of us," I pointed out. "Footage that isn't going to go down well in the wrong hands."

"I checked the cameras. You only see tops of heads and hands. You forget, I was the one who figured out the security system on those elevators. I did it for a reason. Unless you point blank look upright into the camera, you can't see faces, and as far as I'm aware, you don't walk around with your head tipped back all the way."

"Smart ass," Brennan grumbled.

"*I'm* the smart ass?" Conor snapped. "Fuck the lot of you."

Aidan grabbed Conor's elbow when he made to stand. "Stop being so prickly."

Conor huffed but took a seat again. His ass jolted the benches around the table, and Aidan flinched, making me question how he could still be so sensitive to pain all these years later.

Was there something wrong with him that required more surgery?

Should he still be experiencing this kind of agony?

"I think you should force her out into the open."

Brennan shook his head at Declan's statement. "I think you should find out what she's doing."

"It isn't as easy as that," Conor claimed.

"I'm not saying find out her motives, I'm saying trace her steps. See where's she's been. According to you and the bullshit you spew, once it's on the net, there's no escaping it. It will always come back to bite you on the ass."

Conor rolled his eyes. "Unless you have a very skilled brother who can hide things for you."

"Yeah? Shame we don't have one of those then, huh?" Brennan countered, but his eyes danced. He was the hardest on us, to be fair, but if there was a brother who always had our backs? It was Bren.

My lips twitched, but I didn't follow through with the laugh.

"Okay, less of the arguing," Aidan groused, rubbing his temple. "I ain't got the patience for it."

"Leave you fuckers alone for ten minutes and you get beer and start bitching?"

I shot Finn a look as he strolled over with Jacob on his hip and a beer in the other hand. "Like you weren't taking advantage of Ma watching Jacob."

His lips cocked up in a smirk. "Trust me, you have to make the time when they're this young."

I grimaced. "I hate kids."

"Ignore him, Jacob," Finn told his kid as he hitched a leg, kicked it over the bench and took a seat on the picnic table with us. "He'll like you when you can shit autonomously."

"I make no promises."

Finn rolled his eyes, took a sip of beer, then asked, "What are we moaning about?"

"The hacker I was telling you about, Finn."

Conor and Finn worked together. Both of them were heavy into the Five Points' finances, and bounced off one another on a daily basis.

Finn pulled a face. "What's she called again? Lonestar?"

"Lodestar," Conor corrected. "She's a pain in the ass. Brennan wants to see what she's been doing up until she decided to target Eoghan."

"What made me the lucky one, huh?" I groused, but I didn't really care. No one could touch us, not with as many Feds, cops, politicians, and attorneys on our payroll.

We altered reality, and no one would question it.

"Must be that ugly face of yours," Finn retorted, but he shot Conor a considering look. "Did you talk about what you wanted to do?"

"No." Conor shrugged his shoulders. "These fuckers were too busy griping at me—"

"Get on with it," Aidan snapped, and his tone wasn't the least bit playful.

We all stared at him, long enough for his pasty features to blanch a little more. "Headache," he muttered.

"And we know why," Brennan retorted. "Fucker. When are you going to admit—"

"Don't go there," Aidan growled, his arms bunching like he was getting ready to start swinging his fists. "I don't need your shit."

"Don't you? Who the fuck did you call when you were puking—"

I slammed a hand on the picnic table. "Enough. Aidan, we all know you're suffering, man. But the only way we can help you is when you decide to stop being so fucking stubborn. Now, Conor, what did you have in mind?"

Conor, while my elder brother, usually deferred to me on this shit, and he hunched his shoulders after glancing at Aidan, and mumbled, "That we bring her in."

"You know where she is?" Declan asked, brow cocked, even as he switched his gaze between Conor and Aidan. Our eldest brother looked like a deflated balloon.

Not because of the confrontation, but because, evidently, by the end of the day, whatever he'd used to prop himself up to get through the meal was starting to wear off.

They said that the only way you could help an addict was if they admitted to themselves they had a problem, but we weren't like regular people, and I saw that then.

While we were men, forged of bone and flesh like everyone else, we could bend laws, ignore government edicts, and rule our roosts like gods.

Aidan wasn't about to do shit, not when he could afford to pay for his habit. The only thing that would fuck with him in the end was if he fucked up on the job, and then Da would be the one ramming his face into the table and dragging him to rehab.

The notion bore merit, because since the last time I'd seen him, he'd lost more weight, and looked wearier and more drained.

Trouble was, with war running on our sidelines, there was no worse a time than now for him to be stuck in some artsy fartsy rehab clinic in Connecticut.

Even as I rubbed my chin, I muttered, "Do you have a lock on Lodestar's location, Conor?"

"No. But I can find it. I just need some time."

"If her intentions aren't aggressive, just meddlesome, then you have time. But the second things change, you need to change too," Brennan intoned, and everyone heard the dominant vibe to the words. Normally we listened to Aidan. As the eldest and the heir to Da's throne, he was in charge.

But Aidan was sick, and that was clearer now than ever.

Brennan had always bossed us around, though, so his command didn't piss any of us off.

Finn shot his best friend a look, because he and Aidan were tight, but he agreed, "You're right, Brennan. Look for her, Conor, find her place, and be ready for her to change tactics in the interim."

"What do we do with her when I find her?" Conor inquired uneasily.

"Your walk-in fridge still working?" Declan questioned dryly.

Conor wrinkled his nose. "I hate putting people in there."

"Tough shit," I retorted. "I hate storing dead bodies in my spare room. 'Them's the cards that fall.'"

When he flipped me the bird, I hid my grin behind the bottle of beer and took a deeper sip.

As I did, Aoife—looking flushed and with a definite bounce to her step thanks to the quickie she and Finn had just had—and Inessa wandered out of the house, mugs in their hands.

Finn's gaze tracked his wife, and I had to admit to doing the same. They were night and day. Aoife so wholesome and womanly, Inessa so slender and regal.

They ignored us, even though they had to know we were here, and while I was a little piqued, I was also grateful because the sight of that fucking hickey, combined with the thought of what we'd just done in my favorite car, had my dick twitching. Last thing I needed was a boner in front of my brothers.

That was freshmen year all over again, and what a fucking nightmare that had been.

"You two seem to be getting on well," Declan rumbled slowly, and I saw he was watching Aoife and Inessa too. Not in a way that made me want to slap him upside the head, but in a protective way.

The notion had my brows rising, because Declan was weird about women. Ever since Deirdre had died—his childhood sweetheart—he'd been a manwhore. Aoife and Jacob had softened him up some, and whatever had gone down during the visits with Inessa's family seemed to have created a liking on his part. We were protective of our women anyway, but it pleased me to know that Declan would kill for them just as much as I would.

Who the fuck knew what Brennan would protect if the apocalypse came, and Conor? He avoided guns, preferring joysticks to real weapons, but I figured he knew when to fight and the time would be when our women were in danger. Aidan? Too strung out to be of much use, but I'd seen his response to Inessa's bruises. The fucker would back us if he could stand up without shaking.

I plucked at my bottom lip as I stared at my wife in that crazy outfit she wore. How something so prim and neat—boring, really—could get my dick so hard was both satisfying and a pain in the ass.

"She suits me."

The three words might have been a declaration of love for the way my brothers—Aidan included—responded.

All of them, Finn too, and hell, he was more of a brother than a friend, gaped at me.

I scowled at them. "What?"

"*She suits you?*" Brennan mocked.

"She does." My shoulders bunched around my ears. "She kind of slotted in well."

"You blew her father's kneecaps off the other day, Eoghan. I think that's the opposite of slotting in well."

I glared at Declan, but no one else showed much surprise, which told me news had spread...around my brothers' circle or into my father's ears, I wasn't sure.

"He deserved it."

"The fucker definitely deserved it for those bruises I saw," Aidan growled. "Her face was like the fucking *Technicolor Dreamcoat*. I've beaten thieves less than what that cunt did to her."

My temper surged, even as I forced it to flatline. "He isn't King Dick now."

"You saw him today? His guards let you in?"

"Went with Inessa."

"You're a mean motherfucker," Brennan rumbled. "Why would she want to see her da like that?"

"Because he's a fucker? Because her enemy is down?" Conor shrugged. "I'd have thought she'd get closure from the visit."

"She did. She isn't afraid of violence. Wouldn't say she was bloodthirsty, but she's not frightened of revenge."

Declan scratched the stubble on his cheek. "That gift of hers was a nice touch."

"Weird though."

I snorted at Conor's statement. "I was as surprised as you were."

"Aren't you the lucky one? Now Ma has an open invite, she'll be around all the time."

I flipped Brennan the bird, but he just grinned at me. "Might not be a bad thing. Will help her acclimate. She's out of place. Fish out of water." I leaned more of my weight onto the elbows I'd stacked on the table. "Seems to think the apartment is some kind of prison."

"You know what they treat their women like in the Bratva."

Dec's remark had me sighing. "Pretty dolls."

"Sounds about right," Brennan said gruffly. "Fuckers."

"I'm sure Vasov is saying the same about us."

Finn's lips twitched. "I'd have paid to see you blow his legs to pieces. That fuck makes your da look normal." He grunted, pulling a face at a memory unique only to him—he'd been the one there when the details for my nuptials had become set in stone.

None of us were strangers to violence, but sweet fuck, for Finn to look a little queasy said it all.

Vasov deserved his fate.

Not that I was feeling guilty or anything, because I wasn't.

He shouldn't have hurt Inessa.

If he'd left her alone, he wouldn't be needing a bag to collect his piss.

As I let my gaze drift up her long legs, to the ass that bounced when we fucked, and to the honey between her thighs as she shifted around when Aoife and her decided to take a seat at a small lounging area by the pool, I knew I was a fucking goner for her.

I wouldn't say she had my prick in a vise, but for the moment at any rate, she had it in her fist, and I was more than happy for it to be there.

"Another one bites the dust," Conor commented in a lilting voice that had me shooting him a look.

I didn't argue though.

What was the point in arguing the truth?

EIGHTEEN
INESSA

"HOLY FUCK!"

Eoghan's statement had me tensing and looking up from my text convo with Lisandra.

She'd been asking about how the family meal went, and I'd been telling her how everything had gone really well. Eoghan had been right—I loved Aoife.

She was awesome. Kind, friendly, but with a bit of snap that kept Finn in line, so I knew she had more bark to her than she let on, and we had the same love of books. She'd sent me a couple of recommendations via text when we'd exchanged numbers, and I was looking forward to delving in.

But Eoghan's comment had me breaking off from my conversation and peering ahead.

We were heading back to Hell's Kitchen, but for some reason, Eoghan had brought us back through the Bronx.

Something he was evidently regretting as he revved the engine and pulled some *Fast and Furious* moves to get us the hell out of the area.

Not easy when the other drivers were just as freaked.

Because there, in plain sight, a gunfight was going down right on the border between Little Yemen and the Bronx.

Pedestrians were screaming as they took shelter, ducking behind cars, and using their hands to cover their faces and heads like that would save them as they screwed themselves up into tiny balls.

But nothing could save you from the spray of an AK-47.

"Sweet fuck, your father's a madman," Eoghan growled, even as he managed to turn us away from the battle royale in the center of a busy street.

I couldn't argue with him, not when I'd seen faces and tattoos I recognized—Bratva.

"The Italians?" I whispered, twisting around to watch as much as I could before Eoghan managed to get us the hell out of there.

Sirens came next, lots of them. A shit ton of them.

Cop cars raced out of nowhere like they were on tracks, sliding toward the fray.

A lot of lives were going to be lost today, and not all of them deserving.

My brow puckered as I stared at him. "He's going ahead with the war against the *Famiglia*."

Didn't take a genius to figure it out. "Yeah," he grunted. "He is. But the fuckwit... What was he thinking?"

"I guess he was thinking of war," I whispered softly.

A war we'd started.

Because Eoghan and I were in this together.

I hadn't hidden my bruises, and while Eoghan hadn't been expected back so early from his trip, and it could be said that—

No.

I hadn't hidden them.

And if I'd wanted to, I wouldn't have. I'd wanted him to see the marks, and I'd wanted him to act. I'd wanted him to avenge me, to live out the promises he'd made me.

And he hadn't let me down.

While he'd backed me to the hilt, and I was so beyond grateful for that, I had to blow out a shaky breath, my entire being starting to tremble with the repercussions of what I'd just seen.

Of what we'd caused together.

Then, Eoghan's hand reached for mine as he steered one-handed, and as our fingers bridged, I stared down at the connection. One that was physical but morphing into something else.

Emotional too.

Another shaky breath escaped me as he stated, his tone cool and calm, "This has been brewing for ten years, Inessa. We kindled a fire that was already starting to burn."

"People are going to get hurt."

He sighed. "People always get hurt. It's what they do."

I bit my lip at that. At the weariness in his voice. "Don't you ever get sick of it? Of all the death?"

"A wise woman told me something recently, and she was right—there's no running away from this world... It will consume you until you take your final breath, Inessa. The only peace is in death, and I still have a hell of a lot I want to do with myself, and you're younger than me, you still have plenty left to do." He cut me a quick look. "Now probably isn't the best time to tell you this, especially when I'll have to increase your guards—"

The news of extra guards didn't come as a surprise. Being watched every time I left the house was the story of my life. It was why sneaking out with Lisandra had been so much fun—fraught with terror at being caught, which I almost always had been. But it had been worth the punishment.

So, bored with talk of guards, I interrupted, "Tell me what?"

"I never intended for you to stay locked up in the penthouse, Inessa. You're free to live your own life. The only stipulation, and this goes for both of us, is that the penthouse is our base."

I knew immediately what he meant.

No going to NC State with Lisandra.

But...regardless, fuck. My eyes pricked with tears as I stared down at our hands.

"You mean that?" I asked softly, quietly, hoping he wouldn't hear the pathetic emotions in my voice.

"Of course. I have no desire for you to be a doll I take down from a pedestal to play with from time to time. Quite frankly, if I was the center of your life, you'd not only be bored shitless, you'd drive me insane."

A sharp laugh escaped me. "Thanks, I think."

His grin was like liquid fire as he shot it my way before focusing on the streets ahead. Streets that were getting crammed with cop cars. The sirens and the sight of so many police put me back on the edge he'd just alleviated me from.

I hadn't done anything wrong—well, not technically—we were just driving along, minding our own business, but a distaste for the cops was bred into me.

"If you want to go to college, go to college. If you want to do something like Aoife has, do that. I don't care. I'll give you an allowance so you don't have to work—this isn't about money. It's about you not thinking you're living in a prison, because you're not."

I couldn't believe what I was hearing, even as I totally believed it.

Confusing, huh?

It made no sense. After a lifetime of being locked away, I was suddenly being allowed out into the world without having to sneak about. But, also, this was Eoghan.

He wasn't my father.

And he was younger. And he had faith in his team. *Trust* because they were there through loyalty. Which meant I was safe with them, and which meant he could allow me some freedom.

He'd prettied it up by saying the penthouse was both our base, but I knew my reins were still tighter than his. Yet, what he was offering was so much more than I could have ever dreamed of that I felt like I was floating.

Options.

Suddenly I had them, and it was heady stuff.

Not as good as my orgasm earlier, but definitely fucking awesome.

He fell silent, evidently aware that I needed time to process a lifetime's conditioning. I'd thought my childhood, though restricted, would be freer than when I was married, but it was turning out to be the opposite.

I suddenly knew how captives felt when they were allowed outside for the first time, staring with stinging eyes into the sun.

Gilded cages were pretty, they were comfortable and elegant, but freedom?

That was priceless.

We rode home, a penthouse that was starting to feel more and more like that word, not just a label but a feeling, and the second we were out of the car and heading for the elevator, his phone was out and he was texting people. His brothers, I assumed, but I didn't pry.

The business wasn't my place, and neither did I have the desire to know anything about it—toxic as it was.

I plucked at my bottom lip as we soared to the top floor, and when we exited into the living room, and I saw my pretty furnishings, a smile blossomed.

The world might be in an uproar, but this, here? A sanctuary. No longer my prison, but a haven of my own making.

Eoghan, surprising me, snapped his hand around mine and jerked me against him. His phone was forgotten now as he reached up and traced my smile.

He stared at my mouth, at the curve on it, then he connected our lips, a groan escaping him as he thrust his tongue inside me, forcing me to accept him—except there was no force. I needed this just as much as he did.

Somehow, when we were like this, everything made sense in a world founded on chaos.

I groaned back, loving his taste, loving the flavor of him.

I was panting when he pulled back, stating, "I had to taste that smile."

Feelings flooded me. So warm and hot and overwhelming that my heart started to pound like mad. It was a wonderful feeling, good and positive, making me feel like I could climb Everest and vanquish a thousand foes—so long as he was at my side.

I didn't know what to call it, didn't know if I could even put those vague feelings to a name, it just enabled me to reach around his waist, hold him tight, and breathe him in.

My husband.

Mine.

NINETEEN

EOGHAN

I SQUINTED AT THE MONITOR, then squinted harder when I saw Ma's cheerful face peering back at me.

"I know you're there, son."

I grunted. "Do you know what time it is?"

"Time for me to smack Winnie upside the head?"

Shit, I'd forgotten about that, and I thought she had as well, considering tomorrow would be a week since the last time I saw her.

Then I peered behind her, and groaned when I saw Da, Aidan Jr., and fucking Brennan along for the ride.

"You woke us up," I groused, even as I let them into the elevator.

"We remember what it was like to be newlyweds," Da said, and I rolled my eyes, grateful when the intercom stopped transmitting with them tucked inside the elevator.

I didn't wait for them to arrive, just headed to the bedroom where Inessa was curled in a ball, her face toward the door. She'd been cuddled into me when I'd woken up, and I really fucking resented being shoved out of bed for a meet and greet between my mother and the goddamn help.

Grunting, I dropped to a squat beside the bed, and muttered, "Baby?"

Her eyelashes fluttered, and I swear to fuck, she was the most beautiful thing I'd ever seen this early in the day. Her skin was like porcelain, her face delicate, and her eyelashes batted against the upper tilt of her cheekbones in a way that made me want to feel them against my skin.

I was a hard man, but fuck, everything about her got to me.

"Sweetheart," I rumbled when she didn't stir.

A sigh escaped her as she unfurled on the bed, and the sight of her tits playing peekaboo with the sheet had me lifting it slightly and peering under to get the full show.

"Beautiful," I sighed.

"Thank you."

Her whisper had me smiling as our gazes tangled, and even though I was feeling grouchy, I didn't stop smiling as I informed her, "Ma's on the way up. Da, Aidan, and Brennan too. It's a whole fucking gathering."

A shriek escaped her, and she flung herself off the bed. I had to laugh when she got tangled in the sheets and half fell out of it, only saved by my catching her. I copped a feel of her ass, grinned when she shivered against me, her hips rocking like she appreciated the touch—my kinky little mouse—then she moaned, "Why didn't she warn me?"

"Probably to catch you unaware. She's shrewd," I said unapologetically, then I leaned down when she tried to move away, and whispered, "I could fuck you here. Now. While they're outside, waiting on us to come out."

She froze, but she didn't slap my chest, or shove me away again. If anything, I felt the taut wire that linked us together pull even tighter. Unable to stop myself, I reached between her thighs from behind, slipping through her legs, and let my fingers caress her pussy.

Sopping.

Wet.

"Fuck," I grunted gutturally. I'd been teasing, testing, but now I really wanted to fuck.

"Eoghan!" Ma called out, making me grunt again.

Inessa tipped her head back, and her pupils were like pinpricks. "You'd do that?"

"If it got you hot," I replied instantly, and I saw that it did.

I saw that it got her so fucking hot that it was a wonder she didn't goddamn melt.

Reaching up, I rubbed my other thumb against her bottom lip, tugging it down so I could see her teeth just as I nudged her clit. "You like that, huh?"

She shivered. "M-Maybe."

"Eoghan!"

The warning was clear, and I gritted my teeth before I called out, "Five minutes, Ma!"

She grumbled beside my door, "It had better be."

My mouth twitched in a half smile because she knew me too fucking well.

Inessa flinched, but I didn't let her move. "You want to be caught, baby? You like that?"

She licked her lips, and the motion had her tongue touching my thumb. "It's wrong," she whispered.

"Nothing's wrong between us," I countered instantly. "You want it, I want to give it to you. Any way you need it."

Her hands gripped my waist firmer. "I want to be caught."

"But you want me to keep you safe," I countered.

"I know you will."

That confirmed my suspicions. She was too good, too modest to want to be seen that way. But the idea of it? Got her locked and loaded—and I felt the proof of that on my fingers.

I thought about the terrace outside, a space I rarely used, thought about the fantasy she'd admitted to me, and I thought about her humping the desk in front of that fucker Maxim...

Could she get more perfect for me?

I was a fucking exhibitionist too. Sex was the only way I could ever let loose, and I did so with a bang.

Pushing my forehead against hers, and my dick into her belly, I muttered, "I'll always keep you safe."

"I know you will," she replied calmly, even if it was a little breathless from the feel of my dick, I figured.

"But I'm going to test your boundaries. You good with that?"

Her bottom lip quivered, making me wish I hadn't moved my hand. "Will it feel good?"

"It'll feel fucking epic."

She gulped. "Then I'm good with that."

I stopped toying with her pussy, and whispered, "Later, I'm going to make you scream."

"Is that a promise?"

I grinned. "You know it." Then, I pulled away and tapped her on the ass. "You go get showered." I sucked my fingers clean as she watched me, loving the taste of her cunt on them, then I wandered to the closet and grabbed some jeans. "I'll keep Ma away for the moment."

Inessa swallowed, and it was torture knowing she'd let me pin her up against the wall and fuck her, even if I also knew I couldn't do that.

Ma wouldn't allow that.

Climbing into my jeans, I snapped them up over my boner, which fucking hurt, and traipsed out before I let my angelic vixen get the better of me. When I meandered out, my brothers were seated on my sofa, the TV already on, and Da was at the window with the slippers Inessa had bought him on his feet.

"The fuck did you get those?" I grumbled. God, could a man have no privacy?

Da, knowing me too well, peered over his shoulder. "Being a newlywed has made you a dumbass. You got a shoe rack beside the console."

I blinked. I did?

Fuck.

Inessa was messing with my head, and with war at our heels, that wasn't fucking good.

I grunted at that, then glowered at Aidan when I saw he was looking at my boner. "You need a pair of fucking slippers too? Weren't you the ones giving me shit about how they had an open invite?"

Aidan grinned, and from his eyes, I knew he was high. "Had to watch the show."

"What show?"

He cocked a finger at me, and I bent down to his angle, looked ahead, and saw what he meant.

Ma and Winnie were talking in the kitchen, and from that angle, you could just see that Winnie was pinned against the counter with fear on her face, even as Ma was five feet away from her.

Even though I was pissed at my housekeeper, and hated that she was making Inessa uncomfortable, the prospect of getting new staff made me wander over there fast.

"Ma?" I called out, watching as Winnie's focus switched to me, and I could sense her praying I was a lifeline.

I wasn't.

Ma looked at me. "I was just telling Winnie about what a lovely daughter-in-law I've got."

My lips twitched. "Yeah?" Then, I stared at Winnie. "Heard you've been giving Inessa shit, Winnie. That true?"

"It's true," Inessa rasped from behind me. "But I think things will be better now, won't they, Winnie?"

The housekeeper blinked and nodded fast.

I'd finally figured out that Inessa was cooking because of Winnie, so deciding to save my gut, I asked, "You gonna make me some of that cottage pie I like?"

Winnie's nod came fast again. "Of course, Eoghan." She cut Inessa a look, and I saw no malice in her eyes, but Ma evidently did. Inessa, too, because she tensed. "If that's what you'd like, Inessa?"

"I hear you give my daughter-in-law any shit, Winnie, I'll be telling Aidan about that stunt your Brian pulled. You got me?"

My ears pricked at that.

What stunt? I knew Brian was on Brennan's crew, so whatever it was, and knowing my bro, I doubted Brian hadn't already been castigated. But Winnie evidently wasn't aware of that, and she tensed up before whispering, "I got you, Lena."

"Good."

Ma huffed then wandered toward me, and Inessa murmured, "The slippers fit! I'm so glad."

She grinned at Inessa. "They're beautiful, thank you, dear. And right in the entrance! It's nice to know I'll be able to see more of both of you now. Eoghan's a rude little booger. He never invited us home."

There'd been a reason for that.

Inessa cleared her throat, and surprised me by asking Ma, "Lena, in future, would you mind giving us some notice?" Her smile was hesitant. "I'd prefer not to have to rush through getting cleaned up, and I'd like to make sure the apartment is nice and tidy for you."

Approval sparked through Ma's eyes. "I can understand that. Aidan's mother was an old bitch, and she'd always pull moves like that on me." She patted Inessa's arm, even as she leaned forward and kissed her cheek. "I only did that today because of the situation." She meant Winnie. "I promise, I won't do it again."

Inessa's smile practically sparkled. "Thank you." She returned the kiss, then asked, "Would you like to stay for brunch?"

"That'd be lovely. Winnie, Aidan will have his usual, but the rest of us will have whatever you can scrape together." The order was clear.

"Yes, Lena," Winnie agreed meekly.

I grinned at Ma as she moved out of the kitchen, but I tugged her into a quick hug, grateful for her backing Inessa up. "And they say Da is the tyrant."

Her eyes twinkled. "Behind every strong man, there's a stronger woman," was all she said, but I let out a laugh, because what the fuck that said about her, I didn't even want to know.

TWENTY

INESSA

AS I LEFT THE CHURCH, which was only two blocks away, I sighed. Vespers on a Saturday evening was something Mama had always attended, and while I often questioned my faith, to the point where I rarely visited church, I tried to go at least once a month.

Since the wedding, I hadn't been once, so I'd been feeling guilty.

The hieromonk was new, though, so he didn't look at me like I was scum as I alighted from the deep, cavernous church that always made me feel like I was going underground with its low domes and dark vibe.

"Did you enjoy the liturgy?" he inquired in our mother tongue, his eyes crinkling at the sides.

"I did, Father. Thank you." I scurried away, not wanting to get into a conversation with him. I'd missed yesterday's confession, so I didn't want him to ask me if I'd be attending next week.

Eoghan had said I could have more freedom, but did I want to be spending that time in church?

Nope.

Although…I had both our souls to worry about now, didn't I? So maybe I should.

With a sigh, I tugged my silk scarf higher over my head as I moved out of the doorway.

This was Bratva territory, which meant it was under siege from the Italians, so I peered out and saw Eoghan was waiting at the side in the Aston Martin like he'd promised.

I slipped down the sidesteps, aware as he was that I was a good target even if I was now Five Points' property, which would be drawing the Irish into the war with the *Famiglia*. Ducking my shoulders, I hunched behind the scarf until I reached the bottom step. Launching myself through the iron gates, I didn't rest easy, even when Eoghan got us out of there.

From his stern expression, I knew he wasn't happy about the church's location.

"I can go to a different one."

My appeasing words had him grimacing. "I don't want you to have to do that."

I reached over and grabbed his hand. "It's okay."

His nostrils flared, but he slipped his fingers through mine and tightened them. It made me feel tied to him, and because I liked that, I didn't move my hand away, letting him steer like that.

When we didn't return home, my brows rose. They lifted even higher when we approached a skyrise I'd never seen before.

"Where are we?"

His serious expression had lessened somewhat, and he shot me a look that was loaded with so many emotions, I didn't even know where to start.

Something had happened to him, something I didn't know the details of. He'd been a locked door to me, but somehow, I'd used the key, and I felt like I'd been welcomed in...I didn't know if it was to his heart, but with a man like Eoghan? I figured that his trust was probably harder to win.

"This is an Acuig property."

"It is?" I cocked a brow as I peered up at it. The Bratva was rich. I'd known Eoghan's family was too.

But this rich?

Fuck.

I cleared my throat. "Why are we here? On a Saturday evening?"

"You'll see."

"Did your father give you some work to—" They'd been mulling over something at brunch, but when we'd brought out the food, they'd started talking about other things. Normal stuff.

Lena and me, for all that I was younger, were no fools though. Men...always thinking they were smart, when they were shit at hiding stuff from the women in their lives.

He snorted. "We're going to my office. But not for work."

"Your office?" My surprise was clear. "Why does a sniper need an office?"

His laughter washed over me, filling me with warmth. "I'm not down on the company payroll as hired gun, sweetheart."

My cheeks burned with embarrassment. "Oops."

"Yeah. Oops." He shot me a look that showed me his eyes were twinkling, but his expression was hidden from me as we moved down into the basement parking. "Technically, I handle our security."

"Oh." There wasn't much I could say to that, so I didn't bother.

When we pulled into a space that was labeled with his name, I climbed out of the car and peered around. Wondering what we were doing, I moved over to him when he held out his hand, and together, we walked toward the elevators.

As it was a Saturday, and late, the elevator came immediately, and it was empty.

Within seconds, we were surging up through the skyscraper, and Eoghan had moved us so that he was behind me, our joined hands resting on my hip.

I could feel his dick burrowing into my ass, and my heart skipped a beat when his phone made an appearance in his other hand. He held it so I could see the screen, and my pussy began to ache when I read what he tapped out.

Eoghan: Conor. Security lights out in my office. Two hours.

Two seconds later, he got a reply.

Conor: Dirty fucker. Lights out engaged.

I could hear my pulse rushing in my ear, but when the elevator doors opened onto a glass expanse of pigeonhole offices?

It surged higher.

The offices all had clear partition walls, and around the perimeter of the building, where the windows were, you could see into the larger, executive offices too.

The windows overlooked the city, but more than that, office and apartment buildings alike.

A fine tremor whispered through me as he pushed me out into the space, and let me get my bearings, before he moved aside and started to walk me forward.

When we made it, my brows rose, because it was big. Very big. A corner office too. Seemed a damn waste for a position that was only in name and with no position behind it.

It overlooked the rest of the floor, the glass partitions here, too, making the doors really pointless.

He opened one and took a step inside first, making me hover outside. I wasn't unaccustomed to that. Guards swept into a room to secure it, then I was allowed in, but this was different. We were alone.

"Take off your clothes."

My heart plummeted at the command, even as my mouth grew dry and my pussy wet. "W-What?"

"You heard me."

His stern tone had my mouth quivering.

I knew what the term 'lights out' meant—there were no cameras in here, and if guards had been scheduled to do a walkabout, it had been canceled.

But...

I looked over to Manhattan.

The whole frickin' city could see in.

"I'm waiting."

The back of my neck prickled, and I turned to look at him, saw he was seated at his desk. When had he moved?

I gulped, turned on at the sight of him sitting there.

The office, the top floor, the size and space...it was massive, and it spoke of power.

My man's power.

His power over me.

My hands grew clammy as I reached for the buttons on the simple shirt dress I'd worn to church. I unfastened each one, fumbling and feeling stupid and like an ingenue, which made me fumble harder.

I kept my gaze on the floor, unable to look at him as I pulled my arms out of the dress and then let it sink to the ground, puddling around my feet.

"Bra too."

My eyes clenched closed, and my lungs burned as I reached behind me, pulling off the bra.

He's possessive. He doesn't want anyone to see me. Not really. Not like this.

I had the litany in my head, silently on repeat, as I tugged my bra off.

When I stood there, naked except for my panties, my skin tingling as I thought about how anyone could look in through the windows, how someone could use the elevator, and they'd see us—there was no way they couldn't, not with how the floor was set up—I wasn't sure if I wanted to faint, fuck, or fumble back into my clothes and flee.

Maybe he got that, because he asked, "Are you wet, love?"

I loved his gruff tone, and because it grounded me, reminded me of when he was thrusting into me, fucking me, giving me what I needed, I slipped my hand under the waistband of my underwear, moved it between my legs, and tested myself.

A sob escaped me though, and I covered my face with my other hand.

"That wet, hmm?" he questioned softly, then he tutted, and ordered, "Come over here."

I shuffled to him fast, needing his reassurance. Needing to know I wasn't fucking weird.

Pretty much hurling myself at him, I perched on his lap, and he slid his hand under my legs, tugged me closer, and curved me so I was cuddled into him.

It felt like bliss.

True bliss.

I sighed, happy now that I was here, happy to have my face shoved in his throat, to hide from a world that made me this wet.

"There's no need to be embarrassed, Inessa," he rasped, his hand sliding over my arm, making gooseflesh surge and fall in a wave.

"I'm weird," I whimpered, needing him to tell me I wasn't.

"If you're weird, then I am too."

Well, that wasn't reassuring.

I stiffened, then when he laughed, I moved my face from his throat and glowered at him.

"There's my woman," he rasped, and somehow, that word got to me like nothing else could.

Not his wife.

His woman.

There was a massive difference, and we both knew it.

I swallowed thickly, suddenly the exact opposite of ashamed and uncomfortable.

He wanted me.

Not that slut I'd seen on our wedding day.

Not a random whore.

He wanted *me*.

"I do have some work to do," he murmured, "and you? You're going to hump the desk while Manhattan watches."

My cheeks flushed with heat, and I knew this was both a punishment and a gift for what I'd told him about Maxim.

This was about him replacing Maxim in that memory, and it was about giving me what I needed.

I didn't argue, even though I was embarrassed.

"I never did it naked," I whispered, head ducked.

"No, but you will for me. That's why your panties are on," he said matter-of-factly, as he tapped my thigh and directed, "Go on, get."

Shivering a little, I scrambled to my feet, then moved around the desk as he turned on the computer that sat at the edge of the glass surface. It wasn't a sharp corner, more of a blunt one, and I propped myself on the edge, hitching my pussy above it.

When I looked at him, I saw he was focused on the screen, so I stared outside, and my eyes flared wide when I saw some people in the opposite building. They were having a meeting. Their focus wasn't on me, but it felt like it was.

My heartrate surged, but so did my arousal. And I rocked my hips. Rubbing hard, grinding down into the corner. It was weird, but he wanted me weird.

He wanted me.

I felt my skin prickle again as I used the desk to get myself off. Behind my panties, my flesh grew impossibly slick, and I knew the white fabric was probably going translucent.

Feeling myself getting a little frantic when I could sense how close I was, and how soon, I whimpered, and let my gaze flicker between Eoghan and the meeting across the way.

When I saw he wasn't watching, not at all, his fingers tapping on the keyboard, my mouth worked.

Did he want me to come?

Or didn't he?

I whimpered, "Eoghan?"

He hushed me. "I'm busy."

"B-But..."

"But nothing. I'm busy."

His tone was harder, and that made me more uncertain. Did he want me to get off? He hadn't said the words, hadn't told me to. But I needed it.

Badly.

I shuddered as I ground down on my clit with a force that would normally cause an orgasm, but I could no more stop the outpouring of ecstasy that washed through me than I could stop my heart from taking its next beat.

The cry that escaped me was glorious. I'd done this twice before. Each time it had been hurried and shame filled, and I'd had to be quiet.

Now?

I could be noisy.

I loved being noisy.

My ecstasy had my back arching, passion pounding through me as I recognized this wasn't enough now. I needed more.

I needed his dick.

When I came down from that high, I saw he was watching me. At long last. His focus was off the screen, his gaze glued on me, even if it was narrowed and kind of ferocious—all the sexier for it.

"Take your panties off."

On shaky legs, I moved back, and dropped the underwear to the ground.

"Get back on the desk."

My eyes widened, but I obeyed. The glass was slightly warm, but still cool against my pussy.

"Grind down on it." A slightly squeaky noise escaped me with my obedience, and he murmured, "Look at that dripping cunt." His voice was thick. "Come here, Inessa."

He patted the front of the desk as he pushed away. I got off the desk again, moved, on wobbly legs, around it, and sat in front of him.

"Spread your legs."

I did as he asked, my body burning as he helped put my feet where he wanted them—wide apart, so my legs were spread—and he moved out of the way so everything was right on display out of the window.

Eyes wide and feeling like I was a deer in front of headlights, I barely noticed when his fingers began to trace my nub before they danced down to my slit. I shuddered when two digits thrust in right from the start, and when he arced them up, I fell back onto my elbows even as I kept my gaze glued right on that damn meeting.

All the people had to do was look up, and they'd see me spread, my pussy on display, my man finger fucking me.

I stared blindly ahead as he messed with me, physically and mentally, not stopping until I was creaming so hard, I could feel the juices puddling beneath my butt.

Oh God, I was going to have to sanitize the desk before I left—

"Fuck!" I screamed, my head finally falling back on my neck as he did something, touched something that lit me up like a firework. My shriek might be heard across the Hudson, but fuck if I cared.

I groaned, almost wanting to close my legs, to deny him access, but even as the thought crossed my mind, everything in me rebelled.

Why on Earth would I want this to stop?

The pleasure was agonizing, and it only stopped when he moved in front of me with his dick out, slipped between the tines of the zipper so he was entirely covered except for his cock, and he thrust inside me.

He groaned, but I let out a litany of, "Oh God, oh God, oh God." I didn't care if it was irritating, I just cared that I was full at last.

And he was fucking me.

Hard. Fast. Wet.

I could hear the squelch of my cunt around him as he shoved into me, grinding harder, better than what I could do with the damn desk.

When I screamed my next orgasm?

I hurled myself upward, changing the angle so I knew we were both going cross-eyed, as I slid my arms around his neck and brought our mouths together. As I thrust my tongue into his mouth, fucking him like he was fucking me, he shuddered his orgasm, exploding inside me as I welcomed him where he was always supposed to be —home.

Inside me.

TWENTY-ONE
AOIFE

"JUST DO IT."

My nose wrinkled. "Since when did you get so bossy?"

Watching Finn's eyes widen had me grinning at him. Then they narrowed. "Since when did you get to be such a smartass?"

I snickered. "Marrying you took care of that."

He mock-growled, then nibbled on my shoulder, making me squeal. His arms came around my waist, and I sighed, loving how tightly he held me, how fierce his hold was. Three years on, a shooting, only God knew how many crises, a baby, and now a war—even if we were only on the periphery of it so far—and Finn still made me feel like I was the only woman he saw.

I nuzzled into him, loving his embrace, before I muttered, "She might not want to go."

"So? If she doesn't, she doesn't."

He sounded so blasé about it that I had to grumble, "How would you feel if you went to a Pats' game with Conor or Brennan?"

"Ah. That bad?"

"Yeah. That bad." Considering they were massive Giants fans, and Finn was considered a traitor to his city, state, and country the way the others went on about his allegiance to a New England team, that was the only way I could describe it.

"But you're not asking her out on a date. You both like books," he chivvied. "She liked the list you sent her, didn't she?"

I squirmed around in his hold, which made Jacob squirm too. He was sleeping after having just finished feeding, and because it was Finn and me, we were all a naked pile in the bed, discussing the stupid anxiety I was having over inviting Eoghan's new wife to a book convention I was going to next year.

"What if she doesn't like me?"

His lips twitched until he saw my genuine concern. "Then I'll shoot her."

I huffed. "Then Eoghan will shoot you. My goal is to keep you alive, not get you killed."

Eyes twinkling, he murmured, "Good to know you still want me around."

"You have your uses," I informed him loftily, grinning when he barked out a laugh.

"Glad to hear it." His brows soared high in amusement, but he reiterated, "It isn't a date, just like a friendship thing. She's even worse off than you, darlin'. I mean, let's face it, she had to get Lena in to sort out Winnie." He rolled his eyes. "If she can't get the housekeeper to like her, then none of the other women will."

"You think we'll have to go into lockdown?" I questioned softly, not liking to ask when we didn't speak about business, but I knew what he was talking about.

When war came to our doorsteps, the women were sent off to a massive house that was tucked away. Like a hotel, we all stayed in there together until it was safe to come out again. The men tended to stay at home, but last time, I'd been injured, and Finn had slept with me. Now, I had Jacob, and the prospect of being away from Finn while I had Jacob? Horrible.

Still, he was right. In that situation, Inessa would be worse off.

The women had tolerated me at first, and now I was accepted. Inessa? Wouldn't get that much consideration.

She needed all the friends she could get.

"Maybe," he said eventually, as he stroked his finger over Jacob's dimpled cheek.

I'd thought I'd known what love was when Finn had come into my life like a wrecking ball. But watching Finn look at our son? It magnified the love I felt for him a thousandfold.

If my husband looked at me like I was the only woman in the world for him, he looked at our son like he'd raze the planet to the ground to keep him safe.

"If it happens, will you stay with us?"

"At night?" He sighed. "I don't think I could stay away."

"Good answer," I rasped, pressing my lips to his as I snuggled into him. He propped me up even as he kissed me, his tongue dragging against mine, bringing my body to awareness in a way that it wasn't prepared for. Jacob was only just starting to sleep a little more regularly, so we were both tired all the time, and now was no different, but I could feel the exhaustion weighing us both down.

It was 3AM, for Pete's sake, and we both had early wake up calls in the morning.

Like he knew that, he nipped my bottom lip and muttered, "I'll go put him down."

My heart thumped as he shuffled our baby into his arms, then once he was off the bed, I watched him move over to the cradle that sat at the opposite end of the bedroom. We'd put a little nesting screen around him because I couldn't have sex when he was there, watching us, even if he didn't have a damn clue what we were doing. I actually thought Finn felt the same way, and I was looking forward to the point when I felt comfortable letting Jacob have a nursery.

I was a clingy mom, and I felt no shame in that. None whatsoever.

I knew what was important in this world, and the guys in the other corner were it for me.

When Finn returned, dick swinging, I grinned at him as he climbed back into bed and dragged me into his arms.

"I can ask Lena to watch him tomorrow."

I felt his attention. "You okay with that?"

It would be his first sleepover, and I was terrified, but I wanted my husband, an orgasm, and a full night's sleep. In that order.

"I'll deal." I cleared my throat. "Plus, if Lena asks to look after him any more times, it's going to get ugly."

He snorted. "Baby mad."

"She's waited long enough for a grandchild," I said dryly.

To that, he just let out a long yawn. "Crap, we need to get some sleep then. I refuse to spend the first night he's away with us sleeping the night through."

I snorted, but I kind of agreed too, so I rolled onto my side, sighing when he curved behind me, his arm coming over my belly. Sure, I sucked it in a little, but he smacked my hip and grumbled, "Less of that."

Nose crinkling, I relaxed, then mumbled, "Do you think Inessa really liked me?"

"I do." He sighed. "She needs a friend, love. Now, go to sleep. I have devious plans for you tomorrow night."

I grinned at that, and when he fell asleep within seconds, I knew I wouldn't. I was too nervous. Jen, my best friend, hated reading. She was a math person, and she had her feet firmly on the ground. She didn't believe in romance, thought it was nonsense, but I loved that stuff.

When I'd seen one of my favorite authors was coming to a convention in the Big Apple next year, I'd bought myself a ticket and had intended on going alone. Inessa and I had similar tastes, though, and I'd steered her to Serena Akeroyd's backlist. From her Goodreads account, where we were friends now, she was whizzing through the books, so why wouldn't she want to meet her?

Still, I found it hard making friends, and Inessa had been so watchful at the last Sunday dinner. I couldn't blame her really. The first real meal with Aidan had gone well, but the second? Sure, they'd met before, but on his home turf? Aidan was a true wild card. And each time she attended, he relaxed more and more, so only Christ knew what could come flying out of his mouth. She'd survived thus far, though, which meant she had staying power.

She'd need it. Not just for what was ahead of us, but the O'Donnelly brothers were teddy bears on a Sunday compared to the bitches who were married to the crew. Well, deadly teddy bears. Shit comparison, but still, on lockdown, she probably wouldn't have Eoghan...

We both needed to cement a friendship between us.

Though Finn held me close to him, I managed to grab my phone from the nightstand.

Looking at the convention details, I sucked in a breath as I copied the link, pasted it into a message, and typed.

Me: Inessa, I know this might be a bit weird, but I'm going to this convention next year. Would you like to go with me? No worries if you don't want to, but it would be really cool to go with someone who'd enjoy it too. Hope you're doing okay, Aoife <3

When I pressed send, I sighed, glad I'd sent it. She was a lot younger than me, but she was sweet, and I liked Eoghan around her. I wanted to be friends because I loved how close-knit the family was, and never wanted the brothers to be torn apart by their women.

Pushing my phone under the pillow, I sighed and settled into my husband's arms to sleep.

The next morning, I grinned when, upon reaching for my phone, I saw her text.

Inessa: Are you kidding me? I'd love to go! I can't wait! Just bought a ticket. <3 <3 <3 Thank you for thinking of me!!

"Should I be jealous?" Finn's amused voice told me he was reading the text over my shoulder.

"She said yes."

"Of course she did," he mumbled, pressing a kiss to my shoulder. When his hands moved over my body, slipping down between my legs, I tensed a little. Not because I didn't want him, but because we had to get up, I needed to open the bakery, he had to get to work, but then his fingers started moving, he began teasing me, and I forgot everything else as he muttered thickly, "Just an appetizer to build up to tonight."

And who was I to protest?

TWENTY-TWO
EOGHAN
A FEW DAYS LATER

"WHAT?" I snarled down the line.

Inessa's legs were spread wide, her pussy was on display, and my dick had just been inside her.

Until the fucking phone rang.

Most people might be able to ignore a phone call, but in my line of work, and with the situation brewing between the Italians and Bratva, ignoring my cell wasn't something I could do right now.

God.

Damn.

It.

Sliding a hand over Inessa's bubble butt, moving my fingers between her thighs to keep her locked and loaded, I snarled some more when Declan muttered, "We have a problem."

"Yeah, I have a problem too."

He grunted. "A big one."

"Spill." I'd blow my top—and not in the way I'd anticipated ten minutes ago—if he said I had to get on a fucking flight.

"Your place is the nearest to the..."

My building was in Sugar Hill, just a drive across the Macomb Dam Bridge to the Yankee Stadium.

Yeah, I'd had my family build my home here, with a fucking killer view of the stadium.

It was the least Da could give me after all the fucking money I'd earned him along the way.

Wondering why Dec had petered off, I butted in, "Dec? What the fuck?"

"Eagle Eyes has been kidnapped by the *Famiglia*."

Whatever I'd expected him to say, it wasn't that.

No guilt filled me. Even if his abduction had to be tied to my hit on Vasov. "One less off the streets, I figure. Competition is a bitch in our market—"

A strangled sound came from Dec. "Yeah, well, this isn't ideal."

"Why not?" I leaned over, pressed a kiss to the delicious curve of my wife's ass, and whispered, "Sweetheart, I'm sorry."

She flung herself over, tits quivering, legs a little spread, and I almost groaned. The move wasn't to entice, she didn't even pout, if anything, she looked concerned which told me she could hear every word Dec said.

Like any well-bred woman in the life, she knew that business took precedence, and that calls that interrupted fucking, that a man willingly let interrupt said fucking, were serious shit.

Fuck, she was perfect, and because she was, that made me resent this goddamn phone call all the more.

As she dragged the sheet over her body to cover up, I played tug of war with her, barely stopping myself from laughing when she glowered at me and wafted her hands as if to say, 'Go on, get.'

Like I'd fucking listen.

What bewildered the shit out of me was how I was okay with her knowing what was being said between my brother and me. Any other bitch, and I'd have moved into another room. Inessa? I just wanted to keep looking at her pretty pussy while I talked business.

"You heard of the Hell's Rebels?"

"MC based in..." My brow puckered as I tried to recall where I'd heard of them. "Texas."

"Look at you, forgetting a conversation."

I rolled my eyes. "I hate MCs, you know that."

"I know why you do too. They're soldiers. Just with no rules."

That had me scowling. "That's the direct opposite of the definition of a soldier. You just described a group of tyrants—"

"Let's not split hairs because your memory's failing you. Is Inessa sucking it out of you?"

"Fuck you," I growled, making him laugh. "Get on with it."

So she could go back to sucking something out of me.

"Eagle Eyes isn't attached to the *Famiglia*. He's a gun for hire."

My brows lifted at that. "So the rumors were bullshit."

"All the best rumors are. Still, it's clear the Bratva heard that rumor and, as planned, are blaming the Italians for the hit on their Pakhan."

I rubbed a hand over my chin, grimacing at the scent of Inessa all over my fingers. Fuck, I wanted to eat her pussy so badly... "There's a reason you're telling me shit I already know, so, I repeat, get on with it."

"Long story short, Aela O'Neill has a position in Providence at the Rhode Island School of Design."

My brows lifted at that particular blast from the past. Aela and Dec's old love had been best buds. When Deirdre had been a stupid cunt and gotten herself killed, Aela and Dec had a massive falling out that had seen Aela leaving our neighborhood and heading for the mother country.

"She's a professor?"

"Apparently." He sighed, but the news came as a surprise. Aela had been part rebel, anti-establishment, and all that shit. A professor? Huh. "The daughter of the Prez of the Hell's Rebels is taking one of her classes. She approached Aela—"

"With violence?" I barked, twisting away from Inessa, who I knew was reading my facial expressions.

"No. Apparently Aela has an Acuig tattoo on her wrist."

My brows lifted at that. "Why? She was never a foot soldier."

"I don't know." And that, right there, was a fucking lie. But I let it drop. "You know how distinctive the tattoos are. This Amaryllis kid saw it and approached her, and asked her for her help, thinking she was in the life."

"And she got in touch with you?"

"Yeah. She did."

"And now someone's driving toward my apartment—"

"Amaryllis and her protective detail, I think."

"Who's Eagle Eyes to Amaryllis? Boyfriend?" I guessed.

"Seems so. He was taken eight hours ago—"

"We're going to find him, aren't we?"

"Her daddy, the Prez, is offering big bucks to retrieve him."

"Since when were we swayed by big bucks?"

"Shit, man, Inessa really has fried your cock off. The Rebels produce ghost guns. Top whack shit. They're not affiliated."

"Until now?" I predicted.

"Exactly," Dec said, satisfaction in his words.

"For how long?"

"Ten years."

"That's how much Eagle Eyes means to them?" I questioned.

"Apparently."

That didn't make any sense, but then also, I knew what people would do for their kids. The lengths they'd go through to keep them safe and happy—which meant the Prez's kid was loved, and that Eagle Eyes was a lucky fucker to be that bitch's man.

I stared over at the Yankee Stadium, and muttered, "We don't have long. If they took him today, he'll be lucky to be alive."

"That's why they're racing like a bat out of hell to get to you."

"You know where Eagle Eyes is being held?"

"Had chatter—Brennan just confirmed it. They're at their compound on the docks."

"Fucking hate that place."

My mutter had Declan snorting. "Yeah. Me too."

His reasoning was different than mine. He had bad memories. Me? I just hated the fucking smell.

"I'll get dressed," I said on a huff.

"Aren't you generous?" he retorted with a laugh. "I'll be there in twenty. I have to crack the armory."

"This is sanctioned by Da, isn't it?"

"Like the original hit was, you mean?" he snarked.

"Fuck you. You and I both know you told Da before I shot Vasov."

He laughed. "Been saving your ass for a long time, bud. Anyway, Da thought it was amusing—"

"Thought he would, to be honest."

"Yeah, well, he likes the sound of us having our own personal weapons. He's already coming up with ideas for unique builds."

"Just what we need—weapons built to Da's specs."

Declan fell silent. "Fuck. I never thought about that."

My lips twitched at the horror in his voice, but I just muttered, "Get here ASAP. Hate having strangers in my place."

"Be there soon."

We disconnected the line, and I turned back to Inessa. Though she was a sight for sore eyes, her hair a tumbled mess, thanks to us writhing all over the bed, her eyes were big in her pale face.

Knowing where her head was at, I immediately said, "Not your fault, sweetheart."

She bit her lip. "Someone else has gotten hurt."

I shrugged. "What did I tell you?"

"That's what people do." Her whisper didn't sound convincing, and I couldn't blame her.

So, instead of getting dressed, which I really needed to do, I crawled onto the bed and settled myself at the headboard. Hauling her into my side, I kissed the crown of her head, and muttered, "I already told you, shit's been brewing for a while."

"The blood is on my hands. You'd never have done anything if—"

"If what? You didn't do shit. Your father is the one who put his hands on you, after I warned him. This is on your father's head. Not yours. And let's face it, his soul is already fucked—"

"If his is, that means yours is too," she whispered, and for some reason, that had her turning her face into me, her nose burrowing into my ribcage.

I might have been offended about the whole 'my soul being in hell already' shit, but I wasn't. Mostly because I didn't believe in that stuff, and I hadn't thought Inessa did either.

But I could feel the moisture leaking from her eyes, brushing up against my skin.

"Hey, what's this?" I rasped, not liking her crying.

Her arm slipped over my waist, and she hugged me tight. "I don't want you to go to hell."

Because she couldn't see me, my lips curved. "I might not. I take out a lot of bad people. Maybe that gives me some cosmic balance," I reassured her.

"I don't think God works that way," she muttered.

I wasn't sure how God worked, and I didn't really give a damn. If fifteen years of Sunday school and a lifetime of being forced to go to church hadn't explained shit to me, I wasn't sure how she could.

"Will you go to confession after?"

I frowned. "I already go."

"I know you. You won't say anything about what you really do."

That she'd figured that out told me she knew me pretty well for someone who'd only been my wife for just under four weeks.

"Maybe if you confess, you won't go to hell."

I had to smile. "If it makes you feel better, I'll confess."

"You're just saying that to appease me," she whispered sadly.

I had been, but her words had me reaching for her, tucking my fingers beneath her chin as I urged her to look at me. When she did, those luminous green eyes of hers stole my fucking heart.

"Why'd you care about whether my soul goes to hell or not?"

Her lips trembled. "N-Never mind."

"Nuh-uh," I countered, not letting her look away. "Why, Inessa?"

The heat that arced between us when our gazes collided once more scorched me, razed me down to the fucking ground until I wasn't a Five Pointer, wasn't a veteran of too many battles to count, wasn't a Catholic, wasn't a sniper, wasn't anything other than one thing—a man.

My heart pounded.

Her man.

I stared at her, my brow puckering as the link seemed to brand itself into me.

"I don't want to be in heaven without you," she rasped, her voice lower than usual, a husky whisper that made every nerve ending in my body come to life.

I hadn't expected her to say that—how could I?

My jaw tensed though, a welter of...God, I didn't even know what. Feelings? Sensations? They whirled through me, left me feeling like I'd been thrown in an industrial washing machine and had been put on deep spin mode.

"I'll go to confession."

Four words, pathetic really, in the face of what we'd just shared, but they were all I could think to say.

It seemed to be enough.

She sagged into me. "Thank you."

My lips wanted to twitch into a smile, but I knew this wasn't funny. She meant it.

And fuck if I didn't too.

TWENTY-THREE
INESSA

THE BUZZER DISTURBED US BOTH. Eoghan leaped off the bed, leaving things mostly unspoken between us. I got it. I did. But still, it felt like he and I had never been so close as we were at that moment, and I only hoped we'd reach that point once more.

As I quickly shrugged on some skinny jeans and a thin Ralph Lauren sweater that was a hell of a lot brighter than my current mood —vivid magenta—I wandered out into the hall to see Eoghan, now dressed in jeans and a tee, waiting at the elevator. He was barefoot, and he was pretty much bouncing on his toes.

I stared at them, amused to think he was about to talk business barefoot.

The elevator doors whirled open, revealing Declan, a woman I didn't know who was glowering at him, and then another woman, more my age, with two bikers in their twenties clustered at her side.

What had I overheard on the phone?

Something about the daughter of the Hell's Rebels' Prez bringing security with her?

Yeah, no chance. They were more than security. Every inch of them screamed over-protective, but it had nothing to do with an edict from their boss.

There was love there.

I saw it in a flash.

My gaze connected with the girl's, and deep in her eyes, there was a misery and a grief so terrifying, it suffocated me for a second.

I felt her pain, felt it so rawly, that I knew, even though she was trying, she thought her man—her other man—was dead.

Unable to stop myself, I cast Eoghan a glance. He was mine, whether he knew it or not, and the prospect of him dying tonight, of this mission going awry, had everything inside me going haywire.

I wanted to cling to him, even as I knew I had to back off. This was business. Feelings couldn't get involved, but there was no way in hell I could let him leave this apartment without trying to show him something of the chaos inside me.

A chaos the other woman shared.

"Been a long time, Aela," Eoghan rumbled, his gaze drifting over the oldest woman in the room. Saying that, she was only in her late twenties, early thirties maybe, and she was gorgeous with an abundance of bright blue hair that gleamed in the hall light like it had glitter in it.

The blue matched her eyes, and the bright red paint on her lips was discordant, but it suited her. She had delicate golden studs all the way down her ear and along to her earlobe, and even though I knew she was Irish from her name, there was something faintly exotic about her. The almond eyes that were heavy on liner, then the scrolling tattoos on her wrist that were like a living bracelet, Acuig swirling through the tatt... She reminded me of Jasmine from *Aladdin*. Except with blue hair instead of black.

She shot Eoghan a smile. "Too long, Eoghan. You look well." She cut me a look too. "Married. Never thought I'd see the day."

"Da agreed, decided to fix things for me," he said ruefully, and before I could get annoyed at being talked about like I wasn't even here, he twisted and held out his hand for me. When his arm slipped over my shoulder, curving me into him, I hesitantly placed my fingers on his belly even as I smiled at Aela.

Eoghan's small squeeze filled me with a confidence I hadn't known I'd been lacking, and I greeted her, "It's a pleasure to meet an old friend of Eoghan's—"

Declan snorted at that. "They weren't friends."

His harsh voice had my brows rising. Declan had always been kind to me, he'd been the one I'd spent the most time with before my wedding. I knew he'd felt sorry for me. Eoghan's refusal to meet me before the day of the ceremony had hurt at first, then I'd started getting pissed, but Declan had always cheered me up on the occasions where we'd been pushed together.

There'd even been times where I wished he was the one I was going to marry, but this Declan was different from *that* Declan.

I frowned at him, and had we not had company, I'd have asked him if he was well.

At his harsh tone, Aela changed. It was like something from a movie about witches. Ice overtook her. Freezing her in place. She turned brittle, enough that she looked like she could snap.

I wanted to smack Declan for that, but instead, I glowered at him. His stern expression didn't give me any mercy though. Eoghan's second squeeze had me peering up at him, but what I saw there told me to back off.

Aela and Declan evidently had a history together, and that was crystal clear.

"Look, this reunion is great and all, but we need to move. Fuck knows how much longer Ink has."

The youngest guy in the room started jangling a set of keys as he snarled the words at us. He definitely had brass balls, because I wouldn't have interrupted that conversation, not when Declan was throwing visual knives at Aela.

"He's right," Eoghan agreed calmly.

Dec growled, "Finn's on his way with Aoife. Should be five minutes, then we can head off. Brennan is already down at the docks, and he has two lieutenants and five soldiers on their way. We should be rendezvousing in the next forty minutes."

The young woman bit her lip, and because I felt for her, I reached out and soothed, "Don't worry. Eoghan never lets people down."

Our eyes caught and held. "I hope that's true."

"He's never disappointed me." Guilt rammed me in the gut when I thought about how her man was suffering because of me, because of how Eoghan hadn't let me down.

"I'm Amaryllis," she whispered. "He's Keys, and that's Saint."

"I'm Inessa." I met the weary gazes of the men, too, as I said, "Pleasure to meet you—I just wish it was under different circumstances."

"You and me both, Inessa." She blew out a breath and began to rub her hands up and down her arms. "I'm not even sure if he's still alive."

The pain in her voice hurt me on a visceral level, but the kid jangling the keys squeezed his arm around her, mimicking Eoghan's hold on me. "Ink's a tough son of a bitch, Ama. You know that, babe."

"I do, Keys, but he's already been through so much." She nibbled her bottom lip, and I knew she was seconds away from tears.

Clearing my throat, I muttered, "Come on, let's take a seat. I think it's going to be a long night."

I had no idea how true that would be.

Within ten minutes, Aoife, Jacob, and Finn were shuffling into the apartment, a yawning Conor after them. The second Aoife and Jacob were deposited safely in the living room, the guys started to get together to leave.

Before they could, I grabbed Eoghan, who'd gone into the bedroom to get some boots, and the moment the bedroom door closed, I hauled my arms around his waist and squeezed tightly.

"Hey, what's this?" he rumbled, even as he squeezed me back.

I didn't have the guts to say it out loud. Didn't have the guts to say another word, so I just squeezed him, and as I muttered, "Stay safe. For me," I silently added, *I think I love you.*

Please.

Don't leave me.

He tensed a little, but he pressed a kiss to my temple. "I probably won't be going into the warehouse," he said softly. "My place is usually on a rooftop somewhere."

"I gathered. Still...take care. For me."

"I will."

Not wanting to cling or embarrass him, I let go of him, and before he could say another word, I whirled away and returned to the living room.

Aoife was nursing a fussing Jacob and staring daggers at Finn, who had hunched shoulders.

"What the fuck are you and Conor going to be able to do out there?" she snapped. "You're not soldiers anymore. You fire computers up, not guns."

"I can help, but Finn, she's right. You should stay here."

Finn scowled at his wife, then at Conor. "I can help."

"Yeah, you can," Eoghan rumbled behind me. "Stay here and keep the women safe."

Declan cut Finn a look. "That's why I wanted you armed. You're not coming with us."

Wondering what had triggered this argument, I murmured, "Finn?"

He shot me a glare, and it was loaded with defiance. "What?"

"Aoife needs you, Jacob does too." I smiled. "There are plenty of other moments where you can be GI Joe, but tonight isn't one of them."

Eoghan snorted. "You never were a foot soldier anyway."

"I fucking was," Finn grumbled, but the tension in his shoulders had leached out some.

"For what? Two months?" Declan chided, but he shot me a grateful look.

"Two years, pricks. You know Aidan's going to be pissed about not being included too—"

"You old fucks can't help out on the streets. Not with—" I got the feeling Eoghan was glaring at him because Declan cleared his throat. "Never mind. Eoghan, we need to get going." He glanced at the guys with Amaryllis. "You coming with?"

"Of course."

Amaryllis tensed, but I figured she knew that getting her men to stay behind wasn't going to happen.

She surprised me by reaching onto tiptoes and kissing the elder of the guys with a passion that was definitely not fraternal. Before us all, she kissed the other kid too, the one with the keys, hence the name I guessed, and muttered, "You come back to me safe."

"We'll bring him home to you, Ama," the youngest one whispered, even as the elder sandwiched her between the pair of them.

Surprised at the PDA and wondering what that actually felt like, my eyes widened. Eoghan caught my glance and laughed a little. As he ducked down to kiss me too, he whispered, "Don't get any ideas," and for the first time, I realized he was truly joking.

Jesus, how dangerous was tonight going to be if he could actually joke around?

I darted up on tiptoe too, and kissed him properly, before breathlessly whispering, "We need to finish what we started tonight," as I pulled back.

His eyes darkened, the pupils turning to pinpricks. His growl was deep and heavy, enough to rumble through my body like an earthquake.

"You got it," he rasped, before he turned abruptly away.

His arms were bunched as he pressed the button to the elevators, and as they opened, he walked in. Our eyes remained linked as Declan and Conor followed him, with Ama's two men at their sides.

I only let go of the link when the doors shut, and Finn, Aoife, Amaryllis, Aela, and I were left alone in an uncomfortable silence.

Aela cleared her throat, and I twisted to see she'd moved behind me, and as she shot out her hand, I realized she wanted to shake mine.

"Declan was being a prick, as usual. But I'm Aela O'Neill."

I blinked at her. "Pleasure."

Her head tilted to the side. "You love him?"

My heart thumped in my chest. "Well, I mean, I think so."

Her lips pursed. "I'd warn you off him, but Eoghan's one of the best. He always did have a good heart."

"You've known him a long time?"

"Since we were kids. I was in the same class as Declan. My best friend and him were sweethearts." Her smile was pained, and I read into it easily.

"You loved him too?"

"I did. It was stupid. Just a crush, but I never could let go of it."

"Why was he so mean to you?"

"That's a long story." She blew out a breath. "I just wanted to tell you that Eoghan's a good man. Even if…"

"Even if, what?"

"He looks a lot harder than he used to be, but people don't change that much." Her mouth tightened, and I got the feeling she was talking more about Declan than she was Eoghan. She seemed to shake off her thoughts by running a hand through her hair. "I need to make a call. Is there somewhere I can talk privately?"

"Of course. There's a bedroom behind the second door in the hall."

She smiled her thanks at me before she followed my directions.

Turning my focus to the others, I stepped over to Amaryllis, and asked, "Can I get you something to drink?"

A laugh escaped her, and I wasn't surprised it sounded a little crazed. "Do you have a few gallons of tequila that will make this night a blur?"

"I think we might," I muttered, thinking about the liquor cupboard in the kitchen.

"I wouldn't bother," Finn stated calmly. "This won't take long."

There was tension in his shoulders from earlier, and I got that his pride was pricked, but he really did have different priorities now.

In my world, it didn't matter if a man had a newborn and was about to go into danger. But this world was different.

I knew it.

From the bottom to the top of the ladder, I knew the Five Points were family oriented.

I stared at Aoife, who was gnawing on her bottom lip as she watched her husband, whose back was to us, his gaze out on the city ahead.

She'd taken a seat in the armchair and was slumped into it as Jacob continued feeding.

I eyed the sight with soft eyes, never having seen it before. That kind of thing went down behind closed doors, but I'd seen her do it at Lena's, albeit, that had been in the kitchen when it was just the women around.

It was in my nature to make things better, to soften things, even if, of late, I'd been a tad more aggressive than usual, and the urge to go over to Finn and try to smooth things over was fierce. But I also knew that where a man and his pride were concerned, nothing would soothe it.

Except maybe a blowjob.

And I wasn't that willing to make peace in my living room, I thought with an inner laugh.

Maybe it was stupid, but I moved over to Aoife, and said, "We have another bedroom."

Her eyes flared as she got my meaning before she snorted out a laugh. "I don't think he's in the mood."

"Aren't men always?" I asked, with a frown.

She tilted her head to the side. "No."

I thought about all the things I'd seen as a kid, on nights such as this...how Mama had dragged Papa away, and we knew not to disturb them.

Tugging at my bottom lip, I just shrugged. "The offer is there."

"Thank you." She grabbed my hand. "Do you have decaf coffee?"

The plea was urgent, and I chuckled. "Yeah, we do."

She blew out a relieved breath. "I was awake when we got the call, Jacob needed feeding, but God, I'm tired."

"You can use the bedroom for rest too," I said dryly.

"Thanks, but there'll be no sleep tonight."

"Has this happened before?" I asked curiously.

"Not often. Maybe twice since I've met Finn. He went off last time and—"

When she bit her lip, I patted her arm. "He got hurt?"

"Yeah. Stray bullet. He was lucky." She squeezed Jacob. "I want him to know his dad."

"Of course you do. Nothing wrong with that."

Aoife huffed. "You'd never tell. You'd think I asked him for a divorce!"

When she glared at her husband's back, I patted her arm again. "I'll get you that coffee."

"Thanks, Inessa. I appreciate that."

With a shrug, I drifted off, wishing now was the time to talk about the convention we were planning on going to, but life was on hold for the moment. It would stay that way until the family was back together again.

"Want to come with me?" I asked Amaryllis, feeling for her, more than she would probably ever know.

She blinked and peered around the room like she hadn't even known she was here, with strangers.

I grabbed her hand and tugged her along to the kitchen, recognizing the signs of someone in deep shock.

"If Finn says it won't take long, it won't."

My attempt at reassurance had tears prickling her eyes, turning them a soft pink. She really was beautiful. All delicate and pretty. We were of a similar build, but she seemed to be more fragile somehow. On her hands, there were flecks of paint, same in the grooves on her nails.

"I-I can't sleep without him," she whispered.

The statement surprised me. "You can't?"

She shook her head. "No."

I wasn't really sure what to say to that, so I murmured, "They're going to get him back."

"You don't know that."

"No, I don't, but I know they'll do their best."

"What good is their best if he's already dead?" she whispered brokenly.

Because I felt guilty and ashamed and a little lost, I did what I wouldn't ordinarily do—I reached for her and slipped my arms around her waist, hugging her.

I knew, in this situation, that was what I'd need.

"You'll sleep again. He'll be okay. He might be hurt, but as long as he's alive, hurt can be fixed."

She tensed, then abruptly sank into me, to the point where I almost staggered back in surprise at her weight as she released all the terror in a heart that was no longer hers, but that belonged with the man who'd been taken by the *Famiglia*.

And because, for the first time in my life I knew what it felt like for your heart to be with someone else, to have given it to another, I hugged her tightly, trying to keep her together until Eoghan could bring her man back home.

TWENTY-FOUR
BRENNAN

THE ITALIAN COMPOUND on the docks was only a mile away, but there were more guards between us than there was distance.

Making our way there had been an effort in torture, but though I lived for this shit, I had to admit concern was riding me. We couldn't use cars, not without triggering their cameras, and sneaking through alleys at this time of night was like asking for nightmares. Well, for a regular person. For someone like me, the horrors that went down in the shadows were my trade.

With every yard we breached of their territory, awareness hit me. The *Famiglia* were in an all-out war with the Bratva, so they were bound to be armed to the max.

Getting in and out of this facility, even though I had recon info from one of our rats that Eagle Eyes was being stored in a small outhouse just off the main compound, was going to be hard as fuck.

Eoghan was already situated a few buildings across the way, and every now and then, I heard the telltale sound of his rifle firing.

Knowing him as well as I did, I had to figure that the fucker was picking off the right Italian cunts in the most strategic of areas.

With Conor in all our ears, I heard him mutter, "I'm into the mainframe. Just give me five minutes to take down the alarms."

I rolled my eyes, but I didn't reply. I knew he'd go as fast as he could without me giving him shit, even if giving him shit was usually what I did best.

I was hard on all my brothers for a reason—someone had to be. Someone had to be the buffer between my da and them. Aidan was too busy butting heads with him to see to our baby brothers, but I wasn't.

Everyone had their place in their family, and mine was as the protector. That the fuckers didn't know it didn't matter.

I stretched my shoulders, even as I rubbed the small of my back. Getting old sucked. Ten years ago, I'd have been able to crouch here for a fucking lifetime. As it was, ten minutes longer and I'd probably have a fucking seizure.

I mean, I wasn't ancient. Only thirty-nine, but Christ, the lives we led weren't exactly easy on the body. Every morning, I woke up well aware of all the shit I'd gotten into in my years, thanks to the painful reminders as gunshot wounds and scars from stabbings made themselves known.

At the moment, it was the place at my hip where someone had sliced into me, not deep enough to fuck with my organs, but to fuck with the muscles.

Maybe I was too old for this shit, but you were only too old when you were dead. Da would be here, heading the raid if he could, and if Ma wouldn't slay him first. In our world, the upper ranks never got soft. Even Finn and Conor, who rode desks, were men I'd want at my back in a gunfight. I knew Finn's pride would be pricking at being left out, Aidan's too, but Finn had a kid and Aidan was fucked on whatever his doctor was overprescribing him...

Our men were used to leadership actually fucking leading, especially out in the field, so I headed the small team, because after Eoghan, I was the one most at ease with this shit. I'd led enough raids to know how they worked, and to know that we were fucked if Conor couldn't mess with their security systems and Eoghan wasn't there, picking off soldiers from his position in his nest.

At my side, there was a twenty-foot tall brick wall topped with glass and barbed wire, behind it, there was the outhouse where Eagle Eyes was being stored. At the other side of the compound, waiting to rush in if we needed them, there were three more soldiers, and the two Hell's Rebels bikers who I wanted as far away from the action as possible—dragging emotion into this shit was only going to make things a thousand times harder.

Just around the corner from where me, Declan, and a lieutenant, Jensen, were waiting, there was a small side entrance that Conor had to hack to find the code to enter.

That was the delay.

"Why's he taking so long?"

I glared at nothing, not even bothering to turn around to snarl at Declan.

I wasn't sure what was riding him tonight. He'd been on edge ever since he'd come into my office at the docks twenty minutes ago, and that wasn't Declan. He was usually calm, and then when shit went down, buzzed. When he was in the zone, he could shoot cleaner than even Eoghan, which was a miracle in itself because I'd never come across anyone with my baby brother's accuracy.

"What the fuck is wrong with you?" I muttered. "Drank too much caffeine?"

"He's got a hard-on for Aela."

Eoghan's voice surprised me, because he tended to stay quiet during these raids.

"Fuck you, Eoghan."

My lips twitched. Aela was one woman who Declan had under his skin. I wasn't sure why he fought it. They were far more suited for one another than Declan and Deirdre had been. Still, there was no pulling the wool from over his eyes. The fucker would think what he wanted to.

"Why's Aela here?" I asked, instead of telling him to get his head out of his ass.

"Apparently, she has an Acuig tatt on her wrist. The Hell's Rebel girl recognized it and asked for help."

My brows lifted at that. "She has an Acuig tattoo?"

"Yeah," Declan muttered, and somehow, I knew this wasn't the first time he'd heard about this.

My brow puckered as I tried to figure out what the fuck was with him, then Conor muttered, "Okay, the code is 87745. You need to get in there fast. The main compound will get an alert in three minutes that there's been an opening in their system."

"Three minutes?" I grinned. "That's a fucking lifetime." Surging up onto my feet, I ran to the entrance, secure in the knowledge that Eoghan and Conor had my back.

It was my place, right at the front of the line, and I owned it.

Inputting the code, I raised my gun, even as I sucked in a quick breath to calm myself, then pushed inside.

Having seen the compound's interior a few times, thanks to a satellite Conor had hacked once, I knew where I was.

To the right, just across a large, asphalted drive that was lined with crates and trucks that were being loaded up with fuck knew what, I knew the main workforce was on a break.

That was why we were breaching their lines now.

I moved toward the outhouse, aware that the guards here would either be higher or fewer in number, dependent on the threat they believed Eagle Eyes carried.

As I stepped down a gravel-lined path, I pulled a face at the crunch, aware that was probably an early, albeit basic, alarm system.

Within seconds, my fears were realized. But Eoghan was there. Three pops and the guards crumpled. I ran over to one, Declan and Jensen moving to the others. We swept their weapons away, and I grabbed the guy's earpiece, untucking it from the folds of his suit as quickly as I could, and palming the set of keys he carried too.

With that in place, and hearing nothing untoward as the guards back at HQ bitched about their bosses and how many had already died in the war with the Bratva, I surged forward toward the outhouse.

It was brick built, a little ratty, and tucked into the corner like it was an afterthought, but I knew it was a common place for them to store their dead. Or soon to be dead.

A few more bullets sounded, making me aware that Eoghan had my back. Muttering, "Thanks, *deartháir*," I carried on, running with the guard's AK-47 in my hand as I smashed my back into the side wall. There was a small window, and peering in, I saw it was empty except for Eagle Eyes, who was in the middle of the space.

I wasn't altogether surprised by the sight of him, even though I knew he was fucked if we didn't get him help quickly.

"Alert Pritchett," I muttered, referring to our med guy. "We need the ER set up."

"Fuck. He's bad?"

Declan peered through the window. "Shit," he hissed.

Eagle Eyes was tied to a chair, and his head was pulled back so his face was directly under the lamp overhead. It was close enough that he had to feel the heat from the bulb, but if he could sleep, he was a better man than me.

His mouth and nose were taped up, and there was the tiniest slit for air to get in. And they'd done something to his head to keep it arced back and his eyes wide open.

His body was a mass of blood. It covered him to the point where I didn't even know where his wounds were.

"Shit," I grumbled, aware I was going to ruin my favorite fucking boots because there was no fucking way that shit wasn't about to coat every inch of me.

"We need a vehicle," Declan stated, and he was right.

"Make it two to be on the safe side, C."

I moved toward the door, glad I'd grabbed the keys from the guard I'd searched earlier when I found it locked.

The second it was open, Eagle Eyes tensed, and that gave me a clue he was alive.

I'd seen that he was naked from outside, and I really didn't want to fucking know why that was.

"We're friends," I called out softly, running forward to start helping the poor bastard.

A quick scan around told me we were alone, but there were some corpses stacked on top of each other on the floor at the sides.

I fucking hated the Italians.

They said we were scum, but our people had burials. We gave a fuck. The men in the corner were their own. I knew some of their faces, even if they were slack from the peace of death.

That they could treat their dead like that said a lot about them—they were the scum. Not us, but that was neither here nor there. Not at the moment.

Knowing we were safe, I rushed over to him, and said, "I'm going to loosen the tape on your mouth. It's going to hurt." He was already in a world of hurt, but fuck, I had to warn him, didn't I?

He grunted, and I quickly tugged at the tape, which was slippery with sweat, blood, and only fuck knew what.

Yeah, this outfit had to go in the trash.

Ripping it off, I was impressed that he only managed to grunt once, but he sucked in a deep breath before asking, "Who are you?"

That he sounded aware had my brows rising. From the level of blood loss, I'd thought he'd be unconscious.

"Five Points."

Declan and I shared a look as we both got to work. Jensen cut away at the tape tying Eagle Eyes' feet to the stool, even as we hacked at the duct tape they'd taped to his hair and forehead and had tied around the stool leg at the back, which kept his head forced in that direction.

I'd seen worse torture victims, but they were usually dead by this point.

"Where are you hurt?" I demanded.

"Gut wound. Sliced and diced me. Nearly cut off my fucking cock, the bastards."

Declan gagged. "Did they succeed?"

Eagle Eyes snorted. "You tell me. But no. They didn't. I think they were heading for their break."

"Fucking *Famiglia*," I rumbled. "Always on the clock."

The sniper grunted, "Well, you won't hear me complaining about that."

"How are you lucid?" Declan questioned.

"I'm a veteran. Was in Kembesh." Eoghan's hiss told me he'd heard, and that the battle in Afghanistan had been a motherfucker. "Seen worse, done worse, been in worse states." He blew out a breath. "I'd really appreciate getting that fucking light out of my eyes though."

The lamp hung low, so I pushed it away by moving my body into it.

He released a sigh. "That probably fucked with my vision."

"Can you see?"

"At the moment, I can only see the light. I tried to close my eyes some, but the tape had no give to it."

Fuck if that wasn't an understatement.

When he was finally free of all the duct tape, Conor muttered, "Eighty seconds."

"Shit."

Declan's declaration said it all.

"Eagle Eyes, this is going to fucking hurt, but I'm going to have to—"

"I get it. I'd help, but they broke my feet."

Goddammit.

I stared at the chair, wondering if it was easier to just heft the chair and carry him that way, but would that take longer?

No time to think, I moved around, shoved my shoulder into his gut, and hoisted him over it.

His cry of pain had me grimacing, but I managed to balance myself with his weight on me.

"Movement by the main compound," Eoghan stated, his voice clinical as hell, his control reined in once more.

Pops sounded, but I heard activity humming to life like the Italians had finally realized something wasn't right, and in my car, I heard sharp muttering as the bees began to buzz.

Acclimating to my new balance, I ground out, "Declan, Jensen, move."

I should have expected it.

Jensen moved out the door first, gun raised, but it was too late.

Declan was at his back, and the bullets that tore through a fucking good lieutenant slammed into my baby brother.

Even as terror filled me, fucking fury overwhelmed it.

I heard the pops, knew Eoghan had gotten there, but it was too fucking late.

"Need back up," I said calmly, even as I kept my eyes trained on Declan all the while.

He grimaced, his hand coming up to cover his chest, and the damage was...

Fuck.

"Need. Back. Up," I snarled.

I heard boots, quickly looked, saw it was our men and the bikers, and watched as Kilkenny hauled my brother onto his shoulder like I had Eagle Eyes, and McNamara grabbed Jensen even though it was too late for him—we never left a man behind.

"He okay?" Eagle Eyes asked softly, knowing something had gone down.

"One dead, my brother was hit."

My voice sounded calm, too calm. I was anything but.

Inside, the panic was clawing at me, and the horror at letting my baby bro get fucking hurt on my watch was starting to overrun my senses.

But I didn't have time to let it get to me. I was in enemy territory.

"Ink," one of the brothers rasped.

"Keys? Get the fuck out of here. Now!" the guy barked, sounding way too put together to be believed.

"Forty seconds until things get really FUBAR," Conor muttered, though I could hear the tension in his voice too.

The bikers took off, their boots pounding into the concrete as I surged forward, running flat out, aware the others were doing the same.

As we made it out, I felt Eagle Eyes reach for something, and was stunned when I heard the blast of a gun and recognized he'd pulled the weapon from my waistband.

He also slammed the outer door shut behind him, making him a very useful hostage victim.

The fuck? In his state? Jesus.

As I ran around the corner where we'd hidden earlier, I saw two cars there waiting. The first had McNamara and Jensen in it, the bikers too, the second had Conor in the passenger seat, and Hutchins, a soldier, behind the wheel. I shoved Eagle Eyes in, he shuffled next to Declan, and the second I could shut the door behind me, Hutchins took off.

As we spun out of the alley, gunshots flew wild, and I was fucking grateful for the license plates on the vehicles—Bratva owned and Mob stolen.

As we raced out of there, bullets flying, I turned to my baby bro and saw his eyes were closed.

My fists furled into tight balls in my lap, and I saw Conor looking at me over his shoulder.

"Get us to the ER," I grated out, and Hutchins, being the smart fucker he was, obeyed and drove twice over the speed limits.

TWENTY-FIVE
EOGHAN

THE SECOND I COULD, I moved away from my nest, packed up, and hurried the fuck out of the apartment building whose roof I'd hijacked for my own purposes.

No one saw me, but then, this wasn't my first rodeo. As I slipped into my car, my heart pounded like I was tripping.

My phone pinged, and I saw the address of the makeshift ER Conor sent me, set it on my GPS, and got the fuck out of dodge.

I made the twenty-minute journey in ten, and by the time I was pulling up outside a Points' owned warehouse, I didn't give a fuck about my car—I left the doors open as I slammed out of it, racing toward the entrance. The guards saw me, lowering their weapons once they recognized me, and let me in.

The space was dark and empty, except for the middle of the room that looked like a hospital.

Plastic had been secured to the ceilings and floor, creating a sealed off interior that was sterile. Inside, it was like any other hospital you might find, there were two beds, and monitors and machinery that made the space as equipped as a clinic.

We had two doctors on call, a few surgeons, and that we had them all here at once told me how fucked up things were.

There were so many people buzzing around the space that I couldn't even see who was on which bed.

My throat felt thick as a hand clapped me on the shoulder. I turned, ready to snarl, then I saw it was Brennan. There was hell in his eyes, and I knew he always took these things to heart. I mean, we all did, but he'd set himself up as our guardian a long time ago, and that Declan had been injured on his watch would be fucking with his head worse than it was with mine.

I was only one set of eyes, but I should have had their backs—should have done better. It didn't matter that I'd been focused on stopping the tidal wave of soldiers heading my brothers' way. I hadn't seen the bastards who'd hit Dec and Jensen before it was too fucking late.

"He'll be okay."

I said it more for him than for me.

His tight jaw said he wasn't so sure, but he muttered, "They asked us to leave them. To go inside the office."

"You making them nervous?" I tried to joke, even as my throat worked, and I could feel my own horror starting to choke me.

It was insane, but at that moment, I wanted Inessa. I didn't want her tainted with this side of our lives, but fuck, like a pussy, she'd make me feel better, and to be frank, I couldn't feel worse.

"Yeah, they say I scare the nurses," Brennan groused, but I let him drag me away and toward a side office in the warehouse.

We had four buildings for this express purpose, but for security reasons, we never left the equipment in them for long, interchanging them so that our enemies couldn't compromise our gear. Finn's place had a makeshift clinic, but these were for when war visited our doorsteps and major injuries required more than a quick stitch.

As we made it toward the side office, I heard the squeal of wheels outside and turned to Brennan. "Da?"

He shook his head. "We haven't told him."

My eyes widened. "The fuck? He'll go insane."

"He'll go even crazier if Declan doesn't pull through, and if the staff are terrified of me, then what the fuck are they going to be when Da's breathing down their necks?"

I grimaced because he was right. "Aidan?"

"Maybe."

But it wasn't Aidan limping in, it was a horde of women.

Aela, Inessa, and Amaryllis.

Inessa veered toward me, running so fast that she slammed into me, her arms coming around me as she squeezed me tight.

"You're okay," she breathed, and fuck if I didn't feel better with her in my arms. "Conor didn't say," she sobbed. "He just told Finn someone was down."

I squeezed her back. "Declan." I could hear the tears in my voice. "I don't know how he's doing. They're working on both of them now."

For a second, I escaped the world by burying my face in her hair, then I heard someone sob. Twisting to look, I saw Amaryllis was being held back by her men—Saint and Keys. She was slapping at them, kicking, trying to get to Eagle Eyes, and I growled, "You calm her the fuck down or we'll sedate her. My brother is in there. If you distract the fucking doctors, you'll all pay. I don't care about any fucking deals you've made—"

Keys glowered at me, but then he stunned me by grabbing Amaryllis by the shoulders and shaking her hard. Once. "You heard him. Do you want to be sedated?"

Her mouth worked as she stared at him, but she blinked, shook her head, and stood there looking like she could crumble away before our eyes. Before she could, he gripped her, tucked her into him tight, and I left them to it now that there was peace.

Automatically, I tracked Aela's movements, and saw she was standing by Declan's bed—how both women had figured out which guy was in which bed meant that I was more tired than I reckoned, because I hadn't been able to tell.

She pressed her hands to the sheet like it was glass and Declan might be able to touch her through it.

She was trembling, one big quiver, and I saw she was crying.

Crying for a man who hated her.

There was more to their story, more than Declan had ever let on, and more than he'd probably ever share. Whatever they'd had together, I didn't know about it, which meant it was well hidden. I knew more shit about my brothers than they could guess, but I'd never seen anything between Dec and Aela, and as a result, I'd never kept an eye on her.

Apparently, that was shortsighted of me.

Too many fucking mistakes... I needed the shit smacked out of me.

With Inessa in my arms, I muttered, "You shouldn't be here." I said that, of course, as I carried on squeezing her.

"Had to come. Wasn't sure if it was you in that bed." She shuddered, her face pushing into my shirt.

"I told you, I stay out of it."

"Didn't know for certain."

"Fucking Conor," I grumbled.

"He's on the phone with Ma," Brennan said, his tone hushed.

Because I couldn't imagine what Ma was doing with herself, not able to come because, if she did, Da would be with her, and then he'd be terrorizing the doctors which wasn't good for morale, I whispered, "Jesus. Okay. I forgive him."

I gave Inessa another squeeze, then muttered, "Come on, let's go get Aela. She doesn't need to see this."

Inessa shivered, but let me go. I didn't bother tugging her along with me, instead, I strode the few steps to Aela's side.

She'd found a small space in the cluster around his bed, one that meant she could see him.

He was awake.

I wasn't sure how that was possible, but even though he was

drugged up, he was staring at Aela with a cocktail of emotions in his eyes.

I could see hate. Could see love. There was want and need, but there was also fear and rage.

"What the fuck did you do to him?" I whispered, never having seen my brother emote so fucking much, and even now, I had to figure he was only showing it because he was on whatever drugs the docs were feeding him.

At my question, she flinched, but when she spoke, she gutted me, so I knew how Declan had to feel all those years ago when, apparently, they'd had more of a relationship than I'd known.

"I let him think I had an abortion."

And like that, a lot made sense, but what didn't?

That an O'Donnelly was somewhere out in the world, and he wasn't in the family's fold.

TWENTY-SIX
AELA

"DO YOU THINK HE'LL DIE?"

I'd spent so many years terrified of Declan, so many years petrified that he'd find me, that he'd catch up with me, that to think I could be free of him wasn't the release I'd anticipated.

I'd always loved him, even if I'd always been terrified of him.

Of the life.

Of his world.

And this was why I'd done what I had. This was why I'd taken Seamus to Ireland, why I'd stayed with my grandparents, who'd disapproved of my unwed state, and who'd made me feel like shit for being a slut. A slattern, as my grandma had called me.

I'd dealt with it to keep my baby safe.

But I'd been stupid. So stupid to come home, to return to the States. I should have known my past would catch up with me. Should have known there was no escaping fate.

"I don't know."

Eoghan's voice was stern, and I couldn't blame him. I knew what the O'Donnellys were like with family—insane—and that was why I'd lied to Declan all those years ago.

They'd never have let me out of the fold, would have forced us to marry, and I couldn't have that.

Deirdre had been my best friend, and I'd betrayed her. Declan had too. And it hadn't just been once. I'd been his side piece for over a year.

Even now, shame filled me.

Deirdre had wanted too much from Declan, had expected too much. But the only reason she'd been sneaking around that day, the day she died, the only reason she'd been following Declan, was because she suspected he'd been fucking around on her.

He had.

But she'd been in the wrong place at the wrong time, and had paid for our betrayal with her life.

As far as I'd managed to piece together, she'd intercepted a drug deal Declan was orchestrating—the other guy had seen her, and had shot her first, thinking she was a cop.

The second our eyes had met over Deirdre's coffin, I'd known that any affection he'd had for me had turned to hate, so the next time I saw him, a few months down the line when he'd asked me if I was pregnant—we'd had a condom scare a week before Deirdre's death—I'd told him I'd had an abortion.

That was when hatred had turned into something else.

For a second, I could remember being terrified he'd kill me, then he'd walked away, and before he could return, I'd run off.

And I hadn't stopped running until I was in Ireland.

Eoghan's hand wrapped around my arm. "Aela," he snapped, jolting me when he shook me slightly.

I realized he'd been talking to me for a while, but I hadn't processed a damn word.

Blinking up at him with dazed eyes, I muttered, "What?"

"Where's the child?"

"He's safe."

"He?" He gulped. "I have a nephew?"

"Yeah, you do," I whispered, kind of touched by how affected he was.

Family...it was one thing these heathens truly valued.

"What's his name?"

"Seamus."

His eyes glinted. "Grandda's name."

I dipped my chin. "Had to honor him somehow, didn't I?"

That was the wrong thing to say. "You could have let him be a part of the boy's life."

"And drag him into this world?" I snarled, suddenly loaded with too much emotion I didn't know how to process.

Ever since Finn had received the text, I'd been seeing the world as though I was looking through a filthy windshield.

Two men down. We're here. Talking to Ma.

That, complete with a live location, had been it. All the information we'd fucking received. When Finn had read that aloud, he hadn't expected Amaryllis, Inessa, and me to rush to the elevator and stir into action.

With Aoife fast asleep, Jacob dozing against her breast, I'd known who his priority was—and quite rightly so—and had seen he wouldn't stop us, even if, as the elevator doors had closed on us, he stated, "Text me with more information the second you have it."

The thought prompted me to say, "You need to text Finn. He's worried."

Eoghan scowled at me, but he drew out his cell and tapped off a message as he ground out, "Where's Seamus?"

"He's safe," I repeated.

"You know this changes everything."

I did.

I really did.

And maybe I was ready for that. Maybe, even as I was terrified about what the future might hold, I needed this to be over with. I was tired of looking over my shoulder, tired of hiding Seamus away like he was a dirty secret.

He wasn't dirty.

He was my world. My everything.

I blew out a breath. "I need him not to die, Eoghan."

"You do? How the fuck do you think we feel—"

"Not like me. I love him. Always have," I whispered. "I even let him come between Deirdre and me."

Eoghan tensed at that. "He cheated on her?"

"Yeah." My gaze was wary, miserable, and loaded with shame as I cast him a look. "I know, I'm a slut." My words were wooden. "But Deirdre was—"

"I know what she was. A pain in the fucking ass." His jaw tensed. "I wasn't going to call you a slut."

"Why not? He called me that."

Eoghan hissed out a breath. "Fucking dumbass."

My lips curved into a sad smile. "That sounds about right." Tension filled me when Declan's eyes finally fluttered to a close. Even in the daze of drugs, he'd known me, he'd seen me, and he'd smiled at me.

Smiled like when we were together back when I was seventeen. Smiled like I made the world spin for him and him alone.

"What's happening?" I snapped, and Eoghan grunted.

"They must have knocked him out finally. He has a high tolerance to meds."

I hadn't known that. Why would I? But there were so many things I didn't fucking know, and it killed me.

I wanted to know it all, and I had no right to it. But, also, he wouldn't want me to know.

He could look at me without hatred overtaking everything else only when he was drugged to the hilt... That said a lot about the state of our relationship.

I sucked in a sharp breath as a movement caught my eye. Watching the doctors slice into him had me wincing, and I let Eoghan drag me away.

I didn't see much along the path to wherever he was taking me, and that was because of just how dark it was in here. The only light came from behind me, in the makeshift operating room, and then a door that glowed with illumination.

When I made it in there, I saw Amaryllis sobbing, sandwiched between her two guys, who both looked wrecked from the night's events.

They were seated on simple plastic chairs that lined the walls, where Inessa and Conor were also sitting. Conor was on the phone, and Inessa was digging her hands into the edge of the seat like she was holding herself back.

The second she saw Eoghan, she was off and practically throwing herself at him. The love in her face was painful to behold, and it reminded me far too much of how I'd looked whenever Declan had graced me with his attention.

I just hoped to fuck Eoghan would never hurt her like Declan had hurt me.

When Eoghan caught her and hugged her tight, no shame in his face at the PDA, no horror at her emotional response to his presence, I figured her heart was safe in his keeping.

No Five Pointer would let a bitch do that if she was only a snatch to him.

Emotions and clinging were the death knell for every relationship with one of them.

Unless they felt the same way, of course. Then it was completely different.

Pain filtered through me, jealousy and happiness for her too, as I mimicked her earlier position—sitting on the edge of the uncomfortable plastic seat, my hands curved around the edge.

Brennan stunned the hell out of me by appearing out of nowhere and bobbing down at my side. When his fingers traced the tattoo on my wrist, I flinched.

With his other hand, he reached for my chin, and though I tried to bow my head, he wouldn't let me.

"He claimed you."

The words had tension filling me. "He didn't do a good job of it, did he?" I rasped.

"He wouldn't have given you the mark if he intended on—"

"On what?" I snapped, and I dragged my arm back, curving it around my waist.

"She had a kid with him, Brennan," Eoghan murmured, making me close my eyes as my entire world collapsed around me.

"A kid?" Conor pretty much squeaked, before he stated, "Nothing, Ma. No! There's no need for you to come down—" He rubbed a hand over his face. "Shit. She's coming down."

"Christ. That means Da is on his way." Brennan blew out a breath. "I'll go outside and wait for them. Head them off." But he didn't move. Not yet. Instead, he stared at me. "He won't forgive you."

"I know he won't," I snarled at him. "I'm well aware of that, Brennan. I don't need your warning."

He shook his head. "What the fuck went wrong with you two?"

"Too long a story to even explain it, and it's old news."

"No, it isn't. He's always been hooked on you—"

"He was hooked on Deirdre."

Conor's statement had me flinching, but Brennan shook his head. "No. This makes much more sense. Fine line between love and hate." Brennan popped his jaw to the side. "Let's just hope he makes it through to see his kid, huh?"

My throat tightened. "He will, Brennan, won't he?" My hand snapped out, and I grabbed his, my fingers slipping between his digits as I clung to him. Desperate for reassurance.

"You still love him," Brennan observed, his surprise evident.

"Never stopped, never will."

He whistled under his breath. "How did you two fuck this up so much?"

I tugged at his hand. "He'll live, won't he?"

"I don't know, little *laoch*, but I'm praying he does."

"What happened?"

His face softened, even as, etched into his expression, I saw his guilt. "He got shot. But he didn't get the brunt of it. We lost a lieutenant."

With my spare hand, I ran it over my face, digging into my eyes. "He has to live." Guilt speared me. I'd been terrified of the day Seamus would learn of his father, but now? I was more scared that my son would never know his father at all.

I'd denied him that. Denied Declan the chance of knowing what a wonderful boy Seamus was too.

There'd been reasons, justifications, but they paled into nothing now.

He sighed, got to his feet, and ran his fingers over my head. "You always were a good girl, Aela. I'll be rooting for you."

When he left, I stared down at my feet. Being surrounded by women and men in love was like pouring salt in my wounds. Amaryllis had three men who evidently worshipped the ground she walked on, Eoghan had actually fallen for his bride—whether he realized it or not, the dipshit—and here I was, sitting and pining for a man who'd never loved me, worrying over a future we might never have together.

One where Seamus wouldn't be a bastard.

Because, if Declan survived this, I knew there'd be wedding bells —whether or not I had to be dragged to the altar.

I had an O'Donnelly boy for a son, that meant my wishes had no sway in the matter.

And for Seamus? I'd do it. Even if his father hated me, I'd make it work.

I had no choice.

Fate had come calling, at long last, and I had no choice but to heed it.

TWENTY-SEVEN
INESSA

"COME ON."

I tugged Eoghan into the bedroom, not stopping until we were both in the dark, cavernous space. He sighed, and the second the door was closed, pulled me into his arms and pressed his face into my shoulder.

I didn't feel any tears, but I knew his eyes were probably burning.

Reaching up and feeling sorry for men in the life like Eoghan who weren't allowed to express their emotions, I ran my hand over his head, letting my fingers curl into his hair. Gently, I massaged him, trying to soothe him. Trying to give him something he could never ask for.

A shiver whispered through him, and I murmured, "We need to get some sleep."

He tensed up, arguing, "I need to stay awake—"

"No, you don't. You can rest. I'll stay awake."

He was living on his nerves, but the adrenaline had worn off a couple of hours ago, and I couldn't altogether blame him. I was feeling wrecked myself, but I'd stay awake for him. Because he needed that from me. Twice, we'd almost lost Declan. Twice, the family had almost crumpled.

I pressed a kiss to his cheek, loving that he needed me, and murmured, "Come on, let's just get into bed."

We wandered over to the mattress, and he looked a little like he was lost as he allowed me to undress him. I tugged at his fly, stripped him out of his jeans, and then let him climb into bed once I'd lowered the covers. I rounded the side of it, crawled in beside him, and within seconds, he'd hauled me into his arms.

I felt him shake and tried to soothe him, but then he rasped, "I fucked up."

"You didn't." I knew that, because Eoghan never made mistakes. It wasn't in his nature.

"I did. Wasn't the first time—" His jaw worked, the stubble scraping my jaw. "Even though my nest is like a second home to me, I fucking hate it sometimes. I was in Helmand Province back in two thousand seven. Wasn't supposed to be there. Was supposed to be hush-hush." He swallowed thickly. "Was supposed to be backing up their forces. It was my first tour, and I was a rookie, but my skill with a rifle had me soaring high pretty quick. The top brass put their faith in me, and I didn't let them down. I actually hit a personal record. Just over three thousand yards on one kill." A shuddery breath escaped him. "Took out two Taliban machine gunners, but it took so many fucking calculations to get the bastards, we lost over forty men before I could get—"

"You expect too much of yourself."

His face turned into my hair. "It's the only way to get anything done."

"What made you think of that?"

"The numbers. So many men surging out, so much blood spilled."

Even as I felt for him, I knew this wasn't Eoghan. This was a part of him, sure, but fuck. This was Aidan Sr.'s fault. My jaw tensed, anger filling me as I thought about his stupid display back at the weird ER setup I'd driven us to after Finn had received the text from Conor.

Raging back and forth, blaming everyone but himself for getting his sons involved in this kind of shit, pinning this on Eoghan and me... Declan was in the life. So was I. It was likely that, at some point, I'd suffer a bullet wound just like I knew Aoife had. And, I imagined, Lena too.

It was how it worked.

Was I upset that Declan was grievously injured?

Terribly.

He was the first O'Donnelly brother I'd met, the only one aside from Eoghan that I knew, and to be honest, I'd liked him for a lot longer!

But this wasn't Eoghan's fault.

I knew it wasn't.

And that Aidan Sr. could blame him pissed me off. Everyone knew he was fucking crazy, but until tonight, I hadn't seen that side of him. It made sense that it would roll out when his son could be on his deathbed, but he'd just made matters worse.

In a matter-of-fact tone, one that belied how irritated I was, I muttered, "I wanted to slap your father."

Eoghan stilled. "I'm glad you didn't."

"Why?"

"Because he might have slapped you back. He was raging tonight. Ma shouldn't have come, shouldn't have let him be there—how the fuck the doctors can work when he's like that, I don't know."

We'd had no choice but to get out of there while Aidan was making a fool out of himself.

We were all fretting for Declan, but blaming Eoghan? Like it was all his fault? Like the mission was all on him?

Brennan had even tried to defend him, and Aidan had smacked him, so yeah, maybe he'd have hit me too...

I squeezed him. "It wasn't your fault."

"I let him down." He rolled onto his back, and although I ached for the small distance he'd put between us, his voice was clinical when he explained, "We hit the compound when the workers were on a break. For whatever reason, they didn't get out fast enough. There were two dozen men just heading their way—"

"You're only one person. Only had one gun. Could only reload so many times within such a tight timeframe."

"They trusted me to protect them."

"And they'll trust you again because, if it wasn't for you, then maybe Brennan would be in a hospital bed too. And maybe Declan wouldn't be in with a chance, period. As it stands, he's being sewn back together again."

Maybe I sounded hard, and maybe that was because I was. No way in fuck was I going to let this weigh heavy on Eoghan, not when he wasn't a goddamn miracle worker.

Because I didn't have anything nice to say, I reached for his hand and connected ours together, feeling the bump of his scar against my sensitive flesh. Maybe it was psychosomatic, but it calmed me down.

"Eoghan?" I murmured, after several minutes passed in which I tried to get my irritation under control. He didn't need this right now. Didn't need my shit as well as all the other crap in his head.

"Yeah."

He sounded sleepy, and I really hoped he was. Really hoped he didn't remember this when I next woke him, and that he managed to get some rest before the surgeons called us in once more with news—good or bad.

"I love you," I whispered softly, but only after a few seconds had slipped by, when his breathing had slowed into a rhythm that made me think he was sleeping for real so he wouldn't know what I'd actually said.

He didn't need to hear the words to know I was feeling that way.

I imbued it in the hold I had him in, in the touches I gave him, in the way I pressed a kiss to his chest.

That was enough.

I let him rest, even as I tightened my arm about his waist and rested my head on his belly.

Tonight couldn't have gone worse for the family, but for me? Eoghan was safe and sound, and while I'd mourn Declan, grieve him fiercely if he passed away, I was starting to think there was no me without Eoghan. No Inessa without him because, in this crazy world we lived in, where bullets fell like rain and death was a constant companion, I knew that the one joy I was granted was this man.

This love I felt for him.

The freedom I felt in his arms.

No, he wasn't perfect, but neither was I.

Yes, he was jaded and filthy, but so was I.

We complimented each other, and I thought he knew that. Believed he could feel it too.

And if he didn't, I'd just keep on trying until he did. Until he wised up and recognized me for what I was—his soul mate.

TWENTY-EIGHT
LODESTAR

FUCK.

Just...fuck.

I stared at the code, started at the fucking Trojan Horse I'd let infect my hardware, and I growled under my breath.

I was rarely bested as a hacker, rarely as in never. I wouldn't let this prick gangbanger get the best of me, but I didn't have time to set malware on his ass, not with Katina here. I'd diverted his spyware and scareware, but that fucking Trojan? Nestled in a goddamn email from Child Services?

Yeah, he'd got me.

He'd got me good.

Motherfucker.

I was too hard to panic, and ordinarily I wouldn't give a shit. I'd survived Kembesh, had endured more fucking shit at the hands of my superior officers than any made man dick could wish to torture me with, but Katina?

She'd been through enough.

And she'd just started sleeping.

Fuck.

Fuck!

I didn't have time to move, didn't have time to isolate the issue.

Staring at the screens as my programs worked on flushing out the malware, I knew I had about three hours before they'd find my IP address. I'd never seen a Trojan like it, and God help me, I wanted to figure it out so I could dismantle it. Normally, that was what I'd do.

I'd take it apart, put it back together again, then use it in my repertoire.

But Katina changed shit.

When it was just me, I'd pick up the one laptop I never left home without, pack a rucksack, and take off, the open road my home for the foreseeable future.

With Katina, I needed to provide an address for state welfare to find me. To check up on me.

I didn't like it, but...

Digging my fingers into my eyes, I racked my brain, going over my next options.

The second Kat's social worker showed up and we weren't here, she'd pull an Amber Alert, which meant I needed to be somewhere the cops didn't go...

I rifled through my memory like it was an index card box, shoving cards aside where I stored tidbits of information on them for a later date. Things were a little messy inside and had been ever since Katina had come into my life.

That little kid had ruined my world in more ways than one, but I didn't have it in me to dislike her for it. She'd lost her mom, her dad, then her sister, and me? I was on the hunt for that sister.

I fucking refused to let that sweet little kid lose everything.

That was how I'd tapped into the Five Points' systems. I was on the hunt for some scum-sucking, Hitler wannabes who were selling women like they were chickens at a market.

I mean, as a vegan, selling chickens sucked too, but this was a thousand times worse.

Just thinking about it made my heart start to pound with outrage.

But like that was the key, I thought about someone else who usually pissed me off.

Maverick.

He was my friend, sort of. He was one person I could tolerate, who tolerated me, and hadn't he called me a few weeks back?

Wanting my help with something?

I'd been neck deep in my hunt for Katina's sister, Alessa, so my brain hadn't been wired right the past few weeks. Just remembering to feed Katina was a fucking miracle.

But yeah... Maverick, and his band of not so merry men, had asked for my help.

They were in New Jersey.

I grunted under my breath.

I'd be crossing more than one pair of state lines if I took Katina out of Ohio, but fuck, I'd committed worse crimes in my life, hadn't I? Plus, I'd signed up as a foster parent under an assumed name so that would save my ass. No way, under my real identity, would any sane fucker have me as a parent, but I was the best thing for Katina even if the state didn't recognize that.

Mentally pulling up a map in my head, I calculated that the Satan's Sinners' compound was about six hundred miles away.

That was doable in a day.

With a huff, and knowing I would have to let this fuckwit aCooooig—what in the fuck kind of handle was that anyway?—win, today at least, I started packing my shit together as I hollered out, "Katina? We're going on a road trip."

Her shriek of glee made me smile, even as I glowered some more at the malware infecting my computer. Then, knowing we were running out of time, I shoved away from my desk, and with my favorite laptop in hand, along with the gear I'd allow myself tucked in a bag that was ready at all times for situations just like these, I hurried up the stairs.

While I could pack in a hurry, Katina was incapable of it, and at the moment, we needed more speed, and both our asses in my Porsche Cayenne as we roared toward the East Coast to the dubious haven that was a one-percenter MC.

Fuck.

Just...fuck.

TWENTY-NINE
EOGHAN

SHE MOANED as I thrust into her, and as the sound washed over me, I grunted, then reached behind me on the nightstand for the two boxes I had there.

Dazed eyes stared up at me as she recognized I wasn't moving anymore, and she whispered, "Eoghan?"

"Hush, I have a present for you."

"Your dick is all I want right now," she muttered thickly, her heels digging into my butt, trying to urge me on, and while I was really fucking tempted, I leaned down and sucked on her throat for a second before I nipped it in warning.

"Patience," I grumbled. She was cock hungry pretty much every day, and no way was I about to complain on that score. She had me harder than a pike with more boners than when I'd been a fucking teenager, and again...no complaints.

Especially when we were alone, in this hotel, in the middle of the Irish wilderness, with no fucking war to worry about, and my family about five thousand miles away.

"I have your birthday present."

She blinked up at me again, her eyes even more dazed than before. "Huh? My birthday was eight months ago."

"Yeah, well, good things come to those who wait," I mumbled, finding it incredible that she'd been my wife for eight months. How had so much time passed? And how the fuck did I crave her more each day?

A laugh escaped her, and her hand moved up to cup my cheek. "You're blushing."

Well, I couldn't believe it'd taken me this long to, A, get us on a real honeymoon, B, get her a birthday present, and C, finally fulfill one of my promises to her. At least, part of a promise.

"First one." I shoved the box at her. She opened it with a gleam in her eyes that told me she was excited, and when she stared at the little dangling ropes forged in gold, I sensed her confusion.

"What are they?"

"Diamonds?" I teased, laughing when she wrinkled her nose at me.

"I mean, I know that, but...where do they go?"

"Clever girl for realizing they're not earrings." I surged up, my dick pushing into her harder, making us both grunt, even as I leaned on one elbow and pinched her nipple with my other hand. Though she squealed, it was more of a token squeal, one that was founded in surprise more than anything else. "Here."

She blinked. "Nipple rings?"

I grinned at her. "I want you to wear them now and for dinner tonight."

A snort escaped her, but she nodded eagerly. "Put them on?"

My little love, so willing to be corrupted.

I sighed, unable to stop myself from bending down again and pressing a kiss to her lips. "Inessa?"

She hummed.

"I love you."

Her smile was everything.

It wasn't the first time I'd told her that, nor would it be the last, but every time I said it, she looked at me like it was.

"I love you too, Eoghan," she whispered, reaching up and running her fingers through my hair. Her smile appeared again. "I remember when you told me that the first time."

I did too, but I teased, "When?"

"At Amaryllis's wedding."

My nose crinkled. "How cliché of me."

"Love was in the air." She huffed out a laugh. "I didn't think you'd ever tell me."

"No? Well, you don't know everything, do you?" I tapped her nose before I reached down and nibbled the tip, making her laugh. "Just like you didn't know what these were for."

Her eyes were back to gleaming. "Ready to learn more."

Her eagerness had me sighing with delight.

Fuck, she was perfect.

How couldn't I have told her I loved her when we'd had to attend a hick wedding down in Texas to celebrate some weird, fucked up, four-way wedding that wasn't even legal...? Her patience was only one facet to her entirely lovable nature.

Speaking of nature... I'd tried to find a hotel with a terrace where I could fuck her out in the open, but this was Ireland. It rained all the fucking time, and while it might sound romantic, fucking in the rain wasn't my idea of fun. So, I'd made do with this ridiculous hotel that I'd known would appeal to her, even if I thought it was all for the tourists, and I dealt with chintz and flowers and little pouf ottomans that I nearly tripped over every time I got out of bed.

It was why I was also dealing with dusty museums, road trips across fields that were fucking wet through to visit castles, and traipsing around stores...

I felt guilty.

She was eighteen. She'd seen nothing.

And me?

Jackass over here?

I wanted to give her the fucking world.

"Hold up your boob," I rumbled, "and keep squeezing your nipple."

The little rings were tiny clamps that had decorative, almost gold filigree embellishments with a substantial, dangling, half-carat diamond.

When she felt the pressure, which was only slight, and was all I wanted really, she moaned, and her pussy clamped down on my dick.

Heaven.

Fuck.

As I gestured to her other tit, I arranged the second ring, sighing when her cunt started fucking fluttering at the sensation.

Wanting to give this up and just fuck her, I had to force myself to grate out, "Happy birthday."

A moan escaped her. "I know how you can finish it off—"

"Not yet," I grumbled, and reached for the other box. This one was bigger.

When I opened it, this time, her eyes didn't gleam, they turned molten.

With tears.

"Oh, Eoghan," she breathed.

"I asked Cammie to sneak it out, you know, before everything went down, and since I'm not exactly allowed onto the compound right now..."

"I don't care. Thank you." She shivered as she reached out, tracing her fingers over the emeralds that were set in clusters of diamonds. "I remember the last time Mama wore it—"

"When?" I asked, when her expression turned a little sad.

She shook her head. "That's for the past. Put it on? I want to make new memories with it."

More than willing, I placed the heavyset emerald and diamond necklace—a piece that made me wonder if Vasov had raided some kind of bank vault because this shit screamed Romanov dynasty—at her throat. It was very awkward, but with some heavy breathing and fumbling because, shit, we both wanted to rip into each other, I managed to get it on her.

When I did?

It confirmed what I already knew.

She was a fucking queen.

My fucking queen.

Unable to stop myself, I reached for her hand, the one with the thick scar on her palm, and pressed mine to it. She sighed, like that grounded her, and fuck if I didn't feel the same way.

"Need you," she whispered.

And I needed her too.

I propped one elbow to the side of her head as I raised our connected hands to the pillow, pinning her in place. Then I dropped my mouth to hers and joined us in a kiss that was like wildfire. It tore through our bones, ripped us apart, even as it merged us together again.

When my phone rang, Declan's ring tone buzzing to life in the kitschy bedroom, I muttered, "I preferred it when he was in the hospital."

She laughed, nipped my bottom lip, then muttered, "Ignore it," as she surged upright, our hands still united so she was on top, and showed me her appreciation for her gifts.

I was a made man. I was a sniper. But through all the blood I shed, through all the violence I wreaked in our war torn city, I was so much more than either of those things.

I was her man.

Hers.

And more importantly?

She was mine.

Forever.

AFTERWORD

A secret has been brewing for fifteen years. Two gunshots changed it all.

Find out more in Filthy Dark.

YOU CAN GRAB Declan and Aela's story here: www.books2read.com/FilthyDark

Thank you soooo much for reading Eoghan and Inessa's story. I truly hope you loved it, and that you're gagging for Declan's scrumptious tale. I'm sure you saw my name dropped in the book—that isn't because my head is massive, but because Julia, my PA par excellence, thought it would be a giggle for me to 'meet' Finn from The Air He Breathes. LOL. You read it here first. So watch out for that happening in one of the upcoming Filthy Fecker books!!

Be sure to join my Diva reader group as, on release day, I'll be dropping an exclusive behind the scenes' snippet in there. www.facebook.com/groups/SerenaAkeroydsDivas

You may recognize some characters from within this book, because I've done several crossovers. They don't have to be read to enjoy the universe, but again, why not if you want more?! :P Remember, this is only a suggestion. :) You don't have to read them as they're ALL standalone.

Suggested reading order:
Bound
All Sinner No Saint (RH Novel. You meet Ink, Ama, Keys, and Saint here.)
Filthy
Nyx
Link
Filthy Rich
Sin
Steel
ALL MY BOOKS ARE ON KU.

MUCH LOVE TO YOU ALL, and thank you again for reading. If you enjoyed it, if you'd consider leaving an honest review, I'd truly appreciate it.

Thank you. <3

Serena

xoxo

PS. To grab a free book, just carry on reading. ;) And, also, carry on to get a snippet from FILTHY DARK.

THE CROSSOVER READING ORDER WITH THE FIVE POINTS

FILTHY
NYX
LINK
FILTHY RICH
SIN
STEEL
FILTHY DARK
CRUZ
MAVERICK
FILTHY SEX
HAWK
FILTHY HOT
STORM
THE DON (Coming Soon)
THE LADY (Coming Soon)
FILTHY SECRET (Coming Soon)

FILTHY DARK
CHAPTER ONE

AELA

Have your eyes ever met someone's across a crowded room?

Have you ever looked into that person's eyes, and somehow known you were theirs?

That they were yours?

I was fifteen when that happened to me.

It wasn't the first and only time it happened either. It kept on happening, only with the same guy. Over and over and over, it occurred.

Our eyes would connect, and it was like the sun would peep out from behind the clouds on a dull day.

I knew it sounded like nonsense, but it actually wasn't.

Every time my gaze was captured by Declan O'Donnelly's, I knew we were meant to be together.

That was what made things so awkward.

I wasn't his.

He wasn't mine.

He was my best friend's.

And that was only the start of all the trouble.

My father had been low down on the totem pole in the Five Points' Mob for most of my life, meaning I'd been pretty much a nonentity. Only when he'd been promoted had I started attending a decent school, and that was where I met Deirdre.

She was the kind of girl who knew everyone and everything, and somehow, she'd taken me under her wing when I arrived at St. Mary's Middle School for Girls.

Nearly twenty years later, I still wasn't sure if that was the best thing that had ever happened to me or the worst.

Deirdre had been kind and sweet to me. Enough so that I hadn't realized what a manipulative bitch she was until I was nearly seventeen.

You read that right—for nearly six years, the cow managed to pull the wool over my eyes. But I didn't do what I did to get back at her.

No, back then I'd been too innocent to be so conniving.

I'd appreciated her friendship when I'd suddenly gone from a regular, run-of-the-mill PS162 school to a private Catholic middle school.

When St. Mary's had been forcibly closed due to—and this always amused the hell out of me—abuse because the nuns used to get whippy with it when you were really bad, we'd had to go to St. John's High School.

A *mixed* private high school.

For girls who'd only been surrounded by other girls all their school life, it had been groundbreaking. For me, it was just normal. Still, I'd been allowed to meet Deirdre's Declan for the first time ever, and when we *had* met?

That was when the whole world crashed and burned to a halt.

All this time later, as I sat beside his hospital bed, I still couldn't believe how powerful that moment had been.

I was an artist now. A mom. I wasn't some dopey kid who had her head in the clouds, her hands covered in paint—although they still were most of the time—and her will easily molded to what others wanted.

With the power of time, a reputation that had been hard-won, and after coming to terms with being a single mom, I was still mind blown by that connection.

I created art in many mediums, had worked in studios around the world, picking up techniques and teaching them, my mind was a hive of creativity... but no matter what I did, I couldn't replicate that sensation.

It was like a lightning bolt between the eyes. It was so strong, it should have killed me, but it didn't. It almost zapped my heart, but hearts were a little supernatural in their ability to regenerate themselves—over time.

Or so I'd thought.

Watching over the man I'd grown to hate, a hate that would always be founded with a seed of love, was proof of that.

I'd thought that was it for me. I was one and done. Guys were a pain in the ass that I had no time for. The only dude I wanted around was my kid. He took up every second of my non-working time, every ounce of my energy. But it took one look at Declan for me to know it was all bullshit. Lies I told myself to make it easier to live without the love of my life.

That was why it was a punch in the gut for him to have almost died.

My hands itched with the need to draw him, to take in the majesty of his face. A hard jaw, a stubborn firm slash for a mouth, eyes that were usually narrowed with distrust. He had a dark face, one built with features that were perfect for his choice of career. Somehow, though it was hardened, it was utterly perfect to me.

So wonderfully complex to draw.

There was a play of light and shadow on his brow, furrowed lines between them too. Either side of his eyes, there were squint lines, making him so much more interesting than he'd been as a boy.

Pitch black stubble made him look even tougher, and while his hair was a tousled mess and should have made him look less hardcore, it didn't. So much so, I wanted him to open his eyes because that would reveal the only softness to his nature. A softness I'd lost any and all rights to access a long time ago—his soul.

Mournfully, I blew out a breath, then jerked when the door opened and my gaze clashed with Brennan's.

I liked Brennan, but unfortunately when I looked at him, we didn't have the same sparks.

I wished we did.

I wished I could be with him.

He was insane, like all the O'Donnelly sons—you couldn't not be when spawned from Aidan Sr.'s seed—but he was the most grounded, I thought.

When I looked at him, I felt calm, felt like my brain wasn't whirring with a mixture of panic.

But I didn't want to paint him, and that was indicative of my feelings for him. Or the lack of them, I guessed.

So I smiled at him weakly as he rasped, "What are you doing here?"

I shrugged. "I don't know."

His brow furrowed. "Hmm." That was all he said, almost making me snort.

Brennan was a man of few words, that was for damn sure.

I pressed my head to the side of the armchair, just resting it for a second.

I wanted, badly, to walk away. I knew when he woke up again, he'd discover the truth and call me chickenshit, but I didn't want to be there when he learned he was a father.

Maybe I should be the one to tell him, but I didn't think I could.

I'd spent so long running, so many years hiding, that I just couldn't do it.

Brennan shook his head at me like he knew what I was thinking. "You need to get out of here, Aela."

I gulped. "I know I do."

"The doctors say they're drawing him out of the coma. When he wakes up, we'll be telling him the truth. You need to bring the kid down here."

"You mean your nephew?" I snapped, irritated by his dismissal of my pride and joy as just a 'kid.'

Brennan wafted a hand. "You know what I mean."

I gritted my teeth. "He's the best O'Donnelly out there," I told him.

"Course he is. He hasn't been tainted by us yet," Brennan rumbled, and his words had me flinching inside.

Because they were true.

And in his eyes, I knew he was being candid and earnest, and it killed me.

For a second, my heart pounded, and the sensation of being trapped was so all-consuming that I wasn't sure what to do.

I'd done the right thing. I'd helped someone in need, but I should have stayed out of it, and now my boy was going to pay the price for that.

Suddenly feeling like I had a melon lodged in my throat, I stared at him and I saw sympathy etched in his features.

Sympathy.

I closed my eyes, clenching them tightly because I couldn't cope with that look.

"Don't even think about running," he warned me, but it wasn't really a warning, it was more of a gentle reminder.

My mouth tightened. "You think I don't know the drill?"

"You forgot it once upon a time," he rasped, making me flinch.

"Because I had sense."

"No, you'd have had sense to stay gone," he told me, and again, his honesty hit me square in the gut. "You always were good people though, Aela. I'll have your back if ever the time comes where you need it."

I gaped at him, unable to believe he handed me that offer.

Everyone knew it was the O'Donnellys against the world. Against the universe. And truth was, they needed to be so tight-knit.

They were the head of the Five Points, the one and only Irish Mob family in the tristate area because, long ago, Aidan O'Donnelly Sr. had taken over every other piece of the puzzle and consolidated it, establishing himself as king of the hill a long time before I was born.

As a result, they were the most powerful family on the East Coast. The billionaires and one-percenters thought they were powerful, but that was nothing compared to the clout the O'Donnellys had.

I'd been born revering them like they were the second coming of Jesus though.

The O'Donnellys, for all they were headed by a psychopath, were good leaders. Everyone respected them, loved them even. It was rare to get a traitor in the midst, and not only because Aidan would cut you like a motherfucker either, but because they earned it.

They treated the commoners like they treated the lieutenants—sure, the pay was less, but the respect wasn't. And for people who did the running, who were the most likely to be tossed in jail or prison for the crap they did for the family, respect meant everything.

Feeling tired, I got to my feet because I didn't want to be dealing with any of this now. I just... I didn't even know what I was doing here.

I should have been running far and wide across the Atlantic, but there was no stone I knew the family would leave unturned now that I was in the picture.

Now that Seamus was in the picture.

My jaw clenched and I started to walk toward the door, toward Brennan.

When his hand reached out to grab my arm, and he turned me to face him, I looked up at him and muttered, "I'll probably need your help in the upcoming weeks. You might regret offering me the olive branch."

He shrugged. "You think I'm frightened of Dec, *laoch*?" His lips twitched, and he revealed the slightest of smiles that, along with his Gaelic endearment, would melt any woman's heart.

Just not mine.

Mine belonged to the bastard on the bed.

The bastard who'd almost *died* on the bed. Twice.

When I'd learned he'd been shot, I'd been unable to stay away. For years, I'd pushed distance between us, uncaring what he did or what happened to him, just living with survival instincts in mind.

But the second I'd known he might be dying?

I'd had no alternative but to come and see for myself.

Thanks to a few misspoken words when I thought the love of my life, the father of my son, was about to leave this world forever, my kid's future was in jeopardy. I'd hate myself for it if I hadn't been traumatized by the sight of Declan as a bunch of surgeons, in this illegal hospital, gathered around him and started to cut his chest wide open.

No one should have to see that.

No one.

"I don't think you're scared of anyone, Brennan," I told him carefully, well aware that was true.

Some might say I was still a dreamer, unrealistic, but I knew how to read people. More than when I was a kid.

I knew what Brennan was and wondered if he knew it too.

He was Aidan Sr. reincarnate.

The thought made a shiver rush down my spine, because that meant he was a psychopath, but Brennan had a self-awareness that was very uncomfortable, and made his kindness all the more perplexing and my trust in him all the more concerning and bewildering.

When Eoghan, Declan's younger brother, had discovered I'd been hiding a son from the family, he'd gone apeshit.

Brennan?

He'd dealt with me—there was that word again—*kindly.*

I gulped, and whispered, "Will you do everything in your power to protect my boy?"

He patted my shoulder. "He's *our* boy," he corrected me, making me shudder. "And you know we will. You should go get him. Bring him here. Not for Declan. We don't want the boy to see his da like this for the first meeting, but the family will want to get to know him."

My stomach twisted, turning sour at the prospect. "I-I have responsibilities up there."

He shrugged once more, and I knew he was about to dismiss a decade's worth of hard work as if it was nothing. "You know they mean shit now."

I gritted my teeth with fury. "I'm a professor at the Rhode Island School of Art, Brennan. Do you know how difficult it was to obtain that position? Do you know what I had to sacrifice—"

He snorted. "Use that argument on Declan, and I'm pretty sure he'll blow his top." Another pat. All the more discomforting. "Your life's been in New York ever since you got pregnant. You've just been procrastinating."

I wanted to wail that I had a life, that I had plans that had nothing to do with the many and various crimes the family committed. That that wasn't my future anymore.

But when I looked at him, I knew what I was seeing.

The stonewalling that would make it so that if I didn't do as I was told, Seamus would be taken from me.

Was it weak to concede defeat?

Or strong to accept it? Because for my boy, I'd kill. And in this world, those words held real-life consequences.

I bit my lip, grinding my teeth hard as I shoved away from him, and when I walked toward the door, he called out softly, so softly that I felt the threat worse than if he'd pressed a knife to my throat. "Don't think to run, Aela. If you do, the consequences will be a thousand times worse."

The statement, and that he'd felt he had to repeat the warning, had me shoving the Velcro-ed sheets that acted as a doorway open, dashing out of the freaky clinic I was sitting in, and running to the bathroom so I could puke my guts out.

The place was beyond weird.

Situated in the middle of a warehouse, clear, see-through plastic had been rigged up to create a sterile space within a space.

Inside, there were two hospital beds surrounded by all the equipment you'd expect in an ER or ICU.

That was the clout the O'Donnellys had.

They didn't need access to hospitals, they had their own. Anywhere, any time. With a team of nurses and doctors and surgeons on hand who'd jump to help, it was all the more disconcerting to be in the web again.

To know the spider was closing in on me, and I was the one stupid enough to come traipsing inside.

When my knees were aching, my body trembling as the aftereffects of fear, stress, and anxiety hit me, I leaned back and away from the toilet, pushing the lever so it flushed.

As I watched my meager stomach contents disappear down the drain, I tried to get my thoughts in order.

Obeying didn't come easily to me.

I was known for my anarchist art, known for my feelings on the current government, and my anti-populist stances. It was all well-represented in my work, for God's sake, and my art was internationally renowned.

I'd created pieces for bigwigs. Made works of art for billionaires and corporate sharks, even a few Saudi princes.

Why?

Because I bled them for all they were worth, for every inch they'd given me to have a piece of Aela O'Neill in their homes, and that money? I gave it back to the people.

I was a modern-day Robin Hood for a reason.

I knew what it was like to be controlled, to be under someone's thumb, and I did my best to protect anyone else from that fate.

Of course, there was no one here to help me now.

My Maid Marian was a dude lying on a hospital bed who'd loathe me the second he opened his eyes, and who'd treat me like crap.

But my fate was entwined with his.

I should have known it would bring us back together—sometimes, wishful thinking just never got you far enough away.

I clambered to my feet, and I washed my hands and face with the soap provided. It cut through a day and night's worth of grease, but I still needed a shower badly.

Blowing out a breath as I looked in the mirror, taking in the black curls, the blue streaks that were my rebellion, the elfin face that was too weak, and the eyes that were exhausted, I shook my head and pushed myself away from the spotted mirror and the chipped sink and headed on out.

Was I surprised when a couple of goons appeared at my side?

Maybe I was.

Maybe I wasn't.

I'd thought Brennan was giving me a semblance of control, making it look like I had a say in this, even though I didn't.

The goons?

Proof otherwise. Proof that I wasn't to be trusted.

Pretty smart of them.

When I cast both men a look, I saw Eoghan in the background, Dec's younger brother, eying me.

And I knew.

He'd sent the goons.

I gritted my teeth. I was grateful that Aidan Sr. and Lena O'Donnelly weren't here anymore. After the old man had slapped Brennan for speaking up, for telling the old man to calm down because he was freaking the staff out with his wild temper, I was grateful that they'd gone to Finn O'Grady's apartment to get some rest. Only having to deal with my babysitters was a boon, but I still ignored Eoghan and stormed out into the street.

There was nowhere to go, nowhere to run, but I had to make sure Seamus was prepared for the future that was coming our way.

Unfortunately for me, he was a teenager.

And teenagers were like mini mafiosos without the murdering power.

FML.

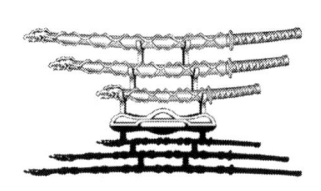

DECLAN

"YOU'RE SHITTING ME."

It wasn't a question. It was a statement.

A statement because I knew Brennan was joking. He had to be, didn't he?

Of course, there was massive concern over the fact that he was the one imparting this news to me.

After all, Brennan rarely joked.

It wasn't that he was somber, it was that he saw the world a little differently. There was nothing wrong with that considering the world we lived in was a shower of shit, but still, he wasn't easily amused.

And he'd never laugh or joke about the fact that I had a son out there.

A son I'd fathered with Aela O'Neill.

My throat tightened at the memories of her. She'd been the one who got away. The one I'd loved. Who I'd *let* get away.

At the time, a part of me had been relieved when she'd gone, so there'd been no blame. No recriminations. I'd even thought she was smart to leave the city.

A lot of people underestimated her, but never me.

She was a little ditzy because her mind was usually in a sketchpad, cooking up various things for her projects, but anyone who failed to see how smart she was deserved to be in the outer circle.

She'd been one of the best people I'd known.

Until shit had gone wrong. Until my past had come crawling up my butt and I'd had to let go of the best thing that had ever happened to me.

"How?

Brennan scowled at me. "How?"

Because I knew why he was scowling, I rolled my eyes even though that hurt, and ground out, "I don't need a talk on the birds and the bees, Bren. I'm just talking out loud."

"Oh." He shrugged. "You were boning her on the side for a while. You were dumb back then. Not too hard to figure it out."

I narrowed my eyes at him. "Fuck off, you never knew that."

His lips twisted slightly. "I know everything about the family."

That had me complaining, "When you and Eoghan say crap like that, it's creepy as fuck."

"Maybe, but you should be grateful. At least I know the stuff that would make our enemies come if they got their hands on our weaknesses."

"You didn't know about my son though, did you?" I wasn't smug about that, because I wished I'd known about him too, but Brennan could be an arrogant shithead sometimes.

He wriggled his shoulders. "I can be forgiven for that. When you were busy boning Catholic schoolgirls—"

"I was a Catholic schoolboy at the time," I groused. "So don't make me out to be a pervert—"

"I was working full-time, and you know I had to work hard to make the docks ours."

I rolled my eyes. "Overachiever."

His lips twisted. "You're taking this better than I thought."

"Probably the drugs. They're wearing off," I replied honestly, staring around the hospital ward that was something from a nightmare.

Or an episode of *The Blacklist*.

I'd only woken up in one of these joints once before, and I had to say, I hated it.

We drew out the big guns when someone was badly injured, *illegally*, and waking up like this was just horrendous and something I wouldn't wish on an enemy. Being in the middle of a black space in a bright area that was covered up in plastic sheeting made me feel like the kid in *E.T.*, when the house was all excluded.

Fuck, I'd hated that movie, and that goddamn alien still visited me in my dreams.

Reaching up to rub my eyes, I muttered, "The drugs make everything bearable, I guess."

Brennan snorted. "Don't get any ideas. We've already got one junkie in the family."

I grunted. "Aidan ain't no junkie."

"You're a fool if you don't think he is. Just because he isn't shooting up and doesn't have track marks all over his body doesn't mean he isn't an addict. We're pussyfooting around him—"

I raised a hand. "I can't deal with this right now."

Brennan winced. "Sorry, bro."

"No. It's okay. We need to do something about him, you're right. But I just got my ass handed to me. You need to remember that."

He pursed his lips. "You were reckless."

"Maybe."

As one of the lieutenants of the Five Points' Mob, I often got my hands dirty. Brennan too. It was part of the job, part of the life.

We were high-ranking—the highest because our father trusted no one more than he trusted his boys—but we were still involved with integral parts of the puzzle, even though in most families like ours, the heirs were untouchable, rarely getting involved in wet work.

Things had devolved a few nights ago. Aela O'Neill—a blast from the past if ever there was one—had been visited by an MC Prez's daughter.

The kid had discovered that her partner had been kidnapped by the *Famiglia*, and the Italian cunts were going to kill him unless we helped rescue him.

While we sure as fuck were no white knights, the Hell's Rebels MC was renowned for the quality and their level of production of ghost guns—a type of weapon that had no serial number on them, so they couldn't be traced.

When we'd cut a deal, we'd gone in and saved the fucker, but I'd gotten shot up in the process. I knew for a fact that we'd lost another of our men too.

A sad day.

And even worse, my body hurt like a fucker.

In my own way, I was used to pain though. We all were. Knife fights, gun fights, fist fights—they were par for the course.

That was my life, and I didn't want—

My jaw clenched.

I shouldn't think about that crap.

Couldn't.

Because if I did, I'd do something stupid. I'd be kind or something. I'd think of the son I didn't know existed and not of the family, and family was everything.

It was all.

That was our creed. Something that had been drilled into us for a lifetime.

But with that creed came the realization that if I didn't protect the boy who I'd never known about, he'd be in danger too.

"What's that look on your face?"

Brennan's question had me blinking at him. "Huh? Nothing."

He narrowed his eyes at me. "What's going on with you, Dec? I thought you'd be wicked pissed. That's why I made sure to tell you on my own. Didn't want you upsetting Ma."

I scowled. "Why do you always think I'm going to upset Ma?"

His lips twitched. "Because you usually do."

"Now you're just pissing me off," I growled.

"That's what I do best." His sage tone had me huffing, before he said, "I thought you'd be furious."

I wasn't.

That was the kicker.

I wasn't furious, and I knew I should be.

I had a son.

And family was everything.

I should have been there for him, should have helped him grow, should have helped form him into the man he was going to be some day.

Instead, I'd had no input, but I got it.

I did.

And I was almost sad for the kid, because now?

He was going to be introduced into the life, and it wasn't a good life.

I could admit that to myself.

I could admit it when I'd never thought a damn thing about what I did for a living before, because what I did was just the way of it.

As natural as night following day.

O'Donnellys worked for the family.

That was it.

How it worked.

Like clockwork.

My da had worked for his father, and his brothers had done the same—not that they were as smart as us, of course. But still. We'd turned the fam around, gotten us out of the penny-ante shit, and turned us into a corporation.

But that didn't take away from the bones of what we were.

And I wasn't sure if I wanted a kid of mine doing that, being involved in this crap.

The dilemma had me wondering if Finn, one of our family

friends and the Points' money man, was feeling the same way about his kid.

His wife had just had a baby, well, a while back, and I had to wonder if he thought about his son doing the shit we did.

"You're not angry."

The simple statement had me blinking at the opening in the ward. It was odd because it was a make-shift door with plastic sheets that were Velcroed together, so the sound of the ripping should have dragged me from my thoughts. It hadn't.

Maybe the drugs *were* dulling everything.

I stared at my brother, Eoghan, and shook my head. "I will be. Just give me time."

But he didn't smirk at me.

He just stared at me.

Christ.

Brennan and Eoghan always saw too much.

I felt like a petri dish with the way they were both gawking at me, and I scowled at them. "What do you want me to do? Go full out Hulk on you?"

Brennan shrugged. "I think that was what I anticipated."

"Did the doctors say he woke up too early?" Eoghan asked Brennan, pissing me off that they were talking around me, not to me.

I heaved an irritated breath. "Look, I'm tired. I need to rest."

I didn't.

I felt wide awake.

I was definitely more mellow than I should be, definitely a lot more chilled about this situation... yeah, had to be the drugs.

Eoghan grunted. "Stay awake for a little bit longer. Ma's on her way. She was shitting herself."

"Not literally, I hope," I rumbled, trying to tease and failing.

Brennan and Eoghan didn't crack a smile—serious fuckers. "Jesus, where's Conor? At least he'll laugh at my crappy jokes."

"He's asleep in the waiting room. We're all exhausted because we've been here for two goddamn days watching over you."

My mouth turned down. "Yeah. I get it."

"No. I don't think you do," Brennan retorted.

I gritted my teeth before I muttered, "Move the pillows out from behind my head. This position hurts."

Eoghan moved toward me and helped shuffle out the two pillows a nurse had stacked under my shoulders when I'd woken up and found Brennan sitting at my bedside.

The instant relief was enough to make me sigh heavily. I allowed myself to rock back and let my muscles settle.

"I'm just going to rest my eyes," I mumbled, suddenly needing the peace of sleep and a spare moment to stop the buzzing in my head that had nothing to do with almost being shot, blood loss, drugs, or the aftereffects of emergency surgery.

A low hum of conversation came next, and I heard the Velcro softly open and close as they left me to the nightmare ward.

I rocked my head to the side, saw the partition between me and the other guy, Ink, the man we'd gone in to save, and saw he was out cold.

Then again, he'd been tortured. I figured it probably wasn't the first time, judging by all the scars I could see on the parts of his body that weren't covered up with tape, gauze, and wires, but still, torture always took it out of a person.

I pursed my lips, rolled my head up to the ceiling where those godawful surgical lights were blaring onto me, and even though it hurt, I reached up and covered my eyes with my forearm.

I needed to reassimilate things. Needed to figure out what the hell I was thinking and feeling.

I was a father.

I had a son.

That changed everything.

I just didn't know how yet.

FREE EBOOK ALERT!!

Don't forget to grab your free e-Book!
Secrets & Lies is now free!

Meg's love life was missing a spark until she discovered her need to be dominated. When her fiancé shared the same kink, she thought all her birthdays had come at once, and then she came to learn their relationship was one big fat lie.

Gabe has loved Meg for years, watching her from afar, and always wishing he'd been the one to date her first and not his brother. When he has the chance to have Meg in his bed—even better, tied to it—it's an opportunity he can't refuse.

With disastrous consequences.

Can Gabe make Meg realize she's the one woman he's always wanted? But once secrets and lies have wormed their way into a relationship, is it impossible to establish the firm base of trust needed between lovers, and more importantly, between sub and Sir…?

This story features orgasm control in a BDSM setting.

Secrets & Lies is now free!

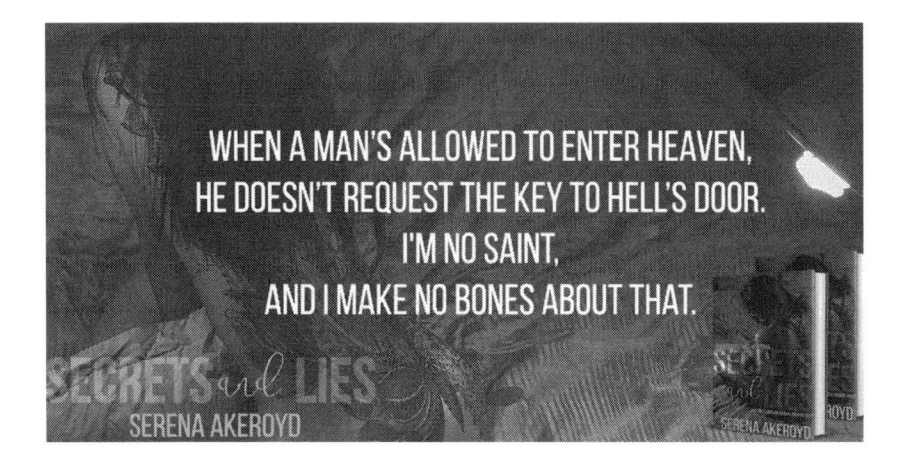

CONNECT WITH SERENA

For the latest updates, be sure to check out my website!

But, if you'd like to hang out with me and get to know me better, then I'd love to see you in my Diva reader's group where you can find out all the gossip on new releases as and when they happen. You can join here: www.facebook.com/groups/SerenaAkeroydsDivas. Or, you can always PM or email me. I love to hear from you guys: serenaakeroyd@gmail.com.

ABOUT THE AUTHOR

I'm a romance novelaholic and I won't touch a book unless I know there's a happy ending. This addiction is what made me craft stories that suit my voracious need for raunchy romance. I love twists and unexpected turns, and my novels all contain sexy guys, dark humor, and hot AF love scenes.

I write MF, Menage, and Reverse Harem (also known as Why Choose romance,) in both contemporary and paranormal. Some of my stories are darker than others, but I can promise you one thing, you will always get the happy ending your heart needs!

facebook.com/SerenaAkeroyd
twitter.com/SerenaAkeroyd
instagram.com/Serena_Akeroyd

Printed in Poland
by Amazon Fulfillment
Poland Sp. z o.o., Wrocław
08 August 2021

24a27cd4-e85a-4f47-a3d6-60237520a0d5R01